Juniper Point

Juniper Point

Philip Austin

Published by Philip Austin, 2023.

JUNIPER POINT

First edition. December 12, 2023.

ISBN: 979-8223040255

Written by Philip Austin.

Also by Philip Austin

The Yellow House
Juniper Point

To Howard and Judy, for giving me the grand idea.

NOBSKA POINT, WOODS HOLE, MASS.

*ENFILADE (*THE ARCHITECTURAL practice of lining house elements in a row)

BEFORE THAT
    nanosecond
    you went missing,
    all the doorways
    in this house
    were perfectly lined
    straight and true as
    loyal guardians
    just right for a
    clear unbroken
    view to the
    open sky
    afterwards...
    while I slept,
    midnight vandals
    with
    sledge hammers
    wrecking bars
    angry saws
    with
    jagged
    rusty
    teeth,
    moved
    each opening,
    not much,
    an inch here,
    an inch there,
    just enough
    to trick my

memory
into losing
the map I'd
made of
you.

Part One

A^{na}

ANA LIEBLING, NEWLY sober millennial, freelance financial reporter for *The Boston Globe* and occasional wedding photographer, woke to the last Saturday of April with a grand idea.

Recently discharged from a well-known rehabilitation center in New Hampshire, her diagnosis, and subsequent treatment, focused on a relentless, and sometimes grimly amusing alcohol addiction. The center was called *Turning Leaves*. Its base cost of roughly a thousand dollars a day had been reluctantly paid for by concerned family members. Part-time *Globe* employees, as the woman in HR had patiently explained, are not covered by its group insurance plan.

Ana's first night at *Turning Leaves* was spent inside a gauzy narcosis. Intake had been dramatic. A few days prior, she had begun to drink straight Stolichnaya in her apartment. Chugging that amount of vodka should have stopped her heart. After lurching about the apartment for several hours, drunk-dialing a handful of friends with a deluge of existential, but unintelligible, questions, she finally collapsed on the floor, badly bruising the soft flesh of one cheek. On the morning of the second day she opened a second bottle, and so on. On the fourth day, a neighbor noticed her mail overflowing in the lobby, knocked five times, then called 911. Things and time began to speed up, as Ana fell under the calm ministrations of crisis professionals. Two burly firehouse paramedics hefted her onto a gurney, gently down the stairs and into an idling ambulance. Its red and blue lights silently strobed against the walls of the Charlestown triple-decker, the curious faces of a few late-night walkers, and the rows of her neighbor's parked cars. Siren off, the ambulance parted the vehicular sea crossing the Leonard P. Zakim Bunker Hill Memorial Bridge, through the Lieutenant William F. Callahan Jr. Tunnel, and into the city. The attending doctor at the Boston emergency room was astonished. He couldn't believe, as he gently placed her slender wrists into Velcro restraints, that anyone's blood alcohol level could be that high and still survive. For weeks afterwards Ana was remembered by hospital staff, with no small admiration, as the "Point-76 girl."

After her family had filed the necessary documents, the next morning Ana was delivered to New Hampshire, still intoxicated, by sheriff's van. She had been sentenced, or "sectioned," by a gruffly unimpressed district court judge in Boston.

Many of the women on rehab had been similarly adjudged. They spent most of their days, in loose-fitting clothes, pacing the perimeter of a nether-worldly, but highly structured, limbo. When not in "group," or waiting in line for "day meds," (powerful, and highly addictive benzodiazepines, or "benzos"), they wandered the high-shined linoleum halls, chemically zombified, and numbly indifferent to the cause and effect of their screaming banishment to these palliative New Hampshire woods.

Each night, the doors to the outside world, a labyrinthine and perhaps unmapped twenty-five acres of thickly wooded countryside, were locked. Escape to these impenetrable wilds was not only impossible, it was laughable. While not technically a lock—down facility, Turning Leaves took the welfare of its clients seriously. It was just far safer, they reasoned, if patients were unable to leave until staff had taken a stab at cobbling together some sort of treatment plan. But for most women it was just another variant of the same compulsions that brought them here; meds and group and cigarettes and caffeine, not to mention boredom, depression, and a stultifying blend of daily self-analysis and pharmacologically induced apathy.

Most came from wealthy families, like Ana. All of them carried a lifetime of addictive behavior, invariably the result of darker, more subterranean abuse. For some women, it had been sexual, often as a child by a family member. Some had body shaming issues, others suffered domestic violence. Most had diagnosed, or undiagnosed, mental illness. These were not poverty's children. Thirty thousand dollars a month was far above the pay grade of common alcoholics. If you couldn't afford Turning Leaves, immunized from prosecution, you would most likely end up in jail.

Sitting on hard folding chairs in the group therapy room, beneath brash fluorescence, atop cold linoleum, Ana quickly became a reluctant dog-paddler in a nearly fathomless sea of women's sorrow. Ana, ever the journalist, learned to recognize key words, constantly alert to trending catch-phrases. Unhappy childhoods, unhappy marriages, a miscarriage here, a battering boyfriend there. After a while, the stories seemed to conflate into a single, misery-fueled narrative. At first, she saw it as *the* story, one she would write about her experiences here. She assiduously took notes and thought of herself as an embedded reporter in the house of pain. She even came up with a clever name. She would be, for the next month, a "felonious monk." After a couple of days numbness displaced curiosity. Ana began tuning it all out. Better to let the drugs blissfully wend their way through her bloodstream.

After the second week came a starkly wondrous realization. She had been cured! (hands in the air!) and all of this had all been a huge mistake. Now she just wanted to go home. At a one-on-one session with a staff psychologist, her earnest attempts at lobbying for early discharge were greeted with a seasoned and cynical skepticism. Turning Leaf clinicians had literally heard some variant of her miraculous epiphany hundreds of times before.

"Tell me why you feel like your treatment has been successful," the man prompted, adding ominously, "after only fourteen days."

He leaned forward, creaking the chair, so close that Ana could smell his deodorant, observe the twitch of his nostril hair. She thought a minute, then pushed back with a question. "Tell me why I'm not allowed to have my laptop or cell phone?"

The psychologist leaned back, triumphantly steepling his fingers.

"Phones and computers are a distraction, Ana," he patiently explained, reciting a line lifted directly from Turning Leaf's playbook. "You're here to work on your recovery, not reinforce the patterns and distractions that brought you here."

Ana shook her head, stood up and stalked from the room. Falling into a kind of cloudy sulk, she spent the afternoon in her room, misunderstood and alone and falsely imprisoned in her tower keep, like some recovering Mary

Queen of Scots. The man recorded the session and tucked a page into her folder.

Liebling, Ana-Patient still exhibits disassociated and overly simplistic notions about her treatment. Argumentative. Suggest more group, possible switch from 100mgs Lorazepam to 400mgs Prozac.

She had climbed that first summit of her denial, like some far-off and vertiginous mountain range, but this was only the first breakthrough. An uncountable number of peaks lay ahead.

By the end of the third week, Ana began to breathe again. She no longer thought of the locked door as keeping her in, but as a gentle barricade, keeping her access to addictive behavior out. She now understood she was a sick woman. A lifetime of abuse had gotten her here; a lifetime of recovery would get her out. The Alcoholics Anonymous group had a pithy mantra: *To get through it you have to go through it.* A month before she would have laughed. Now it sounded suddenly reasonable. She badly needed help, and began to experience what could only be described as a daisy chain of *ah-huh* moments.

Bad things happen to us, she wrote in her recovery journal, *but they cannot be used as an excuse to inflict additional bad things, on ourselves or to others.* So logical, so linear. For Ana, the response to her high school eating disorder, which, in turn, had possibly been caused by her parent's acrimonious divorce at fourteen, had been a decade of addictive wilding. It was the root of her behavior; drunken, reckless, and risky. Somehow, miraculously, within the last thirty days, she had cruised through each stage of recovery and moved on to the next. Anger, denial, depression, and finally, surrender and understanding.

By the end of the fourth week, as her discharge day came near, counselors eyed her carefully. They were checking for either positive change or further cracks in the wall, even though her court-mandated thirty day term of rehabilitation was non-negotiable by either party. After one final group, listening to a nervous, anorexic woman named Janette discuss how her older brother would come nightly into her bedroom to lift her nightgown, Ana met with her case manager.

Carl was an ex-heroin addict, and believed devoutly in the power of redemption. He listened politely, then wrote a positive report. Ana was deemed ready again for prime time, even though relapse and recidivism from such cursory treatment hovers in the high eightieth percentile.

One dreary morning in late April, she was driven to the closest town with a population large enough to have its own post office, in this case Peterborough, New Hampshire. She was dropped at the Trailways bus station with a one-way ticket back to Boston.

Ana's chauffeur was also her case manager, Carl, a devout, sexually closeted evangelical who wore a pendulous gold crucifix over his gray Turning Leaves polo shirt, and talked in a husky, conspiratorial whisper, as if each banality would someday be memorialized in scripture. Steering the shuttle to the curb, he turned and extended his hand, wishing her the best of luck. As an afterthought, he followed Ana out to the sidewalk, throwing his arms around her thin shoulders, embracing her in a clumsy bear hug.

"Jesus loves you, Ana," he whispered, even after he'd been warned twice by the Director of Patient Services about this sort of salvational folderol. "Don't drink," he continued in a queenly baritone, "don't get arrested, don't die. And for god's sake, girl," he added, "don't come back."

Imprisoned in the hug for several long seconds, Ana thought about jabbing him in the rib cage. Then he quickly stepped back, spun, daintily for a big man, and climbed into the van. As he pulled away from the curb Ana saw his lips moving as he gave a quick little wave through the glass.

God bless you.

Carl would have no shortage of passengers. Each Friday, which was discharge day, one or two of those suffering women she'd left behind at the center would take that same long ride to the bus station, sitting morosely in the back seat of the bouncing minivan, staring at the back of Carl's close-shaved head.

ONE WEEK AFTER SHE returned from rehab, but still one week before her grand idea, Ana found herself between assignments at the *Globe*. Her editor hadn't emailed. And nobody was looking for a wedding photographer. She took both as a sign. The HR director might have assumed she needed more time to "get better." Either way, it gave her time to think. She began to spend entire days in her apartment, padding around in her pajamas, balancing a cup of coffee and a bag of Pepperidge Farm cookies. Often, she'd boot up her laptop, check her *Google* feed, randomly scrolling up and down the pages. Every hour or so, she would click again on the *Facebook* icon, a Pavlovian response that rewarded her with an instant scroll of cute cats and cute dogs, trumpeted announcements of complete stranger's birthdays, an endless cornucopia of regurgitated clips her algorithm decided she needed to read. And smiley faces, always the smiley faces. She trolled the Internet, now abuzz with cries and whispers about a slow-moving dumpster fire that was the upcoming presidential election. There were conspiracy theories and talking heads spooled onto infinite 24/7 news loops.

After a while, Ana stopped tapping the icon. *Social media is an inch thick, and a million miles wide*, she mused into her journal. Like eating nothing but high fructose corn syrup for breakfast, lunch, and dinner.

One article did hold her attention. A sobering expose from *New Yorker.com* about unsafe working conditions in Amazon fulfillment centers, as its distribution warehouses are called. She kept scrolling. Workers, mostly minimum wage hires: retirees living in RVs in Walmart parking lots, high school graduates with no hope or money for higher education, military vets fallen on hard times, all toiling beneath the minimal wage yoke, a business model that stressed ever-increasing production quotas, while ignoring actual human capabilities. It was like some insane hamster wheel sped-up to the point of blatant lethality. Human workers were pitted in direct competition with autonomous "bots," machines that routinely fucked up tasks and sometimes collided with living flesh. Human production was constantly monitored by remote managers. Enough infractions, such as unscheduled toilet breaks or sick days or even an emergency phone call from a child's school, for instance, were grounds for immediate termination. Amazon's safety record was three times worse than any other industry, and workers with aching backs and knees, suffering from repetitive motion injuries and occupational stress, were routinely fired for failing to achieve impossibly superhuman production quotas. Steve Bozos, reputedly the richest human on the planet, was the architect of these cavalier and arcane labor practices. It was a simple business model, based on the oldest instinct, avarice and greed, and it was all happening, globally, in real time. Yet little regulations had been written to address such a systemic atrocity.

Reading the story jogged Ana's empathy neurons, the part of her brain that concerned itself with injustice and fair play. She realized now that writing about the manufactured foibles of billionaires and the vain artifice of hundred thousand-dollar weddings had become a nonessential activity in her life. Her blind fealty to them, in pursuit of a paycheck, had insulated her from critical planetary malaise.

She began to leapfrog from story to story. The keyword was *labor*. Labor rights, labor abuses, labor laws, labor activists, labor justice. A pattern began to emerge. What was occurring in Amazon's fulfillment centers worldwide was merely a symptom. It was the tip of the iceberg, historically speaking. What Jeff Bezos was doing had always been done by men with the same inhumane profit motive. Bezos was the perfect Scrooge for a new world order. If a carton, of, say, women's vibrators, or chocolate bonbons, or computer hard drives, had to be located, stocked and shipped within sixty seconds in Calcutta, or Phoenix or Paris, it was the same as a bobbin of cotton thread that had to be spooled onto a weaving machine in Lawrence, Massachusetts by a twelve-year-old mill worker in 1893. Once the symmetry of such an argument had been shaped, its larger context became crystalline. It was all so "ah-hah." Labor abuses had always existed, and they would always exist. In plain sight, the billionaire class , the one-percenters, was not only devouring, they were also torturing, the ninety-nine per-centers. A simple social imperative was at play. Darwin was right. The new industrialists were the same industrialists, and their new victims were the same victims.

Ana flipped her laptop closed and stared out of the second-floor window. She watched the passing traffic. Every once in a while, a particular car would slow. An Uber driver, one of the anonymous millions of gig economy entrepreneurs, idling at the curb, checking his smart phone. A young black man sprinted from a triple-decker next door and hopped into the back seat. The Uber guy pulled away, a tiny gizmo in the global marketplace's endless conveyer belt. In a few miles, his app would chirp and another rider would materialize from another address. When had it all become so predictable and pre-programmed?

It was dusk. Ana felt weary and suddenly hungry. A month since rehab, after weaning herself from the drugs they'd so eagerly prescribed, she was finally beginning to feel things again. One last drug remained in her system. A nifty little number called Antabuse. A single tiny pill in the morning made her vomit if she consumed alcohol. Lovely. Perhaps someday she could wean from that. But for now, it was a grim necessity. Her street in Revere had at least a half a dozen package stores, grimy, run-down Mom and Pop dispensaries of all manner of liquid pleasures, all within walking distance. Sometimes the only thing between Ana and a full, blackout relapse was that tiny morning pill and faithful old Mr. Coffee sitting by the stove.

She opened a cabinet door. Pasta on the shelf, frozen pizza in the fridge. Not long ago she would have started chugging Chablis by now. Vodka had kicked her ass, but, surely a little white wine couldn't hurt. She bit her lip and fiercely thought about dinner. Outside the window, somewhere out there, the high whooping moan of a city ambulance. Some other soul's dire emergency. Her's was alcohol, relapse, the dark aeries of a blackout. If she said yes, a drink would be in her bloodstream within minutes. If she said yes. Ana slowly opened another cabinet door, peering inside at her meager larder. Peanut butter, a half box of saltines. In a little while, she'd fill a pot with water and turn the burner on, stand before the churning bubbles in a kind of prayerful contemplation, waiting for things to boil.

Part Two

A Grand Idea

CROSSING THE LOFTY automobile bridge spanning the Cape Cod Canal, Ana stole a glimpse down, to the sun-dappled, tide-driven, sparkling waters far below. She had taken a leave of absence from the *Globe*, even though, for part-timers, like health insurance, there were few promises. No job would be waiting. More aggressive wedding photographers would easily fill the small shadow left by her disappearance. The idea, a project still miles in the distance, like some glittering mirage, was still as unformed and nebulous as the cirrus clouds puffing above her windshield.

An ocean-going tug, pulling a string of black, dented barges, passing beneath the bridge just as her little car, an avocado-green Prius, crested the four-lane highway. This confluence of human endeavor felt somehow momentous and right. A recent convert to the notion of magical convergence, she had recently coined her own term for such a notion: pattern recognition. Somewhere, she realized, the hand of God was at work, someone's God, knitting together each exact moment of each person's journey. A glittering watercourse, an iron cable span built by American muscle and ingenuity in the days of national civic pride, and a toy boat towing toy barges full of toy necessities far below. And here was Ana, steering south in a battery-fueled cockleshell, on her way to find a story, *the* story, *her* story. But she would also be part of that story. This, today, right now, was her voyage of discovery. Fuck the *Globe*. Fuck millionaires. Fuck vodka and Chablis and rehab! Fuck snapping pictures of impossibly expensive nuptials that were, statistically anyway, going to implode within the first five years.

For the first time in a long time, she felt poised on the precipice of something great, something meaningful.

Ana pondered her subject. Not yet fully anything, really. Just a glimpse of an idea within an idea. Vaguely, it was the story of a lady doctor during the first decades of the twentieth century, a serendipitous kernel of a factoid she'd glimpsed while randomly scrolling for something entirely different.

Frances Crowningshield was a post-Victorian woman born to great wealth and privilege, but nevertheless, possessing of rare intelligence and a kind heart. *Why not*, Ana asked herself? All stories have to begin somewhere. All great journeys follow a tremulous first step, like rivers from tiny streams. She also firmly believed that if the story were to have personal significance, and narrative power, she must certainly include herself in the journey. Her book might be a kind of biographical *pas de deux*. Here was elegant symmetry. The story of Frances Crowningshield, feminist pioneer and labor activist, and Ana Liebling, insecure college graduate who had suffered from an eating disorder in high school and then graduated to fully blown, alcoholic wilding. There was poetic circularity in their connection. A book! She peeked again down at the distant canal waters. Surely, a description of her first ascent would comprise its beginning pages. A bridge crossing, on a sunny Saturday in April. Here was her Homeric odyssey, here it was in a lyrical, symbolic nutshell.

Also, and this was no small matter, Boston and its *Globe* represented a relentlessly pointless grindstone in her life. It was that same crazed hamster wheel set on high. Was she really any different than an overworked widget stacker at an Amazon fulfillment center? Ana desperately needed a vacation. She hadn't had a drink going on two months. Sobriety was a full-time job, and exhausting in its relentless pursuit of sobriety nearly as obsessive as the disease itself. What she needed mostly was not more denial. What she needed was to embrace *something*.

And that something, she decided, would be Ana, writing.

DRIVING "DOWN" TO THE Cape that morning, as the trip from north to south is often described, as if gravity itself would propel her, traffic was light. By the time she'd reached the bridge, Ana had had made another decision. There, at the top of that bridge, an iron spider work of rivets and girts and suspension cables built in 1929, she decided to simply let the story take her where it might went. It wouldn't be some dry treatise, a thousand words on the upticks and downturns of the money merchants, or some dot-com billionaire's whiny paean to greed and conspicuous consumption. Her story, this story, written in the secret privacy of evenings alone, when she wasn't on some deadline, or hoarding stolen hours by missing parties and friends, hunkered with her laptop at the city library, or scribbling notes on the pebbled strand of Revere Beach, a block from her apartment. No, this would be an exploration of the human spirit, the story of indomitability, of emotional doglegs and switchbacks and perhaps some hidden triumph that other biographers before her had somehow overlooked.

It would be a story about America. No, even better, it would be an *American story!* Yes, she thought triumphantly, here was her working title. Ana smiled through the windshield at her wondrous, unfolding destiny. Financial writing was deadly. It was dreadful and demoralizing. It had, now she knew, in no small measure, been partly responsible for the toxic effluvia of hedonistic self-loathing that her alcoholism had become.

She turned off the radio, on since the city. An earnest NPR discussion about the upcoming election. The last words that jangled from the car speaker were 'swing voters.' Terrible times. Rift and rancor, like some chilly menace of civil war brewing. Beyond the summer, at the chilly margins of winter, the voters would decide, and the news wasn't great. America was on the precipice of making a political error in judgement so vast, by electing a vain, duplicitous liar, a shape-shifting, reality TV stuntman as its president, that the existential footing of the republic might never recover. But never mind that. Ana was weary of politics and money. Only in the writing of such a book that could be the one true thing that unshackled her from such a dim and predictable event horizon. Democracy can wait, she thought. This project, *my* book, is important!

THE PRIUS BEGAN TO descend, finally touching down on the far Cape Cod shore. Ana merged with the rotary, an awkward engineering construct that pinwheeled traffic in an accelerated radius of directions, like some vehicular version of Snap the Whip. She punched the radio back on. Ten o'clock. *Car Talk* was just beginning, which she seldom missed. Ana loved Click and Clack, the Tappet Brothers. They reminded her of her own sprawling and cantankerous Polish family. Visions of her father and her two older brothers in their Chicago driveway, heads down, shoulders bent, trading jovial barbs, deep into the vicissitudes of some Detroit, big-block monstrosity, one of a series of cheap cars the family owned over the years. In *Car Talk* she recognized the same absurdist banter and mechanical devotionals that aerated the deepest male roots of her family.

The GPS chirped, and Ana turned the wheel. Exiting the rotary, a dozen cars and trucks elbowed for lanes in front and in back of her. Rotaries were a dance with the devil, a deadly social contract between tons of moving machinery and their daydreaming masters. She was always amazed that bad things didn't happen more than they did. Directly ahead, a high school girl in a dented Honda was checking her makeup while texting. Behind her, a roaring muscle pickup with a *Make America Great Again* bumper sticker, its bearded, unsmiling driver itching for a fight. It was delicate diplomacy at sixty miles an hour, a dance of life-or-death performed by complete strangers.

She entered Route 28, a four-lane east and west highway that connected the sprawling townships of Bourne and Falmouth. Bourne was a town violently bifurcated by the Cape Cod Canal in 1911; a deep, meandering ditch hand-dug by immigrant labor, then completed by steam shovel when the bosses realized that even ten thousand men with pickaxes and wheelbarrows was simply not enough. She passed the Miracle Mile, or Cape Cod's homely version, a tawdry row of car dealerships. After those an outboard motor shop, a carwash, a gaudy feast of fast food emporiums, Dunkin' Donuts, Subway and Mickey D's, then another carwash, a diner. Then came a second rotary, a military base, a military graveyard, a county jail, etcetera, etcetera. A forested meridian strip separated the east and west highways, keeping the glint of oncoming night traffic from blinding drivers. Only then, after thirty minutes, did the outskirts of Falmouth hove into view. Hospitals, a bagel shop, an architect's office, something called Amvets, where old soldiers went to drink, Seafood Sam's, a place started by a guy named Sam who apparently cooked seafood. And so on.

Ana glanced at her GPS. It silently rebuked her. No major turns ahead, or tricky bits of navigation. Unlike Boston, which existed as a fluid flash-mob of road construction, traffic snarls, and places on the map that simply vanished. No, this was smooth sailing all the way, a gentle glide-path down the sandy, undulating upper flank of Cape Cod.

The tiny village of Woods Hole exists as a destination and a departure; a grand notion with a plain history. The docks for the island ferries cling, like prosperous and tenacious lichen, to the banks of its tiny, deep-water harbor. On the other side, the sprawling complex of WHOI, pronounced *WHO-EEE*, like a child on a swing, the Woods Hole Oceanographic Institute.

The Institute is the home of both the vaunted and the obscure. Robert Ballard, famous for discovering the wreck of the *Titanic,* had once been a WHOI oceanographer. Each year hundreds of marine biology students toil anonymously in its modern classrooms, or tramp the local beaches, digging for specimens, as they always have. The U.S. Navy maintains a not-so-secret research facility here, a glass and steel edifice for testing things like miniature drone submarines and the effects of ship sonar on dolphins and humpback whales. And then there is the Marine Biological Laboratory, known as MBL, an antique, ivy-covered edifice that hosts future scientists each year from around the world.

A science town with a sexy pedigree and long history, Woods Hole was once a farming and fishing village. It escaped the staid conservatism of many Cape Cod towns through its marriage to academia and a deep, protected harbor. Although officially part of Falmouth, the two towns remain as disconnected by cultural and academic disparity as feuding siblings at a Thanksgiving dinner. Once a day, in the high summer months, traffic cops in patrol cars prowl slowly down the narrow streets of the village, many no wider than the original cow path. Occasionally they pause, tuck orange parking tickets beneath windshield wipers, a seventy five dollar fine. The town really has no need, or desire, to be part of Falmouth, which is conservatively blue collar and troubled by modernity. It boasts half a hundred sober houses, and a looming Fentanyl problem. Local businesses are being slowly shuttered, choked out by the nuisance weed of big-box retail. A plastic Dairy Queen sign, faded and cracked, rattles in the wind like a death song. But if you need to pay that Woods Hole parking ticket, or your Woods Hole property taxes, you must drive to the Falmouth town hall. Other than that, the two towns exist in a kind of symbiotic orbit, each mildly tolerating the other.

THE GPS HADN'T SPOKEN since the bridge. Then, just as Ana crested the final hill that led down into the village, it metallically chirped, in the voice of a BBC governess:

Destination ahead, five hundred yards on the right.

The view was changing rapidly. Here was, literally, Land's End. A small bridge and a roadway circled down to the docks. A large, red, construction crane rose straight into the air, part of the new terminal project. The glittering harbor, past that the verdant sprawl of the Elizabeth Islands in the hazy distance. Two white ferry boats, tethered to concrete docks. Rows of parked cars. Baggage carts and idling buses. A line of travelers, half tourists, half commuting locals, are waiting to board. The quiet expectancy of a hundred travelers hangs in the air. This was the Steamship Authority, gateway to the island of Martha's Vineyard, and the reason property taxes here were so low.

Turn right.

An enormous eighteen-wheeler slowed in front of Ana. It made a wide, arcing left-hand turn, nearly clipping the guard rail, onto the bridge that led down to the ferry dock. On the bridge, a small metal plaque with a date: *1952.* Cinched to the truck's bed, building materials, two-by-fours and cinder blocks for the island's construction industry. Ana turned right, pulling into a small, tree-lined parking lot. A weathered sign was planted in the front yard. *Woods Hole Historical Museum.* The museum was an old farmhouse, then a small, sway-backed barn a few steps away. A sign on the barn announced that it was some sort of boatbuilding exhibit, but its weathered wooden doors were bolted shut. The stone town library was the next building over, and beyond that, the studio and offices of WCAI, Cape and Islands Radio, the local NPR affiliate, 88.7, which everybody listened to in the "Hole." The radio station, which provided a hip bouillabaisse of folk, blues, and what is loosely called Americana, also occupied an old farmhouse, bristling with a high-tech nosegay of transmission antennae.

Ana scrunched across the pebbly driveway, unsure of which direction led where. Just then an elderly woman popped out of the house, carefully latching the ancient, scarred door behind her.

"Oh hello," she brightly chirped. "Are you here for the tour?"

Ana shook her head. "I'm actually here to do some research. I'm a reporter, with the *Globe*," she added, to give her introduction some professional gravitas.

The old woman cocked her head. She had the most vibrantly twinkling green eyes. "That's nice, dear. And what is the subject of your research? If you don't mind me asking."

Ana stood there, surprised by the question, car keys dangling. Now was the moment it began. She had been asked, by another person, and she would have to say it out loud. It was the first time she'd spoken the words to anyone.

"Frances Crowningshield," She replied. "Do you know anything about her?"

The woman paused, showing the merest tracery of a smile.

"Frances? Why, yes dear. I do know, *did* know her. Quite well, actually. But I have a walking tour group beginning soon. Could you come back in a few hours? We close at four, sometimes earlier, but I'd be happy to discuss her with you."

Ana nodded. "Yes, absolutely. Is there anywhere close by I could grab a bite to eat."

The woman crooked a finger down the hill towards the village. "You have your choice. Coffee or burgers. But the closest would probably be the little sandwich place next to the post office. It's not far. I myself have never eaten there, but I'm told they have wonderful fare."

Ana smiled. "That would be great. What time should I come back?"

The woman glanced, not down at her watch, but up at the sun, an antique reckoning. "Around two should be fine. We're usually wrapped up by then, if the little darlings don't have too many questions."

A few cars had turned into the parking lot. The Saturday walking tour, off-season visitors, New England antiquity buffs curious about old Woods Hole. Ana thanked the woman, then turned and headed out, on the hunt for the post office. Soup would be nice. The end of April was still brisk, the blaze of a Cape Cod summer months in the distance. Ana's stride was quick and purposeful, a *Globe* writer on deadline, a big-city girl used to the sudden death of city crosswalks.

The sonorous blat of the departing island steamer, backing from the pier, filled the air. Here, now, was where the book could really begin. A small New England village with a secret, or at least a decipherable past. In her mind, the opening chapter unfurled. Descriptions of an old woman leading strangers on two-hour voyages of discovery, an old woman with sparkling emerald eyes, wearing sensible walking shoes.

There, just ahead, the Woods Hole post office. Nestled right next door, an inviting-looking coffee shop with a brightly crayoned menu board out on the sidewalk. The name of the place was *Pie in the Sky*. Couples sitting at wooden tables outside, sipping coffee, nibbling on croissants, students bent over laptops. Soup would definitely be nice. She could smell the expresso beans roasting. She might almost be in Cambridge. It was her kind of place.

For the next two hours, Ana hunched over a small wedge-shaped table and read, on her laptop, about the life of Frances Crowningshield. A steady rivulet of people came and went. Coffee orders, sandwich orders, counter girls calling out names. The ubiquitous question passed between strangers: Are you waiting to order or to pick up? Out past a large picture window, the island boats came and went. Movement was always in the air. Embarkation, disembarkation, Crowds formed, crowds boarded, and then it began again, as the next trip would slide around the Point. Woods Hole was a place of unseen geographies and the promise of entire civilizations just beyond its watery horizon.

AT ONE-THIRTY, ANA stood up, bussed her table detritus, and went outside to the sidewalk. She still had a half an hour to kill. A large yellow dog was drinking from a deep, chrome water dish, chained to the sidewalk, the dish, not the dog, and new people were sitting outside beneath cafe umbrellas.

She began walking, a brisk downhill jaunt, towards the harbor. A sign told her she was on Water St. As crossed a small iron bridge, the kind that could be raised and lowered for passing sailboats, she passed Eel Pond, where a number of pleasure craft were anchored, a handful of work skiffs, even a few unoccupied houseboats, shingled like tiny farmhouses, with empty flower boxes in the windows. Further down a grocery store, a few restaurants, a small museum, all closed for the winter's annual layover. It felt ritualized, choreographed, as if the village had taken its last summer breath, and now was waiting to exhale.

A block still, she paused in front of a large, three-story brick building. Three words, Marine Biology Laboratory, were chiseled over the front door, then a date, 1910, with a familiar name above that, Crowningshield. Here was where the family's Woods Hole legacy truly began. Ana had read that Frances's older brother Charles had established the endowment to begin construction on the laboratory, known locally as MBL.

Across the street, a few large vessels were docked. These were the research ships from the Institute that would soon be heading out to explore and catalog the world's oceanic mysteries. Fronting the harbor, separating water from land by great links of iron chain, a small, grassy park had been established, with a few inviting wooden benches. On one bench was a life-sized bronze statue of the naturalist Rachel Carson, who had, apparently, once worked here. Off to one side, at the park's entrance, a large, granite obelisk had been placed, some kind of memorial to something or someone.

Ana walked closer, and circled the obelisk. It was apparently a sundial, a verdigris plaque explained, noting its exact longitude and latitude: 41° 31.502' N 70° 40.358' W. Below that, into six faceted sides, exotic sea creatures had been carved. Lobsters and crabs, nautilus shells, dolphins and whales. The sundial had been planted onto a kind of raised concrete dais, with descriptive words of praise for its donor incised along its perimeter. Businessman. Philanthropist. Friend of Science. And so on. A gift, again, from the town's wealthiest benefactor, Charles Richard Crowningshield. Ana glanced down at her own watch. Ten to two. She exited the park and began to walk back towards the ancient farmhouse on the hill.

THE OLD WOMAN WAS STANDING in the doorway, waiting, as she approached. She looked fatigued.

Ana called to her. "I had a great lunch. Thanks for the tip."

"Not many options this time of year," the woman said. "But I'm glad you enjoyed it."

Ana introduced herself, offering her hand. The woman's grip was surprisingly strong. "So glad to meet you, Ana. I'm Violet. Violet McVicar. I'm what they call the museum's docent, and part-time tour leader. I work here two days a week. The rest of the time, I'm just a lazy, retired widow who lives with her cat, an old, retired mouser."

Ana followed her into the museum. Compact and well-organized, it smelled of floor polish, the mildewed memories of ancient books, and printer toner. Here was where a small town had made a valiant stand against historical amnesia. A stack of brochures lay on the counter, promoting anything from whale watching to contra dancing, next to a small dish of peppermint candy. Not too small, but compact small. Everything in its place small. Like a sailboat, businesslike and purposeful. One could almost hear the sound of the wind in the rigging.

Violet pointed to a small exhibition room, just to the left, as they entered.

"I suggest you start with the photographs," she said. "Then we can talk. Excuse me. I have a brief bit of business I must attend to in the office. But, please take your time."

And then she was gone.

March Hare gone.

ANA BEGAN TO MOVE SLOWLY around the room, carefully examining each image. Large, framed photographs hung on all four walls of what might have once been the farmhouse's front parlor. They were all taken by the same man, mostly in the late 19th century. They were exact in their execution, breathtaking in their clarity, almost luminescent, deceptively simple in subject matter. Ana, who had taken a course in early photographic technology, knew how arduous the old processes were. This was no mere point and click from an iPhone. For early practitioners, their craft was deeply physical, an intimate, time-consuming act. Each glass plate might weigh as much as a half a pound, or more, not to mention the heavy cameras and tripods. Each photograph was a monumental task to plan and complete. Each comprised a sepia testament, irrevocable proof of a subject's existence, whether it be Civil War dead or a farmer, proud of his livestock and his bride, or perhaps some architectural heap long burned or demolished.

The name of the photographer, she read from a card, was Baldwin Coolidge. A talented autodidact who wore many hats, like many Victorians, he had opened his Boston studio in 1878, then spent the next forty years recording scenes around New England. He photographed churches and libraries and public statuary in Boston, woolen factories in mill towns, ships and railroads on Martha's Vineyard and Nantucket, decaying farmsteads in Maine. His subjects were wildly eclectic. An ancient, possibly insane widow in love with her chickens A resolute Wampanoag life-saving crew grouped together in a wrecked surfboat; an urban gentleman in a bowler hat dodging a trolley car on a crowded boulevard. This exhibition concerned itself with the images that Coolidge had captured in and around the village of Woods Hole. They were depictions of village life long disappeared. A sailor rigging a spritsail boat, an extinct fishing craft, in Eel Pond. A panoramic scene of Woods Hole, taken in 1895, from an elevation now a private golf course. A stone whaling warehouse, where spermaceti oil was made into candles, and the Pacific Guano Company on Long Neck which made fertilizer from bird shit and lime.

Ana moved to the right. Here was the *Nereid,* a steam yacht built by the famed naval designer Nat Herreshoff, which had hit a mooring strake sticking from the water. She was now listing on the shallow bottom. Ana peered closely, could just make out the crew of tiny men on deck, frantically dewatering the seventy-six-foot-long yacht. A thick black dash that was the anchor chain disappeared into the black waters of Little Harbor. The next photograph was iconic, taken looking south towards the rail yard. A water tower is in the foreground, the steamer *Nantucket* beyond that. Train tracks end abruptly at the water's edge. A village dog sniffs around the station's planked veranda.

At the end of the fourth wall, she paused. Before her, an image of ten people. They were posed deliberately; some were sitting, some were standing. Four women and six men. One of the women was leaning against an ancient bicycle, as if ready to pedal away. The photograph was titled, : *MBL Embryological Class, Woods Hole, 1894*. Below that, a description. Ana peered closer. She didn't hear Violet McVicar walk quietly into the room. Her soft voice broke the silence.

"Yes, that's her," she said. "Frances Crowningshield. She was all of twenty then. Just a girl." Violet tapped her finger on the glass. "Now count over. See the slim young man with the mustache? There in the middle? He's wearing spectacles, with a white handkerchief in his breast pocket? That's Frank R. Little. Frank was a couple of years older than Frances. The next summer they were married."

Ana turned. "Amazing."

"Would you like to know more about her?" Violet asked.

Ana nodded.

"Let's go upstairs then." Violet turned and led the way, stretching for the rickety railing, adding mysteriously over her shoulder. "There's lots more."

VIOLET MCVICAR SAT down at a long wooden table on the second floor. She invited Ana to do the same, sighing. "Feels good to get off my feet," she said.

They were in the museum's tiny research library.

Violet had laid out on the table a stack of photographs, a file folder, and a large coffee table book of the Coolidge collection, which the museum had designed and had privately produced from public donations. The selling of small-town history has iffy monetary returns, but dedicated volunteers, people like Violet, made sure it never completely vanished.

Violet spread her hands on the table, a medium about to begin a séance. "Tell me, Ana, what is it you wish to know?"

Ana considered the question. She opened her laptop, scrolling down the screen. Google had more than a few mentions of the woman, but many more, of course, of her brother, Charles Richard. He had, after all, once been the ambassador to China. He was known, with no tongue in cheek, as the father of petroleum. He financed the first suspension bridge in Saudi Arabia. His end was untimely. Their father had basically invented the modern sanitary plumbing industry. The Crowningshields were wealthy beyond imagination. They were also powerful. Yet somehow Frances had managed to skirt all of that.

This was complicated. Ana looked up. "I'm not sure, exactly," she began. "I know she had gone to medical school. She was a licensed medical doctor, but chose instead to become a biology teacher."

Violet held up one finger. "Chose? No. Didn't choose. Forbidden. She was forbidden to practice medicine. In those days, women could study anything they wanted to, as long as they didn't practice it. Her family laid down the law, and that was that. Like you. You studied business; I'm guessing?"

Ana nodded. "Actually no, journalism, with a minor in American Lit and Art History."

"But still," Violet continued, "you were free to do what you will with your degree."

Ana shrugged. "I have to pay the rent."

Violet raised her finger again, triumphantly. "Exactly."

Ana nodded. "Frances, I've read, became very religious."

Again, Violet shook her head. Her voice raised a notch. "Her father, Richard the Elder, the scion of the dynasty, as it were, was a Methodist, a staunch Republican Methodist. He was a hard businessman, as unfeeling as stone, an outspoken critic of anything resembling higher education or spiritual belief that didn't comport with his world view. Frances began to see more value, more humanistic value, if you will, in becoming Catholic. Then later on she embraced many faiths. Buddhism, to name one. It was her way of practicing soft rebellion."

Ana stared at her. "Buddhism?"

Violet nodded. "Many faiths."

Ana shook her head. "Unbelievable."

Violet smiled. "Not so unbelievable. She'd lost a child, at birth, you see. That will have a profound effect on a woman."

"It sounds like you knew her well," Ana said.

Violet nodded. "My dear, I'll be ninety-four next month. I knew Frances, yes, certainly, quite well. She was one of the kindest people I've ever met."

Ana glanced down at the stack of photographs. "Tell me about these."

For the next hour they went through the images. Not all were of Frances. Many were of her brother, her father, her nephews and nieces, the good works she performed, like the imposing, stone bell tower she had commissioned on land owned by the Catholic church. Anyone could still see it if they drove down Water St. and looked across Eel Pond.

One photo caught her eye. It was a group portrait of about twenty children, posed on a grassy lawn, moving water in the background, the top yard of a passing schooner, just visible above the scraggly privet of a grassy bluff. A few women stood off to one side, staring shyly into the lens.

"Who are they?" she asked.

Violet placed her finger on the photograph, channeling memory. "Disadvantaged children, a few of them local, but most came from the cities, mainly from Chicago. High risk, you'd call them today. Wretched waifs living on the streets. Homeless orphans, many of them, or abandoned. And through no fault of their own. Heartbreaking."

Her eyes misted over. "Every child had their own story," she added.

Ana leaned closer. "And the women? Who were they?"

Violet smiled. "Oh, they were just people that Frances knew. Friends from the city, society women, I guess you'd call them, but really just good Christians who loved children and agreed to travel here in the summer months to help take care of them."

"So, it was an orphanage?" Ana asked. She bent to her notepad, jotting the word.

Violet shook her head again. "No, Ana, not in the strictest sense of the word. This wasn't an institution. More like a family, you might say. A social experiment, to see how much pure, absolute love could achieve. It had a kind of monastic quality. For Frances, it was the fulfillment of a dream."

"And where did all these children live?"

Violet smiled broadly, lightly caressing the photograph. "Why, up on the Point, of course. Her dead brother's mansion. She called it divine intervention. The children had plenty of room there, and fresh sea air, and good food and just about everything one could needed to flourish. Each child had their own bed, and no more than two to a room. It was just the loveliest place you could imagine. Lifelong relationships were formed, and it was all because of the kindness and vision of one woman."

Violet stood up quickly, surprisingly agile. "Ana," she said, "let's go back downstairs. I want to show you something that might explain things a little better."

VIOLET WAS POINTING down. "See that house? The one with the tower? That's the Crowningshield place."

Ana peered closely. They were downstairs, in the front room occupying one corner of the museum. It might have once been a kitchen. Before them lay a sprawling, intricately painted, glassed-in diorama. It stretched nearly from wall to wall, with just enough space on either end for a viewer to squeeze by.

"This is the town as it was in the 1880s," Violet explained. "The Crowningshield estate was brand new. Of course, back then, it was still called Butler's Point. The Butler family had always lived there. They built a lovely hotel, which sadly burned down, and before that, the first excursion boats to the island landed at Butler docks. They ran the first stagecoach tavern. When Judge Butler died, in 1909, the family sold the entire Point to Charles Crowningshield. He did a lot of fix-up on that old place. Queen Anne Victorians, you see, were no longer in vogue."

Ana stared down at the tiny, intricately constructed world. Tiny houses, tiny sailboats and tiny paddle steamers, a tiny locomotive, cotton smoke streaming from its tiny smokestack, huffing its way down a tiny grade into the village. A tiny, horse-drawn dray, its tiny driver urging two tiny horses down a tiny country lane, delivering tiny goods to a tiny market. Everything was in perfect proportion; late nineteenth century America in miniature.

"Incredible," Ana whispered. "Such detail."

Violet nodded. "Yes, it was built by George Metcalf and Chester O'Brien, two local men. Took them about a year. They had some help, but mostly it was just George and Chester. That was in 1938, the same year Hitler invaded Poland. Day after day, they would come here, after work, on weekends, to get this done for the Centennial. George enlisted in the Army the next year; he died at Anzio fighting the Germans. Chester survived the war, working at the family dairy. He had poor eyesight, don't you see, and couldn't serve. He fell off a barn roof in the 1960s." She clucked once. "Shouldn't have been up there, a man his age, on a ladder."

Ana looked over at Violet. "You know so much about this town, she said. Have you lived here all your life?"

Violet grinned, her emerald eyes flashing. "Not yet," she joked.

Ana laughed. "My grandfather used to say that."

Violet, nodding, still smiling. "Noble minds think alike. So, Ana," she began. "You've seen the museum, you've seen the diorama, you've talked to an old, yacky lady for over an hour. Would you actually like to see the house where Frances lived?"

Ana turned. "Is it close by?"

Violet glanced back down at the diorama, pointing. "See that road? That's Water Street And that's the museum, where we are now. Of course, back then it was still the Jewett farm. But that's how close we are to the Point. No more than a five-minute walk. I'm closing up for the day in a few minutes. Just have to log the receipts, such as they are, then I'm headed home. You're welcome to join me. I could introduce you to the new owners."

"You live there?" Ana asked.

Violet grinned again. "All my life."

JUNIPER POINT. IT WAS the same road it always had been. A few changes, but not many. The old stable on the right was now a private residence. The mill pond was still there, still lily clogged and mysterious and beautiful in its forlorn neglect, an emerald-lagoon clogged with algae and nearly hidden by a canopy of willow and oak trees. A handful of newer houses, those built after 1940, anyway, now hugged the road. The ice house was still standing, freshly shingled, transformed into an artist's painting s studio, in a sandy gully that overlooked Little Harbor. The boathouse was where it belonged, and the massive, timbered horse barn at the water's edge, like the stable, now in different hands and modernized. The sprawling Coast

Guard station occupied the same bit of beach where the old lifesaver's bunkhouse had once stood, bearded men in derbies and suspenders ready to launch surf boats at a minute's notice. Changes, yes. But the effect remained the same. Juniper Point itself would live forever, its human caretakers coming and going as they aged and died, as fortunes rose and fell, as families were created and legacies built and forgotten. But the ground itself? Vanish? Never.

THEY PAUSED AT A SMALL farmhouse. Two windows flanking a door, a configuration known locally as a "Quarter-Cape."

"This is me," Violet waved her arm, taking in a modest bit of dooryard. An ancient mailbox leaned toward the road. **McVicar.** " Home sweet home, for better for worse," she added. "Would you like to come in for a cup of tea, dear, before we head up?"

Ana followed her into the house. It had a musty, but pleasant aroma. The lived-in tang of old wallpaper, lace curtains, mothballs, and soon, tea water simmering. Somewhere from the back of the house, the odiferous astringency of cat litter. An enormous, geriatric tabby emerged from the shadows, arching its back as it slowly sauntered towards their ankles.

"Hello, Atticus, Violet greeted the animal. "He mostly sleeps," she explained. "That's his primary skill set nowadays. But he's earned the right to relax. I can't tell you how many mouse heads I used to find on the front stoop back when he was in his prime." She reached down and patted his dense, well-fed belly. "Now the birds have nothing to fear."

"And you live here alone?" Ana asked.

Violet's face saddened. "Yes, for quite a while. There <u>was</u> a Mr. McVicar, but that's another story. Now, the tea. I have Earl Gray. I have some nice herbs, and an Irish blend. Some people find it strong, but not me."

"The Irish sounds good," Ana said.

Violet nodded towards a couple of comfortable chairs, a soft couch beneath the window. "Please make yourself at home, Ana," she offered, then headed for the small kitchen at the rear of the house.

Sitting down on the couch, Ana retrieved a notepad from her messenger bag. A writing teacher had once opined that stories find the teller, not the other way around. Arriving here this morning, she'd expected something quite different. A book about Frances Crowningshield, an early feminist, pioneering supporter of children's rights, labor activist, a woman with a medical degree who chose instead to open an orphanage in her dead brother's mansion by the sea. It was a story, yes, but was it *the* story? Was it *her* story? A thought occurred to her. She called into the kitchen. "Violet, were you born in this house?"

The teakettle was now whistling. Violet appeared in the doorway.

"I'm sorry, dear. What was that?"

"I asked if you were born in this house."

Violet nodded. "Oh, my lands, yes. 1928. The year before the Crash. Every one of us was." She pointed to a doorway. "Right in the back bedroom, where I still sleep. Everyone except for Patrick, my oldest brother. He was born in New York City. I'm the baby of the family. All the rest are gone now."

"And your parents?" Ana asked. "What did they do?"

Violet pointed one finger skyward, like a schoolmarm explaining a difficult math problem. "Let me get our tea, and some nice biscuits, then I'll tell you all about them."

THE BIG HOUSE ON JUNIPER Point had been on the market for nearly two years when Harrison and Janice Sanderling first walked through the door. Ahead marched a breathlessly enthusiastic real estate broker by the improbable name of Nancy Selling. Nancy worked for the Cobblestone Agency in Falmouth. A sign on her desk was a coy play on words. *I'm Nancy, and I'm Selling...for you!*

Harrison and Janice had known immediately that this was the house for them. They walked from room to room, from one end of the 7,500 square foot mansion, each room with its own unique water view, a panoramic vista on a raised, circular lot that took in Little Harbor, the Woods Hole Passage, the Elizabeth Islands beyond, and finally, tantalizing peeks through the trees of the steamship docks and the sprawling waterfront campus of WHOI. The asking price was four and a half million, which they finally negotiated down to three point five. Nancy Selling's toothy Cheshire smile, incandescent with the kind of mercantile cupidity unique to realtors and used car salesmen, as they sat around a lawyer's conference room table at the closing three months later, had never been brighter. Her commission from the sale would net her a brand-new Mercedes convertible.

Harrison and Janice were the perfect buyers, and since then had become the perfect stewards. Harrison had been a professional woodworker who'd sold his cabinet shop in the city, then bought a bed and breakfast in Falmouth, which he ran for fifteen years. He knew houses, he knew wood, he knew business, and he knew how much grueling labor it would take to make Juniper Point both a home and a profitable enterprise. Janice was a softer version of Harrison. A yoga and meditation teacher from Rhode Island, who'd once transformed an old school house into a home and studio, , she knew things of a different sort. A kind, beatific soul, she knew plants, she knew how to bake, and she understood people. As a team, they were generous and patient, model employers to the army of workmen who came to the house each morning. They had pizzas delivered for the crew on Fridays, and were prompt and fair about paychecks. They never raised their voices, even in the heat of battle. Their lives seemed to well from a place of genuine kindness, and they possessed an almost preternatural belief that from hard work comes great things. The house was a monument to their tenacity; it was perhaps the greatest thing that either one of them had ever attempted.

JANICE ANSWERED THE door at the first knock. She brightened when she saw Violet standing out on the porch. Beside her a young woman she didn't know. But still, it was Violet McVicar, her favorite neighbor on Juniper Point.

"Oh, hello Violet. So great to see you. Has Atticus wandered off again?"

Violet pursed her lips. "He stays inside now. What with all these foxes around. Much too dangerous."

Janice nodded. "I know. They look so adorable, but they're still wild creatures."

She turned to Ana, extending her hand. "I'm Janice, Welcome. I just made some blueberry muffins. Are you hungry?"

"No, thank you," Violet said. "Ana?"

Ana shook her head. "I'm fine, thanks. They do smell delicious, though." She looked around the kitchen. Bright and airy and freshly painted, a large, new-looking commercial stove sat against one wall, the pungent aroma wafting out. The kitchen cabinets were unfinished plywood boxes. No drawers, or doors, but topped by a counter of thick, expensive granite.

Janice noticed her glance. "A work in progress," she explained airily. "But soon."

"Ana is a writer," Violet said. "She works for the *Boston Globe*. Something about finances. But she's here to research a book about Frances Crowningshield."

Janice smiled. "She was an incredible woman."

Ana shrugged. "To be perfectly honest, I haven't completely decided which direction to head. I just want to write something that has a little more meaning than weekly stories about the problems of rich people."

Janice's smile never wavered. It might have been a vague insult to the mistress of a 3.5-million-dollar fixer-upper, but she didn't respond, instead asking, "Would you like to a tour?"

Ana nodded. "Love to. The house is a lot bigger than I imagined."

"I showed her the diorama at the museum." Violet joked.

Janice led the way. Off in the distance, an insistent fusillade of nail guns, the occasional whine of a power saw. "Like I said," Janice called brightly over her shoulder, "a work in progress."

She led them up a narrow set of stairs that emerged on the second floor. "This was the servant's stair," she explained. "The main staircase isn't quite done yet."

They entered a wide hall with a series of closed doors. "Bedrooms," Janice explained. She pointed toward one door. "That was the nursery, these next three were for guests. There were ten all together, if you don't include the maid's quarters on the third floor. Each bedroom had a washing sink in it. The Crowningshield family owned a large plumbing supply business in Chicago. You probably knew that. That's where all the money came from."

She pointed to a freshly plastered wall. Drop cloths covered the floor. "Past that wall is what we call the condo. It's on the market, or will be when we're further along. We're dividing the house in half, or nearly in half. That will allow us to keep our side. In theory anyway. If the right buyer comes along. We don't want to sell to just anyone."

Violet shook her head vigorously. "Oh, heavens no. That would interfere with...what do you call it? The name for the house's spirit?"

Janice smiled. "Feng Shuai?"

"Yes, that."

They paused at the last door. "And this," Janice whispered reverentially, "leads to the tower. It's the reason that Harrison and I fell in love with the house."

They ascended another narrow set of stairs, leading to a small sunlit chamber. Tall, Palladian windows set into the sloping walls peeked out at the four cardinal directions. A statue of a seated golden Buddha occupied one windowsill. "My meditation space," Janice explained. "But up there," she pointed to an iron and wood ladder that disappeared into the bead board-sheathed ceiling, "that's where the magic is."

"You go ahead," Violet resolutely announced, plunking herself into a chair. "I'll wait down here."

Ana climbed skyward, gripping the brass railing, her shoes pinging echoes off the grated ladder. As her head popped through the opening, she gasped. The tower room was like some fantastical lighthouse. Made entirely of arched windows that looked out onto the glittering water beyond, a circular, slatted mahogany bench that ran , an earthbound yacht, the circumference of the tower. A polished brass telescope sat on a tripod, for viewing passing boats, or the stars. A narrow door led outside to the tower's walk-around. Everything was in its place. A snug lookout, meticulously constructed by craftsmen from a different age.

She turned just as Janice was climbing through the floor.

"This is unbelievable," Ana gushed.

"I know," Janice said. "Sometimes I can't believe that I actually live here. We are so incredibly blessed."

Ana stared through the windows. Hand carved cherubs had been placed at each corner. Far below, two workmen were carrying an enormous beam across the yard, which was partially covered by a tall mound of fresh dirt.

"There's still a long way to go," Janice said. "But we knew what we were getting into when we bought this house. It will all get done. It's so worth it. One has to trust."

Ana turned to her. "I totally agree with you. Faith in your choices. That seems to be the secret to life, doesn't it?"

Janice nodded, a mysterious shine in her eyes. "One of them, anyway," she said.

ANA AND VIOLET SAID their goodbyes and began walking back down the steep hill to the road. In the driveway, just as they passed, workmen were tossing bits of wood and plaster chunks into a large green dumpster. Next to it, they'd placed an enormous, lead-lined crate, with cut ends of plumbing pipe dangling from each end. It looked extremely heavy, handmade, primitive but somehow ingenious. Ana bent down beside the crate, examining one end closely. She turned back to Violet. "It's somebody's name written on it. I can barely make out the letters. It's some kind of dark crayon. She wiped the dust away and began to slowly pronounce each letter, as if they were hieroglyphics.

"A...R...T...H...U...R. It says Arthur."

She peered quizzically up at Violet.

"Can you make out the last name, dear?" Violet asked.

Ana turned back to the writing, tracing the delicate, curlicue penmanship. "R...O...U...S...E. It says Rouse," she said. "Then a date after that. 1910."

One of the workmen wandered over. "That was up in the attic," he explained. "Bitch of a time getting it down."

"Do you know what it was for?" Ana asked.

The man nodded. "Yeah, sort of. Some kind of storage tank, gravity fed, that filled up the bathtubs with salt water. Pretty amazing technology for its day. We saved the old electrical system. Pretty cool. The owner wanted to keep it for a memento."

Ana nodded. "Arthur Rouse," she mused. "I wonder who he was."

Violet smiled. "Well, that's easy, dear. He was my father."

THEY WERE WALKING BACK down the lane. "So Ana," Violet said, "tell me, what are your plans? For the rest of your visit, I mean."

Behind them, the looming mass of the big house cast long shadows across the road. Back in her kitchen, Janice had resumed making dinner, slicing carrots and parsnips for the evening's soup. The dense aroma of baking bread wafted from the enormous, six-burner European cookstove. As she worked, she hummed a tuneless melody of thanksgiving. It was the song of unexpected fortune, a song of contented gratitude. She was a woman happy in her life, once a single mother with a crippling mortgage, a failed marriage and a ten-year-old Volvo, now happy in the choices she had made, happy with her husband of three years, happy that the funds had been there to provide for such a miracle. She spent every free moment up in the tower, blessing her circumstance, staring out at a glittering, blue cathedral of restless water.

The workmen had all gone home for the night. They'd return on Monday morning, and so, for now, it was just she and Harrison, approaching their second summer, alone on the hill.

"PLANS?" ANA SHRUGGED. "Oh, I don't really know, to tell you the truth. I thought it would all be so clear by now, this book project, but now, not so much."

Violet reached out, grasping Ana's hands in her own. "Here's an idea. Why don't you spend the night with us, Atticus and II? Driving back to Boston doesn't sound like much fun. I have a nice guest room all set up. I'll make us some dinner. We can talk some more about your writing. Perhaps that would help. I get so little company these days. Perhaps it would be good for both of us."

Ana's face, bathed in the golden dusk. "That's very generous," she said. "I would actually love that. It's been a long day."

Violet nodded, smiling. "My sentiments exactly. Boston will still be there when you return, I promise."

AFTER DINNER, THEY sat together on the couch. "Just to continue our conversation," Ana began, "what of your parents? Where were they originally from?"

Violet regarded her thoughtfully. "Well, Mother, she was from Ireland, a little town in the south country. My dad, Arthur, he was from Scotland. Aberdeen. That's a bit like mixing oil and water, but somehow, they made it work."

Ana jotted this down. "And where did they meet? My parents met in college, out in Ohio. I'm always curious about people's origin stories."

"Ah," Violet said. "Well, actually, my dear, they met right here."

Ana arched an eyebrow, then bent again to her notebook.

Violet continued. "It was their first summer. The summer of 1910. He was a mechanic, a foundry man, he used to tell us. He really could do just about anything having to do with machinery. Mr. Crowningshield sent him here from Chicago to mend the plumbing. Actually to start from scratch. There was nothing here, really, in the way of amenities. Most people back then, in the country anyway, had no indoor facilities. And the poor chambermaids, they had to empty the bed pots in the morning. Can you imagine?"

Ana wrinkled her nose at the image.

"And your mother?"

Violet peeked down at her lap. A sleeping Atticus was snoring, deep in a feline pursuit dream.

"Mother was the family nanny," Violet explained, "come out by private rail car all the way from the Crowningshield's home in Chicago. She was a woman never better suited to minding children, her own or others. She just had a gift." Her eyes were suddenly very far away.

"It's magical," Ana said quietly. "It gives me the chills."

Violet placed one finger on her lips and slowly stood up, carefully brushing the cat to the floor. Atticus shook himself, stretched, leapt into a nearby chair, fell quickly back to sleep.

"Goodness, where are my manners? I haven't offered you a cordial. I myself prefer a bit of peach brandy. It helps me sleep."

Ana stared up at her. "I don't drink. I *can't* drink." She paused. "It's complicated."

Violet considered this. "Say no more. I'll be right back," she promised mysteriously, and hurried away.

Returning with a smallish cardboard box, Violet laid it down in front of Ana, cupping one hand over a yawn. "I'm off to bed soon. But take a look at what's inside, if you like. It will explain things a bit better."

She patted the box, which had once held cans of Campbell's soup. It was tied with a blue, satin ribbon. "You might find it interesting, as a writer. I mean, Frances was a great woman, a saint even, but there has been a great deal already written about her, about the family. Her story is already quite well known, I'm afraid. She lifted the box, handed it reverentially into Ana's arms.

"My family story."

"It's a diary," Ana guessed, her fingertips hovering over the lid. She felt a kind of mild electrical pulse course through her body, as if on the edge of a great discovery.

Violet nodded. "Mother kept it her entire life. It was her secret. Nobody knew about it, not even my father, but it's all there. She wrote down everything."

"Everything...religiously," she added.

Ana stared down at the box. Such a different direction life can carry us. We imagine we are headed there, and we end up here. She recalled the same words she'd thought while crossing the bridge that morning.

"This is an American story," she finally said.

Violet smiled. "Why, yes, I suppose it is. I trust you'll know what to do with it."

ANA SAT UP IN BED READING, the open soup box next to her. Occasionally she would reach inside to lift another paper out. The sounds of the night became the soundtrack for the diary, which really wasn't a diary, a linear document, as in page numbers, an orderly narrative. It was, rather, an assemblage of interrelated discoveries, like shards unearthed from the ground. Brittle stationary, some with the family crest embossed at the top, old postcards, the backs of envelopes, grocery receipts, telegrams, random scraps of paper. Ana knew this wouldn't be easy, collating a lifetime of hen scratches and scrawls. But here, in the aggregate, was precious reliquary, like slivers of the One True Cross. If she could weave it all into a single narrative, if might become a manuscript, perhaps even a book. But she also knew it was up to her alone. Otherwise it would be a tragedy, a loss, an omission, as if the creator of these artifacts, Rosemary Kincaid, once was, and now was gone, as disappeared as morning fog burned by the sun.

The blatting of passing ferries, the clang of a bell buoy, a distant truck downshifting into the village, snuck in through the bedside window, cracked an inch for fresh air. She thought of Janice and Harrison, encamped for the time being on their third floor, the old servant's quarters. But in the morning, instead of greeting an army of house girls and a butler or two, they would wander back down to the kitchen to drink expresso and read the Sunday *New York Times.* She wondered how they would react if they knew the story captured inside these loose pages; written by a lowly nanny, written in stolen moments after the children were asleep and before they woke. She wondered about the Crowningshield family, remnants of a once mighty plumbing dynasty, aged children of privilege who still lived in the same weary houses up and down the road. What might they think? There were two remaining sons, according to Violet. Two brothers who had sold the family home to outsiders, the first since 1910 not a Crowningshield, and Jewish outsiders no less. They were reputedly as miserable and dour as the scion, Richard the Elder, had been.

At two a.m., Ana finally snapped the bedside lamp off. Dark displaced light, but the ocean sounds remained, amplified in the shadowy gloaming.

That night she dreamed. It was informative, and reassuring. Her story had found her, as it always would.

If she only listened.

Tomorrow she would begin.

PART TWO

The Mechanic

CHAPTER ONE

Arthur

Early summer, 1910.

Arthur Rouse, a foundry man from Chicago, was a passenger on a train. Arthur loved trains. He loved their brute might. He loved their mechanical soul. How the engine sounded like a big panting dog as it thundered along the meandering roadbed. The clack of the steel rails that connected, like a telegrapher's dot and dash, New York City and his final destination, the sandy scimitar of Cape Cod, Massachusetts. He loved its dragon's breath, the sooty plume of exhausted steam billowing from its painted stack. He loved the train song of the conductor, the official glint of his brass buttons and chromate ticket puncher, as he sonorously announced each arrival. He loved the whistle's urgent, mournful hoot at each crossing and each arrival.

Arthur loved that train.

He had ridden many on his long journey to the sea.

THE COACH WAS CROWDED, and overheated, and stank of baby shit and luncheon meats, rank sweat beneath heavy clothing and cologne and perfume to cover up the sweat. Arthur was a traveler, just like the others on this train. But unlike many of them, on this humid, blue morning in May, holiday men and women in dime-store flowered hats and jaunty black derbies, he was coming here to do a job, to the small coastal village of Woods Hole. Here is where the iron tracks met the restless sea. Arthur's entire life had been distilled into this day, this hour, this moment.

His usefulness was now in fully realized bloom.

ARTHUR CLOSED HIS EYES and drifted back to a lifetime of labor. Work was his religion. It spoke to him of creation, of mechanical liturgies; the holy trinity of imagination, materials, and invention. He had spent what lifetime God had allotted to him; cutting and hammering, shaping superheated material into new and useful objects. Their complexity often bordered on the mystical. Arthur Rouse was a foundry man, and these were the halcyon days of the Golden Age of Industry. Men like Arthur were the Handmaidens of Progress. They understood both the plain and transcendent. They were not men of academic small talk and dusty theoretical ruminations in the classroom. Men like Arthur were the anointed builders. They lit the furnace, hefted the beam, and got on with it.

IN THE STUFFY CONFINES of a New York, New Haven, and Hartford passenger coach, Arthur felt a dampness drip from his armpits and rejoiced in his aliveness. He was a man with a trade. He was necessary.

Sadly, though, he had never learned to read.

He felt for the timetable book in his pocket. For an illiterate man, it was a complicated affair getting from Chicago to New York City, then from New York City to Cape Cod. There was a precise calculus to traveling. But sometimes the timetable was wrong, or the engine broke down, or jumped the track, and a traveler might miss a connection. In New York, the same timetable in his hand, a small, vest-pocket book he had pulled from a rack by the ticket agent, he had sought out someone, a uniformed attendant, to help with the schedule. They were easy to spot. Helpful-looking men in blue, with scarlet piping down each pant leg the same color as their caps. These men, called Red Caps, were placed around the terminal, *"...to assist passengers with their hand luggage, to direct them to the streetcar lines, to call cabs, to assist feeble persons, and to render such other assistance as may be reasonably required. Those men, however,"* warned the special notice printed in the free booklet, *"will not do porter's work or handle heavy baggage."*

Arthur wasn't feeble. He needed no assistance with his luggage, or someone to procure for him a hackney. He just needed someone to decipher the mystery of the words, the chaotic jumble of letters, so he would know which train went where at what time. All of his life it had been this way. Arthur's difficulty was well-known at the factory. His survival skills were primitive and life-hewn. He had left school at seven, to work in his father's blacksmithing shop, a common enough practice for country boys. Reading and writing was for the educated, for the titled gentry, for soft-handed boys of means, destined to matriculate in one classroom after another. No one had ever bothered to teach him even the alphabetical basics. Arthur moved through the world like a blind man, stumbling over simple obstacles that sighted people took for granted. A document, a letter, a sign.

Traveling on a train was a formidable obstacle.

He walked up to the nearest Red Cap, as he had since leaving Chicago, explained the problem. Within a minute, the man had cheerfully pointed him to the correct track, told him when the train was leaving, and which stop he needed to change for the local. He repeated it three times, and pointed for emphasis. The next, and final, leg of the journey involved a stop at someplace called Fall River. Arthur heard it as Falling River, and thought the name lovely.

Here the man had paused. He was a statuesque, muscular Negro with a kind face and the largest hands Arthur had ever seen. He might have been a laborer like himself, a man used to pushing a barrow or hammering rivets, perhaps helping to build the city's forest of skyscrapers quickly sprouting up. Or he might have been a jazz pianist, reaching for impossible chords, anticipating downbeats, smoothing out the ragged edges of the maddest of tempos.

"Train will take you all day, sir." Here the Red Cap had winked, man to man. "Why not take a steamer? There's a one leaving from Pier 19, around...let me see now... he flipped through the pages of the timetable...yes, here it is. It leaves at five-thirty tonight. Get you there around..." He glanced down again, "Nine-thirty, give or take." Then he looked across at Arthur, smiling broadly. "Get you off that noisy locomotive, sir. Clean air, seagulls, pretty girls, maybe have a tall, cold beer."

Arthur shook his head, reaching for his bags. He extended his own calloused hand of thanks. The black man stepped back, as if burned. Tips, or gratitude, from travelers, were expressly forbidden.

"I like trains," the white man was saying. "Boats sink."

THE DAY WAS UNSEASONABLY warm, the warmest May within memory, and Arthur was a man on a journey watching the scenery roll by. The train cars clattered and swayed, the conductor strolled from end to end. A whistle blew occasionally. He could feel the car's shudder and roll through the soles of his shoes. Life was just past the window. It was a moving picture show. He had no idea what was next, except that he had come here to do a job.

CHAPTER TWO

Rosemary

Rosemary's journey, a day earlier, was just as humid, just as thickly torpid, the unmoving air inside her wood and velvet coach as hot as the factory furnace that paid her salary. It was her first visit to this place; and still a mystery. A small Cape Cod village, a big house on a sandy hill that overlooked a busy seafaring watercourse connecting harbor to harbor. A palace of shingle and stone and brick, with a magical turreted observation tower that guarded a spacious, verdant lawn.

She'd had been brought along as a nanny by a prosperous Chicago family. Her work concerned itself with the lives of three impeccably well-behaved children. Sitting opposite her was an immaculately dressed woman, a mother in her early forties, accustomed to the finest of everything. She sat and read her book, studiously ignoring her children's problems, their occasional cries and needs.

In 1910, upper class parents typically left that role to professional caregivers. More often than not, nannies were white, single, young, and Irish. She might earn less than $3.00 a week, and also typically roomed with the family.

Rosemary's attention moved from child to child; comforting, cajoling, offering calm, constructive explanations to blurted questions. From a large, velveteen traveling bag, she dispensed food and drink, books and toys. But her real gift was patience, love, and understanding. She read them their adventure stories, placated their occasional tantrums, pointed out passing objects of interest: the random cow, a marsh hawk exploding into the blue sky, an amusing cloud overhead, and occasionally bottle-fed and rocked a squalling newborn to the point of blissful narcosis.

The oldest child was no longer a child. Josephine Crowningshield was nineteen, a young woman, with her own baby in her arms. That would have made the baby the grand-daughter of the woman with the book. But to a professional nanny, she was just another child.

Rosemary might have been resentful of her circumstances, to be confined on a moving rail coach with a rich man's children. But she was a good, pleasant-natured woman with a kind heart. She, in fact, loved her work, and went about it with cheerful benefaction, calm and steady as a metronome. The children's mother, on the other hand, was a very different woman. She sat as regal and aloof as a czarina. White kid gloves covered the softest of hands that had never touched a drop of dishwater, pinned a nappy on a squalling baby, or lifted a feather duster onto a chandelier dripping with faceted crystal. She suffered from an occasional bout of moodiness, tectonic dispositional shifts that caused her household staff to be always on the alert.

The mother's narrowed hazel eyes scanned the pages of a popular novel. *The Wild Olive*, by Basil King, recommended by a friend back in the city. *"Finding himself in the level wood-road,"* she read, *"whose open aisle drew a long, straight streak across, still luminous with the late-lingering Adirondack twilight, the tall young fugitive, hatless, coatless, and barefooted, paused a minute for reflection."*

The unsmiling czarina on the train was Cornelia Workman Crowningshield. She had been born a Smythe, of *the* Paterson, New Jersey Smythes. *But, of course.* She and her husband were first cousins, nearly siblings. In 1910, theirs was a common union. There would be no dilution of blood between the Crowningshields and the Smythes. They had named their children, in order of birth: Josephine, Cornelia, Anita, and the youngest, a son, John Oliver.

Occasionally Cornelia glanced up, holding a finger to the place in the book. Her gaze was a silent rapprochement, as she watched her nanny tending to the children, with a soft brogue and whispered ministrations. She understood it was her job, as employer, to be a critical overseer to her lessers, be they Negro Pullman porters or Irish girls fresh off the boat. Rosemary could never be a friend. She was inarguably not her equal. This was a social contract of the times, an insoluble class notion fixated in the Anglo-Saxon roots of all things white and wealthy and entitled. In the deepest American South this same attitude would apply to Negroes, as they were still called in 1910, or by a slur far darker. All ruling class citizens maintained such imaginings, deriving power from their relationship with the subordinate Others. In urban America, in places like Chicago, it was the Irish, the Italians, the Jews, the Blacks, and, of course, all Catholics, coupled with a long list of undesirables, foreigners, including, but not limited to, Mexicans and Chinaman, Gypsies and Arabs, and especially in Chicago, the Polish, who stank of kielbasa and sweat and worked the stockyards.

An Irish girl would get hired as much for servility as for her pale skin. This was as true in America as it was in Great Britain. They would occupy a clearly defined station, and could ascend no higher. Boot firmly on neck, but politely, with noblesse oblige. That is how a proper mistress prevented her staff from unseemly attainments, from ascensions to stations beyond their caste, from interactions with their betters. Both halves understood. The ruling class ruled. The serving class served. It was a story that had been written generations before, and in 1910, before the 20th century began to shake itself free of such hidebound convention, before the Great War and the fall of Gallipoli, before the floor-a-week miracle of the Empire State Building, before air conditioning and elevators and the nattering novelty of television, it was stifling in its antiquated sameness.

THE TRAIN CLATTERED on. The trip, interminable. The children were growing cranky. Their need was to caper and play. Instead, little backs ached against velvet-covered horsehair, little nostrils stung from the constant coal dust streaming through the cracks in the window frames. Food was boring, even created by a private chef in a private dining car, and sleeping...! My God! No human body could quite adjust to the constant serpentine shake and shudder of a twenty-car locomotive rounding a curve at midnight.

NOTICEABLY ABSENT WAS the still-living ghost that was the children's father. Charles Richard Crowningshield was a man who traveled obsessively, and always quite alone. Since he was a teenager, the son of a powerful manufactory owner, he had been a compulsively solitary adventurer. After singlehandedly crossing the Atlantic in a small sloop at nineteen, he had walked across the plains of Siberia at twenty. He had dined with Maharajas and danced in palaces before he was twenty-five. His justification for such worldly, but frivolous, excursions had been a kind of nervous, adolescent exhaustion. The subtext was an overbearing father, who didn't believe in higher education, coupled with an inherently lazy constitution. And so, the habitual and continual journeying and disappearances, stitched together like an infinite mobius strip, that left his marriage and his family in a constant condition somewhere between despair and excitation, between abandonment and reunion. There were trips to Russia, trips to Arabia, to Italy and England and France and Germany. He spoke six or seven languages, and could order dinner in all of them, yet he could barely converse with his own children. No matter. He had seen the sunrise from the tip of a Giza pyramid, had rafted down the Amazon, seen revolutions, supped with Maharajahs and flirted with concubines. There was an exquisite sadness in his privileged isolation, his unquenchable need to always be somewhere far-off and exotic. Marriage and fatherhood had not, would never, change him. He was the Joshua Slocum of his own selfish wanderlust, lost in a solitary voyage of world travel. His joys were the preparations before and the homecomings after, the boastful cork-popping burble with other worldly men in the smoking rooms of the Jekyll Island Club, a private millionaire's enclave in Georgia. He was a rich man's oldest son, and had never worked, not in the desperate sense of dawn awakenings, punch clocks and meager paychecks.

CHARLES'S FATHER, THE great Richard Teller Crowningshield, had been a young machinist from New Jersey. He'd started the R.T. Crowningshield Brass and Bell Foundry with his brother, in Chicago. He made a great fortune in industrial supplies; brass casings, plumbing pipes and fittings, weathervanes, railroad castings, heating systems and finally elevators. But by 1910, the sturdy, uber-achieving patriarch was a forgetful old man who cocked his head to listen to birds and waited for his lunch in a comfortable chair by the window. Soon he would die, of porous arteries, in

1913. His company, and all its children of industry, employees like Arthur, would be a fatherless, but hopefully not rudderless, ship.

In 1910, Charles Richard Crowningshield was a relatively fit, if not slightly delicate fifty-two. He was the eldest and would run the company for another year. But his heart, although healthy, was never really in the business, and so, after a messy public feud, he would sell his half of the company to his younger brother Richard, for eighteen million dollars. He would never have to pretend to work again.

CHAPTER THREE

The Village

Arthur's final train was a local run. It had stopped four times since leaving Fall River. Plymouth, Marion, Falmouth, and then finally Woods Hole. From there passengers could disembark for the steamer to Cottage City, the Presbyterian enclave on Martha's Vineyard. The stately wooden paddle wheeler would then depart Oak Bluffs harbor, head out to sea for the nearly twenty-seven mile voyage, to the whaling island of Nantucket. For those passengers continuing by rail on to Hyannis or further still, towards Provincetown, the locomotive had a simple engineering trick to get the engine turned around. An ingenious planked turntable that rotated using steam power. It was a simple matter to hook back up to the string of passenger coaches, and continue on its return trip.

The Fall River to Woods Hole run was crowded with tourists on holiday, farmers and fishermen, the wives of farmers and fishermen, and their noisy children. A few traveling salesmen, perhaps a drummer, pasting up posters for the coming circus, a gaggle of serious-looking marine biology students returning from a day trip to Boston, and a sprinkling of tourists on holiday. At one table, a trio of Irish house maids returning from their monthly Saturday off. The car was a virtual League of Nations; a soft cacophony of accents: Cape Cod Yankee, Irish brogues, a few Slavic and German and even one Italian. Directly across from him, a tall, distinguished, Negro gentleman sat, with impeccable posture, a leather valise in his lap, gazing serenely out the window. He was a music teacher who gave private lessons to village children, returning from a piano concert he had performed in a large New Bedford social hall.

Arthur loved the train, but was relieved to see the trip end. He had debarked from seven different cars since leaving Chicago. Seven cities, uncounted stations between. Finally, on the morning of the fourteenth, the engine shuddered to a final, squealing stop. They had arrived. Arthur stood up, cricked his neck from side to side, nodded to his brief traveling companion, the black gentleman, who nodded back, almost imperceptibly. Arthur strode purposefully down the aisle. There was no joke to his stride: here was a working man with a job to do. Arthur was a muscular, imposing six feet two inches tall, with an unruly shock of ginger hair that fell into his eyes when he was sorting out a problem. He had an easy, crooked smile, and in his calloused hands he carried two items. Their combined weight was inconsequential, but it might as well have been iron ingots. Arthur wasn't a shopkeeper, or an accountant. He was a giant who toiled on Olympus. He worked in a foundry, hefting unimaginably heavy objects, staring into the blast furnace, accomplishing complex joinery on a massive scale. Yet he could be capable of great tenderness. Once, when his fifty-cent pocket watch stopped keeping time, he disassembled the cursed thing, laying aside tiny gears and springs until the problem was solved, and within a half an hour, it was ticking again. Arthur had a calm, assured relationship with the glorious machinery of modern life that most mortals took for granted.

In his right hand, he carried a large, worn, leather suitcase, tied tight with a loop of butcher's twine. Inside were a change of shirts, a pair of black Sunday pants, several engineering books that Mr. Crowningshield had given him, unintelligible and unread, an old pair of barber shears, a stack of letters, undeciphered and unanswered, tied with a length of blue silk, such as a woman might use to keep her long hair back, and a small, painted child's toy, representing a steam locomotive, cast from pig iron. In the left, he held a course roll of soiled sail cloth, a mechanic's bag crimped towards the middle with a scuffed, leather handle. On the face of the bag, his name was printed in blocky black letters: *Rouse*. Inside were the tools of his trade. These objects represented the entire possessions of Arthur Rouse, foundryman, metalsmith, fabricator of modern sanitary water closets, a mechanical savant of the highest order.

Born in Aberdeen, Scotland, Arthur was now a loyal employee of the R.T Crowningshield Brass and Bell Foundry, a name lately shortened, for ease of public recognition, to Crowningshield Company, or CrownCo, its familiar colophon a graceful, delft-blue motif of intertwined Cs.

The locomotive, briefly finished with its eight-hour journey from New York City, chaffing off clouds of excess steam, sat quietly cooling its boilers. Gray clouds of coal smoke were blown flat by the early afternoon zephyrs that came like clockwork each day across the far edges of Buzzards Bay, and further still, Nantucket Sound.

CHAPTER FOUR

Arrival

Rosemary's train was a private sleeping and dining car owned by the Crowningshield Company, for use by executives and family, by special arrangement with the New York, New Haven, and Hartford railroad. When not so employed, it was kept in its own covered shed at the New York switching yard, right next to J.P. Morgan's larger, much more ornate, covered shed. When the family traveled in the east, their coaches were coupled behind a line of public cars, for traveling convenience and comfort. Richard Crowningshield, the elder, had begun this practice in the late 1880s. It insulated him from the wail of other people's children, as well as sundry, low elements of society that he now very much avoided. The tradition of the private car remained, and by this conveyance the Crowningshield family traveled from the greatest of American cities, New York, although Chicago, they quietly maintained, deserved that rating.

They were scheduled to arrive at a precise hour. Once alerted by the station master, in the form of a village boy pedaling a velocipede, a large, shining motorcar, a two-year-old Model T Ford, driven by a chauffeur in pressed black livery with twin rows of brass buttons and jodhpurs tucked into high-shined boots, would arrive at the tracks to meet them.

With the Crowningshield family, it was all clockwork, all domestic pomp and ceremony. Charles Richard Crowningshield, son of Richard Teller Crowningshield, was a man of diminished work ethic but unshakable routine. Even though he was rarely at home, (he was presently in London, sitting down to tea with Her Majesty's Finance Minister), he demanded rigid adherence to schedule from both his family and employees.

Thusly, during the summer of 1910, forty hired servants, many women, mostly Irish, as well as a lesser amount of grounds and livery men, were engaged in one task or another on the nearly twelve acres comprising the

Crowningshield estate on Juniper Point. Their single, abiding occupation, from pantry maid to head gardener to stable boy, was a simple one, tending to the constant needs and desires of the Crowningshield family.

CHAPTER FIVE

The Foundryman

As Arthur ambled slowly past the locomotive, he absently patted its enormous iron flanks. It was a gesture of intimate familiarity between mechanic and machine. The boilers in the locomotive might well have been built by his factory, the same with the lubricating boxes and the driving wheels beneath. To the average person, the train was a simple conveyance, an iron horse that brought them, on time and with rare breakdowns, from here to there. But to a man like Arthur, a foundry man with a naturally unschooled engineering genius, it was the miracle of modernity. With an almost reverential devotion he blessed its moving parts; it's great valves and pistons, the hammered rivets that sewed the iron skin into a single epidermis. He admired the massive boilers, the elegant copper kettles that heated the steam that moved the valves and pistons that made it all go. To him, the train represented nothing less than the exquisite architecture of the Golden Age of Industry. It spoke to him in the language of the machine builders, both the celebrated and silent men, all capable of endless invention; engineer-capitalists who had made America the sparkling jewel amidst the dung heap of the lesser, darker nations. These were the dreamers who summoned forth an almost limitless flow of novel ingenuity to the masses. Thomas Edison, who changed night into day. Henry Ford, who made every man a master of the motorway, at an affordable cost. These were the bridge builders, the wilderness mapmakers, the river diverters, and the mountain movers, men who had created their masterpieces, not in some dusty classroom, but by hard work, by pluck, and by an almost preternatural vision of the possible.

And then there was Richard Teller Crowningshield, Arthur's original benefactor and mentor, of Paterson, New Jersey, who stood head and shoulders with these giants. Crowningshield was the father of modern indoor plumbing, a mythological hero who had gone to work as a boy of nine in a Brooklyn blacksmithing shop to help support his family. He worked a variety of menial jobs, learned a variety of trades. Sensing a shift in national fortune, he moved to Chicago at twenty-three to help his uncle in the lumber business. But it was foundry work that truly moved him. Finally, he built his own machine shop, on a corner of his uncle's lumberyard, a simple wooden shed, sized twenty by forty feet, hammered together by his own hand, and on the Fourth of July, 1864, a day when the rest of the nation was waving tiny flags and gobbling bratwurst, he'd dug the sandy hole for his first casting pit. It had all been a gamble, this modest beginning. But Richard was not like any boy. At twenty-six he won his very first contract, fabricating lubricating boxes for the railroad. He made brass harness buckles for Union infantry horses in the Civil War, and other items vital to the army effort. His was a true rags-to-riches story. Horatio Alger had actually modeled his plucky novel heroes after Richard Teller Crowningshield.

Arthur himself had shown an early talent for foundry work, arriving in Chicago at eighteen with an inquisitive mind for technical matters, an illiterate natural who only needed the merest of nudges to unravel a mechanical solution. He was a sponge for knowledge and skill. Twenty-two years later, he was known as *the* master mechanic at Crowningshield Company. Even though the gigantic manufacturer, a sprawling facility that covered nearly ten acres, was now in the hands of two feuding sons, neither of whom knew much about the industry they now controlled, it was Arthur Rouse who most embodied the guiding premise of Richard the Elder's original enterprise. There was nothing he could not do, if it involved rolling and casting and hammering steel. Anything that could be imagined could be built by Arthur Rouse. He was considered, by all that knew and worked beside him, as much more than a mere mechanic. He was an authentic genius, that Arthur Rouse, an actual, bonafide *artiste*. The Old Man had said as much, would continue to say it until the day he died.

ROSEMARY, ON THE OTHER hand, toiled in the thankless vineyards of domestic servitude. In the late spring of 1910, she was thirty-two years old.

Old for an unmarried woman, she was still pretty enough about the face and figure to claim admiring glances. A moot point, employment-wise. Married women were considered generally unfit for domestic service, particularly as nannies. The term had yet to be invented, but Rosemary was, by definition and circumstance, a career woman, and her career was other people's children. For this service, on call twenty-four hours a day, seven days a week, she was paid three dollars per week, plus lodging and victuals. She had journeyed to America seeking employment, had worked in a series of upper-class households before she was hired by the Crowningshields. Two in Chicago, one in Minnesota.

Yet Rosemary, by nature a quietly reserved woman, held her secrets. She had begun to keep a personal diary. Each night, and each morning, precious moments that constituted the sum total of her "personal time," she recorded the plain events of her life, which she concealed beneath her mattress. Out of concern for discovery, and dismissal, she used only first names and initials. *Mrs. C, down to breakfast. Toast and coffee. J. with fever. Called doctor. Sunny this morning, but winds and rain in the afternoon. Talked to D. briefly. He is planting azaleas by the front porch. J. is such a pain. I think she hates me. Cramps this morning.*

She wrote of her own life. Her disappointments, daily fatigues, menstrual cycles, unrequited crushes on men: gardeners, chauffeurs, stablemen, shopkeepers, house carpenters, and automobile mechanics. This diary was truly the only place she could just be Rosemary. Her public-facing persona was good-natured employee, god-fearing and hard-working, not the vindictive stereotype of the Irish "Bridget," a foul-mouthed shrew that humor weeklies like *Punch* loved to portray. Yet she also carried a hardened, dark blemish on her heart. Life would never be quite right, just underappreciated labor and the inescapable routine of economic slavery. She resented the harsh cruelties of the modern world, but the smile never left her face. She had seen the signs in storefronts: *Irish not apply,* and harbored a simmering distrust for the emperius English overlords who had subjugated her country, the land barons and their far-off government, wealthy peacocks strutting like potentates. These were the men who had carved the very best farmlands into vast estates, leaving the rest a stony, feudal, hardscrabble existence. They had cruelly triggered the great starvations, thoughtlessly driven the subsequent diaspora of immigrant millions. But the potato famines were long in the past. Now, at the beginning of summer, 1910, Rosemary was a devoted, loyal servant. She had mostly wearied of class hatred, or even of waiting for a husband. She occupied herself with her domestic duties; minding the children, exuding a courteous and pleasant countenance, speaking to her betters in a soft, respectful contralto. She sent half her pay home to a widowed mother, an equally weary woman who never wrote back.

THEY WERE ROUNDING the last curve, climbing the last hill. Rosemary kept vigil on the passing scenery. It was changing, morphing from rural desolation to signs of civilization. They passed an occasional farm house, the march of telephone poles, a gray horse pulling a hay wagon, a solitary man tramping into the village. Leaving Chicago, she had silently rejoiced. Even though the Crowningshields lived in Victorian opulence, it was still a dingy, cacophonous city. She hated the odiferous violence of the stockyards, the scuttling devilry of huge brown sewer rats rooting in rubbish bins. She hated Chicago's namesake river, still toxic from the shitty outfall of human sepsis, that in 1885, was rumored to have caused 75,000 people to die of cholera and malaria. That exact number had proved to be overstated, apocryphal and historically false. Still, the Chicago river remained a polluted river of human and animal effluent.

She loved the first kiss of early May, because it meant leaving these hated things, when the family would escape to some distant idyll. Even the constant choke of coal dust from a moving steam locomotive, as long as it led her away from that urban blight, was a welcome respite.

One day was not much different than the next. Arthur and Rosemary saw the same view through their coach windows, filtered, yes, by the lens of their respective occupations, but the same nevertheless. Scrub oaks and wind-bent cedars replaced the soaring plumage of forests that marked their long inland journey. Salt tang simmered in the heated air. Rosemary's private car lurched around the final bend in the tracks before making its slow, braking descent into the village. As she stood and craned her slender neck for a better view, the children crowded around her, like ducklings to their mother. Rosemary slid the glass open, and tasted the morning. Glorious! She turned and beamed across at Mrs. Crowningshield, who glanced up once from her reading, clucked quietly at this public display of excitement. They were rolling the last hundred feet, the terminus of the rail spur, where the tracks met the sea. A small, tidy station with slatted benches and freight wagons lay just ahead. A water tower, resembling a giant wooden acorn, hugged the spur, and beside that, the enormous wooden turntable. Block letters were painted on the tower's curved staves: *Woods Hole*. But just beyond...and here Rosemary smiled again. Salt water, a bright, glittering bit of ocean, or at least a body of water that led to the ocean. The last time she had seen such a beautifully wild, unruined thing, and here, she and Arthur Rouse, shared the same fading memory—was from the deck of an iron immigrant ship, passing Lady Liberty, at the end of her hope-laden voyage to America.

CHAPTER SIX

Juniper Point

Stepping clear of the tracks, Arthur pondered his course. He'd always prided himself on his navigation skills, an inner compass that rarely failed. His first time in Chicago, after a two-day train journey from New York's Grand Central Station, a mighty hive of unceasing travelers, he'd headed south, instinctively covering a distance of two miles. Then, as he turned a corner, there it lay. The Crowningshield Company was gigantic, more than he could dream a factory could be. Its vast grounds occupied one hundred and fifteen acres, almost half a mile square. It had thirty-nine acres of covered work space, comprising forty-nine two-story buildings, each eighty feet wide and five hundred feet long. An ocean of brick and glass and steel.

Now he turned, just as he had that day, and began walking south. The mid-morning sun warmed his shoulders. It felt fine to be away from the deafening, hammering din of the foundry. But he was anxious to get back to work. Like Rosemary, he concealed a rank hatred of the urban jungle that was Chicago, the human misery on every street, behind every curtain, the constant choke of the slaughterhouses and feedlots in the air. But he stayed because he loved the feeling of tangible accomplishment that each working day brought.

He was deeply loyal to The Company.

A TRAVELER WITHOUT a map really has only four choices, the four cardinal points of the compass. Arthur again unerringly chose the right direction. He trudged up a slight rise, away from the freight depot and passenger docks of the island steamers. Arthur was elated, surrounded by simple, familiar things. Trains, a small country village, the diamond glint of water just beyond. There were islands out there, he knew, somewhere in the great oceanic unknown. Someone on the train had talked about a place called Martha's Vineyard. The man had been a Lutheran minister, headed to a tent revival to preach at the tabernacle in Oak Bluffs. It was exhilarating, to be here, among such convivial tranquility. In the city, an unceasing river of humanity, with a million different stories, a streetcar might run you over, and not a person would stop. A tenement fire might leave you homeless, and you slept in the street. There was a cruel indifference in the city. Here, a solitary seagull swooped and cawed overhead. A man on a bench smiled and waved. A group of boys dove for pennies; naked, wet and slippery as harbor seals, laughing at some shared jest, their toes gripping creosoted pilings, their boned backs arched just before launching into space. Arthur tasted the sweet aroma of salt air in his nostrils. Behind him, the acrid aroma of steam from the train clogged the air, as it slowly chugged away from the depot, heading north.

He turned right, instinctively.

There, just ahead, a turn onto a shaded lane, unpaved by tar or gravel, a traveled driveway of hard-packed earth, just wide enough for a single motorcar. As he entered, he passed an iron gate, held open by an iron latch. It had the same letters to a name he recognized, because he had seen it every day for twelve years above the massive gate that led into the foundry. In looping Victorian cursive, hammered by a blacksmith into delicate intaglio, a single word.

Crowningshield.

He was close.

The lane meandered, rising and falling. Walking still further, he passed a stable. A carriage horse was tethered in a yard, an ochre mare slowly chewing timothy hay from a steel basket. Parked next to it a gleaming black Ford motorcar. The smell of horse manure wafted down, another olfactory relic from his childhood. Arthur's father had been the village farrier dressing the iron shoes of working nags. He routinely drank himself into a stupor, not every day, just on Saturday nights, but enough to cause Arthur's mum, who came from a tea-totaling family of devout Presbyterians, to one day leave him, run off to Glasgow with Arthur in tow. The story caught up to him, years later, that the man had died from the drink. Arthur himself rarely touched a dram, perhaps in honor of his mum, who filled his childhood with a cautionary tale woven of bitter untruths, even though it was a mare's kick that had killed his father.

WALKING STILL FURTHER, he heard the rhythmic timpani of hammers, the steady rasp of sharpened saw teeth. Several carpenters, or chippies, as they were called in the British Isles, banging pine sheathing boards onto the open rafters of a small cottage. Three workmen clinging to a wooden staging plank, engaged in honest industry. Arthur offered them a collegial wave, and they turned to appraise the passing stranger. In the passing Arthur, the carpenters instantly recognized a fellow artisan; his muscular arms, his well-worn roll of tools, his purposeful stride.

Here came another one to do a job.

HE PASSED A SMALLISH pond; a salt water lagoon, surrounded by dense foliage, clogged by emerald-green algae, nearly hidden by a circling canopy of willow and beech, with a partial glimpse of a large barn beyond. The hammering sounds faded. A hundred paces further, he was there. Entering a small clearing, the geographic, and baronial, heart of Juniper Point. The carriage drive looped around, up, towards the formal, water-facing front of the house. A small, painted sign, attached to a post driven into the ground, pointed to the left. *All deliveries and workmen, no peddlers.* Arthur guessed this was the right way to go. He gauged the distance. Another hundred short concrete steps, a crooked, wooden railing. Climbing, several times he paused and looked up. The house towered over him, a monster of wood and brick and stone. Perhaps the same chippies he passed had built this house. Inside, he knew, were the pipes he'd come to replace. Inside the walls, an antiquated plumbing system, or more likely, lack of it. Arthur couldn't know for certain, but no doubt whatever was in that house was a system of water conveyance wholly inadequate for a modern man of industry such as Charles Richard

Crowningshield. What plumbing pipes there were, no doubt, were installed before the dawn of the twentieth century.

The house had been built in 1885. The original owner was a local magistrate named Daniel Webster Butler. His family had owned the Point, always called Butler's, since before the American Revolution. They had built a tavern and lodging for the carriage trade, operated the first steamer dock to serve the island. A grand hotel had recently burned. Esq. Butler had died. The heirs, destitute and tired of the old ruin's upkeep, sold the Point to Charles Crowningshield for a song, who'd renamed it Juniper, after the profligate explosion of ground-hugging conifer bushes and their waxen blue berries.

When he'd' first walked through the mansion, a plumbing supply man, Charles had looked, first, for the bathrooms. Shocked, he'd counted ten bedrooms, and not a single water closet. No, this would never do, he muttered to his newly hired Cape Cod attorney, as they toured the property six months ago. The old Queen Anne style Victorian, architect unknown, was enormous, but run down. Over 7,000 square feet. It had two parlors, one kitchen, plus two large butler's pantry, a grand staircase, a servants' staircase, and six fireplaces, with intricately carved mantels and marble hearthstones. The magnificent, cylindrical observation tower, tapered up over three stories tall. Capped with a conical roof, it had a bronze weathervane in the shape of a prancing horse and carriage. The house, and the tower, had been constructed with the sea in mind, to take the same views and airs and solitude of a ship's lookout.

The old place, of course, also had no electricity within its horse-hair plaster walls. The village still lacked a power dynamo; its homes were still illuminated with kerosene in glass lanterns that had once held sperm whale oil. Food preparation was a trial. Meals were still cooked on a coal-burning stove in the kitchen, perishables were refrigerated with blocks of frozen pond water, kept from melting with bales of hay. Water, for once-weekly baths, was heated on that same iron Glenwood stove. It took hours to fill up the man-sized bathing tub in a small, private chamber at the top of the stairs. Boiling water, heated in large copper kettles, had to be carried upstairs by servants. Well water gushed into a soapstone sink, via a simple lever-style hand pump, an improvement not added until the turn of the century. Daytime calls of nature necessitated a walk to a small, shingled privy building, an outhouse that stood discreetly a short distance from the back porch. Nighttime, it was porcelain chamber pots, hidden beneath feather mattresses. Each morning, the job of housemaids, up at dawn, as they had since the house was new, when Esq. Butler was still alive, to empty the noxious contents into a ditch beyond the yard.

Those water views *were* sublime, and well worth the purchase price, plumbing or no plumbing. Gazing across the water approach to Woods Hole, which emptied back into Buzzards Bay, and, further still, Nantucket Sound and the languid, verdant elbow of the Elizabeth Islands. Little Harbor, a placid inlet of moored catboats and fishing dories, lay down a slight hill and to the left. Great Harbor, with its train depot and steamer docks, lay in the opposite direction, through the trees to the right.

But the plumbing situation would never do. While it might have suited a generation of Butlers, country folk who'd never known any better, for the cosmopolitan Crowningshields, never!

WHEN HE'D FIRST BOUGHT the house, Charles Richard Crowningshield knew it could never be just any plumber. He could think of only one man he trusted to set this enormous, antiquated monstrosity to rights. And that man was Arthur Rouse, his gifted magi of metallurgy. As Charles Crowningshield signed the purchase papers, his thoughts rushed ahead to plumbing fixtures: gleaming brass pipes, polished porcelain commodes and tubs, modern steam boilers, and maybe even the later addition of an elevator. The company had recently purchased a subsidiary that built such devices, to convey visitors from the cellar to the shingled roof.

He sent a telegram to the home office.

Kindly direct Mr. Arthur Rouse, lead man, fabrication department, upon receipt of this message, with all haste, by train to Woods Hole, Massachusetts, then added, as if further explanation might be necessary, *Urgent plumbing job required, details upon arrival.*

Signed, *C. R. Crowningshield.*

ARTHUR TIGHTENED HIS grip on his bags, He was halfway to the summit, like a Himalayan Sherpa. He looked forward to the opportunity to serve Mr. Crowningshield and his family. Anything he could do, he would do. The three Mr. Crowningshields, both sons and father, had done so much for him. He would do anything to make their lives more pleasant and less arduous. His own mum, he remembered, had to carry tin buckets full of drinking and washing water fifty yards each day to their rented family cottage. She, too, carried slops to a ditch dug in the back yard. But it wasn't housemaids doing the lifting and the hauling. Each time he drank, each time he washed, each time he pissed or shat, he owed a debt to the strength in her arms and legs. There was no excuse for the lack of proper plumbing, not in this glorious Age of Industry. It was 1910, and modern times were here. Even though only 14% of American households enjoyed indoor running water, for the Crowningshield family, this would never do. It would be his pleasure to put right to rights.

HE REACHED THE TOP, entered the dooryard, where the ground leveled off. He climbed five steps to a large wooden porch, leading to a screened door. Peering through the metallic gauze, he saw movement inside, inhaling the aroma of freshly baked bread. A kitchen, bustling with activity. Again, memories of an Aberdeen childhood. Saturday was baking day. His mum, arms cloaked in white flour, the drape of her cotton apron, and that heady, pungent aroma of delicious nourishment filling the cottage. He knocked softly on the door, and a middle-aged woman's unsmiling face appeared, sizing him up.

"Don't need no help right now," she told him brusquely, noticing his workman's clothes. She had a thick Irish brogue. "And no peddlers neither," she added quickly. "Didn't ya read the sign?"

Arthur shrugged. "Seems not," he said right back, in his equally thick Scottish brogue. Smiling, he added, "Looks like you've got everything under control."

The woman began to turn away. Lunchtime was a busy time.

"Mr. Crowningshield sent for me," he called after her. "I just come from Chicago, on the train. I come to fix the plumbing. Mr. Crowningshield...sent for me," he said a second time, for emphasis.

The woman turned, mildly surprised by the invocation of her employer's name. Behind her, a small platoon of kitchen girls bustled about. They were loading plates of food onto trays, pouring glasses, bowls of fruit and trays of sweet cakes. The woman frowned, irritated by the interruption.

"I'll have to fetch the missus," she told him, and pointed a finger, like you might warn a dog. "You wait right there, outside on the porch, and don't come in. It's suppertime. You'll just be in the way."

Glancing down, frowning, she added. "And you've got clods on your shoes besides."

The woman turned and marched noisily out of the kitchen. Arthur continued to watch the activity through the screen, as one of the girls, no older than seventeen, dressed in a gray servant's uniform, vigorously pumped well water into a large, cut glass pitcher. A stray damp hair fell from her braided bun. The heat from the coal stove was stifling. They all had ruddy, perspiring faces.

The scene inside the house could have been from the Middle Ages. Chamber pots and hand pumps, coal stoves and yard privies. Arthur was a city man. In Chicago, streets were illuminated by incandescent suns, modern Edison bulbs on each corner. Every prosperous row house and mansion boasted more than one bathroom. He hefted his work bag. Inside were the tools of his trade, tools that would deliver the miracle of modern plumbing, of daily convenience and sanitary conditions to this large, suffering household.

A few moments of waiting brought another woman's face to the door. Cornelia Workman Crowningshield was a tallish woman with regal bearing. Her hair was done in the severe, Gibson style, rolled and tortured into a high bun. She peered through the screen, and Arthur blinked back at her. He doffed his cap, and lowered his head, in deference to her station.

"Good afternoon, Ma'am," he said, explaining simply, "I'm here about the plumbing."

He held out a wrinkled scrap of paper, the single-page reference letter that they had given him in the factory office. The words on the paper were unintelligible to him, but he imagined they contained some sort of salutation, and described his position at the company.

Through the screen, her alert eyes never left him. "Yes, I know. We've been expecting you. My husband sent a telegram, from England. I just got here yesterday myself, with the children, but the staff has been setting things up for the summer. I don't know how we'll manage, honestly." She stared at Arthur. "There are no sanitary facilities here, not one water closet, none at all. Imagine that. Not even running water. I quite frankly don't know what my husband was thinking. Buying this old wreck."

Arthur nodded sympathetically. "They did things differently back then," he offered. "But we'll fix all that, in short order. Don't you worry, Mrs. Crowningshield."

She cracked the screen door, and slipped outside, onto the porch. He could see that she took her role as household matriarch very seriously.

"Let me see, please," she said, nodding at the paper in Arthur's hands. He handed it over, watched her face as she silently read.

To whom it may concern: Kindly extend all consideration to the bearer of this note. Arthur Rouse is a trusted employee of the Crowningshield Company, Chicago, Illinois. Please remit all bills, including the cost of all transportation, victuals, and lodging, for immediate payment, care of the company. It was signed by the chief office manager, with the address of the company. In the days before credit cards and cell phones, a letter of reference was a trusted missive. Strangers traveling in the world could do things like this.

"They gave me the train tickets," he explained. "At the office. But that was three days ago. I had to leave fairly sudden like, with no spending money in my pocket."

Cornelia handed the paper back.

"Tell me," she asked, "have you eaten anything today?"

Arthur shook his head. "No, Ma'am. Nor yesterday, nor the day before. Not since the breakfast I had on Tuesday."

Cornelia shuddered. "Good lord. My husband sends me a plumber, all the way from Chicago, a starving plumber, to boot. Why didn't you eat on the train?"

"Because I had no money, Ma'am."

Cornelia stared back down at the letter. He could have handed it to the conductor, filled his belly. She turned and called into the kitchen.

"Mrs. Carmody?"

The cook appeared at the screen. "Yes, Ma'am?"

"Mrs. Carmody, I know its bedlam in there, but can you please fix a plate for...." she paused and turned inquiringly. "I'm sorry...Mr...?"

"It's Rouse," he said. "Arthur Rouse."

"Of course," Cornelia said. "Mr. Rouse. Can you please fix a plate for Mr. Rouse? He's come all the way from Chicago."

Mrs. Carmody nodded grimly, eyeing Arthur's wrinkled clothes. "As you wish, Mrs. Crowningshield. I'll have Felicia make him a chicken sandwich and some potato salad and cornbread. A spot of coffee as well."

"That sounds fine," Cornelia said. She turned to Arthur. "After you've eaten, Mr. Rouse, we'll discuss things in more detail. You'll be staying in the village, of course. Mr. Crowningshield has secured you a room at the hotel. It's really quite nice. The Breakwater. We stayed there last summer, my husband and I, not the children, of course, before he purchased this house, to visit his sister Frances. Her husband works at the lab, at the marine biological laboratory. Our staff stayed behind. But it was really quite adequate. Cozy, I'd say, but modern. I even had a hot bath every day, if I wanted, and there was a nice restaurant."

Arthur said nothing as Mrs. Crowningshield glanced around her, gazing up at the old, shingled mansion on the hill, of which she had suddenly found herself the mistress. She turned to him.

"Not like this white elephant. You have no idea. But it *is* quite lovely here. The air is clean. You can hear the fog bell at night, and watch the steamers go by in the afternoon. Mr. Jimson, our grounds man, is setting up the croquet wickets today, so the children will have something more to do than jostle each other. They're still pretty worn out from the long train ride."

Her gaze turned businesslike. "But we really do need to get this plumbing situation looked after, and quickly, for all concerned. I hope you understand this, Mr. Rouse." She smiled as she said this, but the smile came and went almost imperceptibly, as if it had a job to do, then moved on.

"And my husband tells me you're just the man for it," she added. It wasn't so much a compliment, but a challenge.

Arthur tipped the brim of his tweed workman's cap. "Don't you worry, Mrs. Crowningshield. I'll set this place to rights."

CHAPTER SEVEN

A Mysterious Stranger

Thursday, 16 May. Woke early today, up with the larks, before Mrs. C. and the children. These are my lodging for now, up three flights to a little painted garret kind of tower, to be near the nursery. It's the highest view in the house. So lucky to not share my room, just like one of those birds in the treetops. From bed I can look out and see that glittering sea. It won't last, just until Mrs. C's cousin F. comes next week, then it's back to the stuffy attic with the other girls. But for now, my own little world, with two soft pillows, a light woolen blanket against the night chill. Summer is here. So lovely, I wish I could stay here forever.

Lunchtime came and went. Out on the lawn, Rosemary noticed the stranger out of the corner of her eye. A tall, muscular man, in workman's coveralls, with a white shirt and tie, slowly perambulating the bounds of the property. She was leading the younger children in a series of outdoor games. Capture the flag, hide and seek, red rover, blind man's bluff.

Mary Josephine, the oldest, sat in a wicker chair in the shade of a tall oak tree, cooing softly to the sleeping baby in her arms. Mary Josephine had been born deaf, but under the instructional of Mr. Alexander Graham Bell, who had invented the telephone and the phonograph, she had learned sign language, just like another of his pupils, Helen Keller. She had gone on to college. Now, she was a young wife and a mother, and quite comfortable in her silent world.

ROSEMARY WATCHED AS the man moved across the yard. He tipped his cap to her, just once, but kept walking. He seemed to be pacing off the property bounds. Searching for something. She noticed his unruly ginger hair, the glittering intensity, even at a distance, in his blue-green eyes, flecked with brown ochre, the colors of the sea and the sand and the sky, the confident, almost effortless way that he moved.

ARTHUR WAS SOLVING a riddle. It was his way of getting acquainted with the house, moving like a dowser coaxing a hidden spring. As soon as Mrs. Carmody's lunch of cold chicken and potato salad and coffee, and more small-talk with Mrs. Crowningshield, was ended, he got down to the business of understanding, what exactly, he was dealing with. This much he knew: the house, an imposing, three story, shingled, Victorian summer place of the Queen Anne style, was constructed solidly, he'd give it that. Little expense was spared in the fancy joiner work, the intricate carvings, the scalloped shingles, the marble and gilt. But he hadn't come all this way to admire the work of carpenters and tile fitters. This place was built long before the advent of modern sanitary plumbing. Servants had always carried and emptied chamber pots, servants had always heated bath water, servants even once hauled large casks of drinking water from a distant well on the edge of the property. It wasn't until 1902 that a crude hand pump was installed, delivered, via crude iron pipe, water into the kitchen sink. A modest improvement, but that was it. This was still rural America, a little picture postcard village at Land's End. Post-Victorians, even wealthy ones, still only bathed occasionally, as people had done for centuries. They used perfumes to mask body odor, and wore black to mask the stains.

ROSEMARY COVERTLY WATCHED the man walk off the perimeter of the spacious yard. The foliage was just beginning to thicken, and she could catch a glimpse of the glittering water past the spring bloom of the twisting oaks and sycamores. Low-lying Juniper berries were everywhere. She wondered why he was here at the Crowningshield's house, this red-headed stranger, or what his job might be. The little ones were playing an exuberant game of *London Bridge is Falling Down*. She herself played this as a girl, but had no idea of the game's origin. The title referred to a superstitious practice, in the Middle Ages, of killing and burying a child at the bridge site to keep it from collapsing.

The littlest Crowningshield child, John, at seven, was serious and shy. She gently urged him forward, to the frolicking center of play, but he clung to the soft folds of her pleated cotton apron, as stubborn as a mule.

"There's a good boy," she encouraged him, "go ahead, it's fun."

But John would have nothing of it. He stayed glued to Rosemary's apron, as tenacious as lichen to river rock.

ARTHUR DISAPPEARED into a sunless thicket. He finally located what he was searching for. The source of the house's water. There, an old iron standpipe, emerging from the mossy ground amidst a tangle of dense bramble and sumac. An artesian well had been dug decades before, by local men with shovels. This was good, an easy discovery. Before he could consider the plumbing, he had to consider the wellspring. He'd drunk a glass of water with his lunch, tasted with a professional appraisal. Slightly brackish, but cool, and mostly clean. Now he fell to his knees, peered down into the black maw of the well head. He dropped an exploratory pebble down its iron shaft. A distant splash echoed back. Good and deep, he thought, but it may have to be drilled deeper. Sand and sediment had probably settled down there over the years. But no matter. This was 1910. Men and machinery, as simple as pickaxe and shovel; that, and a little ingenuity, could fix just about anything.

ROSEMARY NOTICED THE man reemerge from the shadows. He paused, craning his neck to take in the roofline, at least fifty feet above the ground. It was as if he pondering some mysterious calculus that involved the immense house, but of what she had no idea. Most people inhabited a house and grounds unconsciously, like a brute farm animal grazing a hay field. His interest in its secrets held the proprietary alertness of a lover. Rosemary watched the man continued his slow exploratory walkabout, tapping odd shingles here and there, squatting to examine the pink granite foundation, peering beneath the large, elevated veranda and the cool, black void beneath.

He appeared to be taking the measure of the vast building, that seemed clear. A workman of some sort. Here, Rosemary was certain, was a man imbued with an intelligence far more developed than, say, a common ditch digger or bricklayer. Just the calm, assured manner of his methodical examination told her, here was a planner, someone entrusted with the authority not just to *do* the job, but to be the chief architect of that job.

Just then, Mr. Jimson, the grounds man, sauntered over to Rosemary. "The wickets are in," he told her, "if the children wanted to play a round."

She nodded, took John's little hand, and called out.

"Who wants to hit a croquet ball?"

ARTHUR HAD COMPLETED his exterior examination. He now knew things. He knew where the water came from. He knew where it would enter the house. And he knew where the septic gases would exit the roof. Mrs. Crowningshield's butler had given him a tour of the entire house. He knew where each bedroom was, and which anteroom would become which bathroom. He knew which walls divided which rooms, and how each wall supported which roof line or floor above, and how far each hallway extended. He'd poked his head up into the dusty attic, full of forgotten reliquary: Butler family mementos, Christmas decorations, ancient rocking horses, bundles of newspapers, rusted steamer trunks left behind. In his mind, he began the job; drilling holes, threading lengths of brass pipe through each hole. He began to mentally install the various pieces of plumbing: vitreous china-covered cast iron, wall-hung lavatory sinks, bathing tubs of various lengths, from four feet long, for the younger children, to six feet long, for Mr. and Mrs. Crowningshield and their guests. He even planned out a special soaking bath, using salt water, for a lady's healthful edification. This was one modern innovation that few summer houses yet enjoyed, although the Romans had created it a thousand years before: the piping of both fresh and seawater into each bathtub. He knew where the servants quartered, and where their much commoner water closets would be located. He walked downstairs to the enormous cellar, holding a kerosene lantern to examine the dark mysteries beneath the house. He decided where the steam boilers would be installed, where the coal chute would punch through the thick stone foundation. He calculated the size of the pumps that drove the water from the wellhead, out of the woods and into the house. He envisioned a second pump, an industrial-sized model built by the Crowningshield Company, in its own stone house at the edge of the sea, to carry the salty bath water into the house. He ciphered the lead-soldered copper boiler tanks that would reside next to the furnace, and even the installation of cast-iron heating radiators upstairs, in each room, both large and small, to take the chill from the early spring and fall evenings.

By the end of the day, everything was visualized and designed. Now he needed the materials to do the job.

LATER, AS ARTHUR RETURNED down the road, heading back to the village and his rented room at the Breakwater Hotel, which had originally been built as worker dormitories for the now-defunct Pacific Guano Company, the big house on Juniper Point stayed in his mind. Even after his evening meal, a plate of locally caught haddock and pan-fried potatoes, he remained fixated on one thing, and one thing only.

The work that lay ahead.

Later, he was awakened. It was the toot of the island steamer blowing its whistle. Another thought came. A remembrance of the day. A pretty woman, surrounded by laughing children, larking about. A happy scene, a blue sky, the warmth of the afternoon sun. He wondered what her name might be. Then he lowered his head into the pillow, and in no time at all, fell into a dreamless sleep.

CHAPTER EIGHT

The Luxury Liner

New York City. A ship, an enormous luxury liner, inbound. The dark leviathan ghosted along the serpentine flow of the East River, recently clearing the dangerous and shifting narrows at Verrazano, then Hell's Gate, gliding beneath the black trusses and cables supporting the Brooklyn Bridge, finished only twenty years before.

The Crowningshield Company had provided the iron handrails for the bridge, but most passengers were dreamily oblivious to John A. Roebling's remarkable engineering feat at this early hour. The ship was the *RMS Celtic*, of the White Star Line fleet, a still sleeping Charles Crowningshield aboard. The crossing had been uneventful, from both seamen and passengers' perspective, save for one tense evening of pea soup fog off the Canadian coast of Newfoundland. Icebergs had been reported by ships traversing more northerly routes, but the passengers were not informed. The *Celtic* made up speed the next day, and the massive liner arrived on schedule to dock the next morning, at the ungodly hour of six a.m. Magically, at the appointed time, a fleet of steam tugs appeared, like toys in a child's bath, to nudge and guide the immense, riveted hull safely into her slip at the White Star Line's New York docks, Pier 54.

At eight a.m. a soft knock on the door woke Charles Crowningshield, as was shipboard custom. His morning coffee and scones, delivered by a dining steward, with proper British marmalade, which he'd developed a taste for in London. He touched his throbbing temples, a champagne hangover that would follow him, like a growling cur, for most of the morning. Maritime traditions die hard. It was the beginning of the golden age of luxury liner travel. The last night at sea is reserved for revelry, for dancing, and flowing spirits, and comradely toasts to homecomings and arrival. Charles had drunk too much, caught in the alcohol-fueled zeal of his fellow travelers in First

Class, the well-heeled and the privileged. Far below, in steerage, impromptu celebrations by immigrants, the majority from Ireland, who had miraculously made their way to the White Star Line's Southampton docks on the south coast of England.

The riveted decks above pulsed to the placid strains of the ship's string orchestra, playing from popular sheet music of the day: *Down By the Old Mill Stream. Gee, But it's Great to Meet a Friend From Your Old Home Town. How Can I Love Such a Man. Let Me Call You Sweetheart.* Below, simpler fare, Celtic dirges and reels. A beer-stained fiddle, a mandolin, a small Irish drum called a bodhran. A baby's piercing squall, men playing at cards, their beery pub voices raised in jocular combat. Everyone on board was excited for landfall. For some, their first view of Lady Liberty gliding slowly by, a forest of iron skyscrapers pushing the clouds aside.

For the immigrants in steerage, there would be two debarkations, the first at Ellis Island, to be screened for contagions, probed for lunacy, interrogated for proof of sponsorship. For the First Class revelers, who had paid as much as $50,000 in 1910 dollars for luxurious suites and an army of attentive servants, there were waiting limousines and a hero's welcome uptown, to Park Avenue mansions and dinner at the finest clubs and restaurants. The First Class passengers were smugly ebullient, as if the completion of a transatlantic ocean voyage had somehow been their sole doing, not that of a well-found ship and an experienced crew.

Charles Crowningshield had not danced: he'd merely sat discreetly apart all evening, nodding at circling stewards leaning down to refill his champagne stem or light a fresh cigar. He especially enjoyed playing at cards: whist or poker or solitaire. Although a few young, unaccompanied women had caught his eye, he restrained himself. Charles Crowningshield, at fifty-two, was a married man. He had children. Christ, he was now a grandfather, with another on the way.

Now, the morning. He peered through the bronze porthole, saw a sliver of gray-green horizon, the smokestacks of passing work tugs, the dizzying mast of a distant schooner, clawing for seaway against the tide. The first bite of the hot scone lay sweet in his mouth, the crackle of caffeine slowly igniting his gauze-shrouded neurons. He wished for a *Chicago Tribune* folded in two, offering up city news and social gossip. He'd been away far too long this time. Two months. Charles felt a slight tang of remorse, but only slight.

The cabin steward was still in the doorway, awaiting further instructions. Charles Crowningshield was impressed. A proper servant waits until dismissed.

"I need to send a cable," he explained to the thin, nervous young man, barely more than a teenager, a new hire onboard the *Celtic*. It was the steward's first voyage; he was from Liverpool, and unemployment was high.

"Of course, sir." The steward rushed forward, produced a pad emblazoned with the White Star Line letterhead. He handed him a sharpened pencil, then stood back as Charles Crowningshield scribbled a brief message. Telegraph companies charged by the word, so one had to be succinct in one's communications. Outside the door, in the mahogany-clad companionway, beneath the bright gloaming of a thousand Edison bulbs, the clamor of porters hefting hand luggage, the sound of heavy trunks lifted by a dockside derrick from the cavernous hold. He heard excited, shrill voices of millionaires and remittance heirs and pampered divorcees lurching for the stairs, a well-heeled mob hungry for solid ground, for their own beds, for the security of familiar servants and gated brownstones. This crowd would never lay eyes upon anyone from steerage; the unwashed immigrants had all departed an hour earlier, from a lower gangway, herded onto an Immigration Department steam launch bound for Ellis Island. There they would spend the day, or a few hours, or sometimes weeks, in official detention, held in caged cubicles, grilled by intake officers, prodded by keen-eyed physicians eager to reject and deport.

First Class passengers answered perfunctory questions in their cabin suites. A flash of a passport and a posh address or business card would suffice. Charles had never known the ice-water fear of disembarking onto a foreign shore. His life had been paved with privilege since he'd been born. Now, he sat on the edge of his bed, still in his silk pajamas, covered by a pale blue silk kimono from his last trip to the Orient. He'd recently been appointed United States Ambassador to China by newly elected President William Howard Taft. Newspaper wags had remarked on the coincidence between his substantial donation to Taft's campaign and that plum posting.

Crowningshield handed the message to the steward, then reached behind him for the night table, retrieved a nickel from a slim, leather coin purse. It was monogrammed, in blocky Art Deco script: *CRC*. The steward took the coin, nodded gratefully, and backed out of the door.

Charles took another sip of coffee. In a little while, he would rise, head to the toilet, a small cubicle containing shower, washbasin and commode, adjacent to his sitting room. There he would wash, shave, and dress for the day ahead.

UP IN THE WIRELESS room, just off the bridge, the ship's telegraph operator tapped out the message. It was received, a mere hundred yards away, by the dockside office of the White Star Line's New York branch. From there it was relayed to the tranquil peninsula of Cape Cod, Massachusetts, through a two- hundred-mile daisy chain of copper wire and creosoted poles, in the miraculous space of seconds:

Sender: Charles Richard Crowningshield.

Recipient: Mrs. Charles Richard Crowningshield

Receiving Address- Juniper Point, c/o Woods Hole Station, Woods Hole, Massachusetts.

Message as follows: Arriving soon, Thursday latest. Stop. Have business New York. Stop. Best to you and children. Stop. Please inform Mr. Rouse all necessary supplies arriving tomorrow.

Regards, Charles.

HE RELAXED IN HIS CABIN until 9 a.m., to discreetly allow the other passengers to disembark. Modern cruise ship passengers returning to their home ports are herded like cattle down the gangway, shuttled by bus to distant parking lots, and the turnover begins. But, in 1910, affluent customers, especially Important Passengers such as Charles Richard Crowningshield, were allowed to linger.

The sun was just climbing over the busy river, and the city that began at its muddy, dirty banks was in full urban awakening. At five minutes past nine, dressed for the day, polished and preened, the light scent of lavender talc on his face, he stood at the rail, and scanned the docks below. His trunks had been carefully assembled at the foot of the gangway. A circle of burly longshoremen stood around, knotted muscles bulging, rough stevedores in watch caps idling in the shadows, just far enough for social propriety, smoking cheap cigars and spitting into the filthy water. Behind him, Charles noticed movement on the bridge. The bearded captain, talking to the First Mate, peering down out of the thick glass. Crowningshield had shared dinner and brandy and cigars with both men. Below decks, the crew were preparing the ship for its return voyage to England.

A floating city, with the most modern amenities, comfort and safety assured.

That was what the White Star advertisements claimed. Modern amenities. Charles smiled at the thought. One of the reasons for his trip to England had been to negotiate an arrangement with several passenger lines, White Star and Cunard included, to provide plumbing supplies for several great ships under construction. It was a large, lucrative contract. A modern ocean liner's worth of vitreous china commodes and bathing tubs, wall mounted sinks and shower bases, miles of threaded brass piping, plus freight cars of miscellaneous sundries shipped across the Atlantic from Chicago, all on time and under budget. The negotiations had gone well. Crowningshield Company, which now had a growing product line that topped 30,000 items, stood to gain a tidy profit. His return voyage on the *Celtic* had been a complimentary parting gift of the White Star Line. Nothing had been spared. All modern amenities and comfort. A first-class adjoining suite, with an additional staff of five to meet his every need. Polished shoes by his dressing closet, pressed suits for every wardrobe change, today's menu on the bed table, magnums of chilled champagne, and crystal decanters of brandy kept always full by discreetly invisible stewards.

The British merchant fleet had an expression, an acronym to describe luxurious accommodations: POSH. Port Outbound, Starboard Homebound. This was a reference to the sunny side of the vessel's arrival and departures through the English Channel. The captain gazed down past the wheelhouse glass. He'd received the message from the London office: Treat Mr. Crowningshield with white gloves.

Charles turned his attention towards the pier. Finally, what he was waiting for. An enormous touring car, buffed to a high shine, black and maroon, with beige leather interior, driven by a ramrod straight chauffeur in spotless livery, rumbled over the thick planking. The heads of the longshoremen smoking in the shadows swung on a single pivot, as the automobile, glinting in the morning sun, whispered to a stop next to the small mountain of luggage. They watched, with an expert's silent appraisal, as the chauffeur calmly exited the car, began loading things into the car's cavernous trunk. Charles sauntered down the gangplank, waited as the door was held open to the rear seat, and got in.

An attractive, well-dressed woman was sitting inside. She turned her head and smiled.

"I'm so happy to see you, Mr. Crowningshield. Was the voyage interminable? It was for me. I've been just counting the days."

Charles shrugged, reached across the cool, leather seat to brush her hand.

"It was lucrative." He said. "I had dinner at court. And made a lot of money for my family."

The woman frowned at the crass mention of money, reached up to remove a large, flowered hat, with a rainbow nosegay of ostrich feathers, of the day's fashion. She undid a series of pins and ribbons, then tossed her head, like a dog after a swim. A cascade of silken, yellow hair fell over her shoulders.

Emily Smythe was heart-stoppingly beautiful. Petulant, incendiary, and very rich. In 1910, she was twenty-three years old. The city was her oyster. She was its pearl. She was also married.

"Let's not talk business, Charles."

Her velvety contralto lingered over the words. "Let's take a drive, shall we?" Charles considered this. Hers was an offer of loving compliance. He pictured their embrace, her opalescent skin, the softest lips, that perfumed cataract of golden hair.

"I can't stay long, sweet Emily," he said. "Family obligations await. A day or two at the most."

She formed her lips into what she imagined was a girlish pout.

"Charles, you promised."

He took her hands in his. A large diamond ring sat on one slender finger.

"Two days is a long time," he said, with a smile. "I'm sure we'll think of something."

The driver had re-entered the car. He slid behind the wheel, glancing inquiringly into the mirror. A glass partition separated himself from the passengers. Emily leaned and slid the glass a crack.

"Home, please," she instructed him. Then, turning to Charles, she added mischievously, "Mr. Crowningshield must be terribly exhausted from his long voyage. He needs to rest. Don't you, Mr. Crowningshield?"

CHAPTER NINE

The Job Begins

The earth was cool and dank, a living, mildew aroma, fetid as a dug grave. A sliver of sun and cloudless blue sky over his shoulder blades. A quick climb from the trench, back up a quivering apple ladder, to the sun, but down here, always cool and mysterious, somehow deathlike. Arthur shuddered at the thought of a collapse. One of the local men mentioned that somewhere beneath the yard, an ancient tunnel, once used by pirate smugglers. But it remained only legend and conjecture.

MR. CROWNINGSHIELD had hired several laborers, local men to assist Arthur with the plumbing work. It was hard muscle work: six bodies attached to one brain. There were holes to drill, pipes to thread, tubs to heft, and earth to move. A few of them were farmers, with time to kill, waiting for harvests, and one, an off-duty railroad man, who came on his days off.

Arthur was happy for the help, but he also had impossibly high standards. Already, he chided several men for lapses in attention, for fetching the wrong fitting or the incorrect tool. It was a tricky, delicate job, of not just mechanical aptitude, but public relations as well. The big house was occupied, for one thing. People lived there, some of them were important. A family and staff, anxious to have running water for bathing and cooking and flushing. Still, it was a delicate matter. He counted twenty residents, twenty anxious people he must protect and placate. He must be always polite but industrious. To Mrs. Crowningshield, her children, her servants, an occasional visiting relative. With every move he made, nudging the job closer to completion, this thought, this awareness, could never leave his mind. He constantly reminded his men. One couldn't merely clump through the carpeted living room with clods of dirt on your heel. One couldn't merely drill a hole in a ceiling without first verifying that someone down below, someone prosperous and proper, wasn't sitting down there to be showered with horsehair plaster dust. It was a Sisyphean riddle to solve each day.

By the end of the first week, the first water closet had been completed, carved from a small chamber adjacent to Mr. and Mrs. Crowningshield's beautiful master bedroom, with its breathtaking water views. But there still was a long way to go. First, he had to get water to the house.

SIX MEN HAD LABORED all morning, and part of the afternoon, to dig an enormous trench in the front yard. Running from the deep well that Arthur had discovered the first day, to the cellar beneath the floorboards, it would deliver new threaded brass pipe into the house, and inside that pipe, cool, delicious well water. A large submersible pump, similar to what a ship might use to discharge bilge water back into the sea, was lowered into the trench.

Crowningshield pumps were legendary. During the Chicago fire of 1871, the city had nearly burned to the ground. It was only by the introduction of two gigantic pumps into the Chicago River, drawing water from the filthy river and donated by the Company, that the conflagration had been brought under control.

Next, an iron box with a cover was dropped into the trench. It protected the pump and provided access from above. An electric wire was spooled out from the house, fed into the trench, to provide energy for the well pump. Later, a second pump would serve the salt water system that occupied a small, stone shed by the water's edge.

Arthur knelt down in the narrow trench. The slight tang of desiccated soil and mildew and the vacuous slime of earth worms filled his nostrils. He carefully examined the pump, then began to strip back the rubberized canvas sheathing around each wire. Men with shovels, foreheads glistening, stood at the edge, peering down, unsure of how to help. Every so often, Arthur would request a certain tool. It was slow going, like much of this job. He felt slightly uneasy, trying not to imagine the shoveled colonnades of the trench falling, suffocating him in an avalanche of heavy, pungent earth.

Behind him, two men were taking turns chipping a three-inch fissure in the pink granite foundation of the house. They had no electric drills. Just stone chisels and five-pound sledges. He could hear the high-keened hammering of their labors. There is nothing quite so violent and insistent as muscled men drilling rock.

The pipes for the new bathroom, the first of six planned, had already been hooked to the sink and the commode and the bathtub. The room now resembled a proper bathroom. A small window overlooked the yard, the glittering water beyond. Once the holes for the pipes were drilled, using hand augers, pipes were fed down through the floors and ceilings to the basement. Yesterday one of the carpenters had climbed a tall, spindly ladder to install the copper roof vent that would eventually exhaust septic gases from the house.

Their next task was to run the new pipe from the well into the basement and energize the power to the pump. The men had started digging a cavernous hole in the yard for the cesspool, fifty yards to the east. The cast iron waste pipes, and the main stack that exited the roof, had already been dropped into the cellar. There was a lot to it. It was complex joinery between mechanic and materials. One didn't simply waltz into a house that previously had no sanitary facilities, or even running water, and snap one's fingers.

But in Arthur's gloriously unschooled but natively ingenious brain, all would be accomplished, and in a timely manner. Granted, the men that Mr. Crowningshield hired were unskilled, dumb draft horses, not the men that Arthur would have chosen. But his own father, the long-dead farrier, had always said, "It's a poor workman that blames his tools."

HE TOUCHED A BARE WIRE to the pump, heard a pop, smelled ozone. A bright spark, then a faint, gurgling sound underground. The pump was pulling water from the deep, dark well at the edge of the woods. Good, he said quietly to himself, removing the wire from its terminal. The gurgling immediately stopped. A good sign, he thought. We have spark, we have suction, and there's a house full of people waiting for me to perform miracles.

CHAPTER TEN

A Meeting in the Drive

June 20, 1910—Arthur is his name. Arthur Rouse. He's the factory man from Chicago that Mr. C. sent, and now he's making up the plumbing here. Today we talked, just for a short while, out in the drive. The children are absolutely bewitched by all of this activity. He's from Scotland, Arthur is. I enjoyed our little talk. Perhaps again tomorrow. I hope...

The horse-drawn freight wagon rattled up the lane, hauling a houseful of plumbing supplies. It sagged beneath a half ton of brass piping, wooden crates containing chromated faucets, drain assemblies, traps and vents, couplings, copper roof boots, vitreous china-covered cast iron tubs and toilets and sinks. All wore the same name and delft colophon, Crown Co. Chicago. ILL, incised into them. Arthur stood in the drive for long minutes, struggling to cipher the contents of each bundle and crate, until he felt frustration growing. At the factory, it was obvious, each piece out in the open. Here, in the drive, each carefully labeled box mocked his illiteracy.

WORKMEN SEEK ROUTINE. With routine comes job security, and predictable pay. But Arthur knew this was not forever, this lovely idyll by the sea, that someday in the near future he would again be on the train, heading back to Chicago. There was nothing to keep him here, once the pipes were in and the taps flowing and the toilets flushing.

He thought on this sometimes, on his evening tramps back to his room at the Breakwater Hotel.

Then today, early this morning, he finally met her. There were no formal introductions, just a distantly called name.

"Rosemary," Mrs. Crowningshield's voice, "please go down to the drive and see if Mr. Rouse needs any assistance. I think he's having trouble with the ladings." she said.

It was 8:30 a.m., a Tuesday. Charles Crowningshield had had already left the day before, on the New York steamer. The chauffeur had driven him down to the village, with his suitcases and a large leather and brass trunk, containing a gentleman's necessities for travel abroad. Day clothing, a tuxedo for state functions, leisure wear, from the playing of lawn tennis to riding with the hounds. There were fifty ties, five pairs of shoes, ten pairs of trousers, twenty shirts, even a pair of spats, and a brand-new pith helmet, with mosquito netting, this purchased from Abercrombie and Fitch. There was a shaving kit, various skin potions and bottles of cologne. There were ten leather-bound books. Dickens and Wordsworth, a large illustrated history of China, with maps and photographs, plus numerous trade periodicals, to keep abreast of developments that may have interest to Crowningshield Co.

From there to the Orient, on a great ocean liner, after a day and night in the city with his young mistress.

Rosemary had watched his departure. Her employer, the ghost of the household. She exhaled a secret sigh of relief. It was their marriage that worried her. She'd heard the arguments, sometimes nightly. Behind-doors quarrels hard for staff to ignore. Muffled voices raw with acrimony, denials, tears and more denials. A large household of servants, powerless to intervene, or even discuss, is a psychological petri dish. The marital trials of Juniper Point's master and mistress made them uncomfortable. It felt like the opposite of job security.

ROSEMARY WALKED DOWN the long concrete steps to the drive. Her Mr. Rouse was standing by a large freight wagon, pulled by an enormous yellow horse. The driver sat quietly, whip laid across his lap, smoking a cigar and watching Arthur scan several shipping receipts. Arthur scratched his head, then turned to the approaching Rosemary, his eyes quizzically pleading.

"Can't make heads nor tails of any of this, Miss," he explained. "Would you mind putting the words to each crate?"

She took the papers from him, noticing the hard calluses on his hands. He wore the same workman's overalls, but also a clean white shirt and black tie, in the English tradition. Luckily, each crate matched an item, or multiple items, on the document. It wasn't difficult. She went down the list. There, that's the right one. Okay, yes, this is it. The shipping clerks from the factory had been very meticulous, as if they knew who was on the other end to receive it. It had taken nearly a half an hour, but finally Arthur was satisfied everything was in order. He didn't want to cost his benefactor one penny in missing materials or one second of inconvenience.

He turned to Rosemary. "Well, that's that. I thank you. Imagine, a grown man, in this day and age, that can't even read one word on a damned piece of paper."

She shrugged, smiling. "Worse things have happened, Mr. Rouse. I myself have no idea what makes the water come out of a tap."

He smiled back at her. They were both just beaming like idiots. "Fair enough," he said. "But still, it's a handicap I'd prefer to be rid of."

She continued smiling, even as she turned to climb the stairs. The children would be finishing up breakfast.

"Maybe there's something to be done about that, Mr. Rouse." She kept smiling down at him, this great ginger-haired man with the work-worn hands.

"Arthur," he called back at her. "Mr. Rouse was my father. Just Arthur, if you please."

Halfway up, she turned. The sun caught a stray tendril of her own ginger hair, the flash of emerald eyes. "Very well, Arthur it is. And you, sir, can call me Rosemary."

CHAPTER ELEVEN

Her First Bath

Cornelia, Mrs. Charles Richard Crowningshield, stood naked and alone in her new bathroom and silently wept.

"Charles," she whispered, but there was nobody there.

"Husband," she whispered again. "Where are you?"

Still in her dressing gown, she had yet to go down to breakfast. The children were long up, somewhere with Rosemary.

Thank heavens for a competent nanny.

The workmen were already hard at it, she knew, but the house was relatively quiet. Not all of plumbing work was the clanging kind. Charles had gotten one thing right in all of this. He'd sent them Arthur. There was already hot and cold running water in the kitchen, and a small half bath off the hall for the staff during the day. Arthur was like some parlor magician, working surreptitiously, with such knowing grace, moving about the house, installing this thing and that thing with the greatest of ease. She had had her doubts. About all of it. Juniper Point, when the Scotsman had first arrived, was like some drafty medieval castle, and she was the unwashed queen of the realm. Imagine, having to walk out to the yard, like some common dog, to do her business in a rude little shack. How could Charles have done this to her? She reached out, lightly touched a chromated brass faucet. Her bathing tub had four such handles. Two for fresh water, hot and cold. Two additional ones for salt water, again hot and cold, although those had yet to be hooked up. She had asked Charles specifically for this additional luxury. Salt water soaks were all the rage in 1910, as they had been in Rome two thousand years before.

She down to the fresh hot water faucet and turned it counter clockwise. A clear stream of water emerged. She placed her open palm beneath it, feeling the rising temperature. Soon it was blazing hot. She twirled the cold faucet to compensate, then let the tub fill.

A morning bath will be absolute heaven.

"Thank you," she said aloud.

Mrs. Charles Richard Crowningshield felt a single salty tear slowly roll down her cheek, falling and merging with the bubbling, nearly scalding bathwater. She turned and stared out the tiny window at the sea. Woods Hole passage was alive with vessels of every size and purpose. The Vineyard steamer on its outbound course to the island. Fishing boats, a few pleasure sailors, catboats performing leisurely tacks between the channel buoys. A research boat from the Marine Biology Lab, heading towards Cuttyhunk with a deck filled with laughing students. Perhaps her sister and brother-in-law were aboard, carrying clipboards, answering questions from students. Somewhere out there, on a ship bound for the Orient, her husband was just waking to his own, private morning. She smiled. Scones and marmalade, his newest passions. Mrs. Carmody had labored over those at her big Glenwood cook stove, opening and slamming the oven doors, and sent a pantry girl to the market for the orange concoction. Shed's returned instead with ordinary strawberry jam, all the country store had on its shelves, sending Charles into a polite paroxysm. His face turned to a scarlet blotch, his linen napkin sliding from his perfectly creased lap, as he rose from his place at the head of the table without taking a bite. Why was that so difficult to understand? Life here in Woods Hole wasn't like Chicago, or even a well-appointed ship at sea. It was...well, limited. There were only three hundred inhabitants, at last census, and most of them farmers or fishermen. The nearest orange marmalade might be New York City, or the galley of a passing ocean liner. One took what one could. But Charles...*My dear, mysterious, wandering gypsy of a husband...*to him, life was a game, a puzzle to conquer, and each puzzle piece must fit perfectly for him to be content.

She bent down to shut the faucets. The little room became suddenly hushed. Mrs. Crowningshield began to undress from her bed clothes, lightly tugging at ribbons and buttons; first a nightgown, then a negligee, until she stood at the tub's edge in only her silken delicates. How long had it been since she'd stood in front of her husband this way? She stepped out of her final undergarment, delicately folded with the others on a brass rack by the door.

She lowered herself into the miraculously heated waters, felt a gentle burn, as her naked body adjusted, displacing the water until it was nearly lapping over the rounded porcelain edge.

"Heaven," Cornelia whispered again, sliding still further beneath the surface, until only her face, quickly flushed, was suspended. Small, translucent beads of sweat appeared on her flawless, white forehead, dripped down to the bridge of her nose. Her cheeks became flushed with a rouged bloom of heat. A thin trail of hair, just the first traces of gray, floated like damp Sargasso behind her.

Mrs. Charles Crowningshield, taking her first morning bath at Juniper Point. In this moment, she is Cleopatra, a hedonistic lotus-eater. All about her is comfort, and nothing else. She is oblivious to the weeks of dirty, grueling menial labor it took Arthur and his unskilled herd of village men to heave the bathtub up the stairs, drill the holes for the pipes, dig the trench and excavate the enormous cesspool to drain the waste away from the house and into the earth. She had heard them in their labors, of course, but as for specifics, no. She thinks only in terms of wealth and the esoteric magic it can perform, but not the energies dissipated by lesser others in the haze of her selfish needs. She feels this way about every aspect of life that swirls around her. Her staff, each chambermaid and liveryman and cook and weed puller, all comprise a solar system of subordinate planets orbiting about her daily wishes. As the pampered wife of a fabulously wealthy industrialist, no matter the hours of isolation she feels, the marital abandonment that his constant traveling imposes on her, Cornelia exists, and would always exist, as the pampered wife of a fabulously wealthy industrialist. Now she dips her hand beneath the crystalline surface of the calming waters, cupping a tiny wavelet onto her face, and whispers again.

"Thank you, husband, wherever you are."

CHAPTER TWELVE

Beneath the Eaves

Arthur, flat on his back, in the coal-black darkness. Uncomfortably folded into the cramped and stifling attic space just above the servant quarters on the third floor, he gauged by faint pinprick of daylight how far he had crawled from the attic scuttle to get here. Beads of sweat stained the arms of his rough chambray shirt, smudged from rubbing his face dry. His armpits were pools of warm brine. It was stiflingly hot up here, invisible to the household moving below. But had had a job to do. Raw brass pipes emerged through the lath and plaster ceiling, pipes stubbed out and threaded, awaiting his foundry man's steady ministrations. He lay there in the hot twilight, breathing softly, listening for sounds above him, just beyond the roof's sheathing boards. Above his head, the dusty, rough-sawn geometry of the house's massive rafters. The rusted iron points of hand-wrought shingle nails punched through every few inches. *Don't sit up in a hurry*, he thought, *your skull will get punctured*. He heard a raspy, clumping noise. Men on the roof, dragging a ladder, then a second weighted object, feet scrabbling on the dew-damp shingles like rats struggling against gravity. The spiraling puncture of a large brace and bit inserted through the boards, spitting out a rain of kindling-dry sawdust into his face. Ernest, most likely, the older chippy, drilling a pilot hole for the keyhole saw. The carpenters were on the roof, and he was just below, waiting for sunlight.

Arthur heard voices, the sounds of men lightly arguing. *Calm down boys.* he whispered. *Too early in the morning*. He wished he could work alone. Alone is where he felt mostly satisfied. Human beings were just too—what's the word?—complex.

Finally, the slit in the roof boards was enough to insert a larger handsaw. He watched, fascinated, as the sharpened teeth pistoned up and down, slowly tracing the outline of a large rectangle, allowing more and more light to enter the shadowy triangle where Arthur lay. *Rsssppp, rssssppp, rsssppp,* the saw spoke, louder and louder, faster and faster. Someone swore, then the sawing continued. Finally, it was getting close to the end, a four foot by five-foot cut-out. Arthur brought his knees level with his face, grimacing from the contortion, and placed his leather shoes against the boards. Not too hard, careful of those rusted cut nails.

Don't want no lockjaw.

The piece would be free soon, would want to fall inward, onto Arthur. These are the thousand decisions a workman makes each day, the risk-charged choreography of survival. A high-walking girder man thinks about each step in front of him. A fisherman watches the clouds, and tastes the air for storms. A coal digger listens for sounds of coming collapse, and counts the steps back to the shaft.

Arthur felt the weight of the roof section on his legs, a twenty-foot square rectangle of pine and cedar, asphalt and iron. It was warm through the soles of his shoes, flat at the heel from a thousand miles of factory work.

I will never own a home. The thought came to him sometimes. Or have a wife. Or children to call him daddy. He of the rough hands, he who cannot read a menu, he who goes dumb and mute when a woman crosses his path.

"Slow now!" he called up to the men on the roof. "Slow." *Thunkkkk...!* The sound of a hammer, finding a fissure in the shingles, finding purchase, leverage. Two sets of hands found the corners, and began to lift.

The sunlight dazzled him. Arthur blinked into the diamond brightness of an early June morning. The heat was already coming on, mid-seventies, maybe eighties, by lunch. He saw men staring down at him. Just like when he was in that earthen trench. Gravediggers saying the last rites.

"Be careful of that roof bit! Don't let it drop off of the plank, Ernie."

Ernie, steady old Ernest Woods of Woods Hole. No relation, he was always quick to offer.

"No worries, Mr. Rouse." Ernie grinned down at him. "Got it under control up here." Arthur grinned back up at him. Then, bent at the hip, he peeked his head through the hole in the roof. The roof was a cut-up bitch, in the words of the shinglers. Not a straight line anywhere. Valleys and hips and triangular cheeks where dormer met ridge. In the language of its original carpenters, the architect had handed them one great painted whore to build. Queen Anne Victorians, popular in their day, the 1880s, were now considered over-done, antique relics, just too fussy and hard to maintain, with all that gingerbread and fancy shingling and different colors everywhere. Mrs. Crowningshield had mentioned to Arthur that her husband had hired a prominent architectural firm from the Midwest, contemporaries of Mr. Frank Lloyd Wright, devotees of his much simpler, but elegant, Prairie Style now so in fashion. They were drawing up plans at this very moment. The remodeling work would begin in September, when the family was back in Chicago. She had emphasized the word *prominent*. Arthur, who knew neither the reputation of Mr. Wright, or the location of the American prairie, had merely nodded.

ARTHUR LOOKED PAST the men toward the end of the thick staging plank. A large wooden box, made heavier by lead sheeting, sprouting rough plumbing connections. The weight of it caused the plank to sag slightly. Somehow, they'd muscled the thing up the ladder and onto the roof.

"Alright, boys," he instructed softly. "Lower away."

It was less of a command and more of an incantation. Gravity was fighting them with every step. Ernest Woods grabbed one corner; the little guy grabbed the other. Together they slid it, slowly, carefully, towards the hole. Arthur ciphered its immense weight, probably over three hundred pounds, and reached out his own tree-trunk forearms. It was about a three-foot drop to get it safely onto the attic floor. When they'd reached the lip of the opening, the men twisted sturdy hemp ropes to create a sling, then slowly lowered it down, again gravediggers to coffin. It dropped a half a foot, the soft squeak of its bindings protesting, but Arthur managed to keep it level and square to its final resting place, four precisely located oak mounting blocks, bolted to the attic floor.

"Good, good. Keep going," he called up to them, heard back only the exerted pants of working men doing hard labor high on a roof. Finally, just an inch to go. A half an inch. Then it was down, dropped precisely onto the blocks with a dusty thud. Arthur was satisfied. There was none of the amateur re-lift and realign. All on the first go, as it should be.

"Well done, fantastic," he called up to the men. Ernie and the little guy let the ropes dangle, sat back on their haunches, onto the warm shingles.

Arthur got to work.

THE PURPOSE OF THE box was simple: a storage container for the gravity-fed salt-water system. It was all Arthur's invention. Ocean water drawn from the swift-moving Woods Hole Passage, a mad confluence of contrary eddies and currents and wind-driven waves, was siphoned into a small pump house at the water's edge. The pump house, made of large stone boulders, was at the base of a steep, fifty-foot cliff. Arthur had already climbed down several times, his face and arms bleeding from the prickle vines.

Juniper Point is a natural defensive barrier. Attacking invaders from the sea would have to scrabble up that same cliff, a maze of poison ivy, loose sand and gravel, and serpentine roots at ankle height, just to reach the front yard. Cannons mounted on the observation tower would take care of any invasion, but that is preposterous, and history has no mention of such an event.

Arthur's system was ingenuous, and deceptively simple. Salt water was pumped into the house, pushed through the coal-fired steam boiler in the basement to a temperature exceeding 160 degrees. From there it was pumped to the attic, where it sat in the box, simmering like warm broth, until a bath was drawn on the floors below. Modern plumbers call this action "hot water demand," a very queenly description of a common hydrological event.

The lead-lined box contained enough water for one luxurious soak below. Then the replenishment system went into effect. Arthur had designed that as well, and the technology was elegant and foolproof.

He bent over the box, completing its final assembly. Sunlight warmed his shoulder blades, as he threaded the fill pipe from the ceiling onto the brass fittings drilled through the wood and the lead. He wound a piece of sticky oakum around the treads, then closed a monkey wrench around the coupling, and spun it in a clockwise motion. Finally, the plumbing was done. Water could enter and fill with no leaks. This was the easy part. Next, Arthur inserted a large copper ball float, attached to a long iron arm, through the side of the box. This was the heart of the replenishment system. Attached to the arm was a heavy, iron counterweight. The theory was as diabolical as any mousetrap or marble chase. As the water level dropped, the copper float, similar to how a modern toilet works, raised the counterweight. As it raised to a certain height, it lowered an electrical knife switch, mounted on a piece of thick oak screwed to a rafter. This caused an electrical surge, which sent power to the pump down at the water's edge. Once the water had again reached the top rim of the box, the copper float again raised the knife switch, shutting off power to the system. In 1910, this technology was like walking on the moon, or the battery cells of a Prius.

"Alright lads," Arthur called up through the hole, "you can close her up now."

Ernie and the little guy were preparing the piece of roof for reattachment; the shinglers were waiting below. The work was now completed on the box. It would supply Mrs. Crowningshield's salt water bathing tub, and hers alone. In time three more baths would be so equipped, for family and guests.

ARTHUR UNCOILED HIMSELF into a crouching position, kneeling painfully after being contorted for so long. After replacing tools into his old canvas bag, he began to crawl, pushing the bag out in front of him. Turning one last time, to review his handiwork, he heard voices through the roof.

What now?

Ernest Wood was excitedly talking to the little guy. Arthur could just make out the words.

"Will you look at that," he was saying. "Ever see something so tall? Must be a hundred, hundred fifty feet up. Damn!"

Arthur stopped crawling. He turned his head, glimpsed just an instant before the roof chunk dropped into place. A triangle of robin's egg blue sky, and against that great dome of sky, a snow-white sail, enormous and billowing. Then another and another. Three sails, rising into the heavens, attached to masts that rose like redwoods from the deck of an enormous sailing ship.

LATER HE WOULD KNOW. It was the steam auxiliary schooner *Alma*, sliding into Little Harbor below. Just arrived after a ten-day Atlantic cruise, she had a British master and a crew pulled from everywhere. Charles Richard Crowningshield was her new owner. He had purchased *Alma* on a mad whim, negotiated in a gentleman's smoking club, from a London yachting syndicate fallen on hard times. She was nearly one hundred and forty feet long, from her clipper bow, with gracefully carved maiden's figurehead, to her hourglass stern. Iron-built, and tightly riveted, she was reputedly very, very fast.

Climbing down the ladder into the cool hallway below, Arthur heard more voices. The children had gathered at the nursery window, legs folded onto a velvet window seat, excitedly peering across the yard at that magnificent monster bobbing lightly in the harbor. She carried a crew of twenty, and that included a gourmet chef from Paris and a ship's carpenter who had studied furniture design at the Sorbonne.

As Arthur walked quietly past, he saw five heads in a row, each gazing intently out at the *Alma*. Rosemary turned just then, seeing her mysterious Scotsman pass. He was hefting a stepladder on his thick shoulder, his tool bag in one hand. She smiled, and waved. But Arthur only nodded once, then walked quickly on. There was more work to be done. The Crowningshields had been good employers, caring and decent. Distractions were a luxury. Just then a grim thought came. He was thinking of that great monster of a ship out there. He was thinking of that deep, dark water flowing beneath her keel. And he was thinking that if she belonged to Mr. Crowningshield, then there was a possibility that he, Arthur Rouse, might end up someday walking her vast wooden decks, or worse yet, down in her bilges, bent over an enormous steam engine, sweating like a carriage horse in August, urging *Alma* on, with spanner wrench and oiling can.

The thought terrified him.

CHAPTER THIRTEEN

Alma

Alma, at eighty-five tons, had crossed the Atlantic. She now lay at anchor, as docile as a birthday pony, her great keel covered in barnacles and tendrils of seagrass, barely clearing the dirty bottom of Little Harbor. The captain, M.A. Brisbee, an aging mariner at sixty-four, was a man who had been to sea for most of his working life, and even before he was born. His father captained fishing smacks and coastal freighters and passenger ferries around the English Channel for nearly his entire working life. In fact, Captain Brisbee arrived in the world, not in a hospital, or a cottage, not even on solid ground, but below decks, on a rocking fishing trawler off the coast of Cornwall, during a raging tempest that killed half the male inhabitants of that diminutive village. Death had come all night and into the morning, from fathers to brothers to sons, until twenty-nine bodies, nearly frozen and nibbled by baitfish, had washed ashore.

Mathias Alphonse Brisbee had arrived with the shrill banshee wind in the rigging and the view of terrified deckhands lashing down, pumping out, and whispering guttural prayers to the God of Seaborne Calamities. The tiny fishing smack had miraculously survived, stinking of rotting fish offal, half keeled over, but still afloat by dawn. His father and crew of three had survived. His mother, a stubborn, tough woman, who misjudged her own baby's nativity by a month, had bravely gone fishing with her husband, pregnant and bloated as a tick. She survived. Most importantly for the baby that was M.A. Brisbee, M.A. Brisbee survived.

During the *Alma's* leisurely crossing, ten mostly placid, sunlit days on the North Atlantic, half of what the White Star's *Celtic* had taken, they witnessed God's hand in the skies above their foamy wake, and afterwards he led a small prayer service on deck to honor The Lord's Great Works.

Halley's Comet crossed the sky on May 20th. Its first appearance was lost to history, but certainly it reappeared on Christmas night of 1758, and every seventy-five years hence.

Captain Brisbee, drinking his morning Earl Gray in the wheelhouse, (just before the *Alma* cast her lines from the London pier where she had languished for nearly a year, due to accounting irregularities on the part of the sailing syndicate that had commissioned her), had read in the *London Times* a short account of an unusual prediction by the American writer Samuel Clemens. He himself had read many of his books, including the one about working on a paddlewheel steamer on the Mississippi. He still had a copy, which he kept in a small, varnished bookshelf next to his berth.

"I came in with Halley's Comet in 1835," wrote Clemons, whose pen name was Mark Twain, after a certain depth sounding on the river, *"It is coming again next year, and I expect to go out with it."*

The next day, *Alma* received a message on the ship's wireless. Mr. Samuel Clemons had left his mortal coil. It was as if his death had achieved worldwide celebrity more for the comet than from all the books he wrote. From the *Alma's* fantail, Captain Brisbee and his crew witnessed the comet. Twenty pairs of eyes excitedly tracking a speeding, flaming ball, followed by a brilliantly iridescent tail. Afterward Captain Brisbee bowed his head and led the others in prayer to the God of Small and Momentous Things. Then he retired for the night, but not before instructing the helmsman on the latest course adjustment that would steer their great sailing ship towards the eastern coast of the American continent, to Cape Cod, to the threadbare and insignificant fishing port of Woods Hole. Alone is his small cabin, just a few steps from the wheelhouse, he imbibed a small shot glass of Irish whiskey, left there by the cook's mate, as was his nightly ritual, as his father and his father's father had done before him. Just before sleep, he pulled his dog-eared copy of *Life on the Mississippi* from the shelf. He read, as he had always done at sea, a few familiar pages. These were words to live by, especially for a professional mariner.

"The face of the water, in time, became a wonderful book—a book that was a dead language to the uneducated passenger, but which told its mind to me without reserve, delivering its most cherished secrets as clearly as if it uttered

them with a voice. And it was not a book to be read once and thrown aside, for it had a new story to tell each day."

As he closed his eyes, and lowered the page, a thought appeared. Perhaps one day he might travel to Mississippi, might step aboard a riverboat, might have a word with the captain, or his pilot, which Clemons had been. Perhaps he might meet someone who had known the great writer.

ROSEMARY STOOD VIGIL on the edge of the grassy escarpment, staring down the *Alma*. Imagine, she thought, that great sailing ship has just crossed the ocean to get here, practically to the Crowningshield's front yard. The children stood at rapt attention beside her. She gripped John's boned, slender shoulders. He was still the baby, and clumsy with danger and heights.

A puff of white smoke emerged from the steamer's iron stacks. As they watched, the *Alma* moved slowly forward, away from the anchoring stream. She was headed towards the Crowningshield's private dock. Rosemary heard the bright clatter of muddied chain links pulled up by the anchor capstan's steam-driven donkey motor, followed by a pair of enormous gray flukes that rode up the steel plates and into a special housing on the bow.

Villagers gathered below, crowding the dirt lane that led around the perimeter of the Crowningshield estate. Government Road was nearly at sea level. It flooded sometimes on moon tides. Thrusting out in the harbor, a large stone jetty, with water deep enough for the massive auxiliary steamer to attach its lines. Rosemary was hypnotized by the intricate display of nautical choreography. The villagers on shore were less enthralled, accustomed to ships docking, lightly murmuring about crops and the price of cod, horse fever and the circus coming to town. Beyond the ship, a hundred yards more, an erratic chorus line of dancing whitecaps, opposing armies of agitated water. The speed of the current was gauged by the speed of the drifting herring gulls.

LITTLE HARBOR IS NOT a gentle body of water, not protected in the traditional sense. A harbor of refuge, but just barely. It is fed and agitated and buffeted by the Woods Hole Passage, a subtly violent seaway of unpredictable tempers. So close to land, yet fraught with danger. The Passage courses with shifting tides, conceals the wanton caprice of fast-moving currents and whirlpools. Uncharted rocks emerge at low tide, disappear just below the surface at high tide. Each can tear the bottom from a ship. Men have drowned merely adjusting a catboat's sail. People slip on the rocks into the shallows, and are swept away. A steamer runs aground in a winter storm, whipsawed by the wind and the seas, broaches and sinks, all but a handful of souls aboard lost. The great suction effect of three sizable water bodies, Buzzards Bay, Vineyard Sound, and Nantucket Sound, appear to pull and push simultaneously.

But the captain appeared to have things well in hand. Rosemary saw the man, white-bearded and bespectacled, bend over the ship's telegraph. Emerging occasionally from the wheelhouse, he gauged his bearings to the shore, signaled back to the helmsman, who jammed the brass telegraph back and forth, to the sound of a hammered clang. *Half Forward, All Reverse,* and then, finally, *All Stop, Done With Engines.*

Lines were quickly tossed ashore, looped onto great wooden bollards, caught by village farmers and shop clerks, and a long steel gangway was lowered to the dock. A few minutes passed, then a line of sailors descended the gangway, some chatting, others silently morose, most just happy to be off that damned boat.

There was something extraordinary about the captain's docking performance. Rosemary found herself marveling at his adept ship-handling abilities, casual and confident as a honeymooner in a rowboat on a placid lake.

She hugged John tighter, cooing down into his scalp, "Isn't that wonderful, John? Look, that's your papa's new ship. It's called the *Alma.* Isn't that a lovely name?"

John finally wiggled free. He whirled and faced her.

"I want to go inside now," he solemnly intoned. "I'd like to read my new books please."

John was currently devouring two at the same time, *The Secret Garden* and *The Emerald City of Oz,* which had been delivered by post the previous week. His grandfather, Richard Crowningshield, after hearing that young

John was a reader, would rather crack a book than build something with his own two hands, was horrified. The old scion was unabashedly anti-education and anti-intellectual. He believed that knowledge was earned by only one method. Rolling up one's sleeves and getting on with it. He'd built his company this way. He openly railed against higher education in the Chicago newspapers, chiding college boys for their soft hands and lack of grit. Young John, in his opinion, with his bookish ways and his childish anxieties, was a product of too much feminine mollycoddling. And perhaps there was some truth. John had few male role models, just the daily obedience of smiling gardeners and chauffeurs and livery men orbiting around him. What he got, emotionally, intellectually, he got mainly from his nanny, from the pantry girls, chambermaids, and Mrs. Carmody, who cooked his favorite foods. From his mother, the distantly chilly Mrs. Crowningshield, he received far less, nor his father, the phantomesque Charles Richard Crowningshield. John was a by-product of his times, born at the tail end of Queen Victoria's staid orbit. Affluent boys, surrounded by an army of kindly, but subservient, men and women, the great vacuum of parental avoidance in-between.

ALL STOP, DONE WITH Engines.

Captain Brisbee perched on a scarred, wooden stool in the wheelhouse and pondered what sort of place he found himself anchored to. The crew had the afternoon off, free to wander into the village, find a meal, get their personal bearings. They'd all be back on the ship by dinnertime, and half of them given their discharge orders by the weekend. Now that *Alma* was safely in port, he could run her with a skeleton crew of six or eight, certainly not twenty, a quarter of them West Indian and the one black boy, the stoker from Senegal.

It all depended on what Mr. Crowningshield wanted to do, exactly, with his new toy. The *Alma* was a blue water race horse. She was built for speed, for stormy crossings in the Channel. A safe, dry ship, not a drop of green water over the rail, though she'd never won, or even run, a race, never rounded a starting buoy.

A syndicate of wealthy Londoners, who had paid the 1908 equivalent of three million dollars to build her, had nearly gone bankrupt from the mounting expenses, and one by one, each subscribing member dropped out. Captain Brisbee, retained as a shipboard caretaker, had kept her in Bristol condition. Then a rich American industrialist came along, with gold in his pockets and a mad gleam in his eye. *All dollars, and no sense*, Captain thought to himself, after shaking *Alma's* new owner's hand.

Crowningshield was some sort of plumbing magnate from Chicago, an impulse buyer who just wanted a family yacht to show off, impress his friends, pick cockleshells off the beach. That sort of drivel. She was a thoroughbred, was *Alma,* the captain always proudly bragged. Built of the finest materials, by master Irish shipwrights, powered by Scottish boilers, and captained by a British master. Not one unnecessary rivet in her bilges. She was appointed below in Burmese teak, old growth mahogany from Africa, gold-plated faucet handles, English crockery with her name proudly embossed in gold leaf. Every modern convenience. She had five separate water closets, one even with a copper bathing tub. The crew shared a stinking pisser in the foc'sle, and bathed with buckets of salt water, after the guests had retired. Her efficient reciprocating engine used half the coal as any similar vessel, and fresh flowers sat in faceted crystal vases. Yet here she was, tied to a dock in a backwater pond, like a broken-down fishing smack.

Brisbee plucked his favorite briar pipe from a shelf above the wheel, struck a match on his trousers, and began to draw smoke. It always relaxed him.

Think, you damned fool. Is this what you want? Going along for the ride? Be some rich man's bath toy captain?

He stared through the wheelhouse glass, still crusted with salt spray from the passage. They had encountered some seas on the way over, but nothing to worry about. Not with *Alma.* When the crew returned, he'd have them give her a proper washing down, get her back to tip-top condition. Who knew how long she'd sit at this damned rock pile. A ship is like a shark. If it stops moving, it drowns. Iron rusted wood rotted, paint peeled, crews mutinied. He knew this, as much as he knew his own heart beating.

Shoreside, the crowd was thinning out. The boys would be here all afternoon, patiently waiting for excitement. A few people boarded a horse-drawn carriage, one man rode a mule, but most walked the half a mile back to the village. The captain glanced up. At the top of a steep overlook, an enormous house, a palace really, baking in the sun. He could make out its newly shingled roof, the tapered observation tower, resembling a lighthouse, half a hundred open windows facing the sea, their lace curtains dancing in the breeze. Through a wide swath in the trees, he could see a young woman leading a small group of children back to the house. Her long red hair swung in a braid behind her, plaited neat as a mare's tail. She was wearing a starched white apron over a long cotton dress, the uniform of a domestic servant. Nanny, the captain guessed from the obedient parade of children. *The hand that rocks the cradle, rules the world.* His own mum had always said that. The redhead certainly was not the missus of the house, he thought. Too young and pretty.

The captain's eyes swept approvingly over the estate, assessing the land and the trees, the neatly manicured grounds, explosions of bright perennials in bloom everywhere. How much he would like to live again in a proper house of his own, not crammed into a tiny berth on a rolling ship.

The owner of that house is a lucky man.

Captain Brisbee absently picked up the brass speaking tube mounted to the compass binnacle, to call down to the galley. Something simple would be nice, just meat and bread and plenty of mayonnaise. No chance of fish and chips, or some bangers and mash, or even steak and kidney pie. He would have given a week's wages for a spoonful of his mum's Yorkshire pudding. The present cook was a chef, not a cook. Christ, he was a Frenchman. He called food *cuisine*, and that was bad for morale. His new employer, Mr. Crowningshield had hired the man, with gushing praise, after a single meal in Paris, with too much wine. Wealthy men did things like that. They were impetuous, they could afford to buy things, and people, shiny impulses that temporarily pleased them. But the crew was starving, after nearly two weeks of cook's delicate bon bons, when a thick fish stew and a roast beef sandwich was what they craved. Everything the Frenchman made was some sort of gourmet trifle, served with a theatrical flourish. Too sweet and buttery, laden with eggs and drowned in cream. They would have to hire a proper ship's cook when everything got sorted out with Mr. Crowningshield. The captain could talk sense into the owner, and then fire that damned frog cook.

He blew again into the speaking tube, then waited half a minute. When nobody answered his muted blat from the galley below, he suddenly remembered why.

He was completely alone on the *Alma*.

CHAPTER FOURTEEN

The River Dee

Arthur's hatred of the water came when he was thirty-two.

Aberdeen, at the mouth of the River Dee, in northeast Scotland. It was a Wednesday, the fifth of April, 1886, the day of a Sacrificial Fast for all Catholics. After Mass, Bridgett, his young wife not yet twenty-one, had wanted them all to go to the annual fair, across the river in the tiny hamlet of Torry. But Arthur had promised his uncle he'd help with a tricky job in his blacksmith shop. You go, he'd begged off, and dropped a few shillings into her small, delicate palm. The baby, Michael Patrick, at six months, was asleep in her arms. It had seemed so effortless. The sky was the bluest he could remember, a light breeze was freshening across the river, which took the heat off. A perfect day. They'll be back by dinnertime. It wasn't like they were crossing the open ocean. Just a wee bit of river. He left them on a stone jetty called the Pocra Quay. The look she gave him, as he'd walked away, he'd always remember. It was the last time he'd see her face.

A ferry boat had operated here for centuries, and been replaced several times. This latest iteration, like all that came before, had no engine. It operated via a wire and pulley system: steel cables attached to the opposite river banks that the boatman pulled to move them through the water. The boat had been built by William Hall, in a local shop, to standard dimensions. Small, at twenty-five feet in length, eight feet ten and half feet width, she drew two feet four inches, but the river was much deeper than that. The official name of such a craft, in the British Isles, was "wire ferry boat." She had no other name, just a doughty, utilitarian, hull with a large wheel and two friction rollers mounted on the bow. Rated at eight tons, she was tested by the Board of Trade, with sixty men aboard, but that left no room for sitting down, which made her top-loaded. Prudently, the boat was licensed by the Aberdeen city council to carry thirty-two passengers. But sometimes rules are bent. Seventy-six passengers were aboard when she entered the river, which on this day was swollen and fast-moving.

Arthur had crested a small hill, on his way to his uncle's shop, then, on impulse, turned and faced the diamond-glittering water. Hoping to locate his wife's face somewhere on the crowded deck, he would wave to her, and she would wave back. And then she would be across the Dee, to enjoy a fine day at the fair. A few hours later, she would return the same way across the river. He would be waiting on the quay. Then he would heft his young son into his muscular, mechanic's arms, and together they would walk the few miles back to their tiny stone cottage on the Aberdeen Road. Later perhaps, in the soft gloaming just before they slept, they would share a marital intimacy that bore no relation to the ribald jokes told at the small casting yard where he was employed, making axles and hitch hardware for livery wagons.

What he saw instead was horrifying. Almost immediately, the ferry boat had begun to list as it headed into the faster current. Perhaps snow melt had contributed to the river's heightened state. Anyone could see the boat was over-crowded. Arthur opened his mouth to cry out, but instead went silent. The cable from the Torry side of the river went slack, allowing the onrushing current to push violently against the hull. The wire suddenly snapped, with a twang like a banjo string, and the little ferry began to quickly capsize and founder. Arthur wanted to run, to careen down the hill to the quay, but instead his legs were paralyzed, rooted by what had just happened to his life. Passengers were slipping into the fast-moving current, splashing, calling out, shocked by the sudden immersion. Some vanished quickly, others bobbed to the surface, and then vanished again. It all happened so quickly. A few strong swimmers, mainly men, began to fight their way back to the quay. A few sailboats in lazy quadrants, a large dory circled, frantically plucking drenched and panicked survivors from the icy water. Arthur scanned the river, continued to scan as his legs began finally moving. But his wife was nowhere to be seen. They had been married less than a year.

LATER, A PUBLIC INQUIRY was held, concerning the cause of the sinking. It was sponsored by the Board of Trade, chaired by Captain Harris of the Royal Navy. They found two conditions mainly contributed to the tragedy in which thirty-four citizens had perished. A fast-moving current, and overcrowding. Amazingly no blame, or liability, was charged. Arthur sat through the hearings, conducted by sober men in frocks and wigs in the Aberdeen courthouse. He was waiting for an explanation. He was hoping for something miraculous, after losing everything. Then it was over. People, mostly survivors and their families, and the families of the victims, and a few members of the press, wandered out into the sunshine, shaking their heads. Something terribly wrong had just happened, and nothing was done to make it right. Funds were raised, through public subscription, to assist victims and their families. Arthur was paid five pounds, ten shillings, the allotted price of his wife and son. It might be enough, if he added that to his savings, for a steamship ticket to America. He took the money without thanks. Aberdeen had become a place of dreadful memories, and he could not remain there. Later, still within memory of that dreadful ferry sinking, more public funds were raised to build a bridge across the river Dee. They named it Queen Victoria Bridge.

EVERYONE IN ABERDEEN knew about the disaster. Everyone knew that Arthur Rouse was now a widower, suffering the greatest diminishment a husband and father could suffer. No great secret there. But he had never spoken of that day, even after his long, nightmarish voyage to America was over. It was the second hardest thing he had ever done, to board that iron steamer, alone, and cross the ocean, alone. The hardest was, of course, burying the bodies of his wife Bridgett and baby John. He allowed himself a week to grieve, which was the same amount of time he spent later at sea, sitting on a wooden bench in steerage, nodding bloodlessly at the others. That was what people did back then. After some great personal loss, they just got on with it.

When Arthur landed in New York Harbor, taken by steam launch to Ellis Island, he was still drowning in grief. Like a sleepwalker, he stood in a long row of anxious passengers, as men in white smocks, carrying clipboards, probed and prodded and interrogated the new arrivals. One examiner checked a box next to his name, *Mechanic,* then asked Arthur if he had secured employment in America. Not yet, Arthur shrugged. He was cleared to enter the country, having no signs of typhus, syphilis, or imbecility. The fact that he was Scottish, not Italian, or Irish, helped immensely.

RICHARD CROWNINGSHIELD Senior was looking for competent men to work in his Chicago foundry, and that's where Arthur had gone, having heard about the job from an advertisement in *Engineering Journal,* which, of course, he hadn't read. But these things happen. Another Scot, a foundry man he'd met on the crossing, told him the particulars, and together they traveled, by rail and by foot, to the company's hiring office. Richard Crowningshield, the owner of the company, of all things, had interviewed him personally. He quickly recognized in Arthur a rough, uneducated diamond, much as he himself had been thirty years before. And that was that.

CHAPTER FIFTEEN

The Sisters of Charity

SOMETIMES AT NIGHT Rosemary thought about Dublin. Her working days were full of the needs of children not her own. She couldn't possibly think of that fearful, confusing, sorrowful time in her life, during the waking hours. To do so would have been the end of peace, and perhaps, sanity.

SHAMUS WAS A LOCAL boy, the oldest son of the village baker. At sixteen, he wore the airs of an adult man. There was a strutting, preening kind of adolescent arrogance about him. But to Rosemary, who was thirteen, on the cusp of fourteen, he was an entrancing rogue. She was his social opposite: lonely, graceless, full of anxieties, and the voiceless shame of the only child of a vanished father and a bitter mother. She avoided mirrors, because the pale, freckled skin on her face was bloomed with bright, roseate acne. She had recently begun menstruating, and nobody had told her about the blood and the monthly distempers it brought. Certainly not her mum, or her aunts, or the nuns. Her dad was a ghostly legend. He was rumored to have landed in the city, living now in Belfast with his second wife, an escapee from a loveless union. And so, at thirteen, nearly fourteen, there was a great haunted and isolating kind of sadness hovering over Rosemary's life. She suffered daily from a confluence of hidden stressors, not the least of which was a father's abandonment and a mother's cold disassociation, what modern psychologists would describe as "collateral damage."

One day, after classes were done, Shamus approached Rosemary. She was a typical Irish schoolgirl. She wore the uniform of The Sisters of Charity

Convent School: white knee socks, green tartan skirt, white blouse, and black tie. On her feet, high-shined, patent leather shoes, which clacked softly when she walked. It was this uniform she was most proud of. It made her, a homely, moody young girl, truly a Sister of Charity. Her secret ambition was to be a nun, a bride of Christ, to serve Him in the best way that He saw fit. Each night she knelt to her prayers, and each morning, as she walked to school, she silently memorized her catechism. She wanted to be ready when chosen.

Shamus was polite, his brogue laced with a kind of sweet gregariousness. He smiled crookedly, then asked if she'd like some company on her walk home. Such a bright, earnest face, just a nice Irish boy. Rosemary nodded. There was nobody on earth who could have protected her at this moment.

And so, they walked. Shamus was attentive, and asked her questions no one had ever thought to ask. He was clever and adroit, focused as a laser onto her insecurities. She felt flattered, honored, suddenly plucked from obscurity. Rosemary had never before walked with a boy alone like this. Only in class, or in church, or at a marriage or a funeral, always in chattering groups. Never alone. They walked on. Shamus was funny, and said things in a certain way she decided she liked to hear. He was taller, attractive in a small-town kind of way. His eyes glittered with mischief. The fall of his dirty blonde bangs, the way he tossed them away, like a curtain lifting, from his face when he was making a point, made her feel something inside. Something warm, and strange, and new.

They left the village behind, and continued on into the farmlands. It was another mile to the stone cottage where she and her mother lived. But between: only haystacks, an occasional grazing Hereford, a tumbledown barn, and off in a distant field, an enormous gray mare nibbling a Timothy stalk, gazing serenely back at them. These were small, insignificant things that Rosemary recalled, after it was over, for the rest of her life. To her, they represented the opening of a door, a key turning, on the wings of some dreadful and unexpected change. They were roughly hewn emotions, from crisis and urgency, just as Arthur had felt, standing on that hill, watching his family disappear beneath the angry waters of the River Dee.

"COME ON," HE'D SOFTLY coaxed, leading her to a rustic, gated courtyard. In the center of the courtyard was a circular, wooden structure. Loosely slatted, perhaps for ventilation, its red paint was faded. A large double door hung on rusted iron hinges. In her memory's eye, always the red paint, the rusted hinges, the creaking door, as Shamus pushed it open, and turned to her, smiling sweetly. He took her hand. Let's sit here awhile, he suggested, as they entered. It's nice, don't you think? Motes danced in the slashes of yellow sunlight that illuminated the dirt floor, pungent bales of rotting hay, stacked nearly to the roof. It was a farmer's silo, for storing summer grasses cut for winterfeed. Shamus was taller, and stronger, and supremely confident. His smile disappeared, as he quickly wrestled Rosemary to the warm earthen floor. In the space of a frightened heartbeat, he was on top of her, began unbuttoning his trousers, probing with dirty, urgent fingers beneath her skirt.

Afterwards, at home, Rosemary sat in her room, quietly assessing what had happened to her. Her pelvis ached, and there had been blood. Shamus had finished quickly, rolled off of her, and vanished.

She knew what happened to loose girls in the village. Not exactly, but she could guess. Loose girls simply disappeared. Never to be seen again. The Catholic church would see to that. She knew its power. Their laws were absolute. Rosemary had once overheard her mum speaking to a neighbor woman, something about a local woman who had gotten herself preggers and been sent away. Rosemary knew next to nothing about how a girl got herself with child, but it, logically, included the participation of both a man and a woman. She didn't even know what it was called, the urgent, thrusting thing Shamus had put into her body.

The next day, she saw her baker's boy again. Shamus said nothing, and moved with the chattering tide toward his class.

IT WAS NEARLY SEVEN months before Rosemary began to show. She was a thin slip of a girl, but her mum already knew, and dutifully informed the village priest. He in turn notified the parish council, and so on and so on.

It was a delicate matter, to be handled discreetly, between church and family and state.

"Tell us the name of the boy," the priest quietly urged, surrounded by his council, aged churchmen of power and influence.

Rosemary shook her head and bit her lip.

"I can't," she told them. The tribunal of churchmen sat in her mum's front parlor on mismatched, uncomfortable chairs, cups of Earl Gray balanced on their knees.

"It wasn't my fault."

The priest leaned in closer. "You mean he forced himself on you?"

She pondered this. "Yes," she slowly answered. "He was older, and stronger. I didn't know what to do."

The men turned to one another. The priest nodded.

"I see." he said. But he didn't. Not really. Before them was an innocent, a fourteen-year-old girl who wanted desperately to serve Her Lord and Savior. She wished to one day cut her long, red hair and wear a sister's habit, to serve the poor and the infirm and the sick, just like Jesus had done. She wanted to be a bride of Christ. She wanted to be a Sister of Charity.

But now she could never. No, nah, never. It just wasn't possible. No matter how many catechisms she knelt to, no matter how many novenas she whispered, or how many Rosary beads she rolled between her fingers. No, nah, never. This, to these men, was her true confession. It was her inquisition. Her young, unmarried body, wickedly ripe with child, was the only evidence they needed. Rosemary Kincaid was a harlot, a fallen woman, a sinning Jezebel that had seduced a decent village boy and gotten *herself* pregnant.

Rosemary, at that instant, knew instinctively that whatever she said next would have absolutely no bearing on the rest of her life. It would not matter in the slightest to these somber men, balancing china cups in the front room of her mother's house.

"Shamus!" she hissed out her attacker's name. "The baker's boy. He was the one that done this."

The churchmen fell silent. Only the soft ticking of the mantel clock, the uncomfortable rustle of black woolen suits, a bluebird outside the window, swaying on a tree branch, leaping to soundless flight. Rosemary, out of the corner of her eye, saw her mother, staring down at the worn carpet, her hands tightly balled into nervous claws. The priest coughed lightly. Then, as a group, they stood and surrendered their cups onto a worn, wooden table.

As they trooped for the door, the priest was the last to the threshold. He theatrically turned.

"We'll be in touch," he said grimly. Then, with a swish of black and lavender hassock, and a jingle of silver crucifix, was gone.

CHAPTER SIXTEEN

The Moving Picture Show

Is it already July? So hot, even in the morning. The glass says ninety-five degrees. Today, saw A., who has been working so hard so that we can have a more comfortable time of it. Mr. C. home again next week. Who knows for how long. Yesterday J. got a case of the poison ivy. Poor little man, his arms and face all painted in calamine, like some wild Indian...

CORNELIA GLANCED UP from her needlepoint, a floral motif she'd have mounted when they got back to Chicago. She sensed the house plumber was nearby. He came and went so quietly, like some inscrutable phantom. Arthur had just completed the work on the downstairs water closet, converted from a small pantry closet, where the kitchen girls could wash up and do their necessaries.

She was sitting in a wicker rocking chair; he was striding across the porch.

"Oh, Mr. Rouse," she called over to him. "Arthur?" He turned; a pipe wrench heavy on his shoulder. He was headed for the cellar. The furnace had been acting up, likely some blockage in the intake.

"Yes, Mrs. Crowningshield?"

Cornelia laid her needlework down onto a small wicker table, next to a pitcher of lemonade laid on a silver platter, dewy from the melting ice inside.

"Arthur, the children and I are going into the village tonight, to attend a moving picture show. Would you like to accompany us?"

Arthur stared back at her. "A moving picture show, mum? Afraid I don't know what exactly that might be."

She smiled. "It's like a magic lantern. But these are pictures that move, just like in real life. Mr. Edison invented it. They have special cameras. There are newsreels, from current events, and made-up stories. It should be fun," adding mischievously, "Rosemary is coming as well."

Arthur, surprised, only nodded.

"I'll have to get myself presentable, Ma'am," he said. "What time would that be?"

"It begins at seven o-clock," she explained. "I'll tell you where to meet us. You've been working so hard, and we so appreciate everything you've done here."

Arthur tried on his biggest smile. "Of course, Ma'am. I'd be delighted. I wouldn't miss it for the world."

WORK DAY DONE, BACK in his room at the Breakwater, Arthur bent over the basin. He turned the tap, splashing cold water onto his face. Dirt and sweat swirled into the drain. This is where he lived. It was just a sad, single man's room. A place to sleep, nothing more. Everything in his life was simple and cheap. He ate always in the same restaurant back in the village, where everyone knew his face but not his name, and the same tired lady, the wife of the owner and cook, set his plate at the counter, then served him the same thing each night. Steak, with two greasy eggs, over easy, two slices of fat white bread, with butter. And afterwards, a slice of cherry or rhubarb pie, with a dollop of vanilla ice cream. It rarely varied. He always drank the same glass of milk, and the one cup of black coffee. Then he always rose, thanked the tired lady, nodded to her tired husband, sweating over the grill, then placed his napkin neatly beside the plate. Next, he dropped a quarter, for the meal, including tip, then strolled back out into the night. It was always the same time when he finally rolled back the sheets and slept. Ten o'clock, unless a party was happening near his room. Then he'd lay in his bed, listening to the cackling frivolity of drunken men and women until it wasn't there anymore. In the morning, it was back to work, back to Juniper Point, navigating his way quietly around the Crowningshield family and their privileged, needful lives. He stared at himself, saw only reddened eyes, the etched worry lines of an old man staring back. He was nearing forty-five. It wasn't a lifetime of heavy labor that changed him this way. It was the river Dee. That, and a desperate loneliness.

Arthur peered down. The sink looked familiar. He never really noticed before, but he probably made this very one, or one just like it. There, stamped into the vitreous china bowl, just behind the faucets, bold as you please, was the Crowningshield Company logo, an upper-case *C* twined to an abbreviation: *Co.*

Half the hotels in America had these same initials on their toilets and sinks. It was what paid for the mansion on Juniper Point, and the salaries of those forty employees that kept that mansion alive. And *Alma,* the auxiliary steamer tied to the pier, and on and on and on. Imagine, such an opulent life for one family, all from the needs of regular Americans to shit and piss and wash.

Arthur sat on the edge of his bed. It sagged and complained on rusted springs. As he slept and turned, a thousand times each night, it made the same rusted-spring sounds every time he shifted his weight. Everything about his life was the same, each day was the same. The only thing that changed was the task at hand, but even that was the same.

Arthur was a workman. He did his work each day, then went home at night. In Chicago, it was another small, rented room. It was the same number of steps each morning to work and each night back. In Chicago, he ate his dinner alone, and in Woods Hole he ate his dinner alone. And then he went back to his rented room, and listened to the sounds of the evening outside his window. There was a radio next to the bed, but he never turned it on.

Here, at this rambling seaside hotel, the old Breakwater, (and it was considered old, even in 1910), a long, narrow structure made from the conjoined dormitories of the bankrupted Guano factory, his neighbors were mostly vacation-goers, passengers from the train or the steamer who journeyed to escape the city's heat and perhaps find some jollity, or even romance. But Arthur had a job to do, bringing sanitary modernity to the Crowningshield family. He'd carried with him, on his journey, two changes of work clothes, two pairs of trousers, two chambray shirts, and two pairs of socks. He alternately washed each day's clothes, then dried them on a wall hook for the next day. He also owned one additional pair of black pants and white shirt, but these he rarely wore. These were his church clothes. The last time he'd worn them was the funeral of his wife and son. But, since he no longer attended church, they hung there, unused, in the tiny closet across from his bed.

Tonight, he reached for them.

AT SIX-THIRTY, MRS. Crowningshield, Rosemary, and the children began walking down the long drive. It was the beginning of a fair evening. The sun was setting, the crickets were tuning up. Later, clouds of no-see-ums, tiny, aggravating chiggers, would make outdoor activities insufferable, and screened porches necessary. Rosemary walked a few steps behind, quietly observing the children and their mother. They were well-scrubbed and well-behaved, and this was all Rosemary's doing. But it was odd, Mrs. Crowningshield's sudden display of maternal affection. The children seemed happy, but equally puzzled. They kept glancing back at their nanny. As their small procession reached the end of the lane, passing the black, wrought iron gate, Mrs. Crowningshield turned her head and called out sweetly, "You know, Rosemary, your Mr. Rouse will be joining us."

Rosemary replied with just three words. "Oh, that's grand," followed by the faint tracery of a secret smile.

ROSEMARY SAT NEXT TO him, and their legs occasionally touched. She smelled clean, scrubbed with store-bought soap. Her long red hair hung over her shoulders in a taut braid. A sweetly familiar warmth emanated from her slender body. It was the first time he'd sat so close to a woman in a long while. He struggled with the memory.

Not since Bridgett.

They were in a church basement. All the windows were covered with black muslin, and no air moved, which made the hall a stifling cave, a dank and dark catacomb. The itinerant projectionist had put up a large white screen. The crowd waited and fidgeted and quietly chatted as he fed the spooled film between a set of oiled rollers, adjusted the lens, inspected bulbs. Arthur turned and watched him work, fascinated. Rosemary secretly watched him, the back of his neck, the muscles on his shoulder blades, a single bead of sweat on his face. After a few long minutes, the projectionist flicked a switch, and the whirring machine clattered to life. It spat out hot light, hurling silent, flickering images onto the screen. Dust motes and the smoke of a dozen acrid cigars wafted into the projector's white beam. Arthur turned and stared straight ahead, breathing in the aroma of human perspiration and cologne, the rank proximity of men and women on wooden folding chairs. Rosemary shifted in her seat, not knowing what to say. She stole another sideways glance. Arthur. Her daily curiosity. Her nightly thoughts. Here was the A. in her diary, now sitting as close as any man could. But his eyes never left that dancing light, like a small child enthralled by a magician's parlor trick. Up on the screen, an enormous locomotive was thundering soundlessly towards them. Smoke billowed from its black, iron stack. A horseman and rider raced beside the train, a cowboy highwayman galloping in double-time. The timing was wrong, everything faster than in real life. It was all rendered in cinematic shadows, only light and shadow, a thousand variations, surreal as a dream. As the locomotive drew near, just before impact, Arthur shielded his face with one hand, an instinctive, defensive gesture. He had never seen such a thing. Beside him, sensing his fear and wonder, Rosemary reached for his other hand, patting it comfortingly. The scene shifted. Next was a montage of workmen on a swinging staging plank, suspended from a vast, cliff wall with steam-powered hammer chisels. It was the Hoover Dam under construction, certainly the next great wonder of the world. Crowningshield Co. was providing the gigantic pumps and valves for this immense construction project. Arthur glanced down. He barely noticed the weight of her small hand covering his enormous one, until she demurely returned it to her own lap. He saw Rosemary in the dull gloaming. She was smiling faintly, pretending interest for the men on the scaffolding. Something had passed between them. Something electric and secret, but still emotionally vaulted. It spoke of possibilities, something to be explored in the fullness of time. He turned back to the screen. Next, an oceanic scene, a three-masted ship, sailing men and fish offal and the mute fury of a stormy passage. There were subtitles. Arthur frowned, until Rosemary leaned in and whispered, "It says 'Greasy

Luck! The whaling schooner Alice J. Stevens, from New Bedford, returning to port with full barrels and happy crew.'"

He nodded silently, his own secret smile tugging at his lips.

AFTER THE NEWSREELS came the evening's feature, a morality tale starring Mary Pickford, directed by D.W. Griffith. Mary Pickford was the moving picture star of the day. Only seventeen when she was first discovered by Griffith, she had traveled west, to California, to join the Biograph Pictures family of stage actors, who produced, on average, a picture a week. It was said that she supported her parents with what money she made. Her talent was being able to emote, without the elaborate, stagy gestures of other moving picture actors, succinctly and clearly, in as few frames as possible, something a budget-conscious producer like Griffith would appreciate. In 1910, films were sold by the foot, one thousand feet of film considered average. Mary Pickford could tell a story in nine hundred or less.

Tonight's feature was entitled *An Arcadian Maid*. The story was an old one. A morality tale, made for the church-going masses. A working girl falls in love with a traveling peddler who visits the farm where she is employed washing clothes. The script plays upon a popular racial stereotype of the day. The peddler is Italian. We know this because he's a smarmy villain with a sweet-talking way with the ladies. He wears a velveteen suit with white piping, common theatrical code for Italian, and either plays an organ grinder or a pickpocket or a con artist. He's the classic grifter. After showing the farmer's wife some bolts of cloth, he works his magic with the scrub girl, an innocent with virtually no street smarts, even less self-esteem. Meet me tonight, he tells her, after giving her a cheap, imitation ring. She does. They meet, they kiss, and then part. The audience in the stifling basement murmur and fidget. A duplicitous dago and a virtuous virgin on a moral collision course, a powerful cautionary tale. Scene two. The conniving Italian is shooting dice and drinking in a tavern, like greasy Italians are prone to do. Of course, he loses, falling deeply into debt. The next night, he confides in the girl. I want to marry you, he says. Then quickly asks, do you have any money? No, she shakes her head, but I know where my employer hides his.

In a sock under his mattress. Great, get it, he demands. Then we can run away together. Of course, she does, of course he doesn't marry her. Instead he takes the money and boards the next train, without her.

In the church basement, the audience of farmers and shopkeepers and fishermen groaned. This is a telling moment in the screenplay, calculated by D.W Griffith to elicit the best response to sell the next reel. Men are shaking their heads in anger; their wife's brows are furrowed. If that was their sweet daughter, or even their hired girl, there'd be hell to pay.

Damned Italians! Damned low-moraled wops!

Arthur turned his head, slightly, towards Rosemary. Her eyes were moist, and she daubed at them with a lace handkerchief. Further down the row, the children were restless. Mrs. Crowningshield leaned down to say something to John. His face, white with calamine, was a spectral mask.

"Don't scratch, John," she softly ordered him. Arthur, slowly, almost imperceptibly, slid his rough, workingman's paw over Rosemary's petite fist. She sniffled once, and gazed full into his eyes. "I'm sorry," she whispered. "Just something about that poor girl. I dunno. It made me sad to think about it."

Arthur remained silent. He sat there, a lonely man gripping an unmarried woman's tiny hand in his. For the first time in a long time, he's not thinking about the river Dee.

CHAPTER SEVENTEEN

The Master Returns

Charles Richard Crowningshield stood at the edge of his yard, staring down at the monstrous steel yacht he had bought in London only a month ago. He'd drunk too much wine, then paid too much money.

"Fifty-eight thousand dollars!" he moaned, turning to Arthur, standing next to him on the grassy precipice. "What is Christ's name was I thinking?"

Arthur nodded. It was an amount of money that he could never see in a lifetime. Still, he offered a compliment.

"She's a fine-looking boat, all the same," he said. "I don't know nothing about them. But she looks fairly well built. Anyone can see that."

Charles Crowningshield looked over at Arthur, and grinned. "You know what I like about you, Arthur?"

"What would that be, Mr. Crowningshield?"

CHARLES CROWNINGSHIELD had arrived on the New York steamer last night. He made it a point to be with his family to celebrate the 4th of July together. All the way from China, somehow returning in time. He was a true patriot, the country's new Ambassador to China, and a great family man. Certain sacrifices had been made.

He continued. "What I like about you, Arthur, is that you see the goddamn lightness in all things. You work hard and you do your job, but you see the goddamn lightness."

Crowningshield continued to stare down at the *Alma*. Her rigging had been decorated with tiny stars and stripes, bright cotton bunting riffling in the breeze.

When he began to speak again, it was in a strange, lament of a whisper. "What I see down there...what I see...I see a captain that wants to return to England, and a damned chef that *never* wants to leave. I see half her crew deserted, the other half drunk, and a giant hole in the water that I will continue to pour money into until she sinks at the dock or I find somebody else dumb enough to buy the damned thing. Jesus, what was I thinking?"

Arthur considered this, not exactly sure how to respond.

"But, still, sir, she is a fine-looking boat, all the same. I'll bet the children will enjoy going on a cruise sometime."

Charles Crowningshield stared out across the water. The children. He hadn't seen them in months. Or slept in the same bed with his wife in years. His voice sounded weary. A man that has traveled ten thousand miles to be in a place not of his choosing, resentful of an inanimate object, an impulse purchase he has never stepped foot upon.

He surveyed the rich panorama of all that he possessed. The Woods Hole passage was alive with other boats, other skippers, all enjoying the day, or at least making a few dollars from the water. Saturday sailors from the yacht club, Captains of Commerce like himself, in immaculate mahogany cockleshells, jibing around regatta buoys, local fishermen in stinking catboats pushing a spread of patched canvas, a lone oarsman in a dory fighting the current, the island steamer threading between the killing rocks, headed for the railroad docks.

When he finally spoke again, his voice was muted and distant. "That they will, Arthur. That they will."

Then he brightened. He turned and clapped Arthur on the shoulder. "You've really done a magnificent job with the house. I could really use you back in Chicago, but there's still a great deal of work left to do here. The architects are drawing up plans for six more buildings. An ice house, a boat house, a second stable, the gardener's cottage, and my daughter has been really patient to have her own place out on the Point. My position with the government is going to eat up much more of my time, and then there's the Company. I really need a good man to look after things here. Can you manage that?"

"Yes, Mr. Crowningshield," Arthur said, "I understand. No problem at all, sir."

Crowningshield, still staring off into the distance, across Little Harbor.

"Thank you, Arthur," he said without turning. "I knew I could depend on you."

CHAPTER EIGHTEEN

At Breakfast

Cornelia, nibbling on a piece of toast, cautiously watched her husband read the morning newspaper, the Sunday *New York Times,* fresh off the morning steamer.

He set the paper down, took a sip of coffee, and smiled the length of the long gleaming dining table. Kitchen staff came and went. The distant clatter of breakfast dishes being washed behind the swinging door, a subdued cacophony of Irish brogues, a downstairs maid arranging flowers on a breakfront, invisible and self-conscious in the lofty presence of the master and mistress. Outside the window, the gardener was tugging weeds from a rose bed. Mrs. Crowningshield continued to nibble. They politely gazed at one another.

Finally, she broke the silence. "Will you be here long, Charles?"

He considered this, took a bite of scone, daubed with a spoonful of orange marmalade. Mrs. Carmody had finally found a supplier in Boston. There'd be no more temper snits over fruit condiments at table.

"I'll be here until next week. Friday, at the latest, then I must be off," he told her. "Business in Chicago, then New York, and then back to jolly old England."

"England?" She was surprised. "Again? Why so soon, dear?"

He frowned. "I thought I told you. No matter. The company has a big contract with the White Star Line. Two big ships on the ways, and a third after that, all the plumbing and steam valves and piping bits. It's a lot of money, Cornelia, a great opportunity, and I have to personally sign the contracts to get the ball rolling."

She nodded, pursing her lips. "Of course, darling. It sounds quite fascinating."

He shook his head, slightly irritated, then slowly laid down the scone.

"Cornelia, I know I haven't been here as much as I should. As much as you would prefer. But what should I do? Just let things...languish?"

She gazed up at the ceiling. "No, of course not, dear. But the children. They ask where their father is. Especially John. He adores you, but each day that goes by... I just don't know what to tell them."

He nodded. "Of course. I understand, Cornelia. You're doing a wonderful job here, with the children, and the house. Soon, I promise. Things are going to settle down. When my brother takes over the company, there will be more time for all of you."

Cornelia shook her head. "Charles, don't flatter me. It's all Rosemary. I'm a nervous wreck half the time. If we didn't have that woman, I just don't know."

Crowningshield reached for the newspaper. For him, the conversation was winding down. He needed to change the subject.

"I've asked the captain to take us all out for a picnic cruise on the *Alma*. Everyone. Including the entire staff. On the 4th. The children should enjoy that."

Cornelia brightened. "Yes, that does sound like fun. I'll get together with Mrs. Carmody, plan out the menu. Heavens, that's a lot of people. Let me see. Deviled eggs and potato salad, I'm sure. Lemonade. Chicken sandwiches. Cucumber on toast. Perhaps we can have ice cream. I'll have her make some nice blueberry pies.

Charles lowered his paper again. A small article had caught his eye. A peasant revolution in China was brewing. An American gunship attacked on the Yangtze. A missionary family had been killed. He'd have to talk with President Taft. It sounded serious.

"That sounds wonderful, dear," he said vaguely. "There is, you may recall, a professional chef onboard. I'm sure he could assist you and Mrs. Carmody with the preparations."

Back less than twenty-four hours. He was already desperate to leave.

CHAPTER NINETEEN

Shipboard

Arthur, bags in hand, stood at the foot of the gangway and felt the metallic taste of bile in the back of his throat. It was his employer's wish that he give up his room at the Breakwater, move onboard the ship, to be closer to his work on Juniper Point. This he could do, if it was his employer's wish. Even though his heart rate spiked, his brow was already dripping, and of course, the septic nausea just behind his tongue was set to retch onto the newly oiled teak decks.

ALMA, one-hundred-and-forty feet long, was less than five years old. Her tenure with the Crowningshield family would be brief. Within two years, she would be sold to a Michigan lumber mogul, Charles Canfield. Later, in 1923, she would be sold again, to George Taylor Fulford, a wealthy member of the Canadian Parliament, who would rename her *Magedoma,* a combination of syllables from the names of his wife and children, (MAry, GEorge, DOrothy, MArtha). After Fulford's death in 1938, the ship would be donated to the Royal Canadian Navy, for use as a training vessel. After the war she would return to the Fulford family, but in greatly deteriorated condition. The ship would finally be sold again, to Fredric Burtis Smith, who would live onboard for many years at Rochester, NY. Finally, in the early 1980s, after his death, an attempt would be made to restore her, by a hastily formed nonprofit organization, called *Friends of Alma.* The project would ultimately fail for financial reasons and lack of public support, and in 1999, the gutted and porous derelict would finally slip below the polluted, gray waters of Boston Harbor.

ALMA, built as a three-mast, topsail yard schooner, was iron framed and plated. She was heavy, but her sail area was over 9,000 square yards, an ungodly spread of canvas that was thought to make her a genuine contender in any offshore competition. Fitted with an auxiliary compound steam engine, capable of seventy horsepower, she had a top speed of just over ten knots, a little faster than a running man. Her bunkers could hold sixty tons of coal, which meant she could steam for approximately twenty days without refueling. She had sumptuous accommodations for twenty guests, twenty spartan ones for crew. Of course, Arthur knew none of this. To him, a master mechanic, she was a curving symphony of plates and rivets, a machine that moved atop the waves, which, to him, was counter-intuitive, that such a weighty contrivance could actually float. He marveled at what it would take to bend steel into such a graceful shape. Deep in her bilges was a magnificent, Scottish-built, triple-expansion steam engine. He had seen ships like her on the Glasgow docks. Fine rich men's toys, syndicate racehorses.

ARTHUR TOOK A BREATH, and slowly made his way up the gangway, gripping the chain railing each step of the way. His feet touched the teak deck, and his hands went from gray link to highly polished rail. A bearded man appeared, popping through a steel door from the wheelhouse. The man was striding purposefully in his direction, holding out his hand.

"Good morning," he said. "Captain Brisbee. M.A. Brisbee, from London."

Arthur shook the captain's hand. "Arthur Rouse. Aberdeen."

Captain Brisbee smiled. "Ah, the Scotsman. Good, that's good. Welcome aboard. I need somebody that can tend to these fine Glasgow boilers in her belly. My engineer up and left me two days ago. Not a fucking word, that Irish, blackguard son of a bitch. And Mr. Crowningshield expects me to take her out of here in three days." He nodded overhead, to the garland of tiny American flags tied to the dizzyingly high rigging, and winked. "Independence Day, for the Yanks, eh, Arthur."

Arthur shrugged. "I don't know much about steam engines, Captain Brisbee. I'm a foundry man. I can probably build you one, but, the plain truth of the matter, right now, I'm a house plumber. Haven't the foggiest notion about the doings of a ship."

"Maybe, maybe not," Brisbee allowed, "but still, you're a good mechanic. Mr. Crowningshield says you can do anything with tools. Look, Arthur, it's pretty simple, once you understand the basic principles. You build up steam, you engage the throttle when I say go, you disengage the throttle when I say stop." He smiled. "What could be simpler? The second mate is pretty handy down in the engine room. He could help you with the basics. And don't forget we've got the stoker. Christ, that black boy's been down there long enough, he could probably get it going himself, except he drinks, and he kneels on a prayer rug three times a day. Jesus, we're just going out for a couple of hours. Just around the Point, then we'll be heading over to those little islands for a picnic cruise. What do you say? Just until I can find someone."

Arthur laid his satchels down onto the deck. His little bachelor's room at the Breakwater suddenly seemed like the dark side of the moon.

"I suppose so, Captain. But I don't need no manuals, or books. I kind of do everything by feel."

Captain grinned and lightly clapped him on the back. "Done, Arthur, wonderful. I'll have the mate show you your berth. You get squared away, take a little tour of the ship, and then you can get started. No worries. We're just taking a bunch of kiddies and chambermaids out for a holiday cruise."

ARTHUR, STANDING ON the steel grating of *Alma's* immense engine room. The second mate was pointing out the valves, the steam pipes that led to valves, the gauges that monitored what was gurgling though those pipes and gauges. It sounded like some enormous, deafening clockwork. The heat stabbed him in the face, and knocked him back on his heels.

"And this one goes into here, and comes out over there," the man was saying, and stabbing his finger, added, "You have to watch this valve, okay? Never let the pressure up over one-eighty. Or she'll blow."

Arthur stared, in rapt fascination, as the ship came slowly to life. The big, oily, reciprocating arms began to pulse up and down, and the dials inside the glass- covered brass gauges began to quiver. Behind him, a stoker, the Senegalese, even darker with coal dust, was shoveling dusty nuggets into an iron firebox. Rivers of sweat ran down his face, staining his ragged shirt.

Alma was waking up.

"And when the captain telegraphs his order down," the second mate was shouting, top-lung now, "you've got to be snappy. Because he means fucking now! Not a minute from now. This ship can be a bitch in a windy channel. She's almost impossible to steer while under sail in close quarters, like we got around here, with other vessels riding up your arse, the rocks, and the current. She's gonna be under steam for most of the time. You have to stay on yer fuckin' toes."

Arthur nodded, never taking his eyes from the gauges and the steady, racketing, metronome of the pistons. In time, he could master anything. A ship's engine was just another engine.

ROSEMARY CAUGHT SIGHT of Arthur just as he was climbing the gangway. She and the children strolled along the dirt road that led them around the lushly vegetated perimeter of Juniper Point. They were going to the beach today, a short stretch of sandy ground cut into the rocky shore. It wasn't a place for swimming, not for adults, never for children. The waters beyond the beach were an angry confluence of contrary tidal currents and dangerous undertows. No swimmer, no matter how strong, would attempt such a crossing, even though the near shore, Nobska Point, with its squat, striped lighthouse, was less than a cable's length away. The beach was a place for wading, for cupping salt water onto your face, for building sand castles, for watching sea birds whirl and dive, for gobbling baloney sandwiches and Mrs. Carmody's ginger cookies. But never for swimming.

Rosemary waved over to Arthur, but didn't call out. It wouldn't be proper. He was deep in conversation with the captain, the jocular, bearded Mr. Brisbee. Perhaps later, they might talk, before he walked back to the village for the night. She wanted to apologize, for being so forward at the moving picture show.

ARTHUR BEGAN TO LEARN his way around the ship. Here, behind this door, was the wheelhouse. Here was the kitchen, or galley, as boatmen called it. Here was the radio room, the chartroom, the captain's berth a few steps from the helm. He met a fussy, young man of Gaelic disposition, the chef from Paris who was baking some croissants in the large ship's oven. He was shown the rest of the crew's quarters, although half of the cabins were empty. Captain Brisbee had dismissed the non-essential men the first few days, paying them off with wages a one-way train ticket to New York. Back to England, that was not his concern. The second mate pointed down a long hall, or companionway.

"Down there, that's owner's country. That's all velvet cushions and silver spoons," he said. "Nobody goes down there, nobody with grease on their clothes anyways."

Arthur nodded, remembering how friendly Mr. Crowningshield had been to him. But now he knew. That was just to get him onboard the *Alma*. So, they could leave this dock and take the family out for a picnic. But that was fine, as well. He could do this. The ship was a large one, as picnic boats go. Walking her decks, you could almost forget that you were suspended over the black, mysterious water.

Later, in his cabin, Arthur realized that no, it wasn't fine. Being onboard, even such an opulent vessel, his worst memories came tumbling back. He never really left that day in Aberdeen, never forgiven himself, standing on a hill, overlooking the river, helpless to save his family.

CHAPTER TWENTY

A Holiday Cruise

Mrs. Carmody, the cook, sat on a varnished bench by the salon door, the wind tugging at her long gray hair she'd neatly rolled into a tight bun. Her hands moved like birds, modestly holding down the hem of her cotton dress. It reminded her, a widow woman from Cork, of coming to America. The salt zephyrs off an open ocean, an iron ship taking her away from sadness, carrying her to a new life. Around her, familiar faces of her household swirled, untethered from their daily roles of servitude: the kitchen girls, the housemen, the chauffeur, the gardener's boys, the chambermaids. Everyone was excited, everyone at this moment occupied the same social station, just fellow passengers on a sea cruise.

Behind the wheelhouse glass, Captain Brisbee signaled down to the engine room. The lines had been pulled aboard, and Chrissake! They were already drifting toward the shore. The telegraph bell urgently clanged three times. *Reverse Engines, Half.* And he waited. *Christ, man!* A half a minute crept by. Just as he was about to send Jenkins, the first mate, down to investigate, half a ton of bronze propeller began to slowly turn, churning up sand and silt. Slowly her hourglass stern began to back into the stream. *Have to be a little smarter the next time around, Arthur,* the captain swore under his breath. He yanked, then pushed, the brass telegraph lever a second time. Two clangs of the bell. The helmsman spun the wheel. *All Ahead, Half.* This time, miracles, it did come quicker, and the big steam sailboat pushed against the current. A few villagers gathered on the shore to see her off, waving tiny flags. Their raised huzzah was soon carried away by the breeze.

AS THE SHIP MOVED OUT of Little Harbor, entering the Woods Hole passage, she began to cross the channel. A tricky bit of ship handling lay ahead. Decisions had to be made. Captain Brisbee tapped the helmsman on the shoulder. Steady as she goes, he softly ordered, adding the compass bearing. The morning sun was now in their eyes, the waters ahead glittered with a billion diamond shards. He went quickly into the navigation room, unrolled a local chart. When they'd first arrived, it was from the south, from the deeper waters of Vineyard Sound. Now their destination was to the southwest, towards Buzzards Bay, and eventually, Nantucket Sound. There were dangers out there not found on any chart. Shifting shoals, hidden boulders, an infinity of ship-killing traps not seen by the naked eye. Over there, the water rippling with froth. A rock ledge, most of it beneath the surface. Over there, where the sea turned from azure to shadowy white, a sandbar below. All uncharted, where ship handling became educated guesses.

They slowly crept around the Elizabeth Islands. Their first stop would be the largest village, Cuttyhunk, population fifty-two. Mr. Crowningshield had requested they anchor there, take the ship's launch to the beach, so passengers could get their feet wet, dig for clams, explore a bit. The captain glanced at the chart. Fifteen feet at mean high tide at the harbor's entrance, then dropping off quickly. That meant anchoring a fair distance from shore. For *Alma*, with her deep, oceangoing keel, you had to keep clear of the bottom. A grounding, on the family's maiden voyage, was out of the question. Finally, after an hour of streaming, he sent the signal below to throttle down, *Ahead slow*. Then a short burst of white water at the stern. *Full reverse*. They neared the edge of the harbor. The captain telegraphed his final order: *All Stop, Done with Engines.*

Good job, old man, he silently praised his fill-in engineer. It had been nothing less than remarkable, how quickly Arthur had learned his way around the ship's mechanical complexities. Captain Brisbee felt a small lurch beneath the deck, as the auxiliary generator was engaged, ensuring the Edison light bulbs below were still burning, the freezer in the galley kept the ice cream from melting, and the radio room magneto still had contact with the lifesaving station in Woods Hole, just in case.

The first mate gave the order to lower anchor. The steam capstan at the bow clanked and lowered down link after link of heavy chain into the placid waters. They were on a benevolent lee shore, a place of refuge in storms. But today, there was no foul weather forecast, and the sun was beginning to pleasantly heat up the decks.

He watched the crew unfurl the canvas from the ship's launch, swing out the davits. It could handle fifteen passengers. People on deck were excitedly lining up to be the first to make landfall.

Arthur appeared at the doorway, smiling, his face damp and bright with sweat. "Sorry about the confusion when we were shoving off," he said. "Won't happen again."

The captain smiled, reaching for his pipe. "You were fine, Arthur."

What Arthur hadn't mentioned: he had briefly frozen down below, unable to reads the words on the engine room telegraph. Luckily the stoker had noticed, and shown Arthur which notch on the throttle to pull. Afterwards, he had learned to count the bells.

Arthur glanced around the deck, bemused. "Why are people abandoning ship? Are we sinking already?"

Captain Brisbee struck a match, chuckling. A tiny cloud of aromatic tobacco filled the wheelhouse. "It's an expeditionary party, gone to explore the island."

Arthur nodded, saw, out of the corner of his eye, Rosemary walking towards him, shepherding the three youngest children in front of her. When they'd reached the wheelhouse, she turned to them.

"Children, say hello to Mr. Rouse. He's helping to make the boat run today. Say 'hello, Mr. Rouse, how are you today.'" The children shyly echoed the greeting.

Arthur smiled. John's poison ivy had cleared up nicely. Only a few scabs on his elbows remained.

"Good to see you," he told the little group, but staring mostly at Rosemary.

"And you too, Mr. Rouse," she sang right back, trying hard to remain the proper nanny. Her need to speak with him was strong. She'd thought of nothing since the moving picture show. "It's a lovely day for a sea cruise," she said. Then, noticing his steam-reddened face, frowned. "I hope it's not too hot down in the engine room."

"Oh, no, Ma'am," he told her, smiling. "It's lovely, downright tropical down there."

Rosemary smiled back, holding her hat down against the breeze. "Well," she said, turning her head, "the children and I are waiting for the second boat to shore. John is excited about catching some kind of sea urchin or something." Arthur nodded, noticing the boy's small glass specimen jar the boy was clutching, along with a large butterfly net.

"Sounds like a good plan, John. I wish you luck in your scientific endeavors."

"His aunt and uncle are both marine biology professors," Rosemary explained, "over at the Laboratory. John wants to follow in their footsteps."

Arthur tipped his cap. "Well, happy landings, everyone. I'll see you when you return."

The launch bumped lightly against the *Alma's* immense white hull, signaling the second wave of explorers to climb down the side of the ship, on the swinging Jacob's ladder, and take their seats for the short journey to the beach. He wanted to meet Rosemary's bright emerald eyes, but she shyly looked away. Over her shoulder, as she led the children to the rail, she called out, "Perhaps I'll see you later."

"I'd like that," Arthur said quietly.

CAPTAIN BRISBEE SAT on his stool in the wheelhouse, puffing fire into his briar pipe. The burnt tang of aromatic tobacco filled the air.

"You're sweet on that girl, Arthur."

Through the glass, Arthur silently watched her shimmy carefully down into the launch, heard a giggle and mock shriek as the ballast of a dozen bodies shifted. He watched the dip of long oars, the silvery wake of the little boat making for shore. He thought he heard the sound of children singing. John, with his specimen jar and his net, sitting straight-back as a deacon astride the middle thwart.

Arthur turned to the captain.

"I don't mean this as an idle boast. But the truth is I would marry her. She's a good, kind, hard-working woman. I would marry her, if I had the chance."

Captain puffed on his pipe. "I do believe you would," he said gently. "Good wives are hard to find."

Arthur nodded, then walked silently from the wheelhouse, a curious smile on his face. He need to climb below to wake the engine, shut down the generator, and build steam.

CHAPTER TWENTY-ONE

Penikese

The *Alma* ghosted by the island, but would not stop. Penikese was thought to be highly contagious. A leper colony, full of medical castaways, unfortunates diagnosed and then sent away by well-meaning doctors to rot and fester away the years they had left. What is known now they hadn't known then. That ninety-five percent of humans are immune to the ravages of leprosy. Yet in 1910, still in the dark age of modern medicine, contracting the disease was considered a death sentence. Islands like Penikese were chosen for their isolation, much as smallpox pesthouses in the 1700s. Sheer distance was the only proof against the contagion.

Captain Brisbee consulted his chart, confirming that Penikese Island was a state-run leprosarium, a place to warehouse society's untouchables. But it may have been the dark side of the moon. People rarely visited, except for one farmer and the occasional health inspector. The farmer rowed his fishing dory nearly two miles to drop off bundles wrapped in oilcloth on the desolate beach. At first, this once-a-week service provided the patients with fresh vegetables and eggs. After a few years, the inmates began to cultivate their own gardens, raise their own chickens, and the farmer and his dory were never seen again.

Brisbee could see them as they passed, afflicted souls moving slowly along the shore; some working on repairs to the buildings, a few scrounging drift wood for cook stoves, but most just aimlessly milling about, staring out to sea. A few waved as the *Alma* steamed by. The sad, barren rock of seventy acres was a lonely, sea-bound prison.

One by one, passengers moved to the rail to view the lepers.

Charles Crowningshield found his way to the wheelhouse. "What on earth is that?"

He pointed over the rail.

"Leper colony," Brisbee explained. "Poor devils. Nobody wants them. I suppose they're sent there to die."

Crowningshield sniffed the air, as if there were invisible leprosy clouds adrift. He frowned, then bellowed, "Well, let's get the hell out of here. The children don't need to see this. Find some happier destination," he ordered, as if happiness could be found on the chart, alongside immense turtles that would devour a crew if their ship sailed out past the horizon. That, and mermaids.

"Yes, sir," the captain answered automatically. He was used to the trifling whims of wealthy owners. Directing the helmsman to a new heading, he squinted up. The sun had reached its midday zenith. It was now directly above the masthead. Noonish. Time for deviled eggs, potato salad and chicken sandwiches. In an hour or two, they'd reach as far as Nantucket Sound, then it would be time to reverse course, head back to Woods Hole, back to the stone jetty.

Later, the fireworks would begin.

CHAPTER TWENTY-TWO

Revelations

Pyrotechnics experts, an Italian fireworks family from Providence, *"launched a colorful fusillade of patriotic clamor,"* gushed the *Falmouth Journal, "that this town has never seen before. And we have to thank our benefactor, Mr. Charles Crowningshield, vice-president of the Crowningshield plumbing supply company, home offices in Chicago, Illinois, for the magnificent display."*

On Juniper Point, after Independence Day, the excitement had fallen to pre-holiday levels. A heat wave crept in. A pantry girl from Cork, Evelyn, nineteen, collapsed from heat prostration while stirring the soup. It was decided, until the weather broke, that staff would prepare only uncooked meals. Cold sandwiches and salads, cereal and fruit.

Arthur resumed his duties on land. He worked on the house each day, returned to the ship at night. But Sundays off were always a problem. Boarding in his rented room at the Breakwater, that meant an entire day of solitude. No work, no distractions. Arthur had no hobbies or friends. But Sundays aboard *Alma* were interminable.

Now that he lived onboard, in close proximity to crew and a captain he barely knew, social problems were compounded and vexing. It was difficult to avoid their company. He took long walks around the Point, might be gone for hours at a time. Sometimes, he meandered into town, ate a bachelor's meal at the village's sole restaurant, peered into storefronts, gazed out at the anchored boats. Eventually he would return to his tiny berth, listening to men snore and fart.

This Sunday, however, things changed. There, just as he emerged on deck, stood Rosemary, at the foot of the gangway.

She smiled and shyly waved.

"Mrs. Crowningshield says I can have Sundays off now," she called across to him. "Isn't that grand? She says I'm working too hard, and the children will survive a few hours without their nanny."

Arthur smiled down at her, shyly mute.

She stood there, rooted as statuary, then offered a casual aside, "And I'd like to spend today with you, Mr. Arthur Rouse. If you please."

He began walking down the gangway, surprised, a little shaken by her bold proposition. By the time he'd reached her, he'd decided. "Yes, I would be pleased, Ma'am. And what is it you'd like to do?"

Rosemary grinned. It was a dangerously seductive word game they had begun, the two of them. "I have no idea, Mr. Rouse. As long as it's with you. There, see? I've made up my mind."

Arthur towered over her, himself grinning like a schoolboy. He took up her coy banter. "So, you've made up your mind, have you?

In reply, Rosemary offered a quick curtsy, and silently offered her gloved, outstretched hand.

IT WAS A DAY OF DAYS. A grand day. No loneliness, sadness, or regret was allowed to invade the few hours they had been granted to spend together. They walked for miles, aimlessly, purposelessly. There was no other place for them to be, except together.

For the first time in her life, Rosemary felt she could trust a man to not hurt or defile or defame her. For the first time since Bridgett's death, a gentle, smiling woman walked beside Arthur, a woman who took his elbow and blurted out whatever thought or emotion popped into her head. It was a heady, spontaneous courtship.

It was as if this was meant to be. This is what the future might look like, if they were both very, very lucky.

They came to a bench, set there for the purpose of viewing the harbor, and sat down. There was lazy movement out on the water, a billowing sail, small wavelets rippled by a light breeze, gulls capering in the cloudless thermals.

"It's lovely here," she said.

Arthur nodded. "I been by here, many times, on my walks back to the hotel. But I never sat and admired the view. Funny. Never really had a reason to."

Rosemary turned and tapped his arm with mock indignation. "Arthur Rouse! You don't need a reason to appreciate beauty."

He nodded. "I know, but it's more than that."

Rosemary leaned in. "What? Tell me."

He cleared his throat. "It happened a long time ago. I don't talk about it."

"Just tell me," she prodded. "Arthur...it's me, Rosemary. Go on. I'm listening."

AND SO, HE TOLD HER. How he had been a young and married man back in Aberdeen. The wonder of fatherhood, the birth of his only son. And Bridgett, such a fine wife. And how that damned ferry boat and that cursed river had robbed him of everything.

It emerged in fits and starts, somewhere between nervous rambling, and apologies.

"Don't," Rosemary finally scolded him, when he hesitated. "Arthur, this is your life. You have every right to feel this way." She took his hand and squeezed.

Arthur stared into her eyes. She was right. No apologies for anything. Especially sorrow. Impulsively, he took her sweet, pale face, with its faint ghost of adolescent freckles, cupped it gently between two enormous hands, like a man admiring a painting, and kissed her. Her lips tasted like circus candy. Softly at first, then harder. They were completely alone on this hard, wooden bench, two strangers randomly chosen by a cosmic dice roll to find one another. This bench, them together, had become the epicenter of a small, nascent attraction. Here was the origin story of new love, and would be retold by generations. The reasons were simple. He had brought water to her parched world. He had said nothing when she needed silence. She, on the other hand, had shaken him loose from his self-imposed exile. She might have been his feminine mirror. In her eyes, he sensed his own pain. Upon closer examination, they discovered they adored one another. It was as simple, or as complex, as they chose to make it. In the heady narcosis of this one moment, for the one, only the other mattered, for the other, only the one existed. Finally, she softly asked, stroking his thinning, flaxen widow's peak, an unexpected question.

"Arthur, are you hungry?"

"I could do with a bite," he admitted. "Had nothing for breakfast. Interrupted by a fair maiden at the gangplank."

"Where do you take your meals, Arthur?"

He named the only restaurant, just around the corner.

"But they're closed on Sunday," he remembered.

She shuddered, crossing her arms. Even though the day had been a hot one, the night was bringing with it a sudden chill breeze.

He remembered something. "They have a dining room, at the Breakwater, where I used to lodge. I believe it's open for guests at night."

Rosemary stood and offered her hand. "Alright, Arthur, lead on. I'm quite famished."

THEY WALKED THE HALF-mile to Penzance Point. To the Breakwater Hotel, Arthur's home for the last few months. Room 225, on the second floor. The entire village, it seemed, was turning in for the evening. The hotel was strangely empty. The night clerk barely noticed when they entered the lobby and headed for the dining room.

"Closes at ten," the clerk, a student at the Marine Laboratory, called after them, but they hadn't heard. He returned to his book, a scientific text, studying for an exam in the morning.

A weary young woman handed them menus. She recited her waitress speech. "The soup of the day is up on the board. No specials tonight. Just stuffed turkey and gravy, and cranberry sauce, with boiled cabbage on the side, and a cup of clam chowder, if you like. Or I can get you chicken salad sandwiches. We have pies as well, and custard, or watermelon wedges, for dessert."

She waited expectantly. "The cook's gone home," she finally explained. "But everything should still be warm."

"The turkey sounds grand," Rosemary said, handing the menu back.

"For me, as well," Arthur said.

They sat together at the worn, wooden table, covered by a checkered oilcloth. They touched fingertips, and stared out the window. Outside, the sun was beginning to dip behind the Elizabeth Islands, looking in the dusk like a distant, violet mountain range. Directly across the harbor, the lights of the Crowningshield house were just beginning to wink on.

"So," Rosemary began, "here we are. I was wondering when you'd finally ask me to dinner, Mr. Arthur Rouse."

He grinned sheepishly. "I'm not much of the asking type. I'm sorry."

Rosemary placed her finger to his lips. "Shhhh. I'm just joshing you, Arthur. Such a serious man you are."

"And you, Rosemary, are a beautiful woman, the most beautiful I've ever seen," Arthur said. He paused, as if suddenly remembering something.

"What, Arthur?"

He stared at her. "I don't even know your last name."

She shook her head. "No matter, but it's Kincaid."

He said it out loud. "Rosemary Kincaid. I like it. No middle name?"

"Nobody knows it but my mum."

"What?" he prompted. "Rosemary blank Kincaid."

"Alright, if you must know, it's Margaret," she admitted. "But I've always hated it."

"It'll never pass our lips ever again," Arthur promised, with dramatic solemnity.

THE TURKEY WAS TOUGH and tasteless, the gravy tepid. The boiled cabbage cold, the chowder even colder. The young waitress was apologetic, seeing them push their plates away.

"I'm sorry. No charge," she told them. "Are you guests here?"

"No," Arthur told her. "Just hungry." He smiled across the table at Rosemary. "We were out walking."

"Oh," the girl said. "Well, it's just we get a lot of newlyweds here, at the hotel. I thought you two might be...I dunno...You have that look, the two of you."

Rosemary smiled at the thought. "And where are you from? Kerry, or Dingle perhaps? From the south, am I right?"

The girl shook her head. "No, Ma'am. I was born right in Dublin. Lived there for most of my childhood."

Rosemary's face went ashen.

"Where in Dublin?" she asked.

The girl stared at her. "Off Dunhill," she slowly answered.

"At the Sisters of Charity?" Rosemary quickly asked. "Was that where you was born?"

The girl gazed down at her shoes.

Rosemary, at this moment, knew. There were thousands just like her. Standing up from the table, she folded the girl into her arms.

"It's alright," she whispered. "You was just a baby."

The girl began to weep. "My dear mum is buried there," she whispered back into her shoulder.

It was a moment. The dining room was completely empty, except for the three of them.

"It's alright," Rosemary said again, gazing hard into Arthur's eyes. "I Know. I been there, too."

ARTHUR LED ROSEMARY up the stairs, down the cheap, threadbare carpet runner to his old room. 225, second floor, rear. He still kept the key, still jangled it with a few coins in his pocket. No one had thought to ask for it back. It was just one of those things. No one would notice. They were invisible until the morning.

He offered her his old bed. The room had no chairs, just that old squeaky bed. It still wore the same thin quilt. On the wall the hook where he had dried his clothes. The bedside radio was still there. Her slight body made an insignificant, rusted-spring noise when it depressed the old horsehair mattress.

She lay down, still crying. Arthur simply waited and listened. After a few minutes, he knelt on the floor and placed his face close to hers. He smoothed away a tear, one after the other. He could feel the heat coming from her skin. He kissed her eyelids, one, then the other. Finally, she sat up, looking around the room, as if from a dream.

"This is where you stayed?" She asked.

He smiled. "Pretty posh, eh?"

Rosemary rubbed her reddened cheeks. "No, it's lovely. And it was just for you alone? I have to share my room with five other girls." She tried a smile. "Some of them snore. Terrible, like."

"I can leave," he offered. "If you want."

She shook her head. "Oh, sweet Jesus, no. Please, I couldn't bear to be alone."

IT WAS A NIGHT OF DISCOVERY. No, not that. Intimacy was for later, perhaps somewhere up ahead in the distance. She told him everything. Beginning in the slatted silo, with the baker's boy. And then being sent away. Betrayals, and lies. Her mother, the parish priest, the entire village, shunning and abandoning her. And then the train to Dublin, guarded by an old nun. A wizened crone riding along like a prison guard. And then the hospital bed, new life sliding out of her, like a warm christened ship down the ways, and how he cried when they pulled him from her arms, the scent of his blooded, downy scalp in her nostrils. At fifteen, they sent her to work in the laundry, at first washing and ironing, later, lace-making, which the church sold to outsiders to pay the bills. Rosemary lived at the Sisters of Charity for nearly ten years, a bleak monastery for unmarried mothers, for unchaste women, for prostitutes and young flirty girls. In all cases, the Catholic church, never the courts, decided who to send away, who was guilty, even if the crimes were imagined.

"I left my baby there," she told Arthur, her face a contorted mask of fresh tears. "I named him James, after King James. We lived in that same awful building, but I never saw him again."

Arthur listened, but said nothing, as she continued.

At twenty-four Rosemary finally escaped. An aged sister opened the door, just a crack, for a delivery man, and Rosemary had charged. She shouldered the bent hag aside and simply ran. For days she hid, but no one ever came after her. Eventually she found work as a seamstress, making exquisite lace for a dressmaker. In six months she'd saved enough for a steerage ticket to America.

Finally, the tears stopped. She looked over at Arthur. "And that's my secret. Are you ashamed, now, to be seen with a fallen woman?"

It was nearly midnight. Night sounds were few, but those few were profound. The low, sonorous whistle of an island steamer rounding the Point. A dog barking, as if left outside, then nothing, as if a door had quietly opened, then shut. After that, silence as thick as the fog spreading over Vineyard Sound.

He shook his head no. Not in a million years, no. Then he walked to the other side of the tiny bed, with a bigger rusted squeak, eased down his workingman's body next to hers. They slept this way, like spoons in a drawer, until dawn.

CHAPTER TWENTY-THREE

R etribution

CORNELIA WAS NOT HAPPY. Sitting in the front parlor, encased in a soft, high-backed chair of lavender velveteen and exotic, carved wood, Mrs. Charles Crowningshield raised a small, silver bell into the air, like a royal scepter. The bell, engraved with the family name, was used for summoning the nearest servant. Mary Lynch, a downstairs house girl, was within earshot, working outside in the hallway, changing the flowers in a large, porcelain vase. The vase was a gift from Mr. Crowningshield, brought back from his last trip to China. It was exquisite, fragile, and very valuable, decorated with delicate peony flowers and snarling lions.

It was past noon, lunchtime in the Crowningshield household. The children were in their own dining room, seated around a low, circular table, quietly eating. John laid a mason jar in front of him, studiously examining several large beetles, living specimens who climbed a mountain of lettuce and small twigs.

Mary Kelly answered the bell almost immediately.

"Yes, Ma'am," she asked, not quite meeting Mrs. Crowningshield's stern gaze. Something was brewing, she knew that. The kitchen girls had been gossiping all morning.

"Mary," Cornelia said, "please go and fetch Rosemary. She's upstairs in the nursery, I believe."

"Yes, Ma'am," Mary Lynch said, and walked quickly away. To reach the nursery, one had to walk down the long hall, from the parlor to the front entry, climb the enormous stairs, built in the grandly bloated Queen Anne style, with its intricate carved curlicues, layers of African mahogany raised panels. Mary walked quickly, but not too quickly. Her hand reached for an elaborately turned newel post, with its sinewy, corkscrewing balustrade, emerging at the top beneath a wide, curving latticework. She had dusted and polished this staircase a thousand times, many times more. The treads were covered by a long, hand-stitched Oriental carpet, called a runner, woven in pale shades of red and blue and gold. Floor to ceiling damask curtains covered each large Palladian window which faced the water.

The nursery was at the end of the second-floor hall. She passed a row of locked bedroom doors.

Rosemary was inside, just finishing up tidying the children's day room, replacing toys and books and dolls back onto long painted shelves, when the housemaid appeared at the door.

"It's the Missus," Mary Lynch explained, her voice low in a conspiratorial, *sotto voce*. Whisper. "She wants you in the front parlor, right now. Don't look too happy. Rosemary, what have you done?"

Rosemary shook her head. "It's fine, Mary. I'm sure it's nothing, really. Thank you for coming to tell me."

Mary screwed her pale, freckled face into a frown. "Don't really have no choice, now do I? Not when she rings that little bell."

CORNELIA, FEIGNING surprise, glanced up when her nanny appeared. "Rosemary, there you are. Please come in, and close the door behind you. I don't want us to be disturbed."

Rosemary obediently shut the door. Mrs. Crowningshield made no motion to invite her to sit down, so she stood erect as a soldier, waiting.

The mistress of the house didn't spare words.

"Rosemary, tell me, please, where were you last night?"

Rosemary stared back at her. Then she lied, as calmly as she could.

"I was in the village," Ma'am. "Visiting friends."

Cornelia Crowningshield slowly nodded.

"And who, exactly, were these friends, Rosemary? Take a moment. Think carefully about your answer."

"Nobody you'd know, Ma'am," Rosemary said quickly. "Just friends."

Mrs. Crowningshield leaned forward. "But Rosemary, you're an employee here. I employ you. Don't you think it's my job to know who your friends are?"

Rosemary stared back at her, trying to will calm into her voice. "It was my day off, Ma'am. You said Sundays are mine now. It's my private business."

Mrs. Crowningshield settled back into her chair, as if that was the end of it. But, of course, it wasn't.

"I see. Yes, of course. It was your day off. One needs their privacy on their day off."

"Yes, Ma'am."

Perhaps this was the end of it, after all. The children would be finishing up with their lunch by now. Their nanny needed to be with them. John was anxious to go to the beach today, continue his scientific experiments.

Cornelia Crowningshield wasn't finished.

"You know, Rosemary," she continued, a hard edge suddenly in her voice, "when Mr. Crowningshield and I hired you, you came with excellent references, and that, you know, was extremely important to us. Trustworthiness. It's the only thing, really. The only thing that truly matters. " She sighed deeply. "We assumed that you were somebody that could handle a great deal of responsibility, and you've done very well, up until now. I mean, when someone is entrusted to look after somebody's children, they must strive to keep that trust. Every day, by actions and words."

"Yes, Ma'am."

"But, and here's the most important prerequisite," Cornelia continued, "Rosemary, they must also have impeccable moral standards."

Rosemary nodded. She now understood where this was headed.

Cornelia Crowningshield stared at her.

"And do you have impeccable moral standards, Rosemary?"

Rosemary drew in breath, then lightly exhaled.

"I believe I do, Mrs. Crowningshield. I've given you no reason to think otherwise."

Cornelia leaned forward again. "Haven't you, Rosemary?"

She clasped her hands together.

"Rosemary, I think we have a problem."

"Ma'am?"

"Yes, Rosemary. The thing is, I truly believe that you have been lying to me."

"No, no, I haven't, Ma'am. Truly."

Cornelia Crowningshield shook her head, lightly laughed. "Truly? Let's just drop the pretense, Rosemary, shall we? I know, for a fact, that you were in the village last night, and you were with a man. Not just 'friends,' as you say. But a man, and that you most likely were involved in some indiscretion with this man, whoever he might be."

Rosemary, in the briefest of seconds, felt her world, the knowable borders of her knowable universe, begin to crumble. She felt this with vertiginous certainly. She was falling off the edge.

Mrs. Crowningshield continued. "You were seen, last night, Rosemary, by a very reputable witness. You were walking in the village with a man. You were observed kissing this same man, and then you were observed walking towards the Breakwater Hotel with him. Now, tell me, Rosemary, if this is incorrect. Was this reputable witness lying?"

Rosemary felt queasy. She might actually faint. She suddenly felt like a convicted criminal, standing in the docket, awaiting sentencing. The feeling was a familiar one. Images of her girlhood, the tribunal of accusers, after being raped by the baker's boy. The village priest, the circle of dark suits, her mother, the Sisters of Charity nuns who locked the door behind her.

Full circle.

"Just tell me, Rosemary," Cornelia prodded. "Admit your indiscretions. That you've lain down with a man not your husband, and you've lied about it to your employer. Can you just do that, please?"

Mrs. Crowningshield waited. Just like in her girlhood nightmare, the sound of the mantel clock, the rustle of rough fabric, a blackbird on a branch about to take flight.

Finally, Rosemary spoke, trying to push her strongest voice out. "Alright. Yes, I did lie to you, Ma'am. I was with a man, a good man. But I never laid down with him. Not in that way you think. I would never, ever, not until I was married. I'm a Catholic, even though I don't attend church no more, for personal reasons. I took my sacred vows at my first holy communion. Yes, I cannot lie to you no more. I did spend the night with him, I admit that, but he was a perfect gentleman. I was a bit upset and I just needed a friend to talk with."

Mrs. Crowningshield sniffed the air. She shook her head. She snorted. It was a triumphant sound.

"TALKED? You just talked? You went to a hotel room with a man not your husband, and you just *talked*? Rosemary, do you really expect me to believe that? Who was this man? Tell me please. What was his name?"

Rosemary shook her head. "I can't tell you that, Ma'am. I'm sorry. Now if you excuse me, I should be back to minding the children."

Cornelia Crowningshield's expression at this very moment. It was perhaps the most terrible look that Rosemary had ever received from another human being, even worse than all the others. It was pure judgment. It was mistrust. It might have been hatred.

Cornelia's voice went low, to a guttural whisper. "Don't worry about the children, Rosemary. Not just yet. Let's finish our little talk."

"Yes, Ma'am."

"Now, Rosemary, my husband is abroad, and so I can't really consult with him on this matter, but I'm sure he'd agree with me. Here's what I've decided. You will continue your duties. For now. With no further Sundays off. You will not see this man again, whoever he might be, as long as you are under this roof. We will be closing down the house in three weeks, and the children and I will be traveling to Lake Geneva, in Wisconsin, to spend a month with their grandfather at his summer estate. You will *not* be accompanying us, Rosemary. At that point you will be dismissed, with no reference. After that day, what you do is none of my concern. Is that clear?"

Rosemary stared at her. She hadn't fallen. She didn't jump. She had been pushed.

Cornelia smiled, but her pale azure eyes bright with malice. "And nothing more will be spoken of this matter. Is that clear as well? Not to staff, nor to anyone."

Rosemary fell silent.

"Rosemary, Is that clear?"

Finally, she nodded. "Clear, Ma'am. Clear as a window pane."

"Fine, you can go now."

Rosemary bowed.

"Thank you, Ma'am."

After Rosemary had left the room, Cornelia Crowningshield sat back in her chair. Queenly, righteous, vindicated. There, it was done. She'd had her necessary talk with the profligate nanny. She'd caught her in a lie, she'd nipped it in the bud, and she'd meted out punishment in a fair and honorable way. Usually it doesn't come to such an extreme end, having to let someone go. But one must maintain the highest moral standards, especially when one's children are concerned. Sometimes the help just needs a little...what's the word? Adjustment. Like when the chauffeur hid a bottle of whiskey under the car seat, or the pantry maid stole a leg of mutton from the icebox. One has to rule with a firm hand. Or else there's chaos in the household. And one can't have that. Charles was depending on her. He would be the first one to approve of her methods. But he wasn't here, now was he? He never was. And it always fell to her to do these things, as much as she hated them, no matter how awkward or difficult.

She picked up her silver bell.

A passing chambermaid, with an armful of upstairs linens, appeared at the doorway.

"Yes, Mrs. Crowningshield?"

"Please tell Mrs. Carmody we'll have roast duck for dinner tonight, with potatoes, baked in the French way. She'll know what I mean, with braided dinner rolls and fresh butter. Also, apple turnovers, with ice cream, for dessert. The children always like that."

The girl hesitated. "It's still awfully hot down in the kitchen, Ma'am. They haven't been using the oven on account of the heat and all."

Mrs. Crowningshield glared. Just another silly, slow-witted, country girl, a new hire, a temporary from the village. She'd be let go in a few weeks anyway. She waved her hand dismissively, with a practiced, aristocratic flourish.

"I know it's hot. Just tell Mrs. Carmody, please. Can you remember all of that?"

"Yes Ma'am," the girl promised, then hurried off.

They would be having roast duck for dinner.

And that was that.

CORNELIA STOOD UP FROM her chair, carefully replacing the silver bell down on a side table. She headed towards the front of the house, out to the screened porch, where the shade was deepest.

A thought appeared. *Lemonade would be nice.* She returned to the parlor to retrieve her bell, then waggled it slowly back and forth as she walked. Its sweet, melodic tinkle filled the breathless air of late summer, summoning, like some modern Pharaoh's wife, whichever slave might be nearest.

CHAPTER TWENTY-FOUR

Swept Away

Rosemary walked, barely walked, in a kind of shocked paralysis, behind the Crowningshield children. They strolled along the dirt path toward the estate's private beach.

Thoughts skittered around her brain, like finches in an aviary.

Arthur, where are you, my darling? Where have you gone?

The children were all wearing their bathing clothes; scratchy, woolen fabrics that became heavy and sodden when wet, comically unsuited for swimming. The girls wore knee-high pantaloons and cotton blouses with puffy arms. John Oliver wore a smart little sailor outfit, with a wide collar and horizontal blue stripes. He carried his specimen jar and butterfly net, intent on adding new discoveries to the glass aquarium that Arthur had built for him out of plumbing cast-offs and old window panes from the cellar.

The sun was bright, far too bright. It was blazing hot, like standing beneath a broiler. The best place for anyone today was on the screened porch, or sitting beneath the verdant stand of oak and Chinese elms that guarded the waterside. But the children had wanted desperately to be near the sea, John especially. Rosemary tried to never say no to their desires, and now that her time with them was short, she would never again.

The beach wasn't a proper beach. Not with dunes and razor grass and shells. Just a modest square of shoreline carved by men out of rocks, with a layer of imported sand, dumped by horse-drawn wagon, to give the impression of beach. A wealthy family's folly. But to the children, it was soft underfoot and inviting. And so, today they walked, on the hottest day of the summer, in the hottest summer of recorded history, to their private beach.

In New York, in Chicago and Boston and Baltimore, carriage and livery horses were dying at an alarming rate. The stench of rotted equine corpses assailed the nostrils. Editorials were written and printed in the dailies, all voicing public complaints at the civic carnage, but what could be done about the weather? People died as well as horses, urban unfortunates from the slums who could never afford to take a train or a trolley to the seashore. It was claimed, on this day, one could fry an egg on the macadam roadway traversing the Brooklyn Bridge. The only places for relief, during the killing heat wave that struck the country in the summer of 1910, were in any body of moving water, be it ocean, lake, or river.

ROSEMARY SPREAD OUT a large quilted coverlet for the children to sit upon. She arranged a stack of towels, and watched absently as they organized themselves for the several hours they'd be here. Francine, thirteen, brought several girl's adventure books. Cornelia, a tin pail and shovel, for the construction of sand castles. John, his specimen jar and net. Rosemary sat on one side of the coverlet, staring blankly at the sparkling water. After a while, the three children got up, walked tentatively to the water's edge. They waded carefully into the shallows, only up to their knees, but no further. The entrance to Little Harbor was fast-moving and unpredictable. It held contrary currents, tidal rips and occasional undertows. The little faux Crowningshield beach was never a safe swimming beach for children, for anyone. Yet Rosemary offered no warning, and unbidden, one by one the Crowningshield children turned and walked out of the sea, curiously eyeing their nanny.

They played quietly by themselves, reading and shoveling, occasionally glancing up to watch the sailboats moving out in the harbor. The big, new island steamer, the side-wheeler *Martha's Vineyard,* paddled serenely out in the Passage, carrying a holiday crowd back to the rail pier. When it blew its brass whistle, the children knew to cover their ears, and laughed.

Rosemary hardly noticed.

All she could think of was this morning was Mrs. Crowningshield's cruel inquisition.

And where was Arthur?

Walking from the house, she'd searched for him, to tell him the awful news. But he was nowhere, or at least somewhere else, which made everything that much worse. She needed to tell him everything, to scream and wail and wrap her slender arms around his giant shoulders. He would say little, of course, but that was what she loved about him. He didn't try and tease her out of her emotions.

Finally, around three o'clock, the children had had enough of the water. Their arms and legs and faces were already beginning to redden from the scorch of the sun.

Rosemary glanced around, as if waking from a dream.

She counted again. One was missing.

"Has anyone seen John?" she asked.

The children shook their heads.

Somehow, during the last hour, he'd left the blanket, began walking towards a destination that existed only in his logical, nine-year-old mind.

Rosemary felt panic quickly risen up. She looked down the path this way, she looked down the path that way.

To the east, past the stone jetty where the *Alma* lay docked, was the shore, the railroad tracks.

To the west, an uninhabited promontory at the very end of Juniper Point, dense with rose hips and scrub oak, ringed by a shoreline of jagged, slippery boulders.

And then that black water. The fast-moving and contrary currents and tidal rips of the Passage.

John had simply vanished.

Rosemary called loudly in both directions, rooted in place. She called out the boy's name, again and again. Then she stopped; she told the children to stay where they were, and began to sprint towards the house.

IN THE LATE AFTERNOON, a small army of searchers; household staff, the gardener and the limousine driver, local farmers and fishermen, men with the government fisheries department, a few off-duty surfboat crewmen, the constable and his deputy, clambered over the rocks of Juniper Point. They beat the bush, probing into the thicket with boat hooks and wooden poles. They yelled themselves hoarse. Finally, just as the sun dipped low in the west, a salmon dusk began to streak the sky, and the air just about the waves was changing to a damp, shrouded mist, an excited voice called out from the water's edge. A man, time has forgotten which, screaming, top-lung and horrified. "Over here! Quickly, over here."

Exhausted, sweating clots of men ran toward the grim discovery.

Cornelia stood alone at the top of the grassy promontory; her view obscured by thick foliage. She knew the terrible news already. It was plain enough by the invisible shouts of the man who'd found her son.

The awful truth: John had ventured too close to the water, slipped on the rocks, then quickly swept out into the Passage. After a while, on the ebb tide, he'd floated back too shore, like a patch of seaweed. Near his body, somebody discovered what was left of his specimen jar, smashed into pieces on the rocks. The butterfly net was gone.

As the constable trudged up the hill to inform Mrs. Crowningshield of her loss, John's pale, waterlogged corpse was carried by makeshift stretcher to the Government Road, where the undertaker's black carriage waited. Back in the kitchen, Mrs. Carmody wiped her sopping brow. It had to be over a hundred and fifty degrees coming off the big Glenwood kitchen stove. But the roast duck would be ready in time for dinner.

CHAPTER TWENTY-FIVE

Aftermath

The heat wave had broken during the night. New York's equine citizens were safe once again; dray nags and hackney high-steppers, haulers of freight, ice, rags, newspapers, fire engines, produce, and humans.

By morning, a mighty rainstorm had also passed. During the evening, after midnight, a thunderstorm out at sea, punctuated with an occasional burst of the brightest, whitest light, then more fusillades of explosive claps and booms. Rosemary sat with the children for hours, watching their terrified, stricken faces, listening to their childish whimpers, as the storm's violence shook the house. John Crowningshield had become a distant memory. His exuberance and curiosity was now an unlived future. Finally, the children slept, but Rosemary continued to guard them, perched in a chair near their beds.

Once or twice, she saw Mrs. Crowningshield pass the doorway. Her ashen face was twisted into a wraith's mask, but she never entered. The nanny would mind her surviving children.

For the time being.

ARTHUR, IN HIS CRAMPED cabin on the *Alma*, couldn't sleep. He'd only heard about the drowned boy when he returned from working on another part of the estate. Installing the new refrigeration system in the ice house, just over a small hillock, he'd been out of earshot of the terrible tragedy. Walking into the kitchen at dinnertime, Mrs. Carmody wordlessly slid a plateful of roast duck and something fanciful made of potatoes in front of him. Her eyes were bloodshot, wild and distraught. The kitchen girls stood back, silently watching him eat. He still didn't know all of it, and his thoughts were only on Rosemary, to find her, to see how she was holding up from their night at the Breakwater.

Finally, Mrs. Carmody sat herself down in a chair apposite him. She took a deep breath, then told him everything she knew. The little boy was dead, and the disgraced nanny was the cause of it. She's been the one minding him. She didn't mention the other thing, how Rosemary had also disgraced herself the evening last. She'd had intercourse with a man. Everybody in the house knew it to be true. She'd been caught in the lie, and would be soon let go, without reference.

BY THE MORNING, IT was as if the world had been cleansed. Poets might say that the sky had been weeping. The lawn, a damp, verdant green with patches of brown thatch, grass killed by the drought, lay beneath a monochrome sky. The air was suddenly brisk and cool, thick with tidal brine.

Mid-morning, the constable arrived. He was led into the parlor, handed a glass of iced tea, and told to wait, hat in hand, on a silk-covered chair. Mrs. Crowningshield would come down, eventually. He was, by social standing, just another hired hand. Finally, Cornelia appeared. Her face was the bloodless parody of a grieving mother. She still hadn't spoken of yesterday, or seen her children, or allowed herself to cry. It was as if all her emotions were distilled into one central nerve ending. Yet it wasn't her son's loss, or the unexpected madness of grieving, or concern for her family, that fixated itself onto her. Everything, every emotion and thought, coalesced into a single dark, emotion; intense, sustained, vitriolic animus towards the nanny, Rosemary Kincaid. She, Mrs. Charles Crowningshield, the mistress of Juniper Point, had caught her in deception. She'd rendered a tough, but fair sentence, magnanimously allowing her to stay under her roof for three more weeks. And how had this Irish harlot repaid her generosity and kindness? Why simply the worst, that was how. The nanny had allowed her youngest child, and only son, to die.

The constable stood up when Cornelia entered, and set about performing his official duties. First, he offered his condolences. Next, he informed her where John's body had been taken, and how the undertaker was taking very good care of him. Lastly, he inquired if there was anything he might do to help her family through this difficult time.

Cornelia stood there, covered only in a filthy dressing gown, hair uncombed, her eyes smoldering with white rage.

"I want that woman arrested," she croaked. It was a direct order, as though instructing a housemaid to change the bedding, or a kitchen girl to clear the table. The constable was a kind gentleman who ran a poultry farm a mile from the village. His eggs probably sat in her icebox.

Now he stared back at her, hat in hand, puzzled.

"Mrs. Crowningshield, arrest her? On what grounds?"

She opened her lips, baring her teeth into a kind of wolfish sneer. Madness had arrived to this home; he could plainly see that. Grieving will sometimes do that. He'd seen enough death in his time, and many of them, in this seaside town, were drowning victims.

"I want her arrested," she repeated. "For murdering my son."

"But it was an accident," he explained, speaking slowly and clearly, as if to a skittish horse. "That's what's going in the books. A terrible, sad accident. Your son slipped on the rocks, and was swept away by the current. I'm sorry, Mrs. Crowningshield, but there it is. An accident."

Mrs. Crowningshield glared at him. "You're sorry? YOU'RE SORRY? Well, I'm his mother, and I'm a lot more than sorry at the moment. I know my rights, and I want that woman arrested. Immediately."

Cornelia Crowningshield knotted her hands into fists. She was visibly trembling.

"Alright, Mrs. Crowningshield," the constable said gently. "I can talk to her, this nanny of yours, if you like. I can do that. Take her statement, for the record. But arrest her, no, I'm afraid I can't do that. Like I said, it's been ruled an accident, by the medical examiner. No foul play was indicated."

He nodded toward the water, a dull gray presence past the lace-curtained window.

"It's a dangerous shore you've got out here. Children shouldn't be playing near the rocks. I'm sure your nanny feels terrible about what happened. But in my opinion, your family should be doing the things that need being done at times like this, not looking for someone to blame. Tell me, Mrs. Crowningshield, do you attend a church here in the village? You should be discussing these things with your pastor. He'll know what to do, how to guide you."

"We're Methodist," Cornelia calmly explained, suddenly lucid, "but we sometimes attend services at the Episcopal church. Our family parish is back in Chicago."

"I see," the constable said. "And what of your husband? Has he been notified?"

Mrs. Crowningshield shook her head, a loose strand falling into her face. She didn't seem to notice the disarray.

"My husband," she curtly explained, "is currently out of the country." She straightened her spine. "He has a very important position, you see, with the State Department. I doubt if there's any possible way he can be reached."

The constable pondered this information, unsure of what to say next. This woman was dangerously close to a nervous breakdown. He'd met with more than a few grieving families, people who suffered great loss, and there was a predictable arc to the sorry business. Women wept, men were usually stoic, children were confused, and easily distracted, but in the end, his official presence was always a consolation. He usually left their dooryard feeling that perhaps he had done some small duty in making a difficult time more tolerable. But Mrs. Crowningshield, she was altogether different. Stubbornly irreconcilable. The woman seemed only focused on one thing. Blame, punishment, revenge. All directed toward the nanny, the sole person she had entrusted with the well-being of her children. It was as if this nanny had stolen something of great value, like a silver platter, from her home. But here was a child who had crept away, on his own, who had climbed on the rocks, on his own, had drowned, again, completely on his own. It was a curious matter. Yes, the nanny had made a grave mistake. She was distracted. Perhaps by the other children, or some personal matter. But it didn't rise to the level of a crime. No, this was just another terrible accident.

"HELLO, ROSEMARY."

The constable introduced himself and stuck out his hand. They were alone, not in the parlor, or even inside the house, but out on the front porch, like peddlers told to wait. The rain had stopped just before the dawn, and seen from the water's edge, a thick, gauzy vapor was shrouding the Passage beyond. Visibility was down to fifty yards, a nightmare for passing mariners. It might burn off by the afternoon. The lighthouse across the harbor incessantly blatted its deep-throated fog warning, telling ships and boats what they certainly already knew. The sea was like a blind man today, and bad things could happen.

He took out a small notepad, folded it open to a blank page.

"Can you tell me, he began, in your own words, what happened yesterday? Don't worry, you're not in any trouble. It's just for the official record."

Rosemary slowly nodded. She was numb from the tragedy. Distraught, and stricken with guilt. It was all her fault.

She took a breath. "We were all at the little beach down there. Me and the children. It was so terribly hot yesterday. You couldn't get your breath. They just wanted to be near the water, to cool off a little bit. That's all."

The constable nodded. "Of course. And the boy? John? Did he go into the water? With the others?"

Rosemary smiled at the memory. "Oh, yes, he loved the water. It was the one place he felt, I dunno, in charge of something. You know, he wanted to be a scientist, just like his aunt and uncle, and study all the things in the sea."

"He sounds like a very special boy. So young, but he'd already figured out what he wanted to be in life."

"Yes," Rosemary nodded. "That he was. But so very, very shy. A quiet boy, John did nothing but read books in his room. But when he got near the sea, and all them living things in it, it was like, I suppose, that was when he came the most alive."

The constable stood there, listening. It was plainly obvious that Rosemary was a good nanny to these children. She loved them all, especially the youngest.

He still hadn't written anything into his pad. "So, tell me, Rosemary. To clarify. You didn't see him leave? Was there something on your mind, some sort of distraction that caused you not to notice he was missing?"

She stared at him, then finally answered.

"Yes. But it was personal. It shouldn't have kept me from doing my job. When you're entrusted with the care of someone else's children, that's a very serious matter." She began to cry. "I mean," she added, "I should have seen him gone. I should have noticed."

The constable reached out to pat her shoulder. "Perhaps. But all the same, Rosemary. It was an accident. A terrible accident. Nobody is blaming you."

Rosemary shook her head, violently, from side to side. She was crying. She wiped a drop of spittle from her mouth, and tried to smile at this man. He had offered perhaps the only kindness she would be given for a long time.

"No, sir. There's one person that blames me for all of this. And that's the Missus. Mrs. Crowningshield blames me, something dreadful."

The constable shrugged. "I must agree. I just talked with her. But she's just upset, that's all. It's only natural."

"No." Rosemary said fiercely. "She hates me. For what I done."

The constable considered this.

"Tell me, Rosemary," he gently inquired, "do you have some other place to go? Friends? Or family, that can take you in?"

She took a deep breath, wiping her reddened cheek. "No, I don't. I honestly have no idea where I'll go. I have a few dollars, but that's all. Most of my pay goes back home."

The constable was measuring what he'd say next.

"Well, Rosemary. You can't stay here, that's obvious. Why don't you fetch your things, and I'll take you into the village? We can talk on the way."

"That's very kind of you, sir. But like I said, I have nowhere to go, nowhere to stay."

The constable smiled. "I think some change would do you some good right now, to get away from this bleak house. Pack your things. I'll wait. We'll sort all of this out."

ARTHUR, STANDING IN the doorway of the icehouse, watched them drive away in the constable's dented Model T. Henry Ford said you can have any color you wanted, as long as it was black.

Arthur knew how upset and alone Rosemary must feel, yet he had done nothing, said nothing. In the morning, amidst the household drama and the black moods of the kitchen staff, he'd eaten his usual plate of eggs and toast with coffee, black, then simply walked away, back down the hill to his job at the icehouse. There he'd picked up his tools and resumed his labors from the day before, as if sleepwalking. Rosemary was suffering. She was in trouble. But he was a man entombed inside unshakable routine. It might be too late for him, too late for love and the needs of others. He was just the house plumber. He'd brought water to a parched world, but little else. Sometimes, the things he never said were just that, not something noble, not silently charitable acceptance, just things he should have said but didn't. Later, after the day's work was done, he should walk into the village, try to locate her, the woman he had vowed to cherish. But not until his day's work was done. Then he would go. But not one minute before.

He had a job to do.

CHAPTER TWENTY-SIX

A New Life

It felt strange to not have the glittering sea outside her window anymore. It felt even stranger to not hear the voices of children. Rosemary wondered if she would ever have another job as a nanny.

The constable's name was Earnest. Call me Ernie, he instructed her, driving out of the village. But she liked Earnest better. It described him best. A kind, honest man. Oddly enough, his wife's name was Charity. Earnest and Charity Spurlock, poultry farmers.

She heard them in the early mornings, just before the dawn. The clucking layers in their hay roosts, the funny gabbling noises they made outside her window. Their ramshackle coops were only a short walk from the dooryard. A thousand brood hens, shaking their rubbery wattles in cackling unity.

This is where she lived now. Earnest had brought her here that day. He'd led her into their tiny farmhouse kitchen. This is Rosemary, he'd introduced her to his wife, she's going to stay with us awhile. Charity had smiled and simply set another place at the table. And that, in its divine simplicity, was that.

The Spurlocks were childless. Rosemary gave thanks for that. That would have been too much, to see children this soon after. Instead, she was given a tutorial by Charity, a gregarious, plump, red-faced woman, on gathering the morning eggs. She showed her how to pack them carefully, with a layer of excelsior, into pasteboard cartons that said **Spurlock Farms**, for shipment to local homes, grocery stores and restaurants. Charity was a good teacher; she instructed her how to check to see if an egg was fertile. This was called candling, and involved holding the egg behind a kerosene lamp, or an electric bulb, if they'd had one, but Rosemary already knew this. She had grown up in the country, and her father, before he'd vanished off to the city, always kept a small brood. All country folk kept chickens.

But she didn't tell Mr. and Mrs. Spurlock. It would make her seem like a know-all.

She counted the days back to the drowning. It had been nearly a week. John would be having his funeral soon, at the towering, brownstone Presbyterian church on Main St. For now, his little broken and bloated body was kept in a small refrigerated room, like a meat locker, at the rear of the undertaker's home.

CHARLES CROWNINGSHIELD was homebound. Somehow, miraculously, he had been located, contacted, by ship's wireless, a message from Washington, aboard the liner that was carrying him back to New York.

This time, he would not spend a few days in the city with his lovely young mistress. Emily was already onboard with him, since leaving the White Star pier in Southampton. They met in London, and were driven by chauffeured car. She was with him when he read the cable from America, informing him of his loss. He cried in her arms, confessing, through racking sobs, "I'm a terrible father."

John's death would forever change his life, in both large and not-so-large ways. And now he was coming home, if the big house on Juniper Point might still be called his home.

Cornelia received the telegram that same day. She read it once, then let the flimsy message flutter to the carpet.

Arriving day after tomorrow to handle funeral arrangements. Stop. Our son John is in my prayers. Stop. Your husband, Charles.

That night, shipboard, he and Emily danced, cheek to cheek, as usual. He drank too much champagne, as usual, and the next morning had orange marmalade on his scone, as usual. Charles Richard Crowningshield, noted captain of industry, was, like his lowly employee Arthur, a stubborn creature of habit.

SUNDAY MORNING.

Arthur tramped the nearly two miles out of town, navigating by following the railroad tracks. A grocery clerk, who happened to be the constable's cousin, a man named Fish, had told him where she was. A small chicken farm you couldn't miss, if you just followed those tracks. Small towns, they don't hold their secrets for very long.

And so, he walked. The sun was already baking into his shoulder blades, and he hadn't thought to bring along a mason jar of water. Arthur smiled to himself. That would be ironic if he, a plumber, were to die of thirst.

Arthur passed a few farmhouses, and counted the telegraph poles. A large Guernsey cow slowly ruminated on a stalk of clover. He turned, cocking his ears, thought he heard the distant roar of a locomotive rounding the bend. But it was only a phantom in the wind, and so he kept counting the creosoted ties that led him towards the farm.

Rosemary.

He wondered what he might say to her. They were changed forever, as a couple, or whatever they were now.

This week, Mrs. Crowningshield had gotten straight to the point, when he discreetly asked, about the nanny's absence. He wanted to hear it directly from her.

"She murdered my son," Cornelia coldly claimed. "And now she's run away. But the law will catch up to her, Arthur. Mark my words. They'll find her, and she'll pay for what she's done. My husband will hire Pinkerton men, if he has to. If the law won't do it, Charles can."

Arthur turned away, sorry he asked.

Mrs. Crowningshield was descending into a special kind of madness. A madness reserved for mothers of lost children, for widows of men who die at sea, for husbands whose wives die in childbirth. She no longer bothered to come down in the morning, dressed and spotless and ready to take charge of the day. When she did, it was still wearing her night dress, stained with food from the trays left outside her door and god knew what else. She no longer bothered brushing her long, silken hair. It was a tangle of unwashed snarls. Her body odor was like a physical presence. When the house girls tried to come in, pull the sheets from her bed, or discreetly pull the toilet handle down, to empty the night's excretions, she screamed for them to leave. Worst of all, for the staff, what happened in the household, or her family, was of absolutely no interest to her.

They responded in kind. Wandering about each day, dusting furniture with desultory swipes, no longer fearing her wrath. The gardener watered the garden, mowed the lawn, but planted nothing new. No one bothered to place fresh bouquets into crystal vases. Mrs. Carmody fed the children, and housemaids took turns looking in on the nursery. The chauffeur was a thinly veiled alcoholic. He was the worst. With nowhere to drive, he began his day with a shot of whiskey, stayed drunk in the stable until the bottle was dry.

It was a terrible thing to watch. After her tirade, Arthur hurried away, anxious to return to work.

ROSEMARY, WASHING THE dishes, heard the soft tap on the door. She felt a strong jolt of anxiety. Earnest and Charity were off for the morning. After church, a leisurely stroll around the village. The constable liked to have people notice him, for them to know that he was there, keeping an eye on things. It made them feel safe, he firmly believed.

She dipped a rag into the bucket of soapy water, saw the flash of a man's face peering into the shadows. Like most of rural America, the house had no indoor running water, or plumbing of any sort. Only a hand pump in the yard, a coal stove to heat the water on, a wooden privy out back, and lots and lots of labor to do anything vaguely domestic. The Crowningshield estate, with its pressurized faucets, salt water bathing tubs, refrigerated ice house, toilets for every bedroom, embodied domestic luxury beyond most people's wildest imagination.

Rosemary walked slowly to the door, opened it. Arthur stood there, perspiring and red-faced, his breath coming in labored gasps. She let the door hang open and turned away, back to her soapy bucket.

"I could really use a glass of water."

She reached for a battered tin cup, and pointed to the yard.

"Pump's outside."

Arthur drained two cups of cool spring water, then returned to the doorway. She still hadn't invited him in. "Chickens, huh?" he said, gesturing behind him towards the motley collection of coops. "I could hear them a mile away. How do you sleep at night?"

Rosemary stuck her hands into her apron, ignoring his banalities, then whirled to face him.

"Arthur, where in the world have you gotten to?"

He put his palms out. "I know, Rosemary. I know. I have no excuse."

She stared at him. "I needed you, Arthur. All this time, this terrible week, I have needed you. I didn't need a plumber, or a gentleman caller. I just needed you. Just Arthur Rouse. Do you understand?"

He examined his dusty shoes. "I'm sorry, Rosemary. What can I say? It's me, not you?"

She snorted. "Hah, I know it's you, you ninny. I also know it's not me. You're just a damned scoundrel, Arthur Rouse, that's what you are. Leaving me all alone the way you did."

Arthur fell silent, inching closer.

"How can I make it up to you, Rosemary? I'm here. It's Sunday, remember, and I choose you to spend it with."

She smiled at the memory of her own forwardness. It seemed so long ago.

"I was a willful, loose-moral woman, wasn't I? Taking advantage of you that way."

He shrugged and winked. "I didn't mind."

Now it was her moving toward him, closer and closer until she was in his arms, her soapy hands wetting his neck. It was the place she'd always wanted to be. Even if he was a strange, keep-to-himself sort of man, this is where she belonged.

They stood this way for a long time. Only the sound of their conjoined breathing, the occasional cackle of a laying hen, and the distant whistle of the New York Limited, approaching a crossing.

CHAPTER TWENTY-SEVEN

Burnt Offerings

Sometimes, Rosemary would open her eyes in the middle of the night and want to scream. At the Sisters of Charity, often she would be awakened by a looming nun, a dark specter of violent cruelties and benign neglect, patrolling the large dormitory where the children slept. It might be midnight, or three in the morning. Either way, the child penitents of the Sisters of Charity were all deeply sleep-deprived. Each morning, they were shaken awake, and if they tarried, a slap in the face or a hairbrush hard across the shoulder blades. Then, at half six, after a prison breakfast of porridge and milk, a forced march, down a dark tunnel into the convent basement, where the convent's mammoth steam laundry was just rumbling to life.

If Rosemary hadn't run that day, she might still be there. Some were incarcerated for life. There were "girls" of seventy or more who'd died inside, often forgetting their first Christian names, at the end tossed into an unmarked grave, dug from a sparse, treeless field beyond the convent. Babies who died were tossed, just as unceremoniously, into a brick incinerator. The Catholic church had created a hell on earth that even Dante wouldn't recognize. What began, a hundred years before, as a relief organization to assist prostitutes, was now big business, depending on slave labor and the perverted acceptance of societal norms. Fallen girls, mentally ill girls, flirty girls who chattered too much, girls abused by family or the parish priest or, in Rosemary's case, raped by a classmate.

THIS MORNING, HOURS before the dawn, Rosemary lay in her bed off the kitchen, what had once been the borning chamber, thinking about that terrible day. John Crowningshield's funeral service was to be held this week at the big Presbyterian church on Main St. His father would have returned by now, would witness his family close to ruins. He had been away too long. He would see his wife's spiraling descent into madness, and Mrs. Crowningshield, of course, would need to be sent away. Arthur told her about Cornelia's loss-crazed demeanor, and this made her sadder than anything. Rosemary herself had lost a child. He was, perhaps, still alive, but in the end, just as gone.

She thought about death, all the funerals and country wakes she attended. The English were much more restrained in their grieving. They kept their sorrow bottled tight, never sharing the truth of the matter. The Irish, on the other hand...on the other hand. They drank, they laughed, and they cried. They danced and they sang, often for days at the time. The body of the deceased was laid out, just like a guest at the party. And after the laughing and singing and dancing had worn itself out, then the talking began. Nonstop, improvised eulogies, from dawn to dusk, fueled by whiskey and stout, a party for the deceased that continued far into the night, and for many nights after. Family members, some not seen for years, would appear, and the party would swell. And then, when a loved one had been properly waked, and the parlor window left open so the soul could depart, the procession to the graveyard began. Six of the strongest men, usually relations, carried the coffin to the road. They loaded it noisily into the undertaker's wagon, like drunken stevedores. And they sang some more, out on the rocky road to the churchyard, a bawdy processional behind the coffin. They sang ancient Celtic dirges, or sometimes simple folk songs. After all, country people are boisterous and unschooled peasants, not refined like the English gentry who stood off to the side, letting the minister handle things. Country mourners hooted in ragged harmony, accompanied by pipes and drums, fiddles and banjos. Each male mourner carried a flask, each female a bouquet of wildflowers, from the ancient pagan beliefs. After it was over, the women gathered in the kitchen, to wash the plates and bundle up leftovers for the travelers. The men smoked outside, and drank some more, down to the last dram, raising toast after toast to the dearly departed.

That was what she most remembered. Death was a happy release, in her Ireland, a time to be freed from a life of care and woe.

Not like what the poor little drowned boy would have in that cold, borrowed chapel. Sitting up in bed, she lit her lamp, and wondered where they might bury him. If she knew, she might have a mind to pay her respects someday.

Just then, the farm's solitary rooster began to crow. She reached for her clothes, no longer the uniform of the proper American nanny, starched waist shirts and aprons, like a government issue uniform, but a plain wardrobe, a patched but clean, farm woman's dress and blouse that Charity dug out of her closet. For the first time in her life, she knew what freedom might feel like. A kindly family had taken her in, had asked only the merest of obligation in return.

It was time to greet the day, time to gather the eggs.

CHAPTER TWENTY-EIGHT

The Big Empty

Charles Crowningshield, the great man, stood, as he often did, at the edge of his sandy cliff, dark-suited and stylish in black derby and tie, and attempted to find an easy summation of what had recently stricken his family.

Arthur Rouse, his most dependable employee, stood beside him, at rapt attention.

Returned two days ago, he was shocked by the state of the world he left behind only weeks before, beginning with his wife. Cornelia was now a woman whose best attributes and sensibilities had abandoned her. Lunacy, to coin a medical term still common in 1910, was afoot.

The village doctor, upon being summoned, offered his honest diagnosis. He prescribed a simple palliative. Mental exhaustion, he told him. She's had a shock. I suggest plenty of bed rest, thrice-daily tinctures of laudanum, and no excitement, in familiar surroundings.

"I don't know," Charles said, staring out at Little Harbor, the ghostly white apparition of the *Alma* docked below. He turned towards Arthur.

"A man loses his only son, and then his wife's mental vitality, all in the same week. What would you do?"

Arthur shook his head. "I don't know, sir. It's a great tragedy, all that's happened to your family. But I'm sure you'll do the right thing."

Charles nodded. Somehow this simple foundryman always said the right words in the moment, and it always comforted him.

"We'll be leaving tomorrow," he told Arthur. "Closing up the house. There is still a great deal of work to be done here before next summer. The architects will be seeing to everything."

Arthur turned toward his employer. "Next summer, sir? I woulda thought..."

Charles smiled. "You thought what, Arthur? That we'd allow this setback to destroy my family's life here. Well, I think not. We are the Crowningshields. Life, Arthur, it always goes on. My wife just needs rest, a great deal of rest. She'll recover, I'm sure quite rapidly. I have no doubt of that. We have the best physicians back in Chicago."

Arthur silently nodded. He had little experience with women's troubles. His own wife had died long before she was plagued with such afflictions.

He thought of something. "Mr. Crowningshield, sir?"

Charles turned. His eyes were bloodshot, his skin blotchy. The funeral service yesterday was sparsely attended. A small, wooden casket set onto the altar dais. A dozen acquaintances, his surviving children, an unsmiling minister who read from John 14.

Do not let your hearts be troubled. Trust in God; trust also in me. In my father's house are many mansions: if it were not so, I would have told you. I go to prepare a place for you.

Cornelia, of course, had not been there. Instead, the doctor administered an extra dose of laudanum, and let her sleep. It was the saddest day in recent Crowningshield memory.

"Yes, Arthur?"

Arthur respectfully held his tweed cap in his hands.

"Well, sir," he began, "what is it exactly you'd like me to do now?"

Charles nodded, still staring absently out at the water.

"Captain Brisbee is preparing the *Alma* for sea." He said without turning. "She's a little too much ship for me, I'm afraid. I've found a buyer, a man in New York, a banker from Scarsdale, of all places, who's interested in taking her off my hands. Then the Captain is going back to England. He's requested that you sail with him to New York, as engineer. It's just a short trip, Arthur. We'll see where you go from there."

Arthur nodded. "I understand, Mr. Crowningshield. And after that?"

"We'll see, Arthur."

THE NEXT MORNING THE family was gone. A dozen steamer trunks, loaded into a freight car of the Crowningshield's private train. In the first car, half of the Juniper Point staff. The other half were local, and had been let go. Charles Crowningshield sat in the club car, sipping cognac. His children were in the last car, under the temporary guidance of his oldest daughter, Mary Josephine, just until they reached Chicago, and could hire a new nanny. She would be a good, intelligent Irish girl, as Rosemary had seemed at the beginning, but imbued with implacable moral temperance, as Rosemary had proven herself to lack.

The great house on the hill was empty, drained of life. Bed sheets covered the living room furniture, the horsehair divans, and parlor chairs. The shining oak dining table, the beds upstairs and down. All the lace curtains were taken down and neatly folded, placed into aromatic cedar chests, with moth balls sprinkled inside.

The *Alma* was set to leave that night, on the moon tide.

"Be back by ten," Captain Brisbee warned Arthur, "in time to make steam." Adding quietly, he said, "That should give you enough time to say goodbye to your girl."

Arthur tramped the two miles out to the constable's farm. He knew Rosemary would be there. She had found her safe harbor there, and had little interest in rejoining the world.

Ernest Spurlock was sitting at the scarred kitchen table when he heard a knock on the door. It was Arthur Rouse, his face flushed, peering in.

The constable stood up and opened the door.

"Hello, Arthur." He stuck out his hand. His voice had a grim edge to it. "Come in." He gestured toward a chair. "Rosemary and my wife are gone out," he explained. "Picking blackberries, to make some pies."

Arthur nodded.

"You're welcome to wait," the constable said. "Can I get you a glass of lemonade?"

"That would be fine," Arthur said. "I seem to pick the hottest days to visit."

The constable thought on this. "But you usually come on Sundays."

"Sundays are my days off from work," Arthur explained. "But today is different."

The constable peered across the table. "Oh? Why's that?"

"I have to go to New York," Arthur explained. "On the *Alma*. I help to run her."

"I see," Ernest said. "That sounds nice. A sea cruise."

Arthur shook his head, grimacing. "It's pretty nasty down in the engine room. I don't get to see much of the sights. Plus, I'm not much for the water."

The constable nodded, then remembered his manners. Walking to the icebox, he pulled a chipped glass pitcher out, poured the lemonade into a tall glass.

The two men regarded one another. The constable had a piece of paper in front of him. He pushed it forward, across the table.

"Read this. It concerns Rosemary."

Arthur stared at it, then shook his head.

"Sorry, but I can't."

Spurlock cocked one thick eyebrow. "What do you mean?"

"I can't read the words, Mr. Spurlock."

The constable had seen plenty of illiterates.

"It's a warrant," he explained. "I won't get into the legal fine print, Arthur. It's for Rosemary's arrest."

Arthur stared down at the paper. "Arrest? But you said it was an accident."

"I know," the constable said. "In my opinion, yes, it was. But this has become much bigger than a small-town peace officer. I'm afraid Mr. Crowningshield has gone and hired a lawyer, or two, and he's pressing charges. And they found a judge to go along with it. For, let's see," he squinted down at the paper, "child endangerment and involuntary manslaughter. Yes, that's right, the two charges."

Arthur turned the glass around in his hands. "This is very good lemonade," he said. "Just the right amount of sweet to it."

The constable smiled. "My wife made it this morning. She really knows her lemonade."

Arthur slowly took another sip. "And so, I guess, they'll be coming for her."

Constable Spurlock shrugged.

Arthur looked across the table. "And you, I suppose, would have to turn her in?"

Spurlock shrugged a second time. "If I was to know her whereabouts, I'm guessing I would."

Arthur considered this. He peered through the window.

"Where did you say they were? Out picking blackberries?"

The constable gestured with his eyes. "Past the dooryard, past the chicken coops, a half mile or so in that direction. Follow the road. You'll find the patch."

Spurlock eyed Arthur across the table.

"And what time did you say you were sailing?"

"Midnight," Arthur said. "One the tide."

The constable nodded. "So, there'd be time for you to stay for dinner?"

Arthur smiled. "If it wouldn't put you out."

CHAPTER TWENTY-NINE

The Midnight Tide

Captain Brisbee noted the time by the ship's chronometer, a large brass clock fastened to the bulkhead in *Alma's* wheelhouse. Eleven fifteen. Getting on. Beneath a cloudless sky, an enormous golden moon hung low over the placid waters of Little Harbor. He stood there, motionless, gripping the spoked mahogany wheel, glanced again at the ship's telegraph. It was set at the resting position. *Alma* was a cold ship. But she had to be making steam soon. The crew was out on the foredeck, smoking and spitting over the rail into the dirty water. He stared through the wheelhouse window, up at the Crowningshield house on the hill. Not a light was burning up there. Bad business, that. The little boy, drowned, and the mother driven mad with grief. He was glad to be finally shoving off, free of this place. Charles Crowningshield knew about as much about ships on the sea to fill a teacup.

Suddenly, a set of jerky headlights illuminated the sandy length of Government Rd. A beat-up black roadster, bumping its way slowly toward the stone jetty. Captain Brisbee watched as it rattled to a stop. Two figures emerged. Arthur Rouse was the first. His engineer. Thank god. Sailing into New York harbor in the dead of night would be no cakewalk. He needed somebody quick on the throttle.

The second figure he had to squint to make out. It was a woman, moving nervously in the dim moonlight. Then he recognized her. The Crowningshield's nanny, which was odd. The family, a processional of sad faces, a river of steamer trunks and hatboxes, had left by train that morning. He hadn't caught her name, the nanny with the kind face. She was probably coming to see Arthur off.

ARTHUR WALKED CAREFULLY up the *Alma's* gangway; Rosemary followed close behind. The constable turned his car around, then, with a brief wave, in a grinding of gears, he headed back down Government Rd. Headlights jumped, as the Ford bounced over the railroad bridge, then man and car were gone.

Captain Brisbee said nothing when they appeared at the wheelhouse door. He sucked on his unlit pipe, watching and waiting.

"Captain, this is Rosemary," Arthur said.

He touched his cap. "Pleased to see you again, Rosemary. I remember you with the children, the day of our little picnic cruise."

She smiled. "It was a grand day, thanks to you."

They stood in the wheelhouse, uncomfortably silent.

Finally, Rosemary broke the spell.

"Captain, I'll tell you the god's honest truth. I'm in trouble, and it would help me greatly if you would consent to allow me to accompany you to New York."

Captain Brisbee turned his briar around in his palm.

"Well miss..." he began.

"Call me Rosemary," she broke in, then quickly added, "I have no money for passage."

Brisbee smiled. He had already made up his mind. If Charles Crowningshield knew what he was about to do, he would...what? Fire him? Alphonse Brisbee was a man of the sea, a leader of men. He had been driven ashore by hurricanes, faced down mutineers, survived raging cargo fires, and had ships impounded by corrupt foreign officials. What was one spoiled rich man going to do to him?

"Alright then," he said. "Rosemary, it is. You're more than welcome to join us." He glanced over at Arthur. "Why don't you show this young lady to her cabin, and give her the best we've got? In owner's country. Then you'd better be heading down to the engine room. We'll be losing the tide."

Arthur nodded gratefully.

Soon he'd be turning valves, checking pressure, waiting by the telegraph for the Captain's orders.

ROSEMARY SETTLED INTO her cabin. It was the finest on the ship, a glorious cabin, finer even than the Crowningshield's house on the hill. It had gilded bath faucets, a copper bathing tub, hand-carved African mahogany paneling, even goose down pillows on the bed. She settled into a silk-covered chair, decorated with strutting white storks and an embroidered filigree of creeping rose bushes. She reached for a leather-bound volume from a nearby bookshelf, and randomly opened it. It was *The Tempest,* by William Shakespeare. Not a first edition, but lovely. She had never before read, or seen, a stage play. She turned to the first page.

ACT I

SCENE I. On a ship at sea: a tempestuous noise of thunder and lightning heard.

Enter a Master and a Boatswain

Master

Boatswain!

Boatswain

Here, master: what cheer?

Master

Good, speak to the mariners: fall to't, yarely,

or we run ourselves aground: bestir, bestir.

Exit

Enter Mariners

Boatswain

Heigh, my hearts! cheerly, cheerly, my hearts!

yare, yare! Take in the topsail. Tend to the

master's whistle. Blow, till thou burst thy wind,

if room enough.

Rosemary was enthralled by the words on the page. It took her mind from her troubles. Here she was, a wanted woman, escaping by sea with her lover. Her sad little existence had become a tawdry penny novel. Where to next? New York City, to begin with. And then after that, what?

Just then the *Alma's* whistle sounded, a sonorous bellow, deep and long. Captain Brisbee pulled the steam lanyard as they rounded Juniper Point, warning any ships coming through the Passage. Rosemary felt *Alma* turn slightly, toward a new course heading. She felt, rather than heard, the beat of the engine far below, deep in the bilge. The Scotch boilers were making the reciprocating pistons gallop hard to gain traction against the current and the waves. *Alma* was now on a southerly heading, released from her shoreside bondage. Like a champion thoroughbred that had been shown the whip, she charged ahead, a frothy bone in her teeth.

It was half past midnight.

After a while, Rosemary replaced the book, careful to put it back exactly where she had found it. She rose from her chair and opened the cabin door, which led to a spacious deck at the stern. Coal dust blew from the single stack, laid flat by the slight ocean breeze. She stood for a while at the rounded fantail, where wealth and privilege lingered, ringed by snow-white wicker chairs and chaise lounges, gazing back toward shore.

The big house on Juniper Point was dark. No comforting glow from shaded Edison parlor lamps spilled onto the yard, no housemaids walking quickly from room to room, answering the soft tinkle of a silver bell. The moon cast a yellow pall over the village, behind them a river of golden phosphorescence that reached all the way to *Alma's* foaming wake. The Crowningshields had departed early that morning. She was leaving at midnight. With God's grace, the Pinkerton detectives, the ones Charles Crowningshield would surely engage once he learned of her escape, would never find her in an enormous city of three million strangers. But wealthy men could afford revenge and had their ways.

She touched the tiny silver cross on her breast, the cross she had received for her first holy communion, at seven, and whispered a sacred novena. It came like a second breath. She said her prayers to Rita, patron saint of impossible causes. Rita protected victims of celibacy, infidelity, abuse of all kinds, and wounds that would not heal. It was onto her she had leaned each day of her sentence at the Sisters of Charity convent, for each rag she had scrubbed, for each time she loaded the laundry into the enormous steam driers, for each lash and insult suffered beneath the cold-hearted brides of Christ, and, finally, for each day she hid herself from the searchers that never came.

Now that life was coming full circle, and that same terrible fear of discovery. She needed St. Rita more than ever.

ALMA surged forward, effortlessly cleaving the gentle seas ahead. Watching the waters rush by, and how delightful the moonlit evening was, Rosemary thought of Arthur, drenched in sweat below, laboring to keep the steam up, his eyes never leaving the signal telegraph, a constant choreography of valve and piston, listening for telltale knocks in the cadence of the engine. He was her savior, this man who had brought water to her parched land. Just as much as Saint Rita.

ALMA crossed Buzzards Bay, and soon began altering course, swinging her bow to the west, into Nantucket Sound, past Rhode Island, into Block Island Sound, past Connecticut, and then on to New York. The danger now came less from rocks and shoals, and more from collisions with transatlantic steamers inbound or outbound for Europe, tugs with strings of barges a mile long, and other yachts like her, all running blind. They entered the shipping lane before the age of radar. Lookouts with brass spyglasses scanned the horizon from the slender loft of the crow's nest.

But it could be cold comfort. Sometimes they fell asleep on the night watch. Captain Brisbee had wisely stationed two men, one at the bow, the second perched on top of the wheelhouse. He sniffed the air. It would be nice to hoist the sails, he thought, save some coal in the bunkers. But the wind was still down.

At the extreme edge of Long Island Sound, he instructed the helmsman to change course, head to magnetic fifty-nine degrees, toward the southwest. The wind had begun to freshen. The open Atlantic lay ahead. Montauk Point light drifted by on the starboard, a blinding white flash at set intervals, one minute on, two minutes silent. From here to the East River, and the Municipal Boat Basin on the Hudson, they were under the care of a complex series of aids to navigation. Bell buoys, lighthouses and lightships, nun buoys, gong buoys, whistling buoys, fog horns and channel markers. Captain Brisbee noted the locations of each on his chart of New York Harbor and Approaches. But they were still a far way off. He peered up through the wheelhouse glass, craning up at the dizzying height of Alma's towering foremast. They were now in the open ocean. The wind was definitely rising.

"Perhaps a spread of canvas," he casually said to the first mate, an Englishman by the name of Parker, who stood by the open door, smoking a Chesterfield. "See if the old girl still has her stuff."

The man grinned, tossed his butt over the rail. "She's picked up some scum on her bottom, Captain, from sitting in that damned mill pond. I doubt if we can make any speed records."

Captain Brisbee nodded without turning. "Still, we can save some fuel, and that might bring a bonus when we get to port. Owners like it when you save them a few dollars."

The first mate snorted. "Bonus? From *him?* Doubt that, Captain."

Brisbee smiled. But his suggestion was no longer a suggestion. It took on a professional edge. "Let's hoist the main, Mr. Parker. Give the engines a rest and save some fuel. There's a fair breath of air out there. No sense killing the black gang below."

ALL STOP.

Arthur was surprised when the order rang down. They still had momentum, and they were still at sea. *Alma's* big hull was rolling in the swells. But an order was an order. After shutting down the engine, he climbed topside, took a lungful of fresh sea air, dipping a bucket on a rope into the cool waters below. As he poured the refreshing liquid over his head, Arthur heard voices on deck, orders loudly given, then the sound of rippling canvas and racketing spars. The massive sails caught and *Alma* began to slowly claw for headway. Now that the steady thump of the pistons was gone, it was only the wind and the waves and the great steel apparition parting the dancing waves.

"I'll be damned," Arthur swore under his breath.

The stoker had followed him up the ladder, and together they lingered there, beneath the swinging wooden boom, an unnaturally slender spar resisting the taut immensity of *Alma's* wind-filled canvas.

"Christ, man," the stoker said, in a thick Senegalese accent, "it's good to not be shoveling for a change. Hope dat wind holds."

Arthur smiled as the man walked away, probably to find hot coffee in the galley. Captain Brisbee poked his head out of the wheelhouse.

"Oh, there you are." He nodded up at the swaying mast. "Well, Arthur, what do you think of our iron lady now?"

Arthur followed his gaze, then back to the line-handlers scrambling around on the foredeck, yanking at thick, hemp cordage and cranking the enormous bronze winches. The great mainsail snapped like a ghostly bird's wing, followed by the jib, then the mizzen, aft of the salon deck. A mile of running rigging in constant motion.

Alma began to lightly heel over.

It was exhilarating.

Rosemary, walking the length of the deck, greeted the Captain and Arthur.

"This is grand," she shouted over the rattling spars, the rippling canvas and the rushing water. "I never knew how beautiful it could be. Out here on the ocean, with nothing but the breezes to carry us."

The Captain smiled. "Well put, madam," he said, then, nodding towards his deck crew, added, "excuse me, the sails need a bit of trimming."

Arthur and Rosemary stood there in polite silence as he hurried away.

"How are you doing?" he asked.

Rosemary took a breath. "Honestly? I've been better. I'm in a state. That's how I am. I haven't the foggiest idea what comes next. I'm wanted by the authorities, yet I'm innocent of what I'm accused of. I think I am. Child endangerment, manslaughter? I have no idea what that even means."

Arthur lightly touched her sleeve. He glanced toward the bow. How much longer *Alma* could sail on, without his assistance in the engine room, was an unknown. But he knew that Rosemary desperately needed him.

"Come," he took her hand, leading her down the companionway towards the stern. Show me where your cabin is. It was an impetuous suggestion from a shy man.

Arthur had never been here. Owner's country, where greasy oilers and ordinary seamen were forbidden. Only servants carrying silver trays of delicacies, fresh bedding and starched shirts, were allowed.

When she opened the door, he gasped. The posh Victorian opulence was as foreign to him as a Maharaja's tent.

He turned to her. "Amazing what money buys, isn't it?"

Rosemary shrugged. "I've seen how the wealthy live, Arthur. I've been in their grand homes. It comes with a cruel price. I'm lucky to be out of it."

Arthur quietly closed the door.

"Will you have to go back soon?" she asked.

"We're under sail for a while," he told her. "The captain will send someone, when it's time."

"When do you suppose we'll reach New York?"

He thought on this. "I'm no sailor. Perhaps half a day, give or take. I'm guessing by mid-morning we should be docking."

"And then what?" Rosemary asked. "Where will we go? What will we do?"

Arthur reached for her hand.

"Don't worry," he said, "we'll figure it out together."

She considered this, then brightened. "There *is* kindness in the world, Arthur. I've seen it. People who will help you when nobody else will. I have to believe that."

When he took her in his arms, she noticed that one of his big hands was badly burned, singed a deep crimson from touching a hot steam pipe. Rosemary leaned down and kissed what must have been a painful injury. He hated the sea, and he hated all ships upon the sea. She knew that. Yet he was doing this, just for her, and for her alone. There was only one word that sufficed.

Love.

THE WIND HELD. CAPTAIN Brisbee, cap in one hand, the ship's bible in the other, gazed carefully into Rosemary and Arthur's eyes. It was still dark outside, and the helmsman kept their course. In a few hours, *Alma* would begin her slow turn to port, moving from the open Atlantic to the first approaches that would lead them towards New York City. But for now, he was in Owner's Country, the best cabin aboard. The Persian carpet was like a grassy meadow beneath his worn shoes.

They had summoned him, as any adoring couple would the captain of the ship, to perform a shipboard wedding.

Why not? Brisbee had thought. Who knew what the morning would bring.

"Are you sure this is what both of you want?" he asked them.

It was a ridiculous question.

The captain thumbed slowly through his old, dog-eared bible. It had been his sweet old Mum's, long cold in a stony Cornish graveyard.

Which verse would best suit the moment? The second mate stood rigidly next to the Captain, conscripted to be their legal witness.

It was from the *Song of Solomon,* Chapter Two. A fitting verse for two so obviously in love, yet so bereft in this moment of hope or glad promise.

My beloved speaks and says to me:
'Arise, my love, my fair one,
and come away;
for now the winter is past,
the rain is over and gone.
The flowers appear on the earth;
the time of singing has come,
and the voice of the turtle-dove
is heard in our land.

The Captain had his finger on the next lines, something about fig trees and vines. Not right. Instead he skipped ahead, to Chapter Eight. He cleared his throat and began again:

Many waters cannot quench love,
neither can floods drown it.
If one offered for love
all the wealth of one's house,
it would be utterly scorned.

He closed the bible. The rest was from memory, even though no couple had ever asked him to perform such a service before. He was a merchantman, not some country vicar. Still, he knew the words that followed.

And do you, Rosemary, take this man, Arthur, to be your lawfully wedded husband?

I do.

And do you, Arthur, take this woman, Rosemary, to be your lawfully wedded wife?

I do.

To have and to hold. In sickness and in health...

Brisbee smiled. He knew there was no ring, on such short notice. But as far as he, Alphonse Brisbee, Master Mariner, duly licensed by the British Board of Trade to conduct shipping business, serving onboard British vessels of unlimited tonnage, a card-carrying member of the Royal Merchant Mariner's Union, under his aegis and authority, they were now officially married.

"You may kiss the bride."

He turned to the second mate. "Let's leave our blessed couple alone now, shall we." He smiled across at them, then met Arthur's eyes. The meaning was clear; the ship would be needing steam soon.

Arthur wrapped one arm tightly around Rosemary's waist. She leaned her head into his broad shoulder, her cheeks dewy with tears.

Her new husband offered his captain a beaming, mock salute.

PART THREE

Into The Dark

CHAPTER THIRTY

Metropolis

Captain Brisbee stood at the bow, staring up at the mountainous steel hull of the U.S.S. *Chicago,* an American destroyer in dry dock for routine maintenance. The *Alma* was like a child's toy beside the immense warship.

They were now berthed in the Brooklyn Navy Yard, an important, bustling place, with thousands of government workers, like ants, tending to the great armada. Charles Crowningshield had spent political capital to secure a berth at a small, out-of-the way pier.

Captain Brisbee was at the gangway, pondering what to do next. In his hands, an official looking paper, handed to him by an unsmiling Pinkerton man, in the company of four other Pinkerton men, plus a small army of naval personnel, and, for good measure, an equal number of New York City police.

They had come for the child-murdering stowaway, Rosemary Kincaid. It wouldn't be hard. They would find her in the owner's cabin at the stern.

The captain had seen them gathered below on the shore when they docked, men in black waiting for the East River tugs to nudge *Alma* against the pilings. He instructed his crew to lower the gangway, and on the authorities marched, fanning out to search for the cunning escapee.

Arthur, still in the engine room, oblivious to the drama topside, was busy shutting off steam, putting *Alma* to sleep.

By the time he'd climbed back to the main deck, the search party had gone. It had all been ridiculously easy. Rosemary, quickly located, had offered no resistance. She simply strolled down the gangway, as grand as any titled lady debarking her personal yacht. A thousand shipyard men had paused to witness her apprehension; they'd seen the cars and the cops and the Pinkertons drive through the gate. A thousand muscled immigrants pushing barrows of iron rivets, burly, mustachioed shipwrights in derby hats and rolled-up sleeves standing on lofty scaffolding. The place was a sea of curious faces, all watching Rosemary's quiet march to justice.

A police sergeant handed Captain Brisbee the arrest warrant, and with it, a flimsy telegram, copied by the wireless operator at the Navy yard.

To: Captain Alphonse Brisbee, Master, SV Alma, C/O Brooklyn Naval Yard

From: Charles Crowningshield, United States Ambassador to China, Shanghai.

Change of plans. Stop. New York buyer pulled out. Stop. Prepare ship for passage to Southampton, England. Stop. Yacht broker New York will arrange details. Stop. Arthur Rouse to remain in ship's company as engineer. Stop. New work assignment White Star Lines, Belfast. Stop. Trust all is well.

Signed, Charles Richard Crowningshield.

The last was a veiled reference to Rosemary. Brisbee was certain. But Crowningshield hadn't wished to implicate his employee any further in this nasty business. He heard movement behind him. Arthur, up from the engine room, staring off into the distance, barely comprehending. His big, rough hands dangled limply by his side. The convoy ferrying private detectives and law enforcement, always the shiny black Ford sedans, crept slowly away, headed for the guardhouse gate. Arthur's eyes saw only Rosemary, her frightened, upturned face in the rear window.

"How did they find us?" Arthur blankly asked. "How did they know?"

Brisbee waited a beat, then offered a theory. "My best guess. Pinkertons must have had men watching in the village. The trains, the steamers. As long as she was at the farm, she'd be safe, but if they knew we were sailing, they must have guessed Rosemary would be aboard, and telegraphed ahead."

Arthur said nothing. Brisbee continued, "I'm sorry, Arthur. There's nothing you could have done. Crowningshield is too rich and too powerful to stop. He's got the lawyers, the police, the Pinkertons and the cops. Hell, he's even got the damned U.S. Navy doing his dirty work."

Arthur's eyes remained locked onto the deck, a tortured soul twisting in a terrible moment. He seemed, to Brisbee, like a man who has just had the wind punched out of him. There was hatred in those eyes, as well, blind hatred and frustration.

"I'm sorry, Arthur," The captain said a second time.

Arthur finally glanced up. The Pinkertons and the cops had vanished, the cacophony of the gigantic shipyard returning to life.

"She done nothing wrong," he muttered incredulously, waggling his head back and forth. "Rosemary loved that child like her own."

Captain Brisbee reached across to pat his shoulder.

"I know. But Crowningshield thought otherwise. And his wife is in a terrible dark place over all this. He needed somebody to blame for their troubles."

Arthur kept shaking his head. "It's not right. Rosemary done nothing to that boy. Just a rich man's revenge, that's all that is. And now she's off to a jail cell," adding bleakly, "in this heartless city."

Arthur, breathing heavily, was close to tears.

The captain nodded. "There's nothing we can do. Just offer our prayers, hope that the judge finds some mercy, and lets her off."

Arthur spat over the rail. Brisbee saw again that strange new look clouding his eyes. Contempt for corrupt power and the impotent rage of a husband who cannot save his wife.

"Mercy?" Arthur snorted, staring past the bow rail at a sea of derby hats and muscled, hammering arms. He thought again of that long-ago tribunal, Aberdeen, the Board of Trade acquitting the owners of that sunken cable boat.

"When has any judge ever done that?" He asked the heavens, then spat again. It was a question with no answer.

CHAPTER THIRTY-ONE

Sentenced!

T*he Court of General Sessions, Judge Timothy J. Gilfoye presiding,*
Date-August 19, 1910
Prisoner # 852973-Rosemary Kincaid
Legal counsel-not represented
Race-White
Country of Origin-Ireland
Age-34
Occupation-Domestic servant
Charge-Child Endangerment and Negligent Homicide
Conviction-yes
Sentence-six months to five years, Blackwell's Island Penitentiary

The trial lasted less than ten minutes. Her jail lawyer who had gone missing; the judge sat high on his carved dais, impatient to lower the gavel. A brief litany of unchallenged charges was read, merely as a formality. There was an ominous subtext. An American ambassador, with ties to the president, wanted his pound of flesh owing to tragedy in his family, and who was he, a low-level city magistrate, to judge? Besides, his morning's docket was overflowing with the unwashed, the destitute, the insane, why, even those few actual criminals who might get off with a few dollars to the court.

Rosemary was led away, her hands and feet bound by heavy iron manacles that pinched her pale, nearly opalescent skin. She had already spent nearly a month in the Tombs, a barbaric holding facility for New York's accused unfortunates. From the courtroom, she was loaded into a carriage called a Black Maria, then to the dock at 26th Street, where prisoners boarded a steamer to the island in the East River.

Blackwell's, in the next century, would be renamed Roosevelt, an official attempt to expunge the memory of such state-sanctioned barbarism. But in 1910, it was the city's multipurpose facility for New York's poor, sick, mad, and criminal detainees.

The Big House at Juniper Point, with its daily routine, as practiced by the Crowningshield family, the pastoral views and sparkling water, the mannered pretensions, was now a lifetime away. The boy's death had set all this in motion, and there could be no different outcome. But if it could be called an advantage, her new life at Blackwell's had a life corollary, a vivid memory of another prison. It was the ten years she'd' spent incarcerated in Dublin, inside the dismal brick edifice of the Magdalene Laundry.

DEBARKING THE STEAMER, after a short voyage across the filthy East River, inmates were marched to the penitentiary. In a large reception room on the ground floor, the hall keeper sat on a raised platform. The particulars of each convict, including religion and distinguishing features, such as knife wounds or smallpox scars, were noted in a large, leather-bound ledger.

Rosemary, along with a dozen other women, many of them teenaged prostitutes or petty thieves, or both, were stripped and washed in a large lead-lined bathtub. The tub contained the cold, foul water of a hundred previous immersions. The corpses of drowned lice, human hair, rat feces, urine, even bits of scabby tissue, floated on the scummy surface. Cleanliness or hygiene was not the objective, certainly not the result.

She was handed a scratchy, striped dress, two sizes too large, to wear.

The comparisons between this horrific repository for human detritus and the Dublin convent were striking, almost scripted. At both, penitents were roused before dawn, allowed two to five minutes for morning ablutions. Breakfast was spartan. The prison's budget only allowed for a starvation diet of moldy bread and weak coffee. The poorest swabs on the meanest ships were treated far better. Then it was off to work, down the stone stairs to the laundry, scrubbing clothes, or back to the prison scrubbing floors.

By day, armed guards in rowboats circled the island. Night watchmen patrolled the cell block with a gun and a lantern.

Rosemary managed to not weep uncontrollably, wounded by Crowningshield's capricious cruelty, confused by the disappearance of her new husband. At trial, the judge was at a loss as to how to exactly sentence the attractive, earnest-looking woman standing before him. There were no child cruelty laws yet in the penal code, and homicide, negligent or otherwise, was hard to prove without motive or witnesses. Last, but certainly not least, the "crimes," if they were indeed crimes, had occurred within a different jurisdiction, across three state lines, and technically outside New York's statutory reach. Nevertheless, the charges had been brought by a close personal associate of President Taft, litigated by career attorneys with the Federal Justice Department. This was politics, and the judge was a Democrat, serving at the pleasure of a Democratic administration. Charles Crowningshield had made large donations to Taft's presidential campaign, and had been rewarded handsomely. His mansion on Juniper Point was even rumored to become the summer white house.

The judge had no choice. Gavel down a guilty verdict, sentence the woman to Blackwell's, even though the crimes were either nonexistent or virtually unprovable.

BY THE THIRD MONTH, Rosemary had witnessed the deaths of seven inmates, and within another month later, three additional ones. Then four more after that. These facts she dutifully recorded in her 'diary', which consisted of scraps of discarded paper hidden beneath her mattress. She struggled to maintain the barest sanity, struggled to maintain physical stamina. The buildings and grounds were an abomination, medieval in concept and construction. The island teemed with large, brown river rats, vermin that sometimes bit inmates in their sleep. Prisoners died routinely from innocuous, curable causes. Diarrhea, pneumonia, pleurisy. Just a common cold was often enough. Causes of death were invariably from poor diet and unsanitary conditions. In the cellar, a bleak catacomb, a single water closet not connected to water pipes. At the end of a blind, lightless hallway, it stank from a continuous buildup of sewer gases. This odorous atrocity made her wish for Arthur's hand, but no plumbers ever visited the island.

Then, in December, a miracle. A passing hall keeper, with a message. "Warden wants to see you," he announced in a flat monotone, then led her up two flights of stairs to a large, airy, well-lit suite of offices. She peered over the railing, at the Dickensian dystopia below, where life was cheap. A pauper's grave awaited those who didn't survive their time here.

WARDEN FITZPATRICK was a large, bearded man, well-fed and jocular. His thin spectacles kept sliding from his nose. The keeper led Rosemary into the office.

"Come in, please, sit," the warden gestured to a chair in front of a large oak desk, strewn with open ledgers and stacks of official documents, the daily detritus of a middling bureaucrat.

Rosemary obediently sat, and waited. Standing beside the desk was another man, taller and better-dressed. His fingers were steepled into a contemplative pose.

"This is Mr. Harris, Rosemary." The warden gestured to the other man.

Rosemary silently nodded in his direction.

The tall man leaned closer. "And how are they treating you in here, Miss Kincaid?"

Rosemary kept her silence. Inmates that spoke out were punished severely, sent to solitary confinement, or worse.

The warden's smile was fading. "Rosemary, Mr. Harris owns a clothing concern. It's on the East Side, in the garment district. He's in great need of skilled seamstresses. It says here in your file...let's see now..." He pushed his glasses up, then stabbed a finger onto a page. "Oh, yes, right here. It says that you are an experienced lace maker. Is that correct?"

Rosemary finally answered, but it emerged in a whispered croak, so unused to the sound of her own voice. She could go for days in silence. "That's right, sir. I was taught the trade by the Catholic sisters, back in Ireland."

The other man was nodding. "Very nice, very nice," he said. He stared down at Rosemary. It was a critical appraisal, like a man debating some expensive purchase. "Miss Kincaid, I know you can't be very happy here.

After all, prison, the very reason for prison, is designed to be a just punishment for habitual criminals. Do you have any complaints here?"

Rosemary struggled for the right words. "I understand that, sir. I'm just trying to serve my time, not be a bother to anyone here."

Harris glanced towards the warden, who blurted, "Oh, yes, she's been a model inmate. No reports whatsoever."

Harris kept examined her face. "And you say you can make quality lace, of the finest sort? No mistakes? I have repeat customers who are extremely discriminating."

Rosemary struggled to meet his gaze. "My work will speak for itself, Mr. Harris. You'll have no worries."

Harris considered this. Finally, he smiled, "Well, I *was* hoping for an Italian. But I suppose an Irish will do."

The warden quickly stood, kneading his hands. "Excellent, excellent. Well, Mr. Harris. I think we can come to an arrangement. Are we agreed? I think Rosemary would make a fine addition to your firm, and with the court's blessing, we can have her out of here by the New Year."

The warden stuck out his hand, cocked his head. "And what did you say was the name of your establishment, Mr. Harris?"

Harris shrugged, almost unperceptively. "I prefer not to say. We're an established firm."

The warden bared his teeth into a kind of canine grin. "As you wish. No matter. It's not my area of expertise, not having a woman around the house. Still, it sounds like a wonderful opportunity for Rosemary. And I'm sure she's extremely grateful. Aren't you, Rosemary?"

She struggled to remember what her own smile felt like, what gratitude felt like. It wasn't a lot to ask of her memory, but it was nearly impossible.

"It sounds grand," she finally answered.

CHAPTER THIRTY-TWO

The Letter

A week passed.

Rosemary stared down at the envelope in her hand. It had obviously been opened. Water-stained, wrinkled, torn, then taped. It looked as if it had traveled a far distance to reach Blackwell's. In childlike block letters, a name, and return address:

C/O Harland and Wolff Shipyard, Belfast, Ireland

Arthur had returned, like some miraculous Phoenix rising. She silently offered her thanks to Saint Rita, fingering her rosary. The keeper who had delivered the letter to her cell had tossed it at her without a word, then moved on. People, both inmates and employees, were a phantom presence here. Both sides of the bars lived hard lives; both wished to be elsewhere. But the inmates had it far, far worse. An aged and infirm woman; her name was Bess Stilton, (or perhaps that was an alias, people had many here), had hung herself Sunday last. No person had entered her cell for perhaps twenty-four hours. It was the stench from decomposition that finally unlocked her door.

My dearest wife, the letter began. *I hope you are doing alright. I've thought of you often, ever since that terrible day on the Alma, when they took you away. It wasn't right, what they did. You done nothing wrong, and that's a true fact. But here we are. I tried to get to the courthouse, to see you there, maybe I could have done something, and the Captain, he figured out where the men had taken you, but nobody there gets to have visitors, and we was told to go away. We did, and that made me very sad. I'm in Ireland now, in Belfast. It's on the northern side, as you probably know. Mr. Crowningshield has me working for the ships they're building, helping to install toilets and sinks and such on two great ships. Its miles of piping, and I'll probably be here forever, or at least until the ships are launched. It's a great, dirty city, where I am, Rosemary. The shipyard is even bigger than the factory in Chicago. But I think you would like it. You can smell the sea, when the breeze is right, past the river, like back at Juniper Point.*

Missus Backus, the landlady at my boarding house, has been helping me with my writing. I wrote down some of this myself. Not all, but some. She's a nice widow lady and very educated. She composed most of it. I recited it, then she wrote it down.

I miss you terrible, Rosemary, and pray that your circumstances change very soon. Being imprisoned is probably the worst thing I can imagine, but I would gladly change places with you.

Please write back, and tell me how you are doing. Do it right now, today, because I'm told a letter takes a very long time to cross the ocean.

Faithfully,

Your husband, Arthur

She tucked the letter carefully back into its envelope. Of course it had already been plucked apart, likely by the warden or his army of overseers. There were no secrets on Blackwell's Island, and inmates, mostly teenaged girls and younger boys, already working as prostitutes and pickpockets, the insane and emotionally damaged, the impoverished debtors, the alcoholics and the opium addicted, rarely received mail.

Rosemary sat there on a wooden bench for long minutes, oblivious to the constant torrent of human misery around her. New inmates arrived daily, but nobody noticed, so deeply were they immersed in their own sad fates. Last week, a young woman, no older than twenty, had passed by her in the corridor. Pregnant, weeks, or even days, from what would someday be called her due date. That day had certainly come, and the prison doctor was summoned. But he only visited the island on Tuesdays, and the poor girl had bled to death, her baby stillborn. Their bodies were quickly hammered into pine coffins made in the workhouse carpenter shop, then lowered into shallow, unmarked graves. Life was the cheapest commodity on Blackwell's.

And now this, a letter from her beloved. And all the way from Ireland, no less. Rosemary closed her eyes, shut them as tightly as she could, as if only blind might she silence the frightened bedlam from the corridor.

CHAPTER THIRTY-THREE

The Morning Post

Chicago.

In the morning came three letters, all addressed to him. Charles Richard Crowningshield sat behind an enormous oak desk, in his equally enormous office at the Crowningshield Company headquarters. He picked up a delicate, silver letter opener cast in the shape of an exotic bird. It had been a gift from his wife, monogrammed with the initials *CRC*, at Tiffany and Co. jewelers in New York City, and delivered in time for Christmas of 1896.

This was all before the darkness had blotted out his family. When he and Cornelia were happily married. Before he obsessively traveled. Before he kept a mistress. Before his only son died. Before his wife went mad from grief.

He turned to the letters. The first was from the private sanitarium where Cornelia had been taken, "as a palliative for mental exhaustion." It was from Doctor Richardson, Cornelia's personal physician at the hospital. In 1910, there was no such thing as patient confidentiality. In 1910, a man's wife's business, even delicate medical business, belonged to him, no less than his property and his bank account.

He opened the first letter.

Dear Ambassador Crowningshield, it began, *I trust this reaches you safely. I was informed by your secretary that you had been away in the Orient on government business, but that you may have returned by this date. Nevertheless, I wish to inform you of your wife's current medical condition, as well as the treatments she has been receiving at this institution. As we have discussed by letter, your wife suffers from a psychopathological condition known as neurasthenia, but more popularly known as mental exhaustion. Her symptoms are quite common: fatigue, anxiety, headache, heart palpitations, high blood pressure, neuralgia, and depressed mood. She has also expressed notions of wishing to end her own life, which, by itself, is alarming, and I assure you the hospital staff is doing their upmost in addressing this particular threat. It is a shared belief by myself and my colleagues that the root cause of Mrs. Crowningshield's illness stems from two areas, these being the untimely loss of your young son, coupled with the various pressures of administering a large household of employees. Obviously, your son's death was what we might call a triggering mechanism for her, but we also believe that it's not the only sole reason for her subsequent breakdown. Dr. Freud, in Austria, has some interesting theories about repressed childhood memories that might be applicable in your wife's case.*

The treatments thus far employed by the institute are as follows: confinement and restraint, isolation, which brings quiet and hopefully a contemplative adjustment, ice water immersions, which has been proven quite helpful in other cases, and electrotherapy, through the employment of mild electric shock, which, again, has achieved successful results with other patients. Our hope is a positive outcome, through these and other methods, and that by Year's End she might have recovered enough to join her family at home for a short visit.

Respectfully,

Dr. Samuel O. Richardson

Illinois Institute for the Treatment of Mental Disorders, Abington, Illinois

Crowningshield laid the letter down. Rubbing his eyes, rolling his neck until it gave a satisfying crack, he reached for the second. He scanned its return address. *Pinkerton National Detective Agency, 57 Broadway, New York, NY*

Allan Pinkerton was a personal friend of his father, who'd suggested getting in touch with the agency to track down Rosemary. Pinkerton, a former barrel maker in Chicago, had become the city's first police detective, turned a single small office into an internationally acclaimed business.

Inside, an invoice, detailing the cost of the agency's efforts to locate the fugitive runaway child murderess. It was quite detailed, including a daily log of their efforts, a stipend for each detective, charges for lodging, meals, and transportation costs associated with the woman's return to justice. Crowningshield reached for a pen, housed in a gilded pen holder, and dipped it into a small golden container of ink. He quickly wrote a personal check, for the amount of four hundred and twenty-six dollars and fourteen cents, made out to the agency, and laid it aside. Delores, his personal secretary, would be sure to be sure and mail it out that afternoon. A smaller square of paper fluttered out of the envelope. It was a personal note from the lead detective assigned to the case.

Mr. Crowningshield, the note said, *I thought you should know that the fugitive apprehended August 19, Miss Rosemary Kincaid, late of your employ, has been recently approved for a prisoner lease, sometimes called pre-release work indenture, into the custody of Mr. Issac Harris, the proprietor of a small garment manufacturing concern in New York City. This concern is located at 23-29 Washington Place, between Greene St. and Washington Sq. East, Manhattan, New York. Her release was approved, supposedly in a legal fashion, by the New York Penitentiary Indenture Board, and she will be employed for a term of three years in the trade of lace maker. I'm sure this news will come as a disappointment to you, owing to the expense and time involved in locating the fugitive, but to reiterate, this action was done in a legal manner. Please advise us if you should have further need of our services.*

Signed, George Dougherty, Chief Detective, Pinkerton Agency. New York, NY

Charles Crowningshield shook his head. Two bits of bad news in one morning. His wife, locked away in a private asylum, then his son's killer let out, free as she pleases, to walk the streets again. He might just write a letter to the president about this. He reached for the third letter, slit it quickly open. Time was short. He had a meeting with his brother, Richard Junior, concerning his involvement with the company. Let him have the damned thing, he'd said privately to his wife earlier in the summer, before all of...*this.* But, he'd added, he'll have to pay.

The third letter was from his sister, Frances. She was an influential member of the Woods Hole scientific community, and had married, in 1895, Dr. Frank R. Little, a zoology professor and future director of the Marine Biological Laboratory, which had been heavily subsidized by Crowningshield donations.

Frances, unable to practice medicine against the wishes of her conservative Chicago family, taught embryology for several summers instead. When the babies began to arrive, (there would be four, plus three more adoptees) she abandoned academic pursuits altogether.

Dearest Brother, she wrote, *I trust you are well, and hopeful, considering what a summer it's been. Frank and I are packing to return to the city in time for his classes to begin. There's simply never enough time. But we're both excited to get back to business, as they say, after lolling around like seals on a rock all summer. Not Frank, of course. He rolls his sleeves up wherever he is, and of course the students at the MBL were entranced, as usual, by his notable lectures and field expeditions aboard the good ship* Nagitta. *I needn't remind you, dear brother, that without your generous contributions, none of this would be possible.*

Crowningshield smiled at the compliment. His sister would have made a splendid diplomat, if women, of course, were allowed to join the corps.

My work with the Mary Crowningshield Nursery continues, she continued, referencing Chicago's first child-care center for working women, founded in 1907, again, with financial assistance from her family, adding, *It's a gift, to be involved in such a selfless undertaking.*

After a page more of pleasantries, Frances got to the point.

Dear Brother, let us now talk of this entire situation, owing to the tragic death of my sweet young nephew John. I cannot begin to emphasize to you how deeply I felt your family's, my family's as well…great, great loss. I wept for you all, and prayed constantly to God above to help find you, and Cornelia's, peace throughout this terrible, dark time. But it has also come to my attention, brother, that the woman charged with your son's care has herself been charged and sentenced and imprisoned. How is this fair, I ask you? It cannot bring back your son, or assist poor Cornelia in her trials. Rosemary Kincaid had done nothing wrong. It was a terrible accident, and to punish her is a separate tragedy. I'm sorry, but I have to forcefully disagree with you on this matter, Charles. Need I remind you what is written in scripture? "To forgive is divine." It also says, "Justice is mine, sayeth the Lord." I know nothing of legal matters, dear brother, but is it truly too late for you to reconsider your actions, perhaps done in a moment of blind grief? If not, I urge you to do so. Let us discuss all this when we see one another again.

I so look forward to sharing some time with you and the children, and of course, Cornelia, when she returns from her treatments.

Your loving sister, Frances

Charles Crowningshield stared at the words on the paper for a long time. They had given him pause, but just a brief pause. It was well past the time for reconsideration, and his sister was naive to think that it was. What's done was done. And besides, the nanny had been given a sort of reprieve anyway. An early release. His conscience was clear. He stood up, straightened his tie, and walked across the heavy Persian carpet. He opened a door with his name painted onto it, in gold leaf, stepped out into the ordered din of the factory floor. He could almost smell the money mixed in with the metal shavings.

CHAPTER THIRTY-FOUR

The Factory

Dec, 28, 1911 Rosemary Rouse
C/O Blackwell's Island Penitentiary, New York, NY

My dearest husband. It seems so strange to call you this, but I am smiling when I write it. I received your wonderful letter two days ago, (thank you!) and have spent an entire day composing a letter back to you in my mind. I want to say exactly how I feel. Also, it took quite a while for the prison to provide me with a bit of stationary and an envelope. Not many inmates write letters, it would appear. I cannot tell you what sort of place I find myself in. They will certainly read what I write before it is mailed out, so all I will say is this. I am doing reasonably well, considering. There are lots of people here in far worse circumstances than I, and I pity them greatly. Again, I shan't go into details, but you can well imagine. Most of what is wrong with the world is poverty and lack of education, and poor, ignorant people seem to get the worst of it. My situation was a tad different than the rest, and I am grateful, all the same, because the Crowningshields treated me fairly, and what happened to young John was just a terrible, sad accident. I do now understand why Mr. Crowningshield did what he did after his only son was taken away. Grief is a powerful force.

I have some good news. By the time this letter reaches you I will be free of this place. A businessman, Mr. Harris, who owns a garment factory in New York City, has made an arrangement with the prison to have me come and work for him. I'm not sure exactly how this all will turn out, but one thing is certain. I will be leaving Blackwell's Island, that's where this prison is, an island right in the middle of the dirty river, probably the day after tomorrow. That's what they tell me anyways. They don't tell you much here, not in the way of details, but I promise as soon as I know more, I will be writing you a letter, dear husband, with a new address so you can write me back. I know I should be more pleased with all of this, but honestly, I'm terribly sad to be leaving these wretched people *behind. And the children. It brings tears to my eyes. I think, why me, given my freedom, and not them? Again, I can't furnish more details, and frankly, life here is not something that should be shared in proper company. Better to just let it go, and send prayers their way.*

I miss you terribly, Arthur. Sometimes, in the darkest night, and this place has quieted down just a bit, I am comforted by fond memories of you, of our brief time together. Sometimes it's all I have to keep the madness from entering.

Anyway, shan't be maudlin. I must hurry and try to get this off on the afternoon boat. My next letter will be much happier, I promise. I'm so proud of you husband, for working so hard on learning your spelling. I can certainly help with that as well, when we are next together again. Be careful on those big ships. I wouldn't want to lose you.

With my fondest regards, your loving wife, Rosemary.

January 2nd. 1911. Rosemary stepped from the prison launch. It was the same pier she remembered after so many months ago, marched from the courthouse to the ominously named Black Maria, a horse-drawn jitney with barred windows, a row of freshly sentenced wretches sitting across from her, chained with the same leg irons and manacles.

But today was a different day, a new beginning. There would be no Black Maria, or manacles, or guards. She was headed away from the river, accompanied by a tall, well-dressed businessman, who had met her when the prison launch docked. Mr. Isaac Harris, who co-owned, along with a man named Max Blanck, a garment factory located in the Asch Building, on the corner of Greene St. and Washington Pl.

He gestured to a polished sedan, parked adjacent to the pier. A Negro chauffeur wordlessly held the door open. He was resplendent in gray livery, with the same row of brass buttons and jodhpurs tucked into high boots as Mr. Teasdale, a white man who drove for the Crowningshields.

As the car pulled away from the pier, Mr. Harris turned to her. On his hands he wore soft, doeskin gloves, gripping a silver-tipped walking stick.

"Well, Rosemary," he said, "how does it feel?"

She turned to him. "I beg your pardon, sir?"

"To be free of that wretched place," he clarified. "Blackwell's. That stony blight out in the river."

"Oh," she nodded quickly. "Thank you, sir. It feels just grand. I am so terribly grateful for this opportunity."

He nodded. "Don't thank me just yet, Rosemary. You'll be working hard. They'll be long hours, and the pay, I'm afraid, is not the best. But our employees are treated fairly."

Rosemary peered from the window as they rode along the crowded avenue. The chauffeur spun the wheel, expertly dodging pedestrians and streetcars, harness horses pulling rag pickers, ice men hurrying to make deliveries before the morning sun melted their translucent, dripping blocks.

Rosemary turned and smiled. "I'm just grateful, sir, for the opportunity."

Harris stared hard at her, as he had back on Blackwell's, then said, "I'm taking a chance, Rosemary. What they said you did, with that child…Still, I believe in second chances. I myself am an immigrant, you see. I came to America, just like you, seeking a better life. From Russia. People like me, Jews, were imprisoned by the Czar. In the pogroms, whole families were murdered. Mine. " Harris grimaced at the boyhood memory.

Rosemary nodded. "I understand, sir. You won't be disappointed."

Harris glanced out the window. A fully loaded streetcar whizzed by, carrying a sea of black derbies and floral hats. They were just were just entering the part of New York that would someday be called SoHo, a chic, artistically populated place to live for the city's well-heeled, bohemian crowd. They were turning onto Greene St.

The driver steered the limousine to the curb. He got out, opening the doors first for Harris, then Rosemary. She stepped out, staring up at the Asch Building; a plain, gray industrial monolith towered over them. Three words: *Triangle Shirtwaist Company*, had been painted onto a sign bolted to the corner of the edifice.

"We're up on the eighth, ninth, and tenth floors," Harris told her proudly. "You'll be working on the top floor, with the other fancy sewing girls. The cutting room is on the eighth the stitchers are on the ninth. Don't worry," he smiled, "the elevators work."

Rosemary shook her head. "Oh, I wouldn't mind, sir. Even if they didn't."

Harris frowned. "And stop calling me sir, Rosemary. You're not back at the manor house. Mr. Harris is fine."

Rosemary smiled. "Very well, sir…I mean, Mr. Harris, sir."

ON THE TOP FLOOR, SHE was shown to her table, the place where she would spend the next twelve hours, five days a week, with a half a day on Saturday. For her labors, she would be paid $15, five times what she'd earned as a nanny. She quickly recognized the tools of her trade. Needles and bobbins, a small velvet pillow, spools of fine linen thread, a stack of patterns for the more common designs. The mustached foreman, Mr. Craddock, nodded toward the table. "You'll be starting on a christening dress," he told her, "for some wealthy brat uptown. And be quick about it, too."

Rosemary leafed through the patterns until she found the right design, then turned to him. "How old would you say this child is?" she quietly asked, adding, with a smile. "Babies come in all sizes."

Mr. Craddock shrugged. "How the hell should I know? A fucking infant, fer Chrissake."

Rosemary wordlessly picked up a spool of thread, her pins, the small horsehair cushion, and a dozen whalebone bobbins. She began winding thread around the base of each bobbin. All day, and into the early evening, she worked quickly, mostly from muscle memory. She hadn't made proper lace since she'd left Dublin, fourteen years before, at twenty.

By the time the caged elevator slid open, and Mr. Harris had stepped out into the tenth-floor workroom, it was nearly seven o-clock. A perfectly flawless christening dress lay on the scarred, wooden table. Rosemary sat back in her hard-backed chair, parched, exhausted, famished. She hadn't eaten, or drunk, since a meager dinner yesterday.

He lifted one edge of the tiny, intricately stitched garment, then slowly laid it down.

"Very nice, Rosemary," he said.

She wearily returned his gaze. "Thank you, sir."

"Mr. Harris," he reminded her.

She smiled, but it was a partially opened door.

"Yes, Mr. Harris...sir."

CHAPTER THIRTY-FIVE

The Shipyard

Arthur Rouse, Chief Sanitary Engineer
C/O Harland and Wolff Shipyard
Belfast, Ireland
Dearest wife,

Received your fine letter Monday last, but have been working such terrible long hours that's its only now I have the time for a proper reply. There are two big ships on the ways right now, them being the Olympic and the Titanic. Mr. Crowningshield's factory is supplying all the plumbing bits for both of them, and they insisted on a company man be there to oversee the installing. I have ten men under me. Imagine that. The ships are both run by the White Star Line, out of England, but the company is really owned by a rich American, Mr. J.P. Morgan. I understand Mr. Morgan and Mr. Crowningshield are old friends, and you know how those things go.

But that's not what I wanted to talk about. I wanted to tell you how happy I am that you're free of that bleak hell of a prison, and they gave you a good job to do in the city. It's truly a miracle. I hope nobody bothers you too much at your new place, and you can rest your mind from your recent troubles.

Well, I'm not sure what else to say at this point. I'm doing fine here. Lots of hard work on the ships, but don't worry, I'm being careful. I just miss you terrible, and wish we could be together sometime soon.

Your devoted husband, Arthur

THE NEXT DAY, AND ONWARD, Rosemary worked at the Triangle Shirtwaist Factory. Each day was a new lace pattern, and she began each the same; grafting tiny bands of linen thread tied to dozens of bone bobbins.

Over and under, under and over, the design emerged, a sleeve or a bodice slowly moving over the velvet pillow. It was fine, intricate work, beneath the brash suns of the Edison lamps.

That first night, Mr. Harris dropped her off at an address not far from the factory. This was her new home, he told her, a grimy tenement shared with six other shirtwaist girls. Ever since, Rosemary had walked to work, rising just after dawn, then had walked back, just after dusk. She rarely saw her benefactor.

Mr. Issac Blanck managed the day-to-day business. A waist shirt, or shirtwaist, was a common article in any Victorian woman's wardrobe. It was basically an unlined blouse, with a turnover collar and buttons down the front, often ornamented with embroidery or lace. It was designed to hug and uplift a woman's bodice. Before there were Playtex Living Bras, there were shirtwaists, and the diminutive Triangle company was one of thousands that manufactured them. Theirs was a wholesale business. They hired immigrant labor, young women, just off the boat. There were no labor unions. Later, these places would be called sweatshops. Prior to electric lights, workers sometimes even went blind, from the poor lighting that cast dim shadows over their Singer machines, a web-like umbilicus of whirring leather belts attached to spinning shafts mounted to the ceiling. The fancy-sewing department on the tenth floor, by contrast, was a quieter place, nearly monastic, but just as stultifying. Time was translated into money, always, and the schedule was unceasing. By February, Rosemary had saved nearly ten dollars, a portion of which paid for her bed in the tenement known as 29 Greenwich St. Blanck and Harris each earned a hundred times more. It was not an equitable arrangement. Still, there was Blackwell's Island. She had no wish to return. Facts were facts. Just as she had been at the Magdalene Laundry, so too had she become a slave at the Triangle factory.

CHAPTER THIRTY-SIX

Dismissals

January 21, 1911. Washington, DC. President William Howard Taft, in the oval office, stared down at the two letters on his desk. A portly, humorless man, his leather chair squeaked as he adjusted his girth, searching for the best sitting position. Both letters had arrived in the morning's mail. The first, from a prominent law firm in New York City, contained an unsubtle threat. The second, from Chicago, contained a preposterous request. Both letters concerned itself with the same subject, Charles Richard Crowningshield, Taft's newly appointed ambassador to China.

Howard, the first letter began. Taft frowned at the pretentious familiarity. He was the President of the United States, for God's sake. Who did Crowningshield think he was? Granted, the man had given his election campaign ten thousand dollars, but it would take a lot more for him to call him by his first name.

The letter began: *I am writing to you in hopes that the Justice Department might intervene on my behalf, concerning the difficult situation with Rosemary Kincaid, the Irish woman who was convicted and sentenced for the wrongful death of my young son, John. It has come to my attention, through private means, that this woman has recently been granted an early work release from incarceration and is now living and working in New York City, apparently with no official supervision. My lawyers tell me this is a common practice, and thought by some to be a liberal alternative to prison. However, I feel, that under the circumstances, that any criminal act deserves proper punishment, and it is my opinion that Miss Kincaid return to Blackwell's Island post haste. She should not be out, free as she pleases, amongst the general public. I'm sure you agree, and it would very much appreciated if you were to instruct the Justice Department to take whatever measures required to correct this miscarriage of justice perpetrated on myself and my family.*

With warm regards,
Ambassador Charles Richard Crowningshield
Executive Vice President, Crowningshield Company, Chicago, Illinois
Taft laid the first letter aside, and opened the second. This one was infinitely more actionable and compelling.

The salutation was more formal. *Esteemed Mr. President,* it began, and that pleased him. Potentates like to be reminded of their power and prestige. Then he scowled, as he read further. This was no bowing and scraping missive from a loyal constituent.

The letter was from the law firm of Bannister, Bannister, and Childs, of New York, London, and San Francisco. They were *the* firm to hire, it was agreed, if one wanted to get results, quickly.

J. Thomas Bannister, its aging founder, and his son, James, along with long-time partner Stephen Childs, had an impeccable winning record in the courtroom. It was said that when they accepted a case, it was already over.

The letter was a simple statement of fact. But the subtext was an ominous threat, auguring a great wave of public indignation and political enmity if he didn't follow its instructions.

The firm of Bannister, Bannister, and Childs represent the interests of Randolph K. Smythe, of Scarsdale, NY and Columbus, Ohio.
Taft knew who Smythe was. He was a timber baron, among other things. He owned vast holdings of logging land in the Pacific Northwest, in Canada, even in Europe. He owned, or was principal partner in several railroads. He owned steel mills, sugar plantations in Bermuda, even several large international banks, one in Zurich, Switzerland. He was an investing partner in several maritime shipping concerns, including the Cunard and the White Star Lines. God knew what else. If Bannister, Bannister, and Childs represented his good name, the recipient of such correspondence, even the President of the United States, might do well to take notice.

Taft felt his blood boil. To receive such a letter, on such a fine morning, early in his term. Only yesterday, the Senate had had passed his anti-tariff bill, the Payne-Aldrich Act, which essentially created a legal firewall to protect industrial combinations, despite his campaign promises as an antitrust crusader. Monopolists like Smythe, who owned large pieces of everything, while paying zero income tax, were deeply indebted to the Democrats. But still, when Bannister, Bannister, and Childs wrote such a letter to the president, they meant business.

Taft summoned his personal secretary for dictation. He grimaced, as if sipping sour milk. The day was beginning badly.

ON TUESDAY, JANUARY 22, 1911, *The New York Times* published a small article. Most casual readers; men in high shoeshine chairs, men in *New York and New Haven* smoking cars, men in gentleman's clubs and corporate offices, unfurled the paper, scanning the baseball scores, peering at stock prices, and probably missed it. The piece was tucked "below the fold," on page six, just below a breathless account of the Yale Expedition, young explorers recently returned to the country, being the first *White Men* (in breathless caps!) to reenter the mountain city of Machu Pichu in over four hundred years.

Ambassador to China Recalled

Charles Richard Crowningshield, President Taft's recent appointment to be this nation's Ambassador to China, was recalled from service yesterday, the State Department confirmed. No reasons were cited other than escalating tensions in the region, and a feared peasant revolution. Mr. Crowningshield is the son of Richard Teller Crowningshield, founder of the Crowningshield Company, the world's largest manufacturer of plumbing fixtures and other sundry products. The company's home office is in Chicago, Illinois.

Just below that, a smaller blurb about an elevator malfunction in New York City.

Skyscraper Car Plunges Six Floors

An elevator car, reportedly made by the Otis Elevator Company, of Cleveland, Ohio, a subsidiary of Crowningshield Co, plummeted six floors yesterday in a Manhattan office building, causing injury to all passengers aboard. Problems with the hoisting motor are believed to be the cause.

OF COURSE, RANDOLPH K. Smythe was the aggrieved and cuckolded husband of Emily Simmons Smythe, the young mistress of Charles

Crowningshield. Rich and powerful men are inherently distrustful, and often employ spies to corroborate their paranoia. In fact, the very same Pinkerton Detective Agency detectives that had brought Rosemary to justice had also discovered an illicit affair between Crowningshield and Emily Smythe. The final accounting for their services came to just over two hundred dollars. That was how ridiculously easy it had been to gather the necessary evidence to complete their investigation. Exactly one third of a business day, a single photograph of Emily and Charles entering her Park Avenue apartment.

President Taft had to make a choice. It wasn't difficult. Discharge Crowningshield from his government position, or risk public exposure to a damning scandal. In 1911, such things mattered. Even a notoriously corrupt president had to appear above reproach. A rich industrialist, with ties to his administration, carrying on with the wife of another rich industrialist, a young, naive, and quite beautiful woman. The press would have a field day. Taft sent a letter to the State Department, instructing them to immediately relieve Crowningshield of his official duties, exiling him back to the life of just another rich industrialist.

And so on.

Six months later, Emily Smythe divorced her elderly husband, citing 'mental cruelty and alienation of affections.' She received no compensation, neither cash settlement or alimony, due to her own history of marital indiscretions. Bannister, Bannister, and Childs were quite thorough. Within six months after that, she had had married another rich industrialist, a senior executive of the Standard Oil Company. Henry Flagler became famous for his ill-fated project, the Florida East Coast Railway, a wildly conceived fever dream of connecting, by rail, Miami and Key West. It was a seemingly impossible engineering feat, costing millions, which later vanished in the hurricane of 1938. He is also credited with building many of the grand hotels in Miami and Palm Beach, but for the railway folly, most of all. Flagler was a spry eighty-one-year -old when he married Emily, nearly forty years her senior. Tragically dying from a fall two years later, some said suspiciously, at eighty-three, he left sixty million dollars in his estate. When his will was read, the entirety of it went not to Emily, his young widow, but to his children, Jennie, Carrie, and Harry Jr.

Two years later Emily died in a drowning accident, swimming off of a private rocky beach in Newport, Rhode Island, in front of the estate where she had recently been employed as a housekeeper.

And so on.

CHARLES CROWNINGSHIELD stared at the two items on his desk. The first, a telegram from the State Department, delivered by Western Union messenger this morning. The message was curt, discharging him from his duties in China, signed, not by the President, or even the Secretary of State, but by the Third Assistant Secretary of State, Alvey Augustus Adee.

He'd been let go like a common field hand.

The second item was today's edition of the *Chicago Daily Tribune,* which had picked up the story of his recall from *The New York Times.* Crowningshield read and reread it. The words made no sense at all. Tensions in the regions. Peasant revolt. None of these reasons were mentioned in the telegram, only that his services were no long required.

He settled back into in his chair, thickly upholstered in soft, brown leather, with brass studs that ran up and down each arm, and pondered the situation. Now what? Only last week, he'd come to an arrangement with his brother, with the Crowningshield Company. His services were no longer needed in the family business, by mutual consent. And for this, essentially an amicable divorce agreement, he would be paid eighteen million dollars, a kingly sum insuring he would never again step foot upon a factory floor, or listen to the gabble of a roomful of stockholders, or haggle over supplier invoices. None of that. He was now free to...do what, exactly? He already traveled about the world as much as he liked. His "work," really, consisted of occasional forays to his office, between trips to the Orient and Europe and the Middle East. It was his brother Richard who was now the guiding force behind Crowningshield Company's global enterprises.

Charles Crowningshield's future hung like a paper moon on a cardboard sky, as the popular song went.

He frowned and thought of Taft, that fat toady. The man had thrown him to the wolves, for whatever reason. Of that he was convinced. But why?

Politics were an ugly business, and Charles Crowningshield's political armor was gossamer thin. He'd lobbied the newly elected president for a position that would feed both his passions, travel and a love of exotic cultures, but beyond that, he hadn't a clue behind palace intrigues.

The late afternoon sun filtered through the thick, damask curtains, laying a golden pattern onto the carpeted floor. The house was deathly quiet, at this hour. The house maids would all be upstairs, tiptoeing into each bedroom with armloads of fresh sheets, after climbing the servant's' stairs from the basement laundry. In the rear of the mansion, in the cavernous kitchen, staff would be busy with the coming dinner. His children, probably off somewhere with the new nanny. Crowningshield stood up, walked to the marble fireplace. He poked absently at the dwindling fire. A golden flame shot up, quickly fell. Glancing at the pile of logs on the hearth, he laid the poker aside. Someone would be in shortly to feed the fire.

Crowningshield folded the light velum of the telegram into thirds, then tucked it into a desk drawer. He carefully folded the newspaper the same way, and placed it on the writing table. It was official. He now had nothing to do and nowhere to go.

Never again would the morning car arrive to carry him across town, to the city within a city that was Crowningshield Co.

His thoughts shifted, and he smiled. Of course. Emily. Her yellow hair falling across his throat as they made love in her Park Avenue boudoir. Emily, how he missed her. He added the hope that her old, doltish husband would never discover their trysts. That might be messy. But no matter. Charles Crowningshield was a handsome, fit man in his early fifties. Not self-made, of course. No, he could never claim that. Fortune had smiled on him on the day of his birth. "Lucky jissum," the chauffeur had privately quipped once, with a bottle at his lips. But, still, he was a good father. A caring husband. He'd found a suitable mental asylum for Cornelia, hadn't he? And she was making improvements, perhaps by spring to return home. He thought himself compassionate, willing to share his wealth with those less fortunate. Didn't he tip the staff at Christmas? Five dollars and a turkey. And philanthropy? He was practically bankrolling the entire damned marine laboratory in Woods Hole, in the name of science.

He thought again of Emily. Her bright, worry-free face, her wide, cobalt eyes, the lilting contralto in her voice, like the tinkling of a silver bell. Who cared now about Taft, and his lying pack of hyenas? Who cared for some ridiculous government job? Who cared about *The New York Times*? Crowningshield smiled. He now had eighteen million dollars in the bank.

And Emily. Of course. He still had Emily.

CHAPTER THIRTY-SEVEN

The Titan

Arthur, perched on a single iron beam, ten stories above the keel, laboring somewhere midships of the great *White Star* liner *Titanic.* It was nearly February, and his hands felt like frozen stumps in the meat locker of a Belfast winter. The ships, she and her sister *Olympic,* lay side by side, like stablemates, miraculously held upright by a vast, improbably slender crosshatching of timber supports and towering gantries that ringed the immense dry dock.

He was feeding brass pipes, from one end of the ship to the other, from stem to stern. Pipes that would service first and second-class cabins. Each cabin would have its private water closet, hot and cold-water taps, a commode, even a spacious shower.

Unbeknownst to him, his benefactor and employer, Charles Richard Crowningshield, had recently divested himself. He was no longer with the company. Arthur had, by extension, become the sole property of the Harland and Woolf Shipyard, and by extension of that, the *White Star Line*, and by extension to *that,* the financier J.P. Morgan. Perhaps through some elegant equalizing effect, it made no difference to Arthur. It was, for him, always just about the job. Just man and materials.

Standing on that slender beam, deep in the bowels of a great ship, thoughts of Rosemary would appear. He had to be careful. Men whose mind wandered sometimes fell, and usually died from their injuries. Eight fatalities since he'd begun work here. He missed the Chicago factory. The predictability of level ground. Amazingly, he never thought a place could exceed the unrelenting din of a working foundry. But the shipyard certainly did. Thankfully, the riveters had all moved on, to another hull in the far side of the yard. That was surely the devil's choir, and his ears still rang from all those hammers racketing at once. He thought sometimes of Captain Brisbee, the gentle agreeableness of the seafaring gentleman who had married them at sea. Brisbee had tried rescuing them. But the Crowningshield grip was simply too tenacious. But he'd tried. There are kind people in the world, as Rosemary always said.

He constantly thought about what he would write to her, his distantly beloved. Tonight, certainly, when he'd gotten home, he would compose a new letter. He needed less and less help from his patient teacher, the old widow landlady.

Life for Arthur was curiously dreamlike. He worked on the great ships, his feet were in Ireland, but his heart was so far, far away, in that great American city on the river.

And what was Belfast?

A thousand grog shops and pubs, a dozen miles of dirty waterfront, ten thousand angry men who missed their wives, the sword of unemployment constantly above them all.

Arthur didn't drink, had never drunk. But he dearly missed his wife, and lately, had begun conjuring a plan.

CHAPTER THIRTY-EIGHT

A Terrible Day

February 25, 1911.

Rosemary woke to the queerest feeling. It began in her belly, and radiated outward. The symptoms were familiar. Months before she'd fought back nausea, then retched into a wash basin. The nausea had passed, but now today, dressing, she'd noticed a pinprick of tenderness, a slight swelling beneath her pale, freckled breasts.

There was no denying it. It was the oldest sickness in the world.

She was going to have a baby.

Rosemary smiled as she dressed for the day. Imagine. A baby, belonging only to she and Arthur. *Ours.* The word was a perfect circle. She would give birth soon, and Arthur would come to her. If the cold and the snow, the long hours at the bobbins and the spools, the starvation diet, and influenza didn't kill her first. She thought about missing work today, but it was Saturday. Payday, and the rent was due.

She must write Arthur, to tell him the news.

Today she would have money in her purse to buy a fresh envelope and stamps.

Besides, it was almost as cold as the street beneath the covers at the rear of the dark, windowless, tenement apartment. The heat from the leaky old coal stove in the front kitchen was barely keeping the milk from freezing. It would be much warmer at the factory. And besides, spring was almost here. Rosemary bent down and laced up her high leather shoes, wrapped a thin, black shawl over her shoulders, and opened the street-side door. It had snowed last night, a light drifting. A killing cold had blown in over the river. A few dime-a-day snow shovelers, ragged, indigent men with stubbled faces employed by the city to keep the sidewalks clear with wooden shovels, had created a fresh path. As she walked, a river of horse-drawn vehicles passed;

delivery wagons and taxi hacks mostly, and the hot, equine steam from a hundred muscular animals filled the air. A few motorcars honked, and the electrified hum and rattle of an apple-green streetcar, slowing to pick up passengers. The factory was only a few blocks away, but the frigid wind that careened between the brick and stone canyons of the East Side cut like a knife through her long, woolen skirt. Rosemary pulled her thin shawl tighter, and kept walking. One more block to go. Finally, she reached the Asch Building. A group of Triangle girls stood out on the sidewalk, waiting for the doors to unbolt, laughing and speaking in strange tongues. Immigrants, most of them in their twenties, some as young as seventeen. Jewish girls, fleeing Russian revolutions and pogroms. Italians and Germans and Yugoslavians, escaping a provincial life of ignorance and poverty. If America was a melting pot, places like the Triangle Factory were the flames beneath.

Entering the building, she smiled to familiar faces at the caged elevators. She waved, a few waved back, or simply nodded. At thirty-four, Rosemary was one of the oldest employees, and the only from Ireland. Most Irish girls were engaged in the domestic trade, working in mansions on the Upper West Side. Only one woman, an Italian, Catherine Maltese, at thirty-nine, was older. Ida Brodsky, a fifteen-year-old from Russia, was the youngest.

Everyone was glad for the end of the week, and the next day would be for resting heir worn souls and bodies. But many had second, or third, jobs, taking in hand sewing, or washing at home, or selling soup and bread on the street. These were the married girls, or about to be married; some had husbands out of work, or burdened with too many children, especially the Catholics. Everyone was struggling, trying to save for a better life. Rosemary had been asked by one of the girls in her apartment if she needed a second job. There was always clothing to mend, or clean. But so far Rosemary had said no. She needed her precious day off. And besides, pregnancy was going to be a full-time job.

Lately, she'd taken to walking about the city, peering into restaurant windows, observing well-heeled diners consume lavish meals of which she only had a vague recollection. One thing about the Crowningshields: the staff were always well fed. But now, on such meager pay, and half of it for her bed alone, she threw in a few dollars and ate what the others, the three other women who shared her room, ate. She'd never tasted a bagel before, or a bialy, or borscht. The girls offered her smoked salmon, and canned pickles, and pickled beets, and pickled boiled eggs, preserved in canning jars brought in their luggage from the old country. The tenement kitchen was always redolent with the smell of peasant cuisine; boiled cabbage, brisket, or challah, from southern Germany. And the breads! One girl, a plump, Italian, twenty-four- year-old named Annina Ardito, held a wooden spoon out and offered her an enormous meatball, slathered in tomato sauce and cloves of garlic. Rosemary took a bite, and beamed. New York City, even at its poorest, was a cornucopia of exotic culinary delights. The same, staid American food that had emerged from the Crowningshield kitchen each night suddenly seemed bland and tasteless.

BY EIGHT A.M., THE factory had already been toiling for nearly an hour. Long rows of identical black sewing machines, with a single word, *Singer*, embossed in gold leaf, made a clacking, whirring cacophony that drowned out the sounds of the city waking up on Greene St. far below. Rosemary, on the tenth floor, began her shift stitching a wedding dress of an intricate design. She hoped to complete it by the end of the day. Bonuses were unheard of, but still, perhaps her employers would notice. There were rumors of layoffs coming, and the threat of strike hung over every shop in the city. Rosemary tried not to notice. She worked hard, and did her job well, as she had promised Mr. Harris that day in the warden's office.

By quitting time, a few minutes before the bell, the completed dress lay on the table, neatly folded for the manager to pick up. Rosemary was bone-tired, from sitting for so long, and her eyes hurt from squinting down at the tiny stitches. Finally, it was done!

A few minutes later she heard muffled screams. Distressed sounds, wafting up, from the ninth floor, where nearly two hundred women were also quitting for the day. But this was different from the usual Saturday afternoon chatter. Perhaps they were being robbed. Rosemary stayed at her table and cocked one ear. The manager, in his tiny cubicle at the end of the room, would tell her what to do. Suddenly, an invisible whiff of smoke filled her nostrils, the thick aroma of something substantial burning. Something pervasive and monstrous and growing. Mr. Blanck rushed from his office at the opposite end of the sewing room, and quickly looked around. His eyes told her everything. The man was terrified. Then he turned and began to walk quickly towards the iron door that led to the roof. He flung it open, disappearing up the stairs. Rosemary knew that many of the factory doors on the lower floors were kept locked, to prevent pilfering, and the water buckets were usually empty. She'd heard the others complaining. The Triangle shop was a death trap, a few had whispered. It had no modern sprinklers. And all those bins of flammable cuttings at the end of each row of machines. By the end of the week, they'd be overflowing.

Rosemary finally stood up. She gave her completed wedding dress a quick glance, then followed Mr. Blanck's escape route into the stairwell. He hadn't given his employees a second thought, or bothered to investigate the growing chaos on the floors below. He'd simply panicked and run.

The screams were getting louder, a chorus of confused voices in the smoky shadows.

As Rosemary reached the roof, the clanging of fire brigades rushing towards the Asche Building were growing louder. The smoke was closer, dangerously closer. It was like the entire world was burning.

On the roof, a group, mostly women, and all from the tenth, were standing around, too afraid to speak. Safety was an obvious illusion. Rosemary knew, from the few times she'd been upstairs, climbed the steep stairway and looking down, at the alley below. There was no way off of here. The rusted and rickety fire escapes ended at the ninth.

The fire below was now a raging inferno. Occasionally an enormous flame would lick out from ninth-floor windows, scorching the outer walls.

Mr. Blanck stood apart from his employees. His eyes were wild, he stood nervously wringing his hands. Another man, one of the floor managers, peered over the stony parapet, but the heat climbing up to them was too strong. He quickly yanked his face back, his eyebrows singed, his face a sooty mask. The fire could easily break through to the tenth, and then the terrible chimney effect would quickly devour the timbers, hungry for oxygen. It would soon run out of victims below, and would be coming for the rooftop survivors.

They stood there for long minutes, but it seemed like hours. One young man tried making a joke, something about hoping the payroll office didn't get burned up, but nobody was laughing. Lung-searing smoke was spiraling into the sky, and a few in the group began to cough and hack up black phlegm.

The top two floors of the Asche Building were rapidly becoming a death zone. The screams of the dying mixed with the screams of the living, the urgent clanging of the fire bells, the excited voices of well-meaning onlookers calling up to the jumpers in the windows. Don't jump, they called, foolishly, because for many young girls, who had minutes before been happily laughing about the end of a work week and spending time with their fiancés, or parents, or simply walking in the park, or shopping for a new hat, there were no longer any choices. Incinerate, for a few horrible minutes, or simply lean out, push off, and die quickly on the street below. Some of the onlookers called out for the jumpers to aim for the nets, absurdly flimsy contraptions of thin canvas, held open by firemen. But that was just as foolish. The first few bodies became projectiles that tore the nets to shreds. Sometimes, when the bells went quiet, and the screaming became more intermittent, Rosemary could hear the sickening thud of another body hitting the sidewalk. Then the screams would begin again, but now mostly from the onlookers. The dying was nearly over for the people at the windows.

For the survivors on the roof, though, survival became a fragile, implausible dream. Rescue ladders, pulled from horse-drawn wagons, were useless. Their highest rung only reached to the sixth floor. A few people began to pray. Ancient Hebrew incantations. Russian Orthodox. The Italians invoked their god of Roman Catholics. But prayers had rarely worked before, and have rarely worked since. They often comfort, but just as often fail. Rosemary knew this. She believed in St. Rita, but that suddenly seemed foolish as well. She thought of Arthur.

He had once brought water to her parched land.

The very ground beneath her feet was burning.

He would know what to do.

CHAPTER THIRTY-NINE

A Decision

Eight men would die building the *Titanic,* between 1909 to 1912. But numbers can be deceptive, and the shipyard bragged that this was a victory. Statistically speaking, they reasoned, the grim calculus of eight dead men was a small price to pay for such a wondrous, technological achievement. What they failed to mention was that, like every industrial concern on the planet built by wealthy men with big ideas, worker safety was placed far below production quotas. A first-class stateroom on the *Titanic* would cost nearly five thousand dollars, while the average worker earned less than ten dollars a week.

Arthur had heard about the first death; it happened nearly two years before he had begun at the yard. A fifteen-year-old, working on one of the countless riveter's teams, usually four men and a boy, hauling red-hot rivets from the slag fires to the hull, had fallen nearly twenty-five feet to the hard, curved belly of the iron hull below. He'd lived long enough for the doctors to pronounce his wounds untreatable, noting his cause of death to be a fractured skull.

There were other stories. Men on scaffolding who lost their grip, a man crushed by an enormous timber, while his son and wife watched, at the great ship's launching, as it slid down the greased ways into the River Lagan.

It was hard, gruelingly physical work, working on those gigantic ships. Harland and Woolf employed over fifteen thousand men, and if you slouched, or became too sick to work, you were out. Even the dead were replaced the very next morning. That's just how it went. Captains of Industry were not concerned with the lives and needs of those who toiled in their factories or shipyards. Harland and Woolf calculated the eight dead, in over three years of construction, and called it good. Hopefully, eight more wouldn't die before the great ships finally set sail on their maiden voyages. Time was money.

THE FIRST TO DIE WAS Samuel Joseph Scott, a riveter's apprentice. He was employed as a "catch boy." His job was to carry red-hot rivets from the furnace to the waiting men on the scaffolding. Those same iron rivets, after forty-eight of them were fished from the wreck site in the 1980s, were found to be low-quality, made from iron mixed with slag, a smelting byproduct that can cause fractures upon impact and in cold temperatures. The same bad rivets that had killed Samuel Scott had certainly doomed the *Titanic*.

The last to die was a shipwright, James Dobbin, who everyone called Jimmy. He was given the coveted job on launch day of helping to remove the huge timbers that held the ship upright on the ways. On Wednesday, May 31, 1911, the *Titanic* was finally ready to be baptized in the river. Nearly ten thousand people were on hand to watch the historic spectacle. A special platform had been constructed for local dignitaries and their guests. Harland and Woolf had given its employees a special workday off, a holiday, without pay, to view the launching. Lord William Pirrie, Chairman of the Board, and his wife Lady Eliza were joined by J. Bruce Ismay, the company's managing director, as well as American financier J.P. Morgan. Next to Morgan sat another American, Charles Richard Crowningshield, who had supplied all of *Titanic's* modern plumbing fixtures. Crowningshield's wife, however, was not on hand, having been recently re-hospitalized for 'nervous exhaustion'.

At precisely ten a.m., two rockets were fired from shore, to warn other ships who might be passing, and the great ship began to slowly slide towards the dark, dirty river. Thousands of gallons of soap and tallow greased the long, sloping slipway. Suddenly, a heavy timber fell, not to the side, but backwards. Jimmy Dobbin was struck down. His wife and son were somewhere in the crowd, but not close enough to see the accident. Rushed in the company car to the Royal Victoria Hospital, he lingered, then died two days later of his injuries, a crushed pelvis and massive hemorrhaging. The company dispersed a full week's pay envelope to his widow, generously not withholding Jimmy's two days absence from the job while in hospital.

Arthur counted himself fortunate. His work wasn't as dangerous as hammering rivets on a high, swinging scaffolding, or clinging to the towering gantries that embraced the hull. Installing water pipes and hooking up toilets in first-class cabins was all done from the relative safety of plate decks. He rarely had to climb a ladder, or stand beneath a swinging hull section. But, still, it was dangerous. James Dobbin's oldest son, James Junior, had also died at the Harland and Woolf yard, but not on the *Titanic.* He'd fallen from the *Olympic,* a plumber's apprentice not a week on the job, reaching too far overboard for a crate of pipe fittings being hoisted up to the deck.

Arthur absorbed these stories, mulling them over and over, until at last, by mid-February, he made up his mind. He hadn't heard from Mr. Crowningshield all winter, realizing now that he'd been cast adrift by the company. The decision was obvious. He would quit the shipyard. He would return to America. In America were plenty of jobs for men with his abilities. In America was his wife. He might even go into business for himself. Why had he waited for so long? Why had he continued to work here, even after Charles Crowningshield had himself retired? The answer was complex, yet simple. Arthur's loyalty was both a blessing and a bane.

In the Harland and Woolf pay office, he handed in his resignation. The clerk barely noticed. Past the gate, the next morning, another man with far less plumbing experience would quickly step forward to take his place.

Arthur spent the next two days preparing to leave the city. The Belfast steamer to Liverpool would be leaving tomorrow, and from Liverpool another ship would take him to New York. It felt good to finally decide, to finally be doing something. It was as if a long, careless string had been unraveled; at the end of that string a new life waited. Even though he was now unemployed, he thought of those wasted lives of his co-workers. Quitting the shipyard was the right thing to do.

EARLY FRIDAY MORNING Arthur returned to the sprawling Harland and Wolff facility, on Island St, to retrieve his final pay. He looked over towards the dry dock, where *Titanic* still sat, an impossibly enormous, gray leviathan that loomed over the city and blotted out the sky, soiled from the smoke of a hundred hoisting engines. Thousands of men crawled over her exoskeleton and her innards from bow to stern. He felt no remorse. He was emptied of nostalgia. His leaving would be unremarked upon.

The Crowningshield factory had been a teeming city, anchored into predictable, solid ground. Worker deaths were so infrequent that a sign had been placed at the gate that counted the days back to the last. No, *Titanic* was a man-killing bitch, a monumental folly built only to serve the rich and the powerful.

But one thing still bothered him. Where was Rosemary? A week past, and still no letter.

As he was headed back out the gates, a yard foreman he knew strolled up to him. The man was holding out a wrinkled newspaper in one work-worn mitt.

"Rouse," he called out in a thick, Liverpool accent. He was pointing down at the newspaper. "I've been trying to find you. You seen this?"

Arthur shook his head, then peered down at the paper. He felt a queasiness in his stomach. Newspapers rarely wrote about good news.

It was today's *Belfast News*. The story was a week old, received by the amazing new invention of wireless telegraph. One word leapt from the headline. **TRIANGLE!** Then another. **TRAGEDY!**

As Arthur began to read, slowly and laboriously, the man waited, still chatting. "I thought you said your girl worked there."

Arthur kept reading. "My wife," he corrected the man without looking up.

"Sorry, mate," the man said, "my mistake."

At last Arthur lowered the paper, a strange glint in his eyes.

The man was still prattling on. "A terrible thing that happened," he said. "A terrible thing."

Arthur handed him back the paper, and wordlessly stalked away.

CHAPTER FORTY

Tragedy!

February 26, 1911.

The *New York Tribune*:

142 Bodies in Morgue. Inspection of Unidentified Victims Began at 1 O'Clock. Delay For Lack of Coffins. Supply Brought from Blackwell's Island Helps in Disposing of the Dead.

The *Brooklyn Daily Eagle*:

Over 150 Persons, Most of Them Girls, Die as Fire Traps Hapless Factory Workers in Manhattan Skyscraper.

The *New York Times*:

141 Men and Girls Die in Waist Factory Fire; Trapped High Up in Washington Place Building; Street Strewn With Bodies; Piles of Dead Inside.

FRANCES PERKINS, LABOR activist, Fanny to her friends, stood on the far side of Greene St. and watched the bodies falling. She'd been attending a tea party when the butler quietly informed the lady of the house that there was a fire. Across the square in one of the garment factories, he explained, without a trace of excitation. Frances leapt from her chair, hitched up her skirts and began to run toward the clanging fire bells. She quickly reached Greene St, and looked up at the Asch Building. It was ablaze and full of people dying. People, mostly women, their bodies outlined by fire and smoke, were crowding the granite edges of the windowsills. The top floors were totally engulfed. The streams of water from the pump hoses were completely ineffectual. Then somebody called out. A few pointed. An object had been tossed from one of the windows, something large, perhaps a large bundle of cloth, which was odd. Fanny peered closely through the smoky air, watching the tumbling weight. She gasped. The bundle became a human body, a young girl, kicking her high button shoes, waving her arms in one last salute as she fell. A few seconds later, she was gone, an unmoving pile of gore, a wild cascade of dark unpinned hair fanning over the iron sidewalk. Perkins looked up. Another, and another. Living people jumping from windows, the meaty obscenity of their bodies smacking the concrete. Frances tried counting, but lost track after thirty. As soon as one body landed, firemen rushed to cover it with a blanket. But by then, another had launched itself. Then they came in twos, sometimes threes. It became a dangerous game for the firemen, timing the descents. Running in, running back. Greene Street was like a gruesome battlefield, a scene of twisted and broken limbs, rivers of crimson coursing to the gutter.

One young man stepped to the widow, like a dancer from the wings. He gave a long, courtly bow to the onlookers below, then reached behind him, pulling a young girl out by the waist. He relaxed his grip and the girl dropped, plummeting as precisely as a bomb. He did the same with two others. On the fourth, that girl turned and kissed him, long and passionately on the lips. Then they stepped from the window together. The papers reported on his spotless tan shoes, and thought him an honorable man.

It was the most horrific thing Perkins had ever witnessed. It was impossible to not watch.

AT THIRTY-ONE, FANNY Perkins was already a seasoned political operative. She was currently lobbying the government to put an end to child labor, lobbying for fire safety in the very factory now burning. But this, men and women jumping to their death, this was something else entirely. The owners of the Triangle factory had a bad reputation. They had so far resisted any attempts at unionizing their shop, even hiring thugs, paid union-busters like the Pinkertons, to keep organizers out. They had refused to install basic safety equipment, like fire sprinklers, and, it was hinted darkly, they purposely torched two previous buildings to collect insurance money. The unspoken subtext: they were Jewish. Arson, gentiles kidded one another, was just Jewish lightning. Yet, so far, nobody had died.

The Triangle was a tragedy waiting to happen.

FINALLY, THE LAST OF the jumpers lay there on the sidewalk, and the firemen were able to begin the laborious industry of dragging heavy canvas hoses up the stairs. Finally they could begin to direct some water on the flames. They stepped on, then over, bodies in the stairwells, the squishy lifelessness of bodies behind locked doors, charred remains, some still sitting at sewing machines, waiting for help to come.

The stench of burning timbers and human flesh hung over the East Side. Survivors of the fire were already rushing home, hurrying from house to house, knocking on doors, to see who had escaped and who hadn't. Still, the onlookers remained, watching in rapt fascination as undertaker's wagons began the grim task of delivering human remains to a temporary morgue. A roofed-over East River pier, where city policemen patrolled with oil lanterns, guarding against looters.

Fanny Perkins remained where she stood, absorbing the tragedy. From across the street, not from the Asch Building, but the next building over, what would become part of New York University, a straggled knot of dazed people emerged. The first man to appear was one of the factory owners, Blanck. She knew him from her labor efforts. A short, balding, officious, and fussy-looking man. Behind him came a grim parade of survivors, mostly women, but a few men. Their faces were ashen beneath soot, their gazes somber, disbelieving, traumatized.

One of the onlookers in the crowd began explaining, loudly, to any who within earshot, the miracle of the tenth floor survivors. Apparently, at the height of the fire, a group of students next door had organized a rescue operation to save those trapped on the roof. Somewhere, they had found a long, wooden plank, and then extended it across the chasm between the buildings, forming a kind of narrow bridge. One by one, people began to crawl across, were hauled to safety. It was one of the few bright moments in one the darkest days the city had ever faced.

As she watched the workers emerge into the street, Fanny counted again. There were at least twenty, maybe more. One woman caught her eye, crossing the street, unsteady on her feet. After walking a few more steps, the woman staggered, then leaned against a lamp post, as if about to faint. Fanny rushed over, caught her elbow, and led her back toward the square, where a ring of iron benches faced the stone arches hovering over the park. In sixty years, this would be a gathering place for political dissidents, a thousand peaceful demonstrators playing guitars and chanting, all protesting the Vietnam war. But in the smoky dusk of February 25, 1911, it was just a place for the woman to sit and try to forget the fire that had just killed one hundred-forty-six of her co-workers.

Fanny eased the woman down onto the bench. She had such a queer expression on her face, and Fanny reached into her purse for a handkerchief, began carefully daubing the woman's cheeks, a mixture of dewy perspiration and black soot. The skin beneath was pale, with a faint tracery of freckles. Her bloodshot eyes were a vivid green. Irish, she guessed.

"Are you all right?"

The woman said nothing, continued staring across the park at the smoking building. Finally, she nodded, as if awakened.

"Yes, thank you very much," she said. "I just need a moment."

The woman drew in a hard breath, and began to cough, a wracking spasm that went on for long seconds. She placed her hand over her mouth, and apologized. "I'm so sorry, Ma'am. It's the smoke. The smoke up there was something fierce. We were so lucky those boys came along."

Fanny nodded, letting the woman compose herself. "Tell me," she finally asked. "Where do you live? I can help you to get home, if you'd like."

The woman turned and stared back at her. "Home? Oh, I don't think so, Ma'am. I don't think I ever want to go back there." She shook her head violently from side to side.

Fanny turned her gaze back towards Greene St. Firemen and morticians and ordinary people were gently loading the dead into police wagons. The sound of horses whinnying, spooked by the smoke. Reporters from the dailies milling around, scribbling frantically to make the evening edition. Photographers at their tripods, busily loading glass negatives, capturing portraits of the carnage soiling the street. The fire had lasted eighteen minutes. Fanny understood the woman's refusal to return home. Each one of those dead bodies had a name, had once been a living, laughing person, and this strange, shattered woman had known many of them. There would be little to return home to.

"I live nearby. You can come home with me, if you'd like."

The woman forced a grateful smile.

Fanny patted her hand. Cold as a mackerel. Shock was settling in. She'd seen it before.

"Call me Fanny. And what shall I call you?"

The woman paused, as if trying to recall exactly.

Finally, a name emerged, in a pained croak.

"Rosemary," she said.

She quickly corrected herself.

"Mrs. Arthur Rouse."

CHAPTER FORTY-ONE

A Dark Dream

In her dream, the crackling of those awful licking flames, soulless hot tongues climbing the walls, the stink of hellfire searching every inch for consumables, both wooden and human. At first the voices below were subdued and orderly, as if this were a perfectly normal way to end the day. Pay envelopes handed out, a polite procession to the elevators. Mr. Rosen, her floor manager, checking everyone's handbag for stolen fabric scraps. Then the voices rose to cries, and the cries rose to screams, and the screams turned to moans. Somewhere, off in the distance, the urgent clanging of fire brigades galloping through the crowded boulevard.

In her dream, Rosemary frowned. She called out, an unintelligible mumble. Her hands were curled into pale fists. Then another hand broke the spell, gently prodding her awake. Rosemary opened her eyes, blinking to the bright enormity of the morning after. February 26th. Triangle was only yesterday, but already an indelibly inked memory. All those poor, poor girls, never to return, to laugh, to flounce, and jabber in their strange foreign tongues.

"Hello," the voice was saying. A woman, sitting in a chair beside her bed. "Good morning."

Rosemary stared groggily back at her.

"I'm Maude." The voice explained. "And you?"

Rosemary told her.

The woman was Irish. How long had it been since she'd heard another's familiar brogue. She thought hard. Not since Juniper Point. The Crowningshields hired none but. It kept the proper English mythology alive. Irish boys and girls, bred as servants, toiling all their lives without complaint, until they were gone, to be replaced by the next batch.

The woman smiled. "So very pleased to meet you. We've all been so worried. You slept a long time. Nearly twenty hours."

Rosemary grimaced. Yesterday wasn't yet done with her.

"You're Irish," she finally said.

The woman grinned. "Guilty as charged. Maude O'Farrell, from County Kilcare. I'm a friend of Fanny's."

Rosemary, confused. "Fanny?"

Maude explained. "Fanny...Frances Perkins. But everyone calls her Fanny. The woman who brought you here last night. After the...."

Rosemary nodded. She still wore yesterday's clothes, she stank of soot, of burned timbers, of death. Someone had scrubbed her face, though. Her skin smelled of lavender.

"Can I get you anything?" Maude asked. "Coffee? Tea? How about some breakfast? Or lunch?"

Rosemary thought on this, and then answered dully. "I should be hungry. But I'm not sure. Could I trouble you for a glass of water? My throat is awful dry."

Maude rose from her chair. "Of course." She said. Another woman had appeared at the door, anxiously peering in. "Ah, you're awake."

Rosemary nodded. "I remember you, from last night. In the park."

Fanny Perkins walked into the room. She gestured down at the chair. "May I?"

Rosemary was still anxious and drained, although her injuries weren't exactly injuries, just a ragged throat and filthy clothes.

Fanny lowered herself into the chair. She reached out, with a motherly gesture patted the quilted covers.

"Tell me," she began. "How are you doing?"

Rosemary thought on this. "It's coming back," she said, "piece by piece, but it's as if my brain is pushing those things back down. To protect me somehow."

Fanny nodded. "Mr. Freud calls that compensation. It's a way we keep ourselves from getting overwhelmed. Share if you need to, or not. Either way is fine. We're here for you."

Rosemary had no words. No person had ever spoken to her this way. No person, that is, but her Arthur. Never those exact words, but supportive, in his own way. And where was he at this very moment? Did he know, all the way in Belfast? No, of course not. It would take a week or more for a ship to carry news across the Atlantic.

"Thank you," was all she could think of.

Maude appeared with a glass.

Watching Rosemary drink, the two women exchanged glances. The Triangle fire was a fresh, horrific wound on the city. It wasn't the first one, and it wouldn't be the last. None of this would end until new labor laws were written to protect the workers from the abuses and outrages perpetrated by factory owners like Harris and Blanck. Those two men were the worst offenders. Their callousness was legendary, in a city of crass, economic self-dealing.

Rosemary handed the empty glass back, began folding back the covers. "You're very kind," she said, as she struggled to sit up. "But I must be going."

Maude frowned. "Going? Where? You said yourself last night you had no wish to return to your lodgings."

Rosemary sat up on the edge of the bed. "Yes, I know, but still...there's my pay. I'm still owed from last week."

Fanny shook her head and snorted, "Pay? Hah! Those two sons of bitches. They're both in hiding right now. The entire city is up in arms about what they did. I doubt very much they'll be showing their faces."

Rosemary knew this. She'd seen Mr. Blanck run from the office, a strongbox under one arm, as he made for the stairs. Mr. Harris? Probably uptown, in his grand house with his army of servants. Nothing bad would come to those two. Those with all the money called the piper every time.

She heard voices, muffled, excited voices, coming from somewhere outside the bedroom.

"It's the steering committee," Maude explained. "Here to organize a public meeting tomorrow night. They've engaged the Metropolitan Opera House. Can you imagine?"

Rosemary shook her head. No, she couldn't imagine. She was a lace maker who earned five dollars a week. She'd never been to an opera house.

"Would you like to go?" Fanny asked quietly, locking eyes with Maude. The two women thought alike. Their partnership, both personal and official, was deeply about the movement, and the moment was finally upon them.

The Triangle fire was just the catalyst it needed. Things could change. An actual survivor at the meeting would draw attention to the cause.

They would do anything for the cause.

Rosemary stared back at them. "You mean some kind of political meeting?"

Fanny and Maude, excitedly nodding. "Yes, Rosemary," Maude added quickly. "It's important work. You're certainly welcome to join us, if you're up to it."

Rosemary shook her head. "I couldn't. Triangle employees are forbidden to attend union meetings. It's grounds for instant dismissal."

Fanny sighed. "We know all about Triangle's so-called rules. The unions have been fighting them for years. Rosemary, you should really be there tonight."

Rosemary thought on this. Triangle was now dead to her. It had gotten her out of Blackwell's. But she'd never go back even if she could. Not with all them dead girls, the blood of all those innocents on their hands. Harris and Blanck? They could go to hell!

"I would be honored to attend," she finally said. She looked down at herself, a smudged shirtwaist and wrinkled skirt. The hem, torn by the rescue plank. Her shawl, left on the back of her chair when she'd run for the door. "But my clothes...they're a shambles."

Maude moved closer, examining Rosemary. Her mother had been a seamstress, and she could guess a lady's size. "We'll find something for you to wear. I'm a bit stouter than you are, but I see you've got company in there. Tell me, dear, when do you suppose your little one will arrive?"

Rosemary began to weep. Such kindness, these two women. And women in charge of such important issues. Men's issues. This was all so new.

"I don't really know. I've not been to the doctor."

Fanny gently reached out and patted her shoulder, glancing back at Maude. She stood up.

"Rosemary, we're going to give you some privacy. You've had a terrible time of it." She pointed across the room to a door. "Please, take your time. Wash up. Run a nice bath. Soak in that delicious hot water. We'll find you a nice wardrobe. When you're feeling better, and the rabble-rousers have left, we three will have a nice lunch and you can tell us more about yourself."

As they left the room, Rosemary quietly called after them. "Thank you both, for your kindness."

Down the hall, the muffled voices had risen, wafting from a room at the front of house, the sound of men arguing over a point of order. As she closed the door, Fanny placed her finger to her lips, then mouthed a single word.

Sisters.

After they'd left, Rosemary began to cry. She lightly convulsed and shook and cried some more. Yesterday was upon her again.

Later, another word. As it always did.

Arthur.

Saying his name she felt calm.

Yesterday began to slowly subside.

But, she knew, it would be coming back.

CHAPTER FORTY-TWO

A Night at the Opera

The meeting at the Metropolitan Opera House was meant to be about reform. It was meant to be about establishing and protecting workers' rights. Condemning the greed of the factory owners. Creating a grassroots organization that would address and rectify an entire universe of civil rights abuses in the garment industry. Instead it was, from the start, an evening of fracturing allegiances and braying enmity between classes. Discord between the working poor in the gallery, who preferred the direct action of street marches and confrontation, and the fur and jewel crowd, New York's limousine liberals, rich democrats who wished only for quiet and orderly political reforms.

Fanny and Maude were horrified. They saw the evening of goodwill and proposals on behalf of the Triangle Fire victims coming apart at the seams. Standing between them, Rosemary could only gawk at the palatial grandeur of the opera house. All around, in the gallery, a sea of the working class, hungry for change. Above her, in a glittering semi-circle, the city's well-meaning elite gazed down from the subscription boxes, a polite pattering of white glove applause.

Rose Schneiderman strolled to the lectern. Jewish, born in Sawin, Poland, an early crusader for women's rights, Rose was a staunch trade unionist, an avowed socialist, and founding member of the ACLU. No lace-curtain liberal, but an immigrant who had once made a living as a lining stitcher in a Lower East Side hat factory, and then worked as a cashier in a department store. Rosemary stared up her. A diminutive, fiery orator, with flaming red hair that cascaded in circlets about her head, Rose spoke softly, so quiet that audience members fell silent, leaning forward to make out her opening words.

"I would be a traitor to those poor burned bodies," she began, "if I came here to talk good fellowship. We have tried, you good people of the public, and we have found you wanting. This is not the first time girls have been burned alive in the city. Every week I must learn of the untimely death of one of my sister workers. Every year thousands of us are maimed. The life of men and women is so cheap and property is so sacred. There are so many of us for one job, it matters little if 146 of us are burned to death."

Rosemary glanced behind her, at the audience. She scanned their rapt faces for signs of pity, of understanding, of some native intelligence, and was gratified to see it all. Even in the heavens above, among the jewel and fur crowd, she saw genuine tears. This was all so new. Her life with the Crowningshields was such a distantly quaint, historic artifact, a vanishing horizon of time and space. She closed her eyes, and saw them all. Juniper's vast legion of voiceless workers; kitchen girls, Mrs. Carmody thanklessly sweating over uncountable meals, a parade of bed linens sent to the subterranean basement laundry. And dusting, always the dusting. She saw Mrs. Crowningshield, a haughty queen with a little silver bell, casting judgment and distain for anyone and everyone. And then Mr. Crowningshield. God knew who, or where, he was. Only the money, and the power, and the abuse that both inflicted on the servile world. She thought of her Arthur, building ships for the mighty to sail the seas. She thought of the Triangle girls, their first days, their last days. Something was happening, like the percolation of hot liquid inside her. Bosses like Harris and Blanck no longer seemed consequential. Women like Fanny and Maude, and now Rose Schneiderman, made sure of that. Someone had once written that, in life, there were the torturers and there were the torturable. She could never go back.

Rosemary gazed back up at the stage, intrigued by the subtle persuasion of Rose Schneiderman, openly chiding the empty patronage and stingy largess of the fur and jeweled crowd. More than one socialite was tugging uncomfortably at a starched collar or tiara.

"We have tried you citizens, we are trying you now, and you have a couple of dollars for the sorrowing mothers, brothers and sisters, by way of a charitable gift. But every time the workers come out in the only way they know to protest against conditions that are unbearable, the strong hand of the law is allowed to press down heavily upon us."

Rosemary felt both of her hands gripped simultaneously. Fanny and Maude, in sisterly solidarity, caught up in the moment. Strong, unafraid women.

New, all so new.

"I can't talk fellowship to you who are gathered here. Too much blood has been spilled. I know from my experience it is up to the working people to save themselves. The only way they can save themselves is by a strong working-class movement."

Rose Schneiderman nodded to the audience, quickly gathered up her notes and strolled off the stage. Behind her, enormous painted scenery floated, fantastical backdrops for the Met's current production of *Aida*. Then the applause began, a single clap, then quickly a second. The whole house erupted. Three thousand souls, ashamed but inspired.

One of the last speakers was Fanny Perkins. She stared unflinchingly out at the faces, and adjusted her notes. Then she lowered them to the lectern; they were unnecessary. She began to extemporaneously speak.

"There's not much I can add to the words of tonight's speakers. The Triangle Fire, only yesterday, but now firmly attached to the long history of labor struggles in this country. Yes, slavery has been abolished, so many years before. But in places like the Triangle factory, and a hundred non-union factories just like it, the practice still exists. What we are fighting for...what we are all fighting for, each in own way, but united by our commonality...is the belief in human decency, in fair labor practices, in humane business models that promote worker safety and well-being over short-term profits. Yes, all of that. And I believe, like all of you believe, that these practices, in the form of laws that protect not just the owners and the stock-holders, but the workers themselves, and by the inclusion and adoption of labor unions, that this is all within our grasp, right now, this moment in history."

The audience again erupted, and stood for several moments. Fanny allowed it to subside, then continued.

"I'll keep this brief. It's been a long evening. On a personal note, I should mention one extraordinary thing. Yesterday, quite by accident, I happened to witness the tragedy at the Triangle factory. You all know how horrific and heartbreaking it was. For the victims, their families, indeed for the entire city. But to actually witness such an event, and read about it in the newspaper, these are two very distinct things. At the height of the fire, I met a woman, a factory employee who had miraculously escaped the flames, through God's intervention, or just blind luck. She's here with us tonight, to share her story. Rosemary, can you please come up here."

Rosemary slowly stood, rooted by surprise. *I can't*, she mouthed up to Fanny, who shook her head, beckoning, insistent. Three thousand heads strained forward to look at her. Maude took her hand, and led her to the stairs. It seemed like an eternity to walk across the stage to the lectern. Finally, she was standing next to Fanny, illuminated by the bright sun of the footlights. She gazed out over the audience, past the empty orchestra pit, then up towards the boxes. Polite applause washed over her.

"Rosemary, we're all so glad to see you here tonight. This is Mrs. Rosemary Rouse, ladies and gentlemen. Up until yesterday, she was employed as a lace maker by the Triangle shirtwaist factory. Today, she's out of a job. Yesterday, she lost a hundred and forty-six of her friends."

Fanny turned, still smiling.

"Rosemary," she prompted.

Rosemary nodded nervously.

"My name is Rosemary Rouse."

"Louder!" a man yelled from the back.

She began again.

"My name is Rosemary Rouse. I'm just a worker. I haven't done anything really worthy of mention. I've always been a worker, ever since I was a little girl. Until yesterday, I worked for Mr. Harris and Mr. Blanck, who kindly employed me at the Triangle making lace. And that's what I did. Twelve hours a day, rain or shine, I made lace, and tried to do a good job for the company. For that I was paid five dollars a week, sometimes less if I was slow, or made a mistake. I haven't got my last week's pay, and might not ever get it. But lots of women, and men, I know, they won't get theirs as well, or even draw another breath, because of that fire. Mr. Harris and Mr. Blanck, they told the managers to lock the doors, all except the one, and the fire pails were all empty, and those cutting bins were only emptied once a week, and that's why that place burned so quick and why so many lost their lives. It was just greed, plain and simple. It was them putting profits before people. That's the way I see it anyways."

The audience erupted. A standing ovation, longer than the rest. Looking down, Rosemary could see Rose Schneiderman clapping along, her bouncing red hair bright as plumage. Maude, standing beside her, gave her a quick kiss on the cheek. She saw Rose turn and kiss her right back, but on the mouth.

Rosemary held up one hand, as she had seen the others do, and the clapping slowed.

"But I've done nothing to be worthy of your applause, Not really. I survived, and that was just luck, like Miss Perkins said. If those boys across the way hadn't come along with that plank, I'd be like all the rest. Dead in the street. Just like all those poor boys and girls who jumped."

Here, she paused. "But I'm glad, all the same, to see that something will be done about this terrible tragedy, that good people are working together on the problem. That the lives of all those workers, some of them children, won't have been wasted. That's my hope anyways. Thank you, good night, and good luck."

Fanny was beaming across at Rose and Maude. The audience had risen again, nearly apoplectic with soldierly unity. The inclusion of Mrs. Rosemary Rouse, survivor, to the evening's program had been a masterstroke.

The labor movement had its newest heroine.

CHAPTER FORTY-THREE

The Cortege

Arthur, ashore after eight days at sea aboard the *White Star Line's RMS Celtic.* Hired off the Liverpool dock, bound for New York as a second-class oiler, despite the lack of a union book. But competent crews were scarce this time of the year, and this was a winter crossing. Arthur was a shipyard man, a first-class mechanic with steam experience. Not like some of them soused-up dockhands lying their arses off just to get a warm berth and a few shillings further down the road. Arthur didn't mind. For eight days, he was stuck down in the engine room. Which, for once, was preferable. Icy needles from the North Atlantic blew right through woolen layers on deck watches. It reddened skin, and there was the constant risk of frostbite. But below, down five echoing flights, in the ship's belly, near the giant fireboxes and the ratcheting pistons, the weather was sub-Saharan.

Celtic was a tired, doughty old ship. Launched in 1901, she had no business this far at sea in early March. But she was built by Harland and Wolfe, like the best always were, and her hull was still stout. On December 10, 1928, she would die, run aground on some Canadian shore, and that would be that. But for now, this crossing, the rivets would hold. The voyage had been uneventful. Two winter tempests, seas like mountains, luckily no icebergs, and three hundred first-class passengers sick in their berths. That, and no radar, or even a wireless. Just the brute navigation of dead reckoning, antiquated sea charts and a silver-haired captain's educated hunches. Sometimes, when the clouds parted, an occasional sun sight, through the mirrors of a sextant held steady by a shivering mate on the bridge wing. But only when the clouds parted. Which was almost never. The rest of the time, they sailed by compass alone. Mostly they got where they were pointed. All in all, a miserable crossing. Finally, they sighted the New York skyline, slowly wended their way up the East River. Finally, the aging *Celtic* was tethered, with no parade or whistles or reporters elbowing closer to spot some famous celebrity, like an exhausted nag at the end of the *White Star's* dock.

AND NOW, CREW PAID off, the ship was done with her ceaseless rolling and pitching. Quickly re-provisioned for the return voyage, an army of longshoremen loaded a river of supplies: fresh water and coal for the bunkers, a ton of lobster tails and stuffed duck and champagne, uncountable leather and brass steamer trunks and even an automobile or two. Whatever else a well-heeled transatlantic pilgrim might decide they could not leave home without.

Arthur stomped down the crew's gangway, not the upper one, where socialites and remittance men and gossip scribblers might congregate, but the lower one, three decks down, where coal-stained shovelers, greasy oilers, and able-bodied seamen, red-faced and bleary from all the midnight dog watches and frozen fusillades that numb the skin, even under layers of good Scottish wool.

He quickly found his land legs, lugging the same bags from when he'd first trudged up the lane towards Juniper Point. Bags full of mechanic's tools, those same engineering books, no longer unintelligible, letters from Rosemary, laboriously read and reread in his bunk between shifts, plus a few raggedy changes of clothes, and of course that same toy locomotive he'd carried since an Aberdeen boyhood.

Where was he? New York, of course, but more precisely, the big ship docks, and even more precisely, *White Star's* brand-new Chelsea Piers, on Fifty-Fourth Street, which had been built to accommodate the newest great ships. *Olympic,* still unfinished, would be sailing soon, by early summer, followed the next year by the mighty, unsinkable *Titanic.* The world was changing. Ships were bigger, and faster. Skyscrapers vied for the title of tallest. But for now, the seven-hundred-foot long pier would shelter the older, slower, smaller liners such as the tender, antiquated, vomit-inducing *Celtic.*

At the divergence of two busy streets, he pondered his choices, his inner compass undecided. Where was Rosemary? Her letters came from a place called Henry St. And the Triangle? He knew that was on the corner of Greene and Washington Place. New York was a matrix of interconnected histories. The ghosts of the Dutch and the English and the Algonkian still haunted the city through its street names. Arthur pulled a dog-eared street map from his pocket. Sitting on a bench that overlooked the river, an unceasing parade of tenders and schooners and tugs with filthy barges in tow, a hundred smoky plumes of coal fires blackening the sky. He unfolded the creases, placed his thumb on Fifty-Fourth St., then his forefinger on Greene St. He mouthed each word, quickly guessed at the distance between. A few miles, give or take a few blocks. Yes, he could easily walk that.

IT BEGAN TO RAIN, HARDER now, but Arthur kept walking, skirting the deepest puddles, chill droplets falling from the brim of his tweed cap.

Closer now, he began to notice fliers pasted upon each lamppost he passed.

They were written in English, in Hebrew, in Italian.

Fellow Workers! Join in a last sad tribute of sympathy and affection for the victims of the Triangle Fire. THE FUNERAL PROCESSION will take place Wednesday, April 15th. at 1 p.m. Watch the newspapers for the line of march.

April Fifteenth. Amazingly, that was today's date. How had he quit his job at Harland and Wolff, learned about the fire, crossed the stormy ocean, and ended up in New York on the precise day that the city was publicly grieving its great and reasonless loss?

He hailed a man on the street.

"Excuse me, sir. Can you tell me where the funeral parade is?"

The man gazed somberly back at him. He was wearing a black armband. He held out his arms, as if to embrace the entire sorrowful universe.

"Why, look man," he pointed, "it's here. It's all around you."

Arthur turned and stared up the street. Thousands of New Yorkers lined the curbs, as far as the eye could see. There was a strange, deathly stillness. No shouts, or murmurs, or the usual huzzahs of an impatient throng, waiting for the clowns and the elephants to pass.

He and the man stood together, bonded by their chance meeting. The silence was unnerving. Arthur, entombed in a racketing, ear-splitting engine room for the last twelve days, could almost hear his own heartbeat.

The man adjusted his scarf, and closely examined Arthur's face.

"Have you lost someone?" he asked.

Arthur shrugged. He stared out across the empty boulevard. A hundred thousand faces stared back.

"I'm not sure," He finally answered the man.

The man seemed to understand. "This procession," he explained, "it's for the unknown workers. The ones that nobody has identified. There's eight, they say. All young women. Nobody to mourn them, nobody to remember their names. Probably came here alone. So, this is what we do. We mourn them all like family."

Arthur daubed the cold rain from his cheeks. He kept staring down the street.

Then, in that dreariest margins of time, the approaching clopping of hooves. It was raining even more heavily now, a thick downpour that fell upon the mourners, who stood like penguins dripping miserably on an icy precipice, those closest to the street toeing the gutters. Some in the back climbed on each other's shoulders, or shimmied up lampposts. Faces peered from apartment windows, aproned shopkeepers stood on their stoops, smoking cigars and watching. There were no umbrellas, or overshoes, or even hats. Just a vast sea of the bare-headed, a sea of black great coats, silk scarves, leather shoes. Everyone at the curb was wearing their Sunday best. It was the largest, saddest, most indelible farewell in the city's long memory.

The cortege was coming closer. Eight undertaker's wagons, one for each unknown, each pulled by six white stallions, carriage nags covered in black netting for the somber occasion. On each side of each hearse, a half-dozen men, their hands reverentially caressing the rough wooden sides of the pine caskets.

Two men marched at the front.

A man spat into the street as they passed. Other men began to spit; great, furious gobs arcing over the cobblestones, merging with the cold rain.

The factory owners passed, Harris and Blanck, stiff-backed and unapologetic.

"If I was them, I wouldn't be showing my face in public," Arthur's companion mumbled.

"MURDERERS!" A woman's shimmering taunt cut through the torrent, soon joined by others. Policemen, some walking, some aloof and aloft on horseback, looked from side to side, glaring with official distain, scanning the crowd for suspicious characters. These same men had been paid to crack the skulls of union organizers.

"JEW BASTARDS!" another man called out.

"FUCKING GREEDY KIKE BASTARDS!" someone else screamed. Which made no sense. Many, mostly girls less than twenty who died in that fire, were Jewish. They were all immigrants. The paradox was nonsensical. Black and white, victim and villain, right and wrong. The public needed familiar contrasts. The people on the sidewalk, yelling those racial slurs, as the cortege of netted horses and grieving factory girls passed, all mired in the primitive abstraction of bigotry.

THE TRIANGLE OWNERS had a reputation for arson. They had burned other shops for money, or lack of it. But nobody had ever died, not till now. The fires that brought the insurance checks were always before the dawn or after midnight. Arson, if deliberate, was nonsensical. The Triangle was a moneymaker, the most successful of all the city's sweatshops. A jewel of modern manufacturing, it had the latest belt-driven machines, and the women were paid more than other garment workers. To work at the Triangle was a step up, like a field hand reporting to the big house. Edison bulbs hung from the ceiling, and enormous windows fronted the busy street below. Sometimes even a random slash of sunlight would warm the women's shoulders as they stitched mountains of cloth into mountains of shirtwaists. The Triangle was a source of pride and steady revenue for its owners, finally, after all those years of financial struggle. But still, the doors *were* locked, for fear of theft. And the fire escape was a rusted relic that creaked and collapsed, spilling twenty girls to their death. When panic overcrowded the single working elevator car, an antiquated cable affair, it fell ninety feet to the stony shaft floor, killing twenty more. Barrels of sewing machine oil ignited into blazing cauldrons.

Anger or shame. It all depended on which side of the pay envelope you were standing.

But Arthur heard none of it. He stood there at the curb, hat in hands, a ginger-haired giant, fresh off a British steamer. Coal dust still inked the creases in his face. He was scanning the marchers intently.

The politics of the moment were one thing. Surely all this anger would grow and coalesce into a true labor movement, something that might change the world. Someday, it would effect repairs to the bleak, soulless, killing machine of industry that ground the very bones of its minders. There would be more Triangle fires. Every day for all of eternity, people would die in harness, at the whim of the bosses, scratching for a living.

But Arthur heard none of that.

Today he was just a worried man.

A man searching for his wife.

CHAPTER FORTY-FOUR

The Photograph

March the 7th, early morning. Charles Crowningshield, sitting at his library desk. The tea half drunk, now cold, a copy of today's *Tribune*, unfolded again to Page Six, open across the polished mahogany. Strikers had walked off the job at the foundry yesterday, slowing business, and evoking interest in the press. But factory concerns were of no concern to him anymore. He shifted his weight and the chair lightly creaked. A nameless house girl quietly dusted a row of books, leather-bound classics, Dickens and Thackeray and Bronte, unread books as virginal as the day they were printed. Charles Richard Crowningshield lacked, to use the kindest expression, intellectual curiosity. He reacted to everything in one of two ways. Either blasé disinterest or mildly agitated. His survival instincts, what someday would be called "fight or flight," were dull and disused. With eighteen million dollars in the bank, who needed instincts?

He rattled the newspaper to the next page, covertly glancing over at the house girl. She was vaguely pretty for an Irish girl. Not yet twenty, she had an attractive face, and even noticeable beneath voluminous layers of starched linen, an attractive turn of figure. But his father, Richard the Elder, always warned of dalliances with servants. Have your fun outside the house, he advised. And preferably far, far away.

Sound advice for the proper post-Victorian man.

That was the primary reason he traveled.

But Emily, of course, had broken it off, months ago. Without one valid reason, just as he had been dismissed from Taft's diplomatic corps. Just a curt note that informed him his services were no longer required.

Charles turned back to the paper. A brief article at the bottom caught his eye. A single paragraph, and a small, grainy photograph, describing some funeral procession in New York City for unknown factory fire victims.

Terrible thing, he said aloud, when he'd first heard about it, then thought nothing more of it. Workers knew the risk when they were hired.

He squinted down at the photograph, reaching for a magnifying glass, the letters CRC entwined on the silver handle. The girl was done with the dusting, now quietly closing the door behind her.

He was alone.

Holding the glass close to the paper, the image grew larger, hazily pixelated.

He bent closer. It was a photograph of a processional. A hundred and twenty thousand mourners, the article explained. Impressive, he thought. And on a workday. The image was of a group of women in the street. They were holding a large banner. It towered above them, and could have been golden letters sewn onto purple silk. The banner announced, in block letters:

LADIES WAIST AND DRESSMAKERS UNION

LOCAL 25

WE MOURN OUR LOSS

Unions.

Charles shuddered. He was done with the company his father had built, but still, in his own home, he employed a staff of over twenty. And at Juniper Point, nearly forty. Imagine if all those servants suddenly decided to organize. Grievances over working conditions and wages, that sort of rubbish. He would be inconvenienced, to say the least.

He stared down at the paper, at that unsmiling rabble of Jewish dressmakers. They were standing in the rain, standing beneath a shuttered storefront window painted with Hebrew lettering.

Bolsheviks!

The word came out of nowhere. He'd once dined with the Romanovs, met Emperor Nicholas the Second and his family. By 1918, they would all be dead, every vestige of the Russian aristocracy killed by violent revolution.

Unions!

He shuddered again.

But still...he peered closer, squinting through the glass. One woman caught his eye, that one on the left, almost out of frame. She looked so familiar. She didn't fit with the others. He adjusted the glass, and kept staring down. The woman stood like a ghost, the way she passively regarded the camera. A distant, melancholy expression in her eyes. Even in the foggy distortion of the newsprint, that much was obvious.

Charles Crowningshield laid the silver magnifier aside, and took a gulp of stale air. The room was warm, perhaps a little too warm, but he gave not a thought to the origins of such a heat. That he was either comfortable or uncomfortable, that was sufficient. Deep in the cellar, a sweat-drenched Irishman named Eddie something-or-other, a dollar-a-day laborer, was stoking dusty shovelfuls of coal through the blazing maw of the furnace trap.

Then it came to him, and he exhaled. Of course. The woman was *that* woman. It was his former nanny. His child's killer, Rosemary Kincaid.

CHAPTER FORTY-FIVE

Beneath a Falling Sky

Rosemary hadn't wanted to march. Or hold a banner skyward. She didn't feel angry, just weary and lost and alone. There were no words. She just wanted to be by herself, hidden in some dark, safe place.

What she wanted was to cry.

But Fanny and Maude and Rose wouldn't let her go to that safe place. These were the times, the important ones, right now, and there was little place for selfish emotions. Of course, they never said those words, but they were meant all the same.

So, she marched.

The size of the outpouring was breathtaking. Thousands. Hundreds of thousands. A million, perhaps. Who could count?

A hard rain was falling.

And she walked. Frances took her arm, and they were joined together for several blocks. But then they became separated. She found herself walking with a group of Jewish women. They were carrying a banner. It identified the union, and what a great loss they had suffered for lack of it. The banner was surely about tomorrow, and all the tomorrows after that. With such a sentiment, and such ferocious dedication, what things wouldn't change?

She kept walking. The stockings inside her high-buttoned shoes were soaked, and her toes were losing feeling.

But still she walked.

On one street corner, the women stopped to rest. They had paused in front of a Hebrew meat market, just as a photographer rushed forward, his tripod clattering. He was from *The New York Times,* he explained. Would they mind posing? Glass negatives took long minutes to form an image. Subjects had to be patient. That is why early portraits are so dire and so pained. Yet they waited, beneath that chill downpour. The world would see.

The flash of the camera lit their faces through the dark mist. A group of immigrant seamstresses, fearlessly holding a banner in the rain.

Finally, they resumed marching. They marched through that downpour. Up ahead, Rosemary heard the dull, iron clopping of horseshoes striking cobbles. It was all so quiet, just the steady falling of the rain, except for the cadenced clopping ahead.

The procession slowed, and then turned a corner. A block more, Washington Square Park, and then they marched a bit more, finally stopping in front of the Asch Building, its ruined top floors, that terrible stench of burned timber and shirtwaist cloth and human beings. On the building's corner, still attached, a sign: *Triangle Shirtwaist Factory.*

The paraders mingled on the sidewalk. Voices in quiet conversation, eyes averted from the great blooded reminders still staining the gutters. The cortege was now officially over, stalled at the foot of the tragedy. Harris and Blanck had slipped away, replaced by a somber congregation, a black sea of mourners beached like a ship after a great storm. Somebody explained that the pine caskets on the wagons were empty. A smaller, second procession was headed in the opposite direction, toward the pauper's graveyard in Brooklyn. A dispute between the organizers and the city had instigated this terrible discrepancy. Even after death, political shenanigans continued.

Out of the corner of her eye, Rosemary imagined she saw movement. It might have been Fanny or Maude or Rose, signaling to her. She turned. Instead, a big man's arms, excitedly waving from the sidewalk. She heard her name, a shout across the rain-soaked cobbles. A man's voice was calling from across that glistened, puddled boulevard. He was wearing a workman's cap, the only man in the crowd not wearing his Sunday best. A man in soiled, rough clothes.

Then this giant, ginger-haired and grinning, gesticulating and weeping, was running towards her.

CHAPTER FORTY-SIX

Revenge

September, 1911. The Ansonia Hotel, at 73d and Broadway, was only seven years old when Charles Crowningshield arrived by car from Pennsylvania Station. He checked in alone at nine-thirty on a Saturday afternoon. The bellman who showed the guest to his suite then accompanied him to the twelfth floor to view the city's first rooftop animal farm. It boasted over five hundred chickens, (morning eggs for the hotel's fourteen hundred rooms and three hundred and twenty suites), ducks, goats, and even a small bear. Crowningshield observed this faux barnyard scene, but yawned and wordlessly walked back to the elevator. Afterwards, the bellman, a small, hunched immigrant with a thick German accent, escorted Crowningshield to the basement, to view the world's largest indoor swimming pool. Offered a pair of woolen bathing trunks and a bathrobe of the softest terrycloth, emblazoned with a stitched monogram, (each guest was treated thusly), a royal blue CRW on the right breast, Ansonia Hotel on the left, he politely refused. He hadn't come all this way to splash around in some mildewed subterranean grotto.

The Ansonia was built by a business acquaintance, William Earle Dodge Stokes, the Phelps-Dodge copper heir, on the site of the razed New York Orphan Asylum. It boasted pneumatic tubes that whisked guest correspondence and lodging invoices from lobby to room in seconds. Each bath had modern sanitary fittings manufactured expressly through exclusive arrangement by the world-famous Crowningshield Bell and Foundry Co, (Charles had negotiated the contract). But never mind all that. Never mind the history, the plumbing, never mind the orphans, or even the new cocktail, recently invented by the hotel's mixologist, now sweeping the country, a heady concoction of tomato juice, lemon, celery, horse radish, and vodka called a Bloody Mary. Never mind it all. Charles Crowningshield had a job to do. He needed to set his knowable world to rights, restore what was rightfully his, take back his life, damnit, if it was the last thing he did. He owed it to his family. He owed it to his children. He owed it to his poor, suffering wife.

THE CITY WAS EMPTY to him now, devoid of company business or State Department duty, devoid of extramarital trysts and the distant perils of discovery. Not that it mattered now. He was free to philander, was Crowningshield, but he'd lost his taste for adultery. A recent letter from Cornelia's psychiatrist had detailed, in the most delicate terms, his wife's further descent into melancholia. Furthermore, a failed suicide attempt, by the stuffing of pillow feathers into her twisted, crazy maw of a mouth, had left her more vegetative than before. Crowningshield had once described the same mouth in a letter, when she was still a Smythe, a slim and alluring ingénue, of *the* Paterson, NJ Smythe's: "Oh, my lips upon your lips," he had gushed, a younger man, hopelessly smitten, "your sweet mystery, your majestic Alibaba's cave of passion fruit."

Now gone, all gone.

HE TOOK THE CAGED LIFT from the basement back to the hotel lobby, attended by a tall, light-skinned carman of dubious heritage, perhaps somewhere in the Caribbean. The carman stared straight ahead, as if meditating on a distant flame. The cage clattered open onto the lobby and Crowningshield strolled toward the street, beneath an autumnal midday glare. The city was still months away from winter. He passed the deskman, who briefly glanced up, noting an important guest, then returned to his dime novel.

As Crowningshield entered the quickened parade of New Yorkers, pedestrianists engaged by some daily occupation, or walking at a slower pace, as if enchanted by the gossamer threads of leisure, any passersby would have barely noticed a well-dressed man in his early fifties. He wore a black serge suit, in the classic Edwardian style. His Brooks Brothers shirt had a high starched collar. On his feet, high-shined leather shoes, on his head a smart derby hat of black beaver fur, banded with silk. They would notice a pale, delicately featured man with a well-trimmed Van Dyke beard with silver flecks, intelligent, hazel eyes, the softest of hands, with recently manicured fingernails. A closer examination would have revealed a vague, unmapped sadness in his expression. In short, to the world, a well-heeled, prosperous-looking stranger, a purposeful gentleman taking his constitutional down the greatest avenue of the greatest city in the world.

GLANCING AT HIS POCKET watch, Crowningshield lengthened his stride. The offices of the Pinkerton National Detective Agency were also located on Broadway, Number 57, but further west, toward the river, the less reputable, business district. Number 57, known simply as The Pinkerton Building, was a forgettable, five-story heap, a nondescript mongrel of uncertain architectural provenance. On the building's front wall was a painted sign. Pinkerton National Detective Agency. Next to that, a large painted eye, with the company's slogan, "We never sleep." The Pinkerton eye was, in fact, the inspiration for the phrase "private eye." Number 57 would be torn down within the year, after a devastating fire raged for several blocks across the neighborhood.

CROWNINGSHIELD WALKED several more blocks. Almost there. He might have been driven to the address by one of the hotel's private chauffeurs, a sole passenger occupying an enormous, high-buffed touring car. But never mind that. He needed time to think. Walking filled his lungs and cleared his head. He had no time for rooftop barnyards nor basement swimming pools. He was here for one reason. It could pass through the head of the pin. Which was to oversee the apprehension and incarceration of Rosemary Kincaid. The woman had been hiding inside his head for the greater part of a year. He was haunted by visions of an employee he'd entrusted, believing in her a moral, upstanding woman, minder of his children, leading them in games and nursery rhymes, tucking them into their beds at night, waking them in the morning. He shuddered at the thought. Trust? Never again!

AT PRECISELY TWO P.m., he was escorted into the office of Samuel Michael Dougherty.

Dougherty was the detective in charge of the manhunt, or rather woman hunt. For nearly six months Crowningshield had seen the man's name on the invoices, describing how his agents had been combing the city for the Irish murderess and escaped inmate Rosemary Kincaid, the conniving nanny who had allowed a powerful industrialist's youngest and dearest son to perish.

Dougherty rose to greet him. Extending a meaty hand, the portly detective noticeably winced.

"Is everything alright, Mr. Dougherty?"

"Fine, fine," Dougherty said brightly. "Be right as rain in a couple days. Nothing to worry about. Took a slug last week. Shootout with the Lennox Hill gang. Probably read about it."

"Oh, I see," Crowningshield said, lowering himself into a leather chair. No, he didn't see. Nor had he read about the Lennox Hill Gang.

With his good arm, the detective shuffled a stack of papers. Crowningshield sat watching him, thinking of his own ordered and gleaming desk back in Chicago. Finally Dougherty found what he was searching for. "Secretary's off today," he explained with an easy lie, handing them across.

"Your invoices, sir, for the last month. I'm sure you'll find everything in order. Had six men on this thing. Quite a time, quite a time, I'll tell you that. No stone unturned."

Crowningshield silently perused the bills. He had a dozen of them already, lining the inside of his office desk drawer. No stone unturned? No dollar unspent, rather. And still no results.

Finally the detective broke the silence. His joweled face was dewy with perspiration, his corpulent chin and cheeks cross-hatched with a thin roseate stitchery, the tell-tale burst blood vessels of a chronic drinker.

"Tell you the truth, sir? They've vanished."

Crowningshield laid the papers down, staring across at him. "Vanished?"

His voice had risen slightly, but not to an unseemly decibel.

Vanished?

Dougherty shrugged. "It's a big city, sir. Sometimes they do. There's evidence they had help."

Crowningshield leaned forward.

They?

"She and the husband," the detective said matter-of-factly. He reached again across his desk for a dirty, well-thumbed report book, began leafing through it.

Squinting down, he found the page, tooted triumphantly. "Right here, it says, a Mr. Arthur Rouse. No warrants, he added a professional aside. In fact, clean as a whistle, although, legally speaking, he *is* aiding and abetting an escaped convict."

Crowningshield said nothing, digesting Dougherty's words. When he finally spoke it came as a question.

"Arthur Rouse, did you say?"

Dougherty nodded. "Positive, sir. Two are traveling together, as husband and wife." He winked, "Incognito, you might say."

Crowningshield stared at him. "He's my employee...*was* my employee. Of course, I'm no longer with the firm, you understand. But I thought...I had every reason to believe, Arthur was still in Ireland. I assigned him to work there. We were under contract with the *White Star Line*, you understand. Still are. I had no idea he'd quit his position."

Dougherty shrugged. "Well, it seems, sir, he's not there anymore. A man goes where his heart goes, now isn't that the truth? You've seen his wife. Even in that mug shot, a handsome-looking woman."

Crowningshield folded back in the chair.

"So now what?"

Dougherty said nothing. He scratched his chin, he scratched an ear, he rubbed his bum arm where the slug and entered, then exited, in the shootout with the Lennox Hill gang. Five men dead, the tabloids had screamed, with only one Pinkerton wounded. A good day for law and order, some wag of a copywriter had added, with just the right amount of editorial punch.

"Well, sir," Dougherty began, "as I mentioned, we believe they had help eluding capture. After that terrible factory fire, there was quite a bit of confusion. A lot of people died, as you yourself know, and some were never identified properly. It was a bad time, a sorry time. But your one, Rosemary Kincaid, everybody thought she died as well."

The detective paused, for added effect.

"But she did, in fact, survive."

Crowningshield slowly nodded. "The photograph," he said softly.

Dougherty was reaching across to another corner of his desk. He tugged a large, holstered revolver towards him. He drew the gun out. It glinted evilly beneath the yellow murk of the Edison bulbs.

"Smith and Wesson," the detective said, smiling broadly, revealing several broken, corn-yellow teeth. "Never leave home without it."

Crowningshield ignored him.

"To reiterate, Mr. Dougherty, what now?"

The detective laid his revolver gently back down, gave the blue steel a light pat. It was a tender gesture for a weapon recently credited with killing at least three desperate men.

"Well, sir," he said, "we're pretty sure it was the labor organizers who helped them."

"Jew communists," Crowningshield muttered.

Dougherty gazed curiously across at him.

"Jewish?" He shrugged again. "Probably. Some anyway. A lot of them in the union movement are. But you also got your Eye-talians, you got your Germans, even got some Irish agitators. Troublemakers and complainers, if you ask me. Like to stir the pot. Strikes, picket lines, shop walkouts, all that fancy speech-making horseshit about the rights of common workers. Fucking communists," he swore, his own eyes bright with the notion. "Damned right they are, the whole lot of em. I myself have busted quite a few heads of *that* bunch."

Crowningshield took a hard breath. The office reeked of stale cigar smoke, of man sweat and farts, the rank effluvia of delicatessen salami and gun oil. He wanted suddenly to pay his bill, escape these dingy four walls, be done with this cloddish, yammering gumshoe. He wanted to inhale some good, clean oxygen just outside this ancient relic of a building, walk back to the hotel and bask in the familiar aromas of the good life.

Instead he said, slowly and with as much authority as he could manage, "This...woman...must...be...returned...to...justice, Mr. Dougherty."

Dougherty paused a beat, the briefest flash of anger in his eyes. He licked his lips, an oddly pornographic gesture. He laid one baleful and worldly eye upon this man. To another man he might have bellowed, he might have slapped, he even have shot him dead, but instead his reply came a respectful notch below all of these. Such was the nature of the business. To placate the childlike mewing of the wealthy and powerful, weak men who came to him with their insipid, but highly lucrative problems. Cheating wives, labor unrest, larcenous business partners, runaway daughters, rascally sons. Every insolvable conundrum of the civilized world eventually funneled their way down to Pinkerton's National Detective Agency.

We never sleep, the eye on the wall promised.

"Impossible, sir," Dougherty replied.

Crowningshield blinked. *Impossible!* It was a word rarely, if ever, spoken in his presence.

"Excuse me?"

Dougherty picked up the revolver again, absently rolling the barrel between two pudgy fingers.

"Well, sir, to begin with, the problem is...we have on good authority they're in the Kitchen."

Crowningshield blinked again.

"Where? The kitchen, did you say?"

Dougherty smiled. "Hell's Kitchen, sir. That's what they call it. A bad place. Run by gangs of thieves and murderers and rapists. Hard men, many of them Irish, I might add, although it pains me to say it, coming from the old sod myself.

"Where, exactly, is the Kitchen? "Crowningshield asked the detective, as if to an inept cartographer.

Dougherty shrugged. "Well, not to put too fine a point on it, because the borders tend to shift from day to day, but you could draw a rough square around 4th Street, to the south, 59th Street to the north, then add in Eighth Avenue, which borders on the east. Finally, if you walked straight into the

Hudson River, to the west, that just about covers it. A pretty big area, sir, all in all. Might as well be trying to catch a fucking squirrel in Central Park."

Crowningshield's eyes narrowed. "So, if we know where they are, why not go in there, Mr. Dougherty? Beat the bush until they're apprehended. Aren't the police involved? She's a wanted fugitive from justice, after all."

Dougherty nodded. "Couldn't agree with you more. But nobody goes in the Kitchen. *Nobody.* No cop, or Pinkerton, or god-fearing white man. Nobody goes in the Kitchen. Especially the Pinkertons." He smiled, adding, "Especially an *Irish* Pinkerton.

"Oh? Why is that, Mr. Dougherty?"

The detective laid his gun back on the desk. "It's the gangs, Mr. Crowningshield. Like I said, especially the Irish. Vicious trash. Opium addicts, sons of whores, all crazy as bedbugs. And they would surely slit your throat as look at you. They're a law unto themselves, sir, down there in the Kitchen. If your runaway nanny or your man Rouse have gotten themselves mixed up with those criminal knockabouts, they're either dead or under their protection and there's nothing we can do about it. Not with an army of coppers, or sitting in an office on Broadway." He paused, then continued in a softer voice, "My suggestion, sir, respectfully, leave New York and go back to your fine life in Chicago. Try to forget about this whole sorry business."

Crowningshield said nothing. He sat with his hands folded in his lap, docile, eyes down, simply listening as Dougherty droned on. "I'm truly sorry for your loss, sir, for your family's loss, for the loss of your son. But spending all this money, paying us dearly to chase down ghosts, that won't bring him back, sir, won't fix the hole in your life, and certainly won't change a damned thing that has happened in the past."

Crowningshield finally looked up, across at this big, rough, loud-mouth across from him. His eyes had misted. Dougherty's words had touched him. Still, he kept pushing.

"But what about the police? Surely, they won't allow a wanted felon to walk free."

Dougherty shook his head. "Not a damned thing, sir. The police have better things to do than chase them two. Even if there was a warrant, which there isn't. Rosemary Kincaid, in the eyes of the State of New York, sir, or anyone else, is as good as dead. *Corpus delecti*. She died in that fire, and that's that."

Crowningshield sighed. "I understand, Mr. Dougherty. I thank you for your candor."

The detective rubbed his hands and stood up. "Good, good," he said, then yanked open a desk drawer, pulling out a bottle, half full, of brown elixir.

"Now, how about a drink, sir? A wee dram of Mr. Jameson's finest, to bring some color to your cheeks."

NINE P.M. CROWNINGSHIELD, exhausted from the afternoon, ordered room service. He was strangely hungry, nearly famished. Twenty minutes later, a light tap on the door. A man entered pushing a kitchen trolley, laden with a gleaming collection of silver, domed lids, each covering a large dinner plate. An assortment of aromas filled the room, as each lid was lifted by the attendant, resplendent in a white starched jacket, for his approval. Alongside the plates, a large glass. His evening's cocktail, the ghoulishly named, newly invented Bloody Mary. It was all the rage in Manhattan. Crowningshield fingered the celery stalk. Curious, he took a sip.

The meal was meant to be served in multiple courses, but his came in a heat-saving rush from the kitchen to the lift to his suite, hurrying down a carpeted corridor. Raw oysters and assorted hors d'oeuvre, followed by consommé Olga (a veal stock soup flavored with sturgeon marrow). Next was a lightly poached Atlantic salmon topped with a rich mousseline sauce. For the fourth and fifth courses, filet mignon Lili, sauté of chicken Lyonnaise, lamb with mint sauce, roast duckling with applesauce and sirloin of beef with chateau potatoes. The attendant waited off to one side, hurrying forward to silently lift each successive lid as Crowningshield signaled, almost unperceptively, he was finished with the last. By the end of the meal, and the large glass of vodka and tomato juice, a warm glow had supplanted the chill shroud of abject helplessness the Pinkerton man had lain over him. As the attendant wheeled the trolley from the suite, (not a single word had passed between them), Crowningshield stood up, walked from the sitting room to the bedroom, and lowered himself into a soft Louis 15th armchair, upholstered in burgundy silk. Next to the chair was a small mahogany side table, ornate with excised abalone marquetry of plumed birds and exotic flowers. On the table lay a leather satchel, held shut by brass latches. He reached for the satchel, undid the latches, and pulled from it a voluminous sheaf of papers, handwritten notes, all held together with ingenious metal clips. The papers were divided into two sections. On the first, a heading, the words *Background Material,* then a name, *Rosemary Kincaid.* On the next, the same, then the name of a second, *Arthur Rouse.* He was holding in his hand the life and times of the two wanted and, as far as the law was concerned, unremarkable fugitives. He fingered each dossier, hefting its weight, Someone, Dougherty, but probably someone further down the chain, had gone to a great deal of effort in compiling the enclosed information. Dougherty had handed him the satchel as he was leaving.

"Read what's inside," he'd suggested, but the words sounded more like a demand, "before you do anything further."

Just as Crowningshield opened his mouth to reply, the phone rang. Dougherty raised his good arm for silence. The last time he saw the detective, the big man with the fresh bullet wound was leaning in, buttocks draped over his cluttered desk, discussing the particulars of a new case, his loud Irish brogue peppered with American expletives.

CROWNINGSHIELD SAT beneath the dim yellow dusk of the shaded Edison lights in his private suite at the Ansonia, miles, he felt, from the clamor and din of the Broadway traffic below, His children were far away, in Chicago, watched over by a new nanny, an older British woman with impeccable references. Cornelia would be unconscious in her spacious bedroom at the asylum, dreamlessly bobbing atop a pharmacological sea. The big house on Juniper Point had remained empty all that summer, the furniture sleeping beneath cotton sheets, untouchable as ghosts, moonlit as snow-covered Alpines. The astringent aromatics of mothballs strewn by parlor maids as they'd departed for the dismal train ride to New York still hovered in the dark gloaming of the unforgiven empty. On the second floor, in the playroom, a row of juvenile books lined one entire shelf, his lost boy's abandoned library. On the first floor, in the parlor, a small, silver bell, on a serving table beside her chair, with the initials, CWC, silent and unrung within recent memory.

Crowningshield began to read. Occasionally he would pause, pour a dram from a cut glass decanter, take a sip of port wine, then continue reading. By midnight, or perhaps a bit later, he was finished. Each page of each dossier carefully stacked, in order, now occupied opposite sides of the table. He sat awhile, sipping quietly. Then, after a brief, indeterminate while, he carefully returned the papers to the leather satchel. Finally he stood up, opened his gentleman's traveling wardrobe, and began dressing for bed.

CHAPTER FORTY-SEVEN

A Knock at the Door

May, 1912. Hell's Kitchen.

Husband. **She still loved saying the word. It meant protection, emotional safety, and the power of their conjoined strengths. She held such a deep, abiding affection for him it sometimes took her breath away.**

Rosemary, as usual, woke to her baby's strident howl. Wet, hungry, usually both. But never cold. Arthur, up with the larks, hours before the dawn, always stoked the coals before he left for work. And then a long commute, across the river, two street cars and an elevated train ride away, to a job building trolley cars in Weehawken.

Never mind their windowless tenement flat. It was old, and dark, and drafty, and smelled of boiled cabbage from the kitchens above. Never mind the poverty, or the bickering of other husbands and wives noisily and often violently fallen out of love. Never mind the constant worry over rent, or keeping meat and bread on the table or coal in the stove. Never mind the unceasing din of motorcars and construction and conflicts just past their door. Never mind the gangs, Irish madmen who killed one another for a single coin, or imagined slight, or the capricious invention of territory.

Never mind all that.

She and Arthur and Patrick, now a chubby, bubbly, wobbly one-year-old. That was all that mattered. Safe and secure and irrevocably together. That was all that mattered.

Family. Her second favorite word.

She padded, barefoot, to Patrick's makeshift crib, a large wicker basket that once held bread loaves, and lifted him out. His demanding howl slowed, then ceased entirely, replaced by noisy smacking as she lowered the bodice of her nightdress to his hungry mouth.

He fell back to sleep.

The day could start now.

JUST BEFORE NOON THERE was a knock on the door. Three insistent raps. Rosemary paused, perched in an ancient rocking chair by the stove. A drowsing Patrick, sated by her engorged bosom, lay across her shoulder like a flour sack. A knock on the door, in the middle of the day, rarely brought good news. The landlady, in broken English, impatiently demanding rent. Or perhaps the milk man, looking for his weekly two bits. Or a homeless beggar, drunkenly weaving with his palm out. She still feared the Pinkertons, the private dicks who haunted her dreams, the blue and brass thuggery of the New York City police. In another life, it was her mother answering the knock of the parish priest, beginning a tribunal between rapists and their apologists. She preferred to imagine, after the burned factory, and all those unidentified, that no one was looking for a dead woman.

But still.

Three more raps, then a woman's muffled voice.

"Rosemary? Rosemary Kincaid?"

She held on tighter to Patrick, uncertain and afraid.

"It's Frances Crowningshield. We've met. Would you mind opening the door?"

"It's Mrs. Rouse now," Rosemary called softly toward the scarred and cracked door. The gas jet behind made a low, hissing sound, like a snake, her face polished bright by a crack of coal flame. The woman behind the door fell silent, as if pondering this piece of information.

Rosemary waited.

"I'd really like to talk to you," the voice said. A pause, then, "Please."

Rosemary slowly stood, shifting Patrick's tiny bulk in her arms. Resigned now to the knock, to inquisitions from the outside, walking a few steps, she carefully drew the latch. The door swung open. Outside, a cloudless sky, causing her to blink into the brilliant midday sun over the woman's shoulder. She rarely left the flat. They had escaped to this dark place, to the criminal jungle of the Kitchen, where fugitives could vanish, but just barely. With the gangs, or the threat of prosecution, it was always safer in confinement.

Frances Crowningshield peered into the murky interior, recognizing Rosemary's familiar silhouette. It was the nanny of her brother's children. But Rosemary's face, no longer a young woman's, now worn from troubles. Here and there, amidst a conflagration of red hair, a faint memory of youth lingered. Here and there fluttered an untethered silver strand. In the last year, she'd aged ten.

"May I come in, Mrs. Rouse?" Frances asked.

Rosemary silently nodded, holding the door open.

"Call me Rosemary," she allowed, then a slight smile. "Like Arthur always says, 'Mrs. Rouse was me mum's name.'"

Frances stamped the sidewalk dust from her shoes, shivered as she entered the dimly lit flat. Glancing around the narrow kitchen, she took in the tiny dining table, its checkered oilcloth cover. She noticed the cracked plaster, triangles and meanders of random chunks broken loose, leaving flecks of chalky lath behind. There, an ancient rocking chair by the stove, and the only piece of art on the wall, a dime-store souvenir of a tawdry shamrock field beneath an impossibly golden sky. Down the hall, through an open door, a neatly made marriage bed, sagged to the middle, an old quilted coverlet, with a small golden crucifix hammered into the wall. She turned back to Rosemary, the chubby, cherubic Patrick now fallen back to sleep, limp in his mother's arms.

"Would you like a cup of tea?" Rosemary inquired, smiling down at her son, explaining, "He does this all day long, most of the night as well. Like he can't make up his mind. Can't get a bit of sleep myself. Thank heaven for my husband. He takes over nights sometimes. But I really hate to wake him. Mostly."

She smiled again. Husband. There, the word she loved best of all.

"Tea would be lovely," Frances said, nodding toward Rosemary's swollen belly. "Lovely baby. And another on the way, I'd guess. I'd say you're due around August. Pregnancy in the heat of summer can be trying."

Rosemary stood there, stroking Patrick's downy skull. "Oh, I don't mind. I was lucky with him. He was a May baby. No problems whatsoever. Such a good little man."

Frances met her gaze. Both women, stiffly standing, anxious to get on with it.

"I'm so happy for you," Frances finally offered. "Motherhood is a gift."

Rosemary was bending to carefully lay Patrick back into his bread basket. Frances noticed his tiny pillow, an intricate lace weave from an artisan's practiced hand.

Rosemary turned back to her. "He was about the only good thing about last year. Him and my Arthur."

"Tell me all about *that*," Frances prompted, adding, "if you don't mind. Arthur...he was the plumber, am I right?" She watched as Rosemary lay teabags into two cracked cups, then walked to the stove. She lifted up an old copper kettle, releasing a waft of steam from its dented spout.

Rosemary ignored her question until they had both sat, regarding one another across the red-checked cloth.

Rosemary took a sip. "Arthur was always, I dunno...he just seemed...perfect for me. He's quiet, reserved like. I can be kind of bossy."

Frances leaned in. "But it must have been difficult. That summer. I mean, domestics are discouraged from...."

Rosemary nodded grimly. "No good word for it, Mrs. Crowningshield. I was sacked. Without reference. And then...."

Her eyes were suddenly moist.

Frances reached across to pat her hand. "I know...I know. But it wasn't your fault. It was never your fault. John was a very inquisitive little boy. He was an explorer. He had a habit of wandering off by himself."

Rosemary daubed her eyes with a corner of her sleeve, but said nothing. She took another sip.

"So, Miss Crowningshield, what exactly did you want to speak with me about?"

Frances laid her cup down. "It's Mrs. Little, actually. I married Frank several years ago. He's a scientist, a doctor like myself. He...we... both teach at the marine biological laboratory, in Woods Hole."

Rosemary stared at her. "You're a doctor?"

Frances nodded. "I have my degree, from the University of Chicago. But I've never practiced. My family was a tad, what's the word? Old fashioned...about such things. But I really do enjoy my work at the laboratory." She smiled. "All those eager young faces, sponges for knowledge."

Rosemary took a final sip, laid her cup down, waiting.

When Frances spoke again, her own eyes had grown moist.

"Surely, you know about the *Titanic?*"

Rosemary glanced up. "Unsinkable, I heard."

"That's what they said," Francis said.

Rosemary retrieved the cups and walked to the sink.

"Arthur said it was bad rivets or something," she said over her shoulder.

Frances fell silent, then said quietly, "My brother was on that ship."

Rosemary shivered. A dark thought fluttered in. A fear, not so very distant. Arthur was supposed to have been aboard as well. To mind the plumbing on a maiden voyage. She turned, wiping her hands.

"I am so very sorry, Mrs. Little. But tell me, which brother was it?"

Frances reached into her handbag for a handkerchief. "Why, Charles, of course. Richard couldn't take time off from the business, so Charles, who really had no job anymore, volunteered to represent the company. I mean, the *White Star* people had gone to a lot of trouble to arrange things. It was a very important event. The biggest, the fastest, the poshest. All of that. And so, he went." She looked up, and Rosemary saw the tears in her eyes. "Which was right," Frances hurried on, "don't you see. Everyone knew how much he enjoyed an adventure."

She snorted into the handkerchief.

Rosemary reached across to pat her hand. "We never buy the newspaper. I know they printed the names. But we never thought it would be him, not Mr. Crowningshield. Arthur was supposed to be onboard as well, for her first time across. But then..."

Frances caught her meaning. "I know. The fire. Such a terrible tragedy. Senseless. That explains why Arthur left his job so suddenly, to come to New York."

Rosemary nodded. "It was for me. He had to know that I was safe. That's why he came back."

Frances tried a smile, but it was a taut grimace. "Such a good man, your Arthur. A good husband."

Rosemary folded her hands in front of her. "And Mrs. Crowningshield...was she aboard as well?"

Frances shook her head. "Cornelia, I'm afraid, is still a very ill woman. She *has* been home, of course, for brief periods, but she still requires constant hospitalization. She knows nothing of the sinking, or my brother's death. That would be simply too much."

"I'm so sorry to hear that," Rosemary offered quietly. "In all truth, I hold no animosity towards your family. And feel no satisfaction at their present circumstances."

Frances nodded. "I know that, Rosemary. There is really little anyone can do to help either one of them now. Which leads me to the reason why I'm come to see you today. Tell me, Rosemary, and please answer me truthfully. Are you content here? In the city? You and Arthur, are you really content?" She glanced around the kitchen again; the cracked plaster, the chipped cups, the old rocking chair.

Rosemary shook her head. "Oh, no, Ma'am. It's not like that. It's really not that bad. Arthur has a good job. It's a long way to travel, I know. Sometimes he doesn't get home until past seven. But we get by."

Frances took this in. "I understand what you're saying, Rosemary, but what about Patrick? And your next little one. Do you really want them growing up in a dirty city with such terrible crime all around you? I've read about the gangs here that run things here. Hardly an ideal environment for young children."

Rosemary shrugged. "The gangs don't bother us. Arthur wouldn't let them. But we really have no choice, Mrs. Little. Not until Arthur can start his own business. This is just where we are for the moment." She smiled, adding brightly, "Besides...we have each other."

Frances leaned closer. "Rosemary, there's something you should know."

Rosemary stiffened. "I'm listening."

Frances glanced up towards the ceiling, daubing away a lingering tear. "Well, to begin with, you know my brother hired men, detectives, to try and locate you after the fire."

Rosemary nodded. "I know."

Frances continued. "And he wanted you back in prison, and spent quite a bit of time and money to see that happen."

Rosemary shrugged. "I knew that as well. But not about the money. I'm sure hiring detectives can't be inexpensive."

"He was extremely distraught," Frances continued, "I don't think he was thinking it all through. But, nevertheless…"

"I'm truly sorry for what happened to John," Rosemary said. "He was such a good boy. I meant him no harm."

Frances quickly nodded. "Of course. It was an accident. A terrible, unforeseen accident."

Rosemary fell silent. Only the low hiss of the gas jet, the dense heat wafting from the coal stove, the distant murmur of a busy thoroughfare just beyond the latched door.

Frances sighed.

"I should explain. After my brother's death at sea, when they were certain he was gone, I had to travel to Chicago. It was up to me to manage his affairs. I had to care for his children, release the servants, close up his house, pay his bills. One of the last things I did was to go through the contents of his office. I discovered something very peculiar, in among his correspondence, invoices from the detective agency, letters to important people. What I found has to do with you and your husband, Rosemary, and may explain why, in the weeks before he set sail on the *Titanic,* he changed his mind about you."

Patrick began to stir, his little arms preparing to pinwheel again with hungry agitation. Rosemary again lifted her blouse, as she did a dozen times a day.

"I'm sorry," she said. "Do you mind?"

Frances smiled. "Of course not. I'm a doctor, after all."

After Patrick had fallen back to sleep, Rosemary stood and slid him again into his bread basket, tucking his arms, smoothing the coverlet. She turned to Frances. "So tell me, Mrs. Little, what was it you found, and what does it have to do with us?"

Frances wordlessly reached into her handbag. She slid out a small leather satchel, then slowly handed it across.

"These papers inside," Frances explained, "were given to my brother by the Pinkertons, to conclude their investigation. Inside, you'll find your entire life histories, both you and your husband. I sat down at Charles's desk and read the entire report. It took me several hours, but I read every word. It's extremely personal, Rosemary. I learned about how you were sent to the Dublin work house, then having your baby taken away, at such a young age. I learned about your husband's tragedy as well. Please forgive me for reading it."

Rosemary placed the satchel, unopened, on the table, then asked, "Why is this important?"

Frances paused, gathering her thoughts. The memories of her previous winter, the hole in her family growing larger, were a burden still not done.

"I think having this information changed my brother," she continued. "I believe it softened his heart towards the both of you. It made him realize that tragedy and sorrow were not his alone. Of course he lost a child, but you and Arthur each lost your children as well. And aren't we all just human beings coping with life's loss? Knowing this not only opened Charles's eyes. I believe it opened his soul. Knowing this made it impossible for him to continue with his vengeful obsession."

She fell silent, her lips a thin line, then continued. "My brother sent me a couple of letters last winter. There was something about the tone of his words. They were different, kinder. He talked about his children. He talked about Cornelia. He talked about getting back to Juniper Point in the spring. He was excited about traveling again, his upcoming trip to England to board the *Titanic* on her maiden voyage. Imagine, the biggest, fastest, grandest ship on the ocean. But not one word about you, or revenge. I should have understood. Something had changed."

Francis smiled. "I'm just grateful that you and your husband are safe and together again."

"Thank you, Mrs. Little," Rosemary said quietly. "I appreciate you sharing all of this with me." She stared down at the satchel, which lay there like a small, dead animal. She might never open it.

Frances brightened. "Now, to change the subject. I have a little proposition for the two of you. It could be a wonderful opportunity, and I want you to talk it over with your husband tonight. And then you can decide."

Rosemary nodded. Then, for the next twenty minutes, as Patrick slept, oblivious to the machinations swirling around his untroubled world, she merely listened.

CHAPTER FORTY-EIGHT

A Decision

Arthur returned that night from work, stamping his shoes on the granite stoop, as he always did, then sat down to supper. It was a familiar ritual. Beef stew perhaps, a loaf of freshly baked white bread, a plate of butter, sometimes a baked potato, fewer times a small cut of meat, if there was enough grocery money in the jar. Rosemary sat across the table, and watched her husband eat. Tonight, unusual for Patrick, the one-year-old was still awake. He too silently watched his father. Finally, Arthur laid his napkin aside, took a sip of black Irish tea. He might have preferred a spot of whiskey in the cup. Work had been hard today, a man had been injured, but there was none. Besides, his wife disapproved, and he loved his wife. He gazed expectantly across the table. Rosemary had said little since he'd returned.

Finally, she spoke, nervously smoothing the tablecloth with her palm.

"We had a visitor today."

"Oh?"

"Frances Crowningshield," she explained. "Mr. Crowningshield's sister. She's married to Mr. Little now. She's a medical doctor, she told me. But she teaches at the science laboratory."

Arthur nodded. "I remember her. But I did not know that she was a doctor. Must be a very smart woman."

Rosemary gazed across at her husband. There were dark rings beneath her eyes, from sleep deprivation, from anxiety, from the daily strain of a life imprisoned mostly inside this bleak tenement flat. She parted the soft hairs on Patrick's head with her fingertips.

"She has a proposition for us, Arthur. I told her I would talk it over with you."

Arthur regarded her carefully.

"And what would that be?"

"She wants us to move back to Juniper Point," Rosemary said, as if that was the easiest thing to explain. She hurried on. "But not like it was before. She talked about her brother, and him drowning out at sea. I pretended not to know, pretended to be surprised when she told me. I didn't want her to think we had stony hearts by not sending our condolences."

Arthur reached in his pocket for his briar pipe, a habit he'd picked up at the shipyard. He struck a wooden safety match on his rough corduroys, slowly puffed it into life. This always bought him time to think. He shrugged, then leaned forward, pointing the briar like a scepter.

"Wife," he asked, with eyebrows arched, "why would you go back to *that* place, after what that family put you through?"

Rosemary inhaled. "I dunno, Arthur. The way she explained it, it could be very good for us, for our family. I mean, there was another stabbing today on the block. The gangs are getting worse."

Arthur shook his head. "Ah, they never bother us. That's just between criminals, not the ones minding their own business."

Rosemary stared back at him, then persisted. "But when Patrick gets older. And then the baby. I'm afraid sometimes."

Arthur tamped the pipe's ashes into his teacup. "We'll be long gone of this place, Rose. Soon. When I get my own business started. We could maybe move across the river, live in the countryside."

Rosemary bit her lip. "Perhaps."

Arthur stared back at her. "So, what is this proposition? You can't go back to being a nanny, not with a babe on the breast and another on the way. And what would I do for work in that wee village?"

Rosemary gazed across at him. "There's another thing. We would have our own place, Arthur. A nice new house they built last year for the gardener. But he moved away to take care of his sick mother. They won't be hiring anyone new, Mrs. Little said. She said the house would be all ours. Really ours. She would write up a proper deed and all. Isn't that grand?"

Arthur snorted, incredulous. "You're saying she would just *give* us a house? Free and clear?"

Rosemary nodded. "And there's a job waiting for you, a good job at the science lab, taking care of all the buildings and machinery and such. You could walk to work again. No more train rides, and late dinners."

Arthur rubbed his stubbled chin. "And what, exactly, would you do?"

She smiled. "Well, that's easy, Arthur. I'd be a mother. I'd be your wife. I'd cook, and clean, and mind the house. Our house."

He shook his head. "There's got to be a catch. People like the Crowningshields don't just give houses away. Not to the hired help."

Rosemary peeked down. Patrick was beginning to rouse back to life. She hurried on, probing for a seam of persuasion.

"I don't think she sees it that way. With her brother gone, and Mrs. Crowningshield living in an asylum, I think she wants to do the right thing, do some good for the world. That big house, its legally hers now to do what she likes. The other brother has no use for it. He owns a much grander house, a castle even. Mrs. Little told me she wants to turn the place into a kind of orphanage, a nice, decent home for poor children to come and live. It could be very nice, don't you think? To see Juniper Point become a place of hope for those with nothing."

Arthur smiled at his wife's enthusiasm, at the idea of some joy coming their way. If it were all true, that is. He reached across the table for her hand.

"Rosemary," he began, searching his weary brain for exactly the right words. "We have to be careful. People like the Crowningshields...to them life is a game. What they say, or promise, today, might not be true tomorrow."

Across the scarred table, Rosemary listened, carefully mapping the contours of her husband's face. His was a face she would recognize even if she were struck blind. They were married. Husband and wives, the ones who stayed together through all of it, made decisions together. If they had lived a thousand years ago, in a land without borders, when what is now Ireland and what is now Scotland encompassed one vast Celtic empire, Rosemary's womanhood would have afforded her certain unalienable rights. She could own land, without the permission of her husband. She could go to court, without the permission of her husband. If their marriage was a disagreeable union, a woman could easily sue for divorce, which consisted of merely abandoning their nuptial lodgings, free to marry another man. In battle they were fierce and unrelenting, according to the Roman historian Ammianus Marcellinus, who observed:

"A whole band of foreigners will be unable to cope with one Celt in a fight; if he calls in his wife, stronger than he by far and with flashing eyes; least of all

when she swells her neck and gnashes her teeth, and poising her huge white arms, she begins to rain blows mingled with kicks, like shots discharged by the twisted cords of a catapult."

Rosemary said nothing more. She shifted Patrick, then bent to retrieve the leather satchel by her feet, which she placed on the table. Wordlessly, with one free hand, careful to not disturb her sleeping son, she reached deep, passing over the thick dossiers the Pinkertons had created, and retrieved a single item, which she slid across to Arthur.

He stared down at the object, a small envelope, then back at her.

Finally she spoke, a taut, hoarse command. "Husband, we have to leave. Not tonight, maybe not tomorrow, but soon. There'll be no arguing about this." She nodded toward the envelope.

"Open it."

Inside was a telegram, addressed to Mr. Charles Crowningshield, Chicago, Illinois. Its delivery date was April the sixth, 1912.

Since telegraphy companies charged by the word, senders tended toward the succinct, and wasted little in the telling. This one was no different.

Arthur read each word laboriously. Then he read them a second time. Rosemary watched his lips moving as he slowly deciphered the letters printed on the paper.

Sir, it began, *We notify you the following. Stop. Arthur Rouse, mechanic, accidentally, repeat, accidentally, located due to investigations different suspect. Stop. Employed Lummus Steam Co. Streetcar Manufactory Newark, New Jersey. Stop. Employer indicates Rouse residence 1126 West 39th Street, 1st Floor, New York City. Stop. Believe wife same address. Stop. Per our conversation recommend alternate agency to apprehend. Stop. Pinkerton policy operations in Kitchen district untenable. Stop. Please advise. Stop. Good luck.*

George Dougherty, Chief Detective, Pinkerton Agency, New York, NY

Arthur laid the telegram back down on the table. He creased the flimsy paper carefully, sliding it back into its envelope. Without a word, he stood up from the table, crossed the room to the coal stove. Cracking a small, iron door, he tossed the envelope into the bright flames, watching it quickly curl to orange char. Rosemary averted her eyes. For the rest of her life, she would remain uncomfortable around fire. Arthur returned to the table, sat slowly back down.

Finally he spoke, "Well, that's that," he said, quietly adding, "I know he's gone, killed by that monster ship, but this was bound to happen. He probably never even read it. I'm guessing the *Titanic* was well on his way to New York. But all the same...."

Here he paused, imagining Mr. Crowningshield, his old employer, for whom he held no great animus, a great man on a sea cruise, now certainly traveling alone, bereft of his lost love, the impossibly beautiful Emily Smythe, traveling as a guest of the great *White Star Line*. He would be excited to be moving again, him of the youthful, wandering spirit. Excited with thoughts of sailing aboard the world's newest and greatest ocean liner. The biggest, the poshest, the fastest. All the superlatives in the dictionary could never do that ship justice. Her Majesty's Royal Mail Ship *Titanic*. Unsinkable. To be included in such an historical moment, what could be a greater honor?

Rosemary completed his sentence. "But we wouldn't want the world knowing our business."

Arthur nodded toward the stove. "Exactly. And *she* gave you that telegram?"

"Yes," Rosemary said. "Mrs. Little discovered it among Mr. Crowningshield's papers, and thought we should know. Otherwise she never would have come here. She never would have found us." She hurried on, her pale face flushed, a kind of joyful madness come to her eyes.

"Don't you see, Arthur? It's a sign. It's St. Rita, looking after us. Don't you see? It's...a miracle."

She waited a beat, then continued ominously, "I won't stay here, Arthur. I'll leave by myself, take our son, even if you won't. I'm sorry, but there it is."

Arthur stuck his unlit pipe in his mouth. Rosemary's piety and devotion were endearing, even to a nonbeliever. The cruelty of the River Dee had surely made him one. But still...his wife was the strongest person he knew. Her last words were the closest to non-negotiable she had ever spoken.

"Alright, Rosemary," he finally said. "Agreed. I'll leave my job and we'll move to your wee village by the sea. Take up Mrs. Crowningshield on her offer. We'll give it a go. Begin a whole new life. If that's what you want."

"That's what I want," Rosemary prayed softly.

Arthur waggled his pipe back at her, smiling coyly at his wife.

"And no more silver bells from the Missus?"

Rosemary carefully peered into her husband's eyes, then down at Patrick, awake again, the cupid's bow of his tiny mouth an expectant frown, the spread of his tiny fingers reaching for her primly buttoned waist shirt.

"No more silver bells," she agreed.

It was a fierce promise.

PART FOUR

The Book

THE LIBRARY

Ana Liebling stood behind a gracefully carved oak lectern, listening as a cheerful, elderly woman introduced her.

"Tonight's speaker," the woman gushed, "we, the Friends of the Woods Hole Library, are pleased to present Ana Liebling, the author of a brand-new book, *Crowningshield: An American Story*. There are plenty of signed copies for sale in the back," she said, adding with a twinkle, "We *all* must support the arts."

The woman nodded toward a stack of books arranged on a low table at the rear of the room.

About twenty-five people, mostly elderly, were sitting in rows of uncomfortable-looking chairs. They politely clapped. Ana thanked the woman, she thanked the library, and she thanked them all for coming out tonight on such a rainy night to attend her reading. Oh, yes, she added, dutifully praising the largess of the Friends of Woods Hole Library, for the coffee and cookies. The audience laughed and turned to wave at the two silver-haired women tending a large coffee urn and paper plates of brownies and cookies. Ana smiled at this folksy gesture. Small town libraries were fading repositories for civil decorum and literary appreciation in an increasingly detached and digitized world.

Ana glanced down. Her notes, written, in no specific order, scribbled on file cards, and a copy of the book, sprouting tendrils of yellow Post-its marking certain pages and passages.

Her hands were shaking imperceptibly, and she laid them firmly onto the lectern.

Ana took a breath; nerved up, jangly, her heart was racing. She'd never written a book before, and nobody, much less a public library, had ever asked her to speak before.

"This," she quietly began, "really wasn't my idea. My original subject was about a fairly well-known woman, a kind of celebrity in these parts anyway. Anyone who's ever walked by the stone bell tower on Eel Pond, or the Marine Biological Laboratory, would know immediately who I was referring to. I could have easily written about Frances Crowningshield Little. Then I happened to meet Violet McVicar, an amazing woman in her own right, at the museum just next door. She completely changed my direction, such as it was, and the idea for *An American Story* was born. I'm a newspaper writer, or used to be. I wrote about finance. I had no idea how to put together a book. I owe my thanks to so many people along the way who did know how. My editor, Laurie Chang, at Harcourt Brace, my wonderful agent, Denise Gifford. So many people saw this story as important. But to Violet I am the most indebted."

A few people in the audience nodded appreciatively. A few were holding copies of the book in their laps, its cover image, the old Butler estate dominating a foggy crag off in the distance.

Ana continued, "I'm sure many of you knew Violet. I was so sorry to hear about her recent passing. I would have loved to see her smiling face out in the audience tonight. I considered her, in so many senses of the word, my co-writer."

A few people nodded at the mention of their friend and neighbor.

Ana paused. When she continued, her voice was cracking slightly. "*An American Story* is an immigrant's story. Violet's parents had both come here on immigrant ships, Rosemary from Ireland, Arthur from Scotland. And they met right here, somehow, miraculously, just a short walk up Juniper Point Road, where they both worked for the Crowningshield family. Arthur was a foundryman; he had a natural genius for anything mechanical. Rosemary's genius was children."

Ana hesitated, gauging her audience. They were still with her, that was good, but the coffee and cookies awaited.

She continued, "The book really began when Violet handed me her mother's diary. It was an old box full of paper, all kinds of paper. Delivery receipts, family stationary and envelopes, some with canceled stamps from all around the world, from Charles Crowningshield's many travels. Rosemary wrote her diary in secret, after her day's work was done, and the children were asleep. She wrote in the mornings, before they awoke. She wrote in a kind of veiled code, because in those days it was considered unseemly to record events in the lives of your employers. But Rosemary had an abiding need to describe things that happened around her, and to her. She was a natural storyteller. She used pages from an accounting book, wrapping paper from the grocer. It took quite a while, I'll tell you, just to get it into some kind of chronological order. Repeat, *quite* a while. I can only imagine what she would have written if she'd had a laptop."

The audience laughed.

"As I've said, theirs was an immigrant's story, Rosemary and Arthur. But it's also very much an American story. A wealthy family in those days was a microcosm of labor relationships, of class distinction and of economic servitude. How families like the Crowningshields treated their servants in those post-Victorian times, how factories treated their employees. The cruelty of an ancient, inviolate caste system was very much still in place in 1910, when Rosemary and Arthur first came to Juniper Point. It is a caste system that for many around the world, still exists. Rosemary and Arthur had a front row seat to history. After Rosemary was sentenced to Blackwell's Island, unfairly, after a child in her care accidentally drowned, she went on to survive the infamous Triangle Shirtwaist Fire, an industrial tragedy which changed labor laws in American virtually overnight. Her benefactor, Fanny Perkins, was an early feminist who helped bring about those changes. Arthur was also a product of his times. He was an unschooled, illiterate kind of renaissance man, an autodidact of many skills who could build or design anything mechanical. He installed the first private indoor toilet in Woods Hole. He worked on the *Titanic,* at the Harland and Wolff shipyard in Belfast. He saw men fall to their death; industrial accidents quickly forgotten by management. Both he and Rosemary were profoundly changed by their times. Their story is shared by so many immigrants. And lucky for us, Rosemary's humble literary efforts, which constituted a kind of soft rebellion, the words of a lowly house nanny, preserved their incredible story to the ages. We owe a great thanks to Rosemary Kincaid Rouse, diarist, and her youngest daughter, Violet, for keeping those writings safe all these years."

Ana gathered up her file cards. She hadn't once looked down at them.

"Thank you all," she said in closing.

After the applause, an elderly woman hurried to the lectern. "Would you be so kind as to read us a selection from your book?" Turning to the audience, she asked, "Would we all like that?"

More applause filled the room. Ana nodded. "Of course," she said, opening the book to a pre-marked page. It was the section about Rosemary, as a young girl, imprisoned in a nunnery, working in the dank cellars of the

Magdalene Laundry, a rape survivor suffering from PTSD a hundred years before the clinical concept was developed.

She began to read.

Sometimes Rosemary thought about Dublin...

As Ana read, the audience went from jovial to stony-faced. They began shifting uncomfortably in their hard-backed chairs. Rape was not a happy subject to accompany free coffee and cookies. But they stayed with her, stayed with Rosemary's words. Many in the audience had never even known such a thing existed. But, in fact, the last of the Magdalene laundries shut their heavy, prison doors as recently as the 1990s.

Afterwards, Ana wandered out into the room, the author's requisite meet and greet, pausing to chat here and there. She signed a handful of books at the little table, and thanked the library again for sponsoring her trip down from Boston. All in all, a worthwhile evening.

"Lovely turnout," the older librarian said, discreetly handed her an envelope, a $50 honorarium, paid by check from the Friends of the Woods Hole Library.

The crowd was thinning, and Ana had a two-hour drive back to the city. Her publicist had arranged a modest book tour, beginning in a Boston Barnes and Noble the following week, and ending a month later in Chicago. *Publisher's Weekly* had printed a favorable review, and there had even been a whiff of a movie option in the air. But best to stay focused and not let these things distract, her agent had advised. Get busy on the next one, before people forget your name.

After the crowd had thinned, hurrying out into the drizzle, a woman who had been waiting on the edges approached Ana. The sound of warming car engines wafted in. Ana recognized Janice, new mistress of the big house on Juniper Point. She was holding a copy of the book.

"I loved it," she said. "Harrison couldn't make it. He's been working so hard on the house. Would you?" She offered over a thin silver pen, opened the book to the title page. After Ana signed her name, she glanced up.

"I was so sorry to hear about Violet. I talked with her on the phone only a month ago."

Janice, a pained look in her eyes, nodded. "She was in the hospital for a few days. Just a really bad cold that just worsened into full-blown pneumonia. The doctors in Falmouth did what they could. After all, she was ninety-five."

Ana nodded. "I know. She was amazing for a woman her age." She shook her head admiringly. "Yeesh, those walking tours would wear me out."

"But she couldn't stop talking about you," Janice continued. "She wanted desperately to see you finish the book, and was really happy and proud when you sent her an advanced reader copy. She came up to the house to show it to us."

Ana smiled. "That's so sweet."

Janice rummaged in her handbag, finally retrieved a small manila envelope. Handing it over to Ana, she explained, "Violet really wanted you to have these. It took me forever to find them, after she passed away. And then, voila, there they were, in a kitchen drawer, underneath the cheese grater and the spatulas." She grinned. "What kind of person keeps her valuables in a kitchen drawer?"

Ana took the envelope, thanking her. "And how are you doing?"

Janice smiled. "Well, we have a new cat now, but he's pretty old. After Violet passed away, Atticus wandered up to our kitchen porch, and hasn't left. But plans have changed for us. We're selling the house. Disagreements with the family, the Crowningshield heirs, weird rules and regulations they're imposing on us and whoever buys the property, have been simmering. Now, they've come to a head. Petty stuff, really, but we think it goes deeper."

"Oh, really?" Ana said. "Why is that?"

Janice shrugged. "After Frances died, the house fell back into the hands of her brother's children. They kept it in the family until we bought it. But there were lingering resentments. Harrison thinks it's because he's Jewish, for one thing, and some WASP, old money types still have a problem with that. It may explain things. Who really knows? Either way, the vibes are toxic. It's time for us to leave."

Ana waited for more, but Janice was done explaining. It was time for her to return home. Harrison was waiting for his dinner. Then Janice brightened.

"Thank you so much for writing this book, Ana, and for your wonderful reading tonight. Hopefully we'll see you again soon. Perhaps in our new home, wherever we land."

"I'd like that," Ana said.

Then Janice was gone. Volunteers began gathering up rows of chairs, dismantling the coffee urn, replacing unsold books onto a rolling cart. Ana, standing alone in the room, stared down at the envelope, then slowly upended its contents into her palm. A glint of metal emerged, then a fine, silver chain cascaded out. She stared at an intricately formed silver crucifix, turned it around, squinting down at a row of tiny incised letters. There, a name. *Rosemary Margaret Kincaid, First Communion, Kilcare, 1896.*

She shook the envelope and a second item slid out. It was a sepia photograph, an image of a man and a woman, blinking uncomfortably into the lens. The woman was slight. She was dressed in the clothes of another era. A long skirt, a shirtwaist, a round, feathered hat, and white gloves. Even in the somber brown-scale of the ancient picture, it was apparent she was fair-haired, perhaps a redhead. The man standing beside her was a giant, at least a head higher. He too was fair, like her, also perhaps a redhead. They stood together in the dooryard of a small Cape Cod house. Just past their shoulders, the soaring, shingled turret of an enormous Queen Anne Victorian, its prancing mare weathervane pointing north. The Crowningshield place. The farmhouse in the photograph was the same house Ana had once spent the night in. Violet's home, where she was born, then lived her entire life. Ana felt a slight chill. It was the divine goose flesh of serendipity, of pattern recognition.

Ana turned the photograph over. Of course, here they were. *Rosemary and Arthur Rouse,* somebody had scrawled. *Woods Hole, 1913.* Then, almost as an afterthought, a giddy epitaph to the modest dwelling just over their shoulders: *Ours!*

Ana turned the silver crucifix around in her palm. It felt right, somehow, the weighty coolness against her fingers. It made no difference whose God it represented. She carefully undid the clasp and slipped it over her head. Wearing it now didn't make her a Catholic. Wearing it merely brought her closer to the woman she had struggled to understand, to decode, for the better part of a year.

And now the book. Ana was a writer, a fine writer, but these were not her words, not exactly. That was okay. Hers would come later, between the covers of the next book. To be the steward of such an intimate story was a good beginning.

"Hello Mr. and Mrs. Rouse..." she whispered.

Welcome home.

EPILOGUE

Six months later. Ana, no longer living in Revere, on the crowded verge of the city, but the little sea-facing town of Hull, Massachusetts, a sandy scimitar of artists and folksingers, misfits and commuters. She had moved to C Street, part of a matrix of alphabet streets. It was a block from the open Atlantic, sharing a 1920s bungalow with an eccentric ceramics artist, a professional potter usually in the studio or out with friends. It gave Ana ample solitude. Sometimes, they met in the kitchen, sharing small talk over coffee, or occasional impromptu dinners, discussing art, literature, the sad state of American politics. But mostly it was as if they shared a cozy monastery. Each lived alone, planetary bodies in solitary lockdown, orbiting separate suns.

It was a ten-minute ferry ride from downtown Boston, should city business beckon. Life was better, calmer after the whirl of a book tour, occasional radio interviews. Sobriety had become sustainable, a daily vow she guarded fiercely, and she'd begun to date again, but tentatively, rarely. For Ana, it was mostly about the writing. *An American Story* was still firmly on the bookshelves, had received favorable notice, including *The New York Times Review of Books,* and was steadily moving up the Amazon charts. She still had an agent, and her publisher was gently prodding for the next manuscript. Movie talks were ongoing, *Publisher's Weekly* reliably reported, and big names were posited. Nicole Kidman as Cornelia Crowningshield, Russell Crowe as Charles Crowningshield, plus two unknowns from the UK to portray Rosemary and Arthur. But Hollywood moved at a glacial pace. It might take years for a seed to sprout.

American politics were in disarray, but she vaguely noticed, instead burrowing deeper into a cocoon of creative introspection. Healing from addiction, even two years on from her enforced time-out at *Turning Leaves,* was a slow, incremental process. Walks on the stony beaches of winter, cups of calming herb tea, weekly therapy sessions. She studiously ignored the siren call of social media, deleting emails and screening calls. These were the things within her power, done to both exorcize and explain the demons that had done so much damage to her youth. In the aggregate, it seemed to be working. Ana rarely thought about her old roommate, the sometimes gregarious, sometimes morose Mr. Stolichnaya. The little town's half dozen package stores would have to survive without her. Moving here, leaving the city, had been a good decision, and in this calming, stabilized environment, a new book was slowly emerging. It was a semi-scholarly examination of the historic cross-pollination between black Africans and Indigenous tribal society, and had a working title: *Black Lives on a Red Road: The Invisible Alliances Between the African Diaspora and Native America.* A few more chapters, and her agent was certain she could extract an advance for her to keep working. It was a busy, productive time. At the urging of her substance abuse therapist, a positive, insightful ex-heroin addict named Gloria, she had begun journaling; recording daily thoughts and discoveries, jotted prayers, recalled dreams, circling the veiled margins of her own crazy time, the alcoholic wilding and genesis of her battles with the bottle. Perhaps someday she would write the story of her own battle with addiction.

ONE MORNING HER IPHONE chirped. Ana glanced down at the screen, thumb poised over the reject button. Her agent, Denise, calling from New York. She got to the point.

"Ana, how's the book coming?"

"Fine," Ana said cautiously, adding, "good...great." There was an edginess in Denise's voice she'd never heard before. "I have to go on the road," she went on, "conduct a few more interviews, slog through more local archives, talk with some more tribal historians. Why? What's going on?"

Denise hesitated. "It's Harcourt, Ana. They feel this new project might not be right for them, given the current market climate."

"Not right?" Ana felt her stomach churn.

Denise rushed on. "Ana, we both know the book business is a fickle, hot mess. Acquisitions absolutely loved *An American Story*. You hit a solid triple your first time out of the box. And they believe in your talent."

"Okay...great...." Ana said. "Now what?"

Denise paused. Ana could almost hear her searching for just the right blend of praise and candor.

"Well," the agent began, "they suggest that we might begin shopping it to another publisher, a smaller imprint. A university press, perhaps. They feel it just doesn't have the broad enough general appeal to invest their resources at this time."

Ana snorted. "You mean it won't be in with the Harlequin bodice-clutchers at the Stop-n-Save? Have you ever noticed, Denise, how every one of those romance novels has a little sticker that says *New York Times Bestseller?*

The phone went silent. Denise, breathing.

"Ana, I'm sorry."

Ana stared at the screen. "So...just like that, Denise? What about the movie deal?"

"Still a solid maybe. Your publisher maintains fifteen percent of whatever your first book fetches in the marketplace. When and if a movie is made. It's in your contract."

Ana snorted again. "When and if. Hah!"

Denise quietly continued. "This is business, Ana. It happens all the time. Authors, especially new ones, can't afford to rest on their laurels. You're only as good as your last book. Writers must constantly reinvent themselves, and often that means moving on, finding creative opportunities for publication. We can't all be Stephen King."

Ana tried not to laugh. "No, I suppose not. But tell me, what do you propose we do now?"

Denise's answer came quickly, as if she'd been thinking hard on it. "Well, here's my advice. Shelve the history book, at least until we can get some interest elsewhere. I have contacts with some of the academic presses. We have a great proposal written, and that's half the battle. In the meantime, start something new, something more personal, or a novel. You can always get back to it later, when we've found you a new publisher."

"Something new?" Ana heard her voice rising. "What exactly does that mean. I've devoted six months of my life, with nothing to show for it. Royalties aren't exactly paying the bills, and I haven't gotten a dime yet for the movie option. Jesus, Denise. I'll have to get an effing job waitressing."

Denise sighed. "I know, I know. It's disappointing. Look. Just take a couple of days. Let's talk soon. You're a gifted writer, Ana. Ideas will come. Give it time."

THE NEXT DAY, ANA WANDERED out to the street to check the mailbox. Peeking inside, most was addressed to her roommate. Postcards from her grown children, a son in Maine, a daughter in Oregon. An L.L. Bean catalog, a few household bills, random junk circulars, and promo offers for nineteen dollar oil changes and magazine subscriptions. At the bottom of the pile, a small envelope, addressed to her. Strange, few people knew where she'd relocated, on advice from her therapist. It was like she'd unfriended the world. Ana slid it free, glancing at the return address. Handwritten in elegant script, it was from Janice, of Juniper Point. Only now, from a different address in Rhode Island. They must have sold the house. Ana walked into the kitchen just as the furnace kicked on. Raising a flame beneath a pot of water, she dropped a mint teabag into a recently hand-fired coffee mug, and sat down at the kitchen table to read.

Dear Ana, the letter began,

I hope you don't mind me getting in touch this way, but for some reason I've lost your phone number, otherwise I would have called. I remember jotting down your address the last time we talked, and that took a while to locate. Things are still a bit crazy with us, with the move and all. We sold the house, finally, but then had to find something fairly quickly, which turned out to be Rhode Island. The new home is very different. It's not on the ocean, for one thing, not too far away from Narragansett Bay, but very private. It has a great deal of land, nearly ten acres, and a few outbuildings as well. It used to be a horse farm, which makes it the perfect location for a future yoga and meditation retreat. Harrison is really happy here, as well. He's started to build furniture again, and of course there's always politics. Republicans! LOL! We're both very much at peace now. All that Crowningshield hostility really wiped us both out. It was like being under siege. But enough about us. How are you doing these days? Please write, or call, when you can. Or better yet, visit. Would love to catch up.

Okay, down to business. Jonathan Blodgett, an attorney from Woods Hole, has asked me for your mailing address. He wouldn't give me the reason, but I told him I'd reach out to you. I know you value your privacy. Enclosed is his name and office phone number, if you decide to call him. My prayers and blessings are with you, Ana. I hope the new writing project, and your life, are going well. I think of you fondly.

Namaste, Janice

Ana moved to the living room, curled up on the couch. She looked down at the letter and slowly tapped her phone. A lawyer? Who knew what he might want. Then a distant voice on the other end.

"Jonathan Blodgett's office." Ana explained why she was calling, then the voice, a woman, said, "Just a second while I put you through." The receptionist lowered her voice to a *soto voce* whisper, "It's been a madhouse all morning, but I know he's been wanting to talk with you."

Ana waited, then a man's pleasant voice. "Jonathan here. Is that you, Ms. Leibling?"

Ana admitted that it was.

"Thanks for calling. Do you have time to talk?"

Ana admitted that she did, trying her pleasant voice. Now that her nascent project had been torpedoed by some distant marketing tribunal, she had scads of time on her hands.

"Fine, great," the attorney said. "And by the way, I just finished reading *An American Story*. Nice job, loved it, very engaging."

"Thanks," Ana said. The day was starting to catch up with her. She felt suddenly deflated. She needed to decompress, go for a walk, try and rediscover her heart's mission.

"My pleasure," the attorney said. "Now, the reason I've been trying to locate you..."

Ana waited. She could almost the papers shuffling.

"It's about Mrs. McVicar."

"Violet?"

"Yes, of course, Violet," he went on. "Lovely lady. We met several times, here in my office, over the last several years. I've been handling her estate."

Ana quietly exhaled. This place where she lived, across the harbor from a bustling city, was where she had landed in search of quietude and recovery. It was just a rented room, but it was a quiet house. Cars rarely drove down C Street, a dead end terminating at the sandy ocean's edge. If they did, they quickly turned around. Over the mantel was an antique parlor clock, a Seth Thomas softly ticking away the seconds and minutes, chiming the hours of each day. Sometimes, a distant front door slammed shut down the street, and at night, the throaty moan of the foghorn of the Boston Harbor light, guarding the rocky, serpentine, shipping channel. The atmosphere in this house was conducive, supportive, nurturing. Yet suddenly, on the phone with this lawyer, she felt untethered.

"It's about her will," he was saying. "In short, you're mentioned."

"Oh?"

"Prominently," he continued. "In fact, you're her sole beneficiary. She had no heirs."

"Oh, I didn't know that."

"It's quite substantial," he explained.

Ana was staring down at her phone, waiting.

Substantial?

The sound of more papers rustling. Then the lawyer's voice again. "Of course, there will be the inheritance tax. Let me see now."

Ana wanted to scream at this man.

How substantial?

"Here it is," he said. "Just under three. Give or take. Not counting the real estate. The market's strong at the moment. If you should decide to sell the house, I'd be happy to help."

"Three...thousand?" Ana pronounced the words. That would help her live for a couple of months, until things got back on track.

Then the lawyer again, his quick, nervous laughter. "Oh, I'm sorry. Did I say thousand? No, the amount is three million. Give or take."

Give or take?

Suddenly, Ana had nothing more to add to this conversation. "Listen, Mr. Blodgett...can you just mail me the papers, or whatever? I'm a little overwhelmed...at the moment. I just need a little time to...process."

"Understood. I'll need your mailing address, Ms. Liebling."

She gave it to him, adding quickly, "Ana, call me Ana."

"Will do," he said. "Ana it is. Thank you. I'll be in touch."

THAT WAS A MONTH AGO. It had all happened so quickly. Now, she stood before the door, key in the lock. It was the same as she remembered, except the mistress of the house was gone. Violet, Mrs. McVicar, dead a year, vanished. March Hare gone, beneath the ground gone, sadness and memory gone.

Someone had opened the house. They'd turned the water back on, and the rooms were comfortably warm. Such an odd sensation, to open a door and walk into your own house. Ownership, something she'd never known. But then, that wasn't really true, not yet; it was still very much still Violet's home. Ana sat down on the couch, as she had that first night, when she'd first seen Rosemary's diary, and opened her messenger bag. Inside were three items. The letter from attorney Blodgett, explaining the terms of the inheritance, along with a copy of Violet's will. He'd also enclosed the house keys. It was all true, just as he said. She stared at the disbursement papers. She still had to sign things, of course, to make it all legal, and tomorrow she'd head down to his office in the village. But there it was. Three million dollars, some of it in a local bank account, the majority in the form of matured stocks. And of course, a small, unassuming Cape Cod house on Juniper Point Rd. Attorney Blodgett listed its potential evaluation, "in the current market conditions."

The amount floored her. Add seven figures to Violet's remarkable generosity.

The third item was a letter. It was written on old stationary, from an old box kept in a dresser drawer, which noted, in flowery script, the correspondent's name and address. She brought the pages up to her nose and inhaled the musty aroma. Lavender. Violet McVicar, such a kind, civilized human being. She could have easily have left her worldly effects to some charity, or her cat, or bought a bigger house or took a world cruise. Instead she'd left it all to her, a relative stranger, the way one would bequeath to an only child. Ana began to read, for perhaps the twentieth time.

Dear Ana,

Hopefully you are here, in your new home. I trust Mr. Blodgett to handle all the details, and advise you, as he has advised me, of the best way to proceed. It's a lot for you to take in, I realize, and on such short notice, but there it is. This house has been a great comfort and refuge for me over the years. It was the house where I was born, the house where my brothers and sisters grew up, and the house where my parents, as you know quite well, lived for many happy years. There has been sadness as well, within these walls, but thankfully mostly joy. And now there's you. I never was able to have children of my own. Mr. McVicar and I had our own happy life together here on Juniper Point. I can't recall if I told you or not, but he was employed for many years by the Crowningshield family, as the estate superintendent, long after Frances died and her brother's children took over the property. And it was like that for many years, the generations of children and grandchildren passing through that grand house on the hill, until my friends Janice and Harrison bought it. To be clear, the money I have left you is not really from me. It was left to me by my parents, Rosemary and Arthur. My father, after the family had moved to Woods Hole in 1913, purchased some stock in the Crowningshield company. Not much, just a few shares each year, from money he'd saved, but eventually, by the time of their passing, it had grown into quite a large sum. The Crowningshield company helped put a man on the moon. I've never touched it; Mr. McVicar and I had few financial wants, since this house had no mortgage, and our combined salaries were plenty to live on. Nevertheless, the house and the money are yours to do as you please. No strings attached. Hopefully it will lessen the plain burdens of life, and allow you the freedom to pursue and perfect your craft of writing, or whatever else you may decide to do. That's certainly what Frances did with hers. Taking in less privileged children, orphans and foundlings from the cruel city streets, offering them a better life here, in her brother's grand home on the hill. And now you. It's your money and your choice. Whether it's through your writing, or perhaps some other worthy charity, I trust you will make the right decision. Like the great writer Virginia Wolfe, a guest at Juniper Point many times, once observed, "A woman must have a room of her own."

And here is yours.

With great admiration, and affection, your friend, Violet McVicar

Ana laid the letter down, a warm tear sliding down her cheek. This, Violet's gift to her, to return to this house, was overwhelming. She looked around, at the four corners of her new home, then stood up, and walked to the kitchen. It was shipshape and clean, everything put away in its place. Sailboat tidy, as if for the last time. Violet must have known, just before she'd called the firehouse boys to take her to the Falmouth hospital, that she'd never return. A fastidious widow who lived alone, her affairs long settled with Mr. Blodgett, trusted family retainer, she knew who would be the next person to walk through the door, and wanted it to be spotless and ready when she did.

Standing at the sink, about to put the tea water on, Ana heard a scratching noise outside. Peering through the gingham curtains, she looked down, at the small porch. Atticus, the cat was staring up at her, softly mewing. He strolled regally past her ankles and into the kitchen.

"Well, hello there," Ana said. Bending down to stroke his head, she noticed his fur was mottled and dirty, stuck with brambles. He had a fresh cut on his rear leg. Coyotes, or perhaps foxes, on the hunt.

"You must be starving."

She peeked into Violet's tiny pantry. Neat stacks of cat food cans lined one shelf, and she spooned out the contents of one into a small silver bowl on the floor. She'd buy some milk in the village later. Again, Violet must have known he'd be back. Everything in its place. After he was done eating, Atticus sauntered into the living room, leapt into his old chair and fell instantly to sleep.

LATER, ANA SCROLLED through her phone, then dialed a number. On the other end, in Rhode Island, Janice picked up, listening as Ana explained everything, beginning with Violet's remarkable gift, adding that Atticus was asleep in his chair.

Janice nearly screamed, "Atticus is back? We looked everywhere for him when we were moving, but he was just gone. I felt terrible. But you know how cats can be. He must have known, somehow, that he could go home."

"I have no idea," Ana admitted, "but there you go. Violet left him plenty of food. Such an amazing woman. I miss her."

"So, Ana, what about you? Will you stay on at the Point?"

Ana considered this. "I don't know. I suppose so. We'll see. I mean, I can't just uproot poor Atticus now, can I? Leave him to the predations of the wild animals here? That would be cruel and unusual."

Janice laughed. "True enough. And the Crowningshields? They can be pretty cruel and unusual."

Ana smiled. "Oh, I think they can be tamed. I'm in Violet's house, not their old family homestead. I'm under her protection. I think they'll stay on their side of the sandbox. Besides, they wouldn't dare come after me. I wrote the book. I know where all the bodies are buried."

Janice laughed again. "Well, you'll figure it out. But whatever you decide, please come and visit."

ONE MORNING, A MONTH later, an older man, walking a small dog, passed the dooryard. Studiously avoiding eye contact, he stared straight ahead as he meandered down the lane. Later, when he passed by again, on his return trip, Ana opened her front door, stepping out to the frosty air.

"Good morning," she greeted the man. "Cute dog. What kind is he?"

The man paused and looked at her, a dour, pinched look of disapproval on his face. "*He's* a female," he said. "A Shiatsu."

"Oh...okay," Ana said. "Anyway, she's very cute."

The man considered this, about to resume his walk.

"I'm Ana," she told him. "Ana Liebling. I guess we're neighbors. You know you're the first person I've seen since I moved here last month."

The man nodded. "You're the writer," he said.

Ana smiled. "Guilty as charged. And you are?"

The man tugged on the little dog's leash. "John," he told her. "John Crowningshield."

"Ah…" Ana said. "Very nice to meet you. Would you like to come in for a cup of tea?"

He shook his head. "I'm late for a meeting. Perhaps another time."

As Ana watched him walk away, she realized her hands were shaking.

THE NEXT DAY, ANA SAW them again. Same man, same dog. On his return trip, she came to the door and waved without opening it. He paused a step and waved back, then kept walking, the briefest of smiles on his face. The third day he passed, he stopped, and waited for her to open the door.

"Perhaps I will have that tea," he said. "If the offer's still open."

Her first visitor. A Crowningshield.

CROWNINGSHIELD GLANCED toward her writing desk, by the window, the laptop open, the legal pads, a cup of cold coffee.

"Working on something new?" he asked.

"Always," she said, smiling, handing him his tea. Then she sat down on the couch, facing him, just as Violet had done that first night.

The man took a sip. From his chair, Atticus cautiously eyed the little dog lying across from him on the hooked rug, but decided it wasn't worth his time.

"I'm working on a cultural history at the moment," she explained.

"Not another family saga?" The man smiled. Ana tried to gauge his question, but couldn't.

"No…well, yes, sort of, I guess. African slaves taking refuge in Native American communities."

The man nodded. "I enjoyed the book you wrote about my family," he said. "I honestly had no idea. I mean, I knew Violet, and her husband worked for my mother, but she never really talked about her own past. It was, to tell the truth, an eye-opener."

"Thank you," Ana said. "I appreciate that, coming from you."

He took another sip, then smiled again. "I can't say the same for the rest of my family, though."

Ana nodded. "I can appreciate that as well. Sometimes the truth can be very hurtful."

He chuckled. "That, Ana, is an understatement."

"So, what is you do?" Ana said. "If you don't mind me asking."

He shrugged. "No, not at all. I'm a doctor. Well, actually, I'm not a practicing physician anymore. I've worked in the past for the World Health Organization, researching infectious diseases, but now I mainly run a clinic in Africa that treats Ebola patients."

"Wow."

The man shook his head. "Actually, the front-line doctors and nurses deserve all the credit. I mostly do fundraising. Give talks, network with other researchers, that sort of thing. And, by the way, just to clear the air, I apologize for the other day. I was pretty rude. I'm sorry."

"No problem," Ana said. "You must have a lot on your mind."

He nodded. "Jet lag usually. But there was just a large outbreak in the region where my clinic is. A lot of people were affected, including staff members. There were...fatalities."

"I'm so sorry."

He fell silent, his mind back in Africa.

Ana leaned forward. "So, tell me...John...do you live here, on the Point?"

He looked up. "Oh, god no. Just visiting my brother. He lives in the old carriage house down by the water?" He handed her back the teacup.

Ana stood up. "Of course, I've been by there. And, what does he do, your brother?"

Crowningshield smiled. "Not much, really. He's retired. Once upon a time he was a corporate lawyer. But now he just works really hard at doing nothing, nibbling away at the family fortune. He travels a lot."

"Like your grandfather," Ana said.

"Charles?" the man asked, then paused. "No. He wasn't exactly my grandfather. But yes, he did love to travel."

He stood up, glancing down at the little sleeping dog. "My brother's. Walking her gives me an excuse to get some exercise."

Ana gestured across the room at Atticus, sprawled on his back, his two front paws dangling. She laughed. "The only exercise he gets is between his food bowl, the litter box, and his chair. Pathetic waste of a good cat."

Crowningshield offered his hand. "It's been lovely, Ana. Perhaps, before I leave, I'll bring my copy of your book over for a proper autograph."

"Any time," she said. "How long are you here for?"

"I leave the day after tomorrow," he said. "Off to Geneva for a symposium. For some reason I'm the keynote speaker."

LATER THAT EVENING, Ana asked *Google* about John Crowningshield. His curriculum vitae was impressive. Graduated from Johns Hopkins, practiced heart surgery for many years, then went on to study infectious diseases. He had worked for presidents, notably Bush Two and Clinton, had joined Obama's medical advisory council, and even helped set up the White House's special pandemic response team in the United States. And then the Ebola clinic. An odd factoid caught her eye. John Crowningshield was not by blood an actual Crowningshield. His own father had been, in fact, adopted. It was complicated. The link was an excerpt from a memoir that John himself wrote in the 1980s. That explained his interest in her literary work habits. Ana read on. John's father, a homeless orphan, had arrived at Juniper Point in 1916, from Chicago. He had lived in a sunny bedroom on the second floor, sharing that room with another orphan from Chicago. Then at some point, he'd been adopted by Frances and her husband, and legally became a Crowningshield. John's biological mother had been, of all things, an opera singer, but died of ovarian cancer when he was six. John's father had been wounded in World War Two and came home a broken man, suffering from battle fatigue and chronic alcoholism. He died in a soldier's home outside Boston, leaving his son, as all things in life are circular, an orphan like he had been. But, for all intents and purposes, John was a bonafide Crowningshield. He'd gone to the best prep schools, spent his summers on Juniper Point with all the other Crowningshield heirs, and even dated Crowningshield cousins. The family had generously paid his way through medical school, and their great wealth opened the right doors at the right time, as they always had. Yet his life became a paradox. After he'd become a doctor, and could provide for himself, John Crowningshield, the namesake of Charles and Cornelia's youngest drowned boy, began to actively seek ways to reimburse the planet for his fantastic good fortune at being a Crowningshield. Exposure to privilege as a young man led him away from that same privilege as a mature adult. It was the same paradox that Frances herself embraced. It wasn't just about the money, as Violet McVicar asserted in her letter; it was what good works one could do in the world with the money.

That night, Ana dreamt, but quickly forgot about what. After the morning teacup was rinsed, and the litter box scooped clean, and she'd sat at her computer for an hour, polishing the same sentence over and over, a soft rap on the front door. It was John Crowningshield, holding his copy of *An American Story*.

"If my brother catches me with this, I'll be disowned," he joked. "But would you mind signing it? I have to leave a day early."

"Of course," Ana said, reaching for the book. She handed it back, asking, "John, I have a question for you."

"Certainly."

Well," she began, "I'm not sure how to phrase this, but does your clinic...does it have any particular needs? I'd really like to help in some way."

He stood there, a tall, dignified, white-haired gentleman in a puffy North Face parka, and thought for a moment.

"Of course, there's always money, but there is something else with which we could really use assistance." He paused.

"Yes?"

"Well, I think it's right up your alley, Ana. It's a bit of a mix, really. Public relations, talking with the public about the kind of work our clinic does. Also, we're filming a documentary and could use a good writer onboard. The pay isn't great..."

"I'll do it," Ana blurted. "When do I start?"

John, startled, asked, "But what about your own writing projects?"

"It can wait," she said, marveling at how effortless the decision had been.

"You'd have to go to Africa."

"Great," she said. "Never been."

They chatted for a bit longer, but John had an Uber coming and a plane to catch. Details would be forwarded to her.

"Thank you," he said, "I'm honored you want to help."

She shook her head. "Sorry, John, no, but your honor pales in comparison to mine. You've been at this saving-the-world thing a lot longer than I have."

THAT EVENING, JUST before sleep came, with the familiar soundtrack of the foghorn, a soft rustling of the cedar trees outside her window, and an occasional freight truck downshifting into town, Ana stared up at the plaster ceiling. She was lying in the same bed that Violet had slept in, the same bed where she and her brothers and sisters had been conceived and born. The room was redolent with memory. In those long seconds before she shut her eyes, Ana composed a prayer.

Goodnight, Violet, she whispered. *Goodnight, Rosemary. Goodnight, Arthur. Goodnight, everyone, even you stuffy, filthy-rich, and so very, very complicated Crowningshields. I couldn't have done it without you.*

Love, Ana.

About the Author

Philip Austin is the author of seven books, including a memoir, *The Paintbox of Everything*. His first novel, *On Bethel Ridge,* a Christmas fable published in 1998, was hailed by Publisher's Weekly as 'a sharply etched tale reaching across cultures with universal spirituality.'